THE BLUE FLAME

NATHAN SHORE

THE BLUE FLAME

Published 2022

ISBN-13: 979-8-9868807-0-9 (Hardcover)
ISBN-13: 979-8-9868807-1-6 (e-Book)
ISBN 13: 979-8-9868807-2-3 (Paperback)

Library of Congress Control Number: 2022916724

Book cover design by Onur Burc

Barque Point Press, LLC
Saint Paul, Minnesota
c/o Nathan Shore
nathan@barquepointpress.com

www.barquepointpress.com

For Jennifer

PART I

Chapter 1

BEN HIRSCH'S CELL PHONE RANG as he sat in his darkened apartment contemplating where he'd gone wrong. The phone lay on his coffee table alongside a half-empty bottle of Knob Creek rye. The chime repeated several times before he snatched up the phone and silenced the ringer. He glanced at the caller ID—it was Kyle Severson, his law-school classmate and one remaining friend.

"It's over," Hirsch said, answering the call. "They yanked my law license today. I'm done for."

"Jesus, it never should've gone this far. It's a first offense—what the hell's gotten into them?"

"What can I say? The Bar needed to make an example of me. Looks like they did. I screwed-up royally this time, didn't I?"

"We both know plenty of guys who've done far worse than this. Not a damn thing happened to them," Kyle said.

"Yet here we are." Hirsch took a long pull off the bottle, savoring the punishing burn as the liquor slipped down his throat.

"What happened to Greg?"

"Greg walked out last week. He caught wind of the disbarment coming down the pike and did what he had to do—took all of our clients with him. Not that I blame them for leaving."

"I don't even know what to say. I'm beyond pissed about this." Kyle paused. "Listen, there's a reason I called. You've had a few rough months. I wanted to ask what you plan on doing next. Are you sticking around Lansing?"

"I honestly don't have a clue," Hirsch said. "I never thought I'd need another career. I figured I'd plug away at this until I retired or keeled over at my desk. I can't afford to live here, that's for damn sure."

"Don't you have any friends there who could fix you up with some work? You're a popular guy."

"*Was* a popular guy. Most of our friends went with Allison after the divorce. Everyone else only knew me from my practice. I'm a pariah now. Fat chance they want anything to do with me. The long and short of it is, I'm out on my ass at the end of the month if I can't make the rent. I doubt Allison will let me crash at her place."

"What if I had a better idea?" Kyle asked.

"Well, I'm all ears at this point. It's not like I have a plan."

"Come home."

"Home? Wait, what—you mean come back to the UP?" Hirsch asked.

"Yeah, it's where you grew up, you know the lay of the land, and people here still care about you. Sounds like the obvious solution."

Hirsch groaned. "No offense, but I swore I was done with that place."

"Seriously, Ben. You gave it a shot in Lansing, and it didn't work out. Maybe this is where you belong."

"Okay that's all well and fine, but last I checked, the economy's in the toilet. What am I going to do for work? It's not like I can work in a copper mine or fish for a living."

"With the whole disbarment, I'd have a hell of a time finding you anything on the books." Kyle served as a deputy prosecuting attorney for Delta County and was a rising star in the UP legal community. "But maybe … nah, never mind."

"Wait, what is it? Seriously, I'm damn near desperate at this point."

Kyle lowered his voice. "Okay, here's the deal—I have a case I could use a hand with. I'm in a bit of a pickle, and I need someone I can trust."

"Sure … I guess I can help. Are you in some sort of trouble, Kyle?" Hirsch asked.

"No, not exactly. Look, I can't talk now, but can we meet and discuss what I have in mind?"

"I don't know how much use I'll be, but you name it and I'll see what I can do."

"Good, I'm glad to hear that, Ben. I have a feeling you're just the man for the job. You're like a brother to me. Closer in some ways. The UP needs guys like you to come home and make a difference."

Hirsch was silent, and Kyle continued, "Tell you what—why don't you drive up and stay with us for a few days. Jess and the kids would love to see you. Worst case scenario, you decide it's not for you and head back downstate."

Hirsch hated the thought of Kyle's perfect family seeing him mope around. He racked his brain for an excuse to decline but came up with nothing. Save for his Toyota pickup and his father's Smith & Wesson .38 Special, he'd sold near everything of value to pay the disciplinary fees.

"I don't know what to say," Hirsch answered. "Like I said, I have a week left on my lease, then I'll be flat out on the street. You seriously think you could stomach a houseguest?"

"Say the word and we'll fix up a room for you."

"Kyle, I can't tell you how much I appreciate this. Life's been an absolute nightmare the past few months."

"Don't mention it, bud. You'd do the same for me. Besides, this may be a blessing in disguise for us both. This is your shot at a new life. Meet me Monday afternoon on the north shore of Ludington Park. Near the historical marker. We'll chat about the job."

Hirsch ended the call and refreshed his glass from the dwindling bottle of rye. He glanced around the bare room. He was finished here. Fate left him with no choice but to start over. And it began with a journey into his past.

A SIX-HOUR DRIVE NORTH ACROSS the Mackinac Bridge and west along Highway 2 brought Hirsch to Kyle's Upper Peninsula hometown, Escanaba. Hirsch arrived at three in the afternoon and crawled through downtown until he reached Ludington Park. Kyle stood alone near the shore, silhouetted against the stucco-gray expanse of Lake Michigan's Little Bay de Noc. Shelves of lingering ice fringed the shoreline while a trio of gulls glided in gentle arcs above the park.

Hirsch parked his truck and navigated a snow-strewn footpath to join his friend. Kyle wore his standard workplace attire—gray flannel trousers, a stark-white dress shirt, a dark scarlet tie knotted tight under his collar, and a knee-length charcoal herringbone wool coat. His patrician appearance struck a contrast with Hirsch's blue jeans and weathered Carhart jacket. Kyle's reddish-blonde hair clipped close to his scalp likewise highlighted how Hirsch's thick head of hair badly needed a trim.

"Good to see you, buddy!" Kyle said as he wrapped his long arms around his friend. "Glad you made it in one piece. Let's walk. I'll bet you forgot how cold it is here," he continued, noticing Hirsch zipping his jacket against the frigid north wind ripping off the lake.

"It still snows in Lansing, you know," Hirsch said.

"Not like here. I shoveled eighteen inches last week—in April, mind you." Kyle paused. "The important thing is you made it. Jess and the girls can't wait to see you. I was worried you might not come."

"You said you might need my help with a case. I've been wondering what you had in mind since we talked."

"I'm glad you asked, I feel like I've run out of options. I suspect two locals are thieving left and right across the county. They work quickly and under the cover of night. They turn around and fence the goods wherever they can—even as far away as Green Bay or Duluth. It started off small time with lifting power tools from utility trucks and equipment out of storage sheds. Now they've graduated to stripping copper wire from abandoned houses and cutting catalytic converters out of cars. Those are damn expensive and a pain in the ass to replace. This is where you come in—I need a smart and trustworthy person to get to the bottom of this."

"All right, I see where you're going with this, but why not

assign a detective from the sheriff's office to investigate—or do it yourself?" Hirsch said.

Kyle stopped and fixed his piercing blue eyes on Hirsch. "Drugs, Ben, drugs. The county's pissed away a boatload of resources over the past fifteen years battling meth. Now they want to get ahead of the opioid crisis before it blows up in our faces. They've got me and our meager staff working those cases to the exclusion of anything else. And don't even get me started on the sheriff's office. I'm telling you, though, if a concerned citizen were to bust this investigation open and catch these clowns in the act, well, I don't need to explain what a coup that'd be for the public."

"I get what you're saying. The thing is, I'm beyond toxic. You said it yourself—there's no way the PA's office could hire me with a disbarment on my record, even as a paralegal or investigator. Besides, it'd be an epic shitstorm if the bar caught me working a case," Hirsch said.

"That's the thing—we're not going to hire you. In fact, I can't even ask you to investigate this. Let me explain. When my father was fresh out of law school, he started out working in the prosecutor's office, much like I did. We were all taught that the police would investigate criminal activity and tee them up for us to prosecute. Dad believed that too until it dawned on him the police could only do so much. Fact is, most folks won't talk to the cops, and—even if they do—they'll outright lie to you or water down their story. Since this doesn't get you anywhere useful, my dad relied on a handful of trusted informants he knew could get people talking. Hell, if I remember right, one of them was this old barfly who couldn't string together more than a couple sober waking hours in a day. That said, he loved to gab and other drunks would tell him damn near anything. Much of what he learned was inadmissible as hell, but nine times out of ten, he'd throw you a legitimate lead. All it cost my old man was a little cash under the table, beer money really.

"What I'm saying," Kyle continued with a glint of complicity in his eyes, "is if a civilian volunteered of his own free will to look into this and turned over whatever he found, well, even the sheriff and the PA couldn't ignore it."

Kyle's scheme clicked in Hirsch's brain, and the lessons learned in his 2L criminal procedure class came flooding back. If a person acting at the express direction of a government official investigated these thefts, then the Fourth Amendment's search and seizure protections would apply. In other words, get a goddamn warrant. On the other hand, a run-of-the-mill busybody has ample freedom to poke his nose into someone else's business. On the downside, the state or county could offer the snoop little or no protection whatsoever—not officially anyway. Kyle was going rogue on this investigation.

"Let me make sure I understand all this, Kyle. You want me to investigate a couple of small-time con artists using no resources and with no official support from the county or the police? Besides, why put your ass on the line over this? Doesn't that strike you as a fool's errand?"

"Perhaps," Kyle acknowledged. "But this could be a great first step in cleaning up this county. Folks are moving away left and right with the economy being what it is. Having a reputation for criminal mischief doesn't help matters. If we can land a big bust, who knows where this could lead. The UP needs a fresh start, just like you."

"Any idea who these deadbeats might be?" Hirsch asked.

"Buddy, I know exactly who they are. Two brothers—Lionel and Marcus Shaw."

"Never heard of them. What's their story?"

"The Shaws are an old family here in Delta County. They showed up when the pig-iron smelter in Fayette opened back in the 1860s. They've been on the Garden Peninsula ever since. From what I understand, the early ones did all right for themselves. The boys' grandfather, Hiram Shaw, was a doctor here in Escanaba. He practiced into his seventies and was well-liked and respected. My Dad spoke highly of him. Whatever grace and charm Hiram possessed had evaporated by the time Lionel and Marcus came along. Lionel's the older and smarter of the two brothers. I understand he even attended Michigan Tech in Houghton. He ran his own heating company—Shaw Brothers Heating, he called it."

"Brothers? Is Marcus in the business too?" Hirsch asked.

Kyle scoffed. "Marcus lasted about a week before Lionel canned him. I guess Lionel kept the name 'Shaw Brothers' because it sounded family-friendly or some nonsense. Anyway, Lionel ran it for close to twenty years before his wife divorced him. She took every last dime he had, including the business. That happened a couple of years ago. Word is he's desperate for cash. Lionel did mighty fine work with his company and knows as much as anyone about heating systems."

Kyle sat on a park bench facing the bay, and Hirsch followed his lead. Normally teeming with tourists during summer, the park was empty save for the two friends.

"Marcus on the other hand, well, I'm not sure where I should even start with that walking travesty of a man. Marcus is an evil drunk who'd throw his own mother under a bus if he thought it'd save his skin. He's a frequent flyer in the criminal justice system. Has convictions for the usual small-time crimes—a couple DUIs, misdemeanor theft, domestic abuse, trespassing. He's what you'd expect from a white-trash thug living out in the country. Spends most of his free time holding down a barstool at a tavern near Garden Corners, if you know where that is."

Hirsch was all too familiar with the establishment—Lily's Tavern, a haven for lowlifes, petty criminals, and outcasts with nowhere else to go. In other words, people like him.

"The thing is, he's beat a few more serious charges, including assaulting a police officer up in Luce County. If Lionel's the brains of the operation, Marcus is the muscle. He pistol-whipped a poor sap in a bar fight, but the victim was too afraid of the family to press charges. Both are middle-aged. Hell, Lionel might even be fifty by now. He owns a run-down farm right outside the town of Garden on the peninsula. From what I've heard, Marcus crashes with him most of the time. I'd need to check the property records, but I think Marcus owns a spot of land on Summer Island. Must've inherited the place, I imagine. I wouldn't expect it's much more than a hunting camp, but he's known to disappear there when the law's on his tail."

"Okay, I'll take the bait. Why isn't Marcus behind bars?" Hirsch asked. "Seems like assaulting a police officer would earn you a few years minimum, even up here."

"And that's where this whole mess gets complicated, my friend. Here's the deal—Lionel and Marcus have an older sister named Catherine. Her married name is Catherine Shaw Winslow." Kyle paused and let his words sink in.

"Wait—not those Winslows, right?" This saga was growing stranger by the minute.

"The same."

Kyle's discretion now made sense. The Winslows stood amongst the foremost families on the Upper Peninsula. They made their fortune before the turn of the century exploiting the western UP's iron range by extracting and refining iron ore. The paterfamilias, Charles Francis Winslow, known as C.F., was legendary for his parsimony and squeezing all he could from his employees. Multiple union organizers fled town with cracked skulls, if they escaped at all. The Winslows maintained their prominence by diversifying into shipping and milling lumber as the twentieth century wore on. With money handed down from one generation to the next, they retained an eminent position in Upper Peninsula society. While several family scions relocated to Milwaukee, Chicago, or points further south to wallow in the family riches, a significant contingent remained and controlled the active empire. Picking a fight with the Winslow family wouldn't end well.

"Yes, Catherine Shaw married Herbert Milford Winslow, a descendant of C.F. Winslow," Kyle continued. "They live in Marquette and lead the town's social set—what there is of one anyway. If you met Ms. Winslow, you wouldn't have the foggiest inkling she's related to her dipshit brothers. I guess she takes after the old doctor. Needless to say, she has the money and means to make problems disappear. Hence the police dropping the Luce County assault charge against Marcus for 'insufficient evidence.' I'd have to think she has little but disdain for her siblings, but family's family, I suppose. Besides, she doesn't need the embarrassment.

"One other point—Catherine doesn't just have money and power on her side; she's smart as well. She has an MBA from Ann Arbor and makes most of the company's executive decisions. Sure, Herb's the nominal chairman of the Winslow Corporation but he'd much rather be fly fishing. Trust me, he'll talk your ear off about it if given half a chance. It's Catherine who's pulling the strings behind the curtain. Do not underestimate her."

"Fair enough, but why are you so interested in these two clowns? I mean, god knows we have no shortage of violent criminals and meth heads to go after. I'm willing to bet most of them don't have millionaire siblings."

Kyle smiled. "That's a fair question. Catherine Shaw Winslow's family has ample money to throw around. They've flung their fair share at the local elected officials right here in Delta County. Corruption like that angers me. Unless we have this investigation buttoned up tight, we can't let it out that we're actively investigating her brothers. True, they're morons, but they're her moron relatives. I guarantee the powers that be would yank our investigation if they knew the Winslows were involved. I need evidence they can't ignore. You have a unique set of skills yourself. I've seen it plenty of times and it's special, damn special. We're asking you to use those skills that made you such a success in the courtroom."

"I … I'm not sure I follow. It's not like I have my finger on the pulse of the town. Besides, what do you mean when you say 'we?'"

"Delta County, Ben. The people of the UP, if it helps to think of it that way."

"Well, what exactly do you want me to do? You know I'm not a PI, right?"

"First, put your ear to the ground and see what you can learn about the brothers. I know you're not a cop, but you've done your share of due diligence and know how to run an investigation to ground. Anything we can find connecting them to these crimes will be helpful. Once you feel comfortable, it couldn't hurt to track them a little."

Sure, ask the half-Indian guy to be a tracker, Hirsch thought.

"Hell, if you catch them in the act, we'll have an open and shut case," Kyle continued. "In the meantime, I'll find you a legit job as a cover—and for a little walking-around money."

Hirsch exhaled. "Let me think it over. I'm trying to clean my life up, not make a bigger mess of things."

"Can I count on you, Ben?" Kyle asked, looking Hirsch right in the eye.

In his heart, the proposed arrangement made Hirsch uncomfortable. Still, given Kyle was the only person saving him from a complete collapse, what choice did he have?

"Yeah, you can. No promises, but I'll do the best I can."

Kyle stood and offered a thin smile in gratitude. "Good. I'm not sure when I'll need your help, but I need you to be ready all the same. In the meantime, I'll see what I can come up with for legitimate work. Come by the house this evening and make yourself at home. Like I said, Jess and the girls are dying to see you. We planned a big dinner in celebration."

Kyle patted Hirsch on the arm and ambled across the park toward the prosecutor's office while Hirsch sat alone on the park bench, dazed at their conversation. Life as an undercover informant wasn't at all what he had in mind when he returned north. Kyle was his one remaining lifeline, and letting him down was out of the question.

Chapter 2

That evening, Hirsch faced the Seversons' Escanaba family home. They occupied a Victorian-era pale-blue house with white trim on Ogden Avenue, only a block from Ludington Park and the lakeshore. A jewel of the venerable neighborhood, it comprised two stories with bay windows, a white-pillared porch, and a delicate wrought-iron fence outlining the home's corner lot. It was Kyle's childhood home, and he returned after taking the job with the Delta County prosecuting attorney's office.

In his left hand, Hirsch grasped the last bottle of Barbaresco from his once-ample stockpile of wine. He opened the gate of the fence and walked toward the porch. Before he even reached the steps, the heavy front door flew open. The Seversons' ten- and six-year-old daughters, Maddie and Jenna, emerged. Their blonde hair streamed about their heads in shimmering golden waves as they ran out to greet him.

"Uncle Ben!" they cried out in unison as they hugged him.

Their exuberance surprised Hirsch. He hadn't seen either in over a year and wondered if they'd even remember him. He wrapped his arms around their shoulders.

"Hi girls!" he said. "Good to see you too. You're both getting so tall."

Indeed, they'd both grown since he'd last seen them. Maddie was a miniature version of her mother with her button nose and aquamarine eyes, while Jenna favored her father's svelte build and Nordic complexion.

Jess Severson caught his attention as she approached the door. Tall with dark blonde hair and a natural smile, Jess sported a pair of yoga pants and a cream-colored sweater that hugged her enviable figure. Hirsch had long admired Jess since Kyle first invited the undergrad and a group of her friends to a law school tailgate during their 1L year. They weren't dating exclusively yet, and Hirsch took Jess out a few times before her relationship with Kyle turned serious. The furthest Hirsch went with her was making out a few times in his car before she broke it off. It was old history, and he knew better than to fool around with his best friend's wife.

"Hey there, Ben," she said. "Good to see you again after so long." She swung the screen door open. "Girls, let Ben go so he can come in out of the cold."

Maddie and Jenna relinquished their hold on Hirsch and escorted him into the house. He handed Jess the bottle of wine and said, "I know it's not much, but I remember you enjoy a good Italian red."

"That's sweet of you, Ben," Jess replied as she leaned in to hug him. "It'll be perfect with dinner. You know you didn't have to bring us anything under the circumstances." Hirsch blanched at the allusion to his disgrace. "I hope you're hungry. I made us spaghetti for dinner. Kyle's in the kitchen slicing the garlic bread."

"Oh gosh, Jess, you don't need to worry about that. I've saved my appetite all day." He omitted that he was too damn broke to splurge on lunch.

"We'd never fail you when it comes to food. I remember how much you ate for Thanksgiving when you and Allison visited. Have a seat here at the table. We'll have dinner ready in no time. I'll bet you could use a drink after that long drive."

Hirsch nodded.

"I'll find a corkscrew and pour us each a glass of this." Jess held the wine bottle aloft, flashed a smile at Hirsch, and ambled toward the kitchen, her pert rear wagging back and forth at him in the skintight yoga pants.

Hirsch sauntered over to an open seat at the table and pulled out a chair to sit down. Kyle emerged from the adjoining kitchen carrying a tray of steaming hot garlic bread in his hands.

"Hey there, buddy!" Kyle said, beaming at Hirsch. He set the bread tray on the table so he could shake Hirsch's hand. Tall and rail thin, Kyle exuded a good-natured charm in the comfort of his home. "I can't tell you how glad we are you decided to join us up here. I said to Jess, 'Ben will always have a place to stay with us for as long as he wants.' You're in for a real treat tonight. It's Jess's special."

"You know I wouldn't miss her cooking for the world." Hirsch refrained from adding that there were other qualities about Jess he couldn't resist.

Jess appeared with a heaping ceramic bowl of spaghetti in both hands. As she set it down at the center of the table, the aroma flooded through the dining room. Hirsch's mouth watered as his appetite went into overdrive.

"Maddie, Jenna, come take a seat at the table," Kyle said to his daughters, precipitating an argument over which one would get to sit next to their honored guest. Jenna won out and inched her chair closer to Ben's. As Kyle and Jess took their seats, the vacant sixth chair caught Hirsch's attention.

"Will your mom be joining us tonight?" Hirsch asked. Kyle's widowed mother, Eleanor Severson, lived with the family in a mother-in-law apartment they'd converted out of a pair of surplus rooms after her husband's death.

"Not tonight, I'm afraid. She's at an Eastern Star meeting and won't be back until later. She's eager to see you though," Kyle added. The Severson family matriarch remained an active member of the community even in her late seventies. Eleanor and her late husband, Judge Severson, belonged to many of the town's civic organizations, including the Elks and the Rotary Club.

Wasting no time, Kyle passed Hirsch the spaghetti bowl and dinner began. Conversation ceased as they fell to eating. Later, as they reached a point of satiation, Maddie asked, "So how long can you stay with us, Uncle Ben?"

Hirsch shot Kyle a nervous glance before replying, "Well … that's a good question, Maddie. I'm not entirely sure yet."

"Ben's going to stay with us for a few days, girls," Kyle said, spotting Maddie's confusion. "He's sick of living down there in the big ol' city. I told him he should come here and visit. Who knows, he might even stay longer for work."

"Is he going to work for you, Dad?" she asked.

"We'll see about that. Ben might be ready for something other than lawyering."

"Where's Aunt Allison?" Jenna asked between mouthfuls of spaghetti.

Kyle and Jess each opened their mouths to reply on Hirsch's behalf, but he preempted them. "Aunt Allison's living down in Lansing now, sweetie. She likes it there and is going to be staying for a little while." Hirsch didn't know how much Kyle and Jess had told the girls about their divorce. He wasn't in the mood to discuss it yet.

"Who wants cherry pie for dessert?" Jess asked, coming to his rescue. The girls and Hirsch all vigorously assented. A sinking feeling settled in the pit of his stomach. No matter where he went, his failures would haunt him. Aided by the wine, he staggered through the rest of the meal and put on his bravest face.

LATER THAT EVENING, AFTER KYLE put the girls to bed, the three adults gathered in the living room to reconnect. Jess emptied the rest of the wine into their glasses. She and Kyle settled into their couch while Hirsch took a leather armchair opposite it. A roaring fire crackled and hissed in the fireplace, flooding the room with warmth and the comforting aroma of wood smoke.

"We're awfully glad you're here, buddy. We wish it were under different circumstances," Kyle said.

"Kyle told me what happened," Jess said. "You got a raw deal if you ask me. The principal at our high school slept with a teacher—both married to other people, mind you—and he only got a suspension. If he didn't deserve to get fired, you sure didn't." Jess's position as an assistant principal at the local high school made her privy to much of the community's salacious gossip.

"Thanks, Jess. I should have known better. It's odd, but it feels like I was another person when it happened. I always warned my clients to behave themselves. But look what I went and did," Hirsch said as he took another sip of the wine. It helped blur the shame of discussing his disgrace. "Maybe this was the wake-up call I needed. I was burning it at both ends there for too long."

"You always did push the extra mile as long as I've known you. I thought about doing the private-practice thing, but I'm glad I took a county job. I can come home and see my kids most nights and weekends," Kyle said.

"I think you made the right choice too. I wonder where I'd have ended up if I'd done the same. Makes me wish I hadn't turned down that DOL job," Hirsch said. The work had sounded interesting enough, but he declined the Department of Labor's offer thinking he could get rich in private practice.

"Kyle mentioned you hoped to find work up here. Any idea what you might want to do?" Jess asked, unaware of Kyle's entreaty to Hirsch earlier in the day. She leaned toward him and pushed her arms together, bunching her sweater at the collar and revealing a hint of cleavage. Hirsch struggled to meet her eyes.

"Honestly, I'm not sure. Lawyering is all I know how to do, and I've royally screwed myself over there. I can't imagine the county has much use for a disbarred attorney."

Kyle sighed. "I considered that too. You know I'd find you a job in a heartbeat here or with the city if I could, but the disbarment is a non-starter, even for a paralegal position. It's a shame because we could use a smart guy like you on a few of these criminal cases I'm working up. It's not all happy-go-lucky folks around here these days."

"Drugs?" Hirsch asked. Meth and opioids had corroded the region in recent years.

"Mostly—and everything that comes with it. Anymore, a young person might be lucky to get a job working checkout at the local Walmart. The pay is crap and they can't make ends meet, let alone get ahead. No wonder they turn to drugs. It's a break from their shit lives."

"Worst part is, it's not only the kids," Jess added. "Last semester they busted a middle-school teacher for hosting an honest-to-God drug house. Her friends would come over and shoot-up heroin. It's gotten so goddamn crazy you don't even know what to say to the students."

"Too bad you can't teach, Ben. Sounds like you'd have a future if that's your competition," Kyle said. Jess slapped his arm and rolled her eyes. "No, I actually thought I'd give my folks' old friend Edgar Trehearne a call and see if he knows anyone who needs a hand. He retired from the gas company several years back but knows near everyone in these parts."

"Oh, good lord, honey. Knowing Edgar, he'll probably find Ben a job scrubbing campground outhouses," Jess said. "I doubt a guy who practiced law for a dozen years wants to toil outside all day for bad pay and no benefits."

"Wait now," Hirsch interrupted. "Maybe I should at least listen to what your friend Edgar has in mind." Desperation made him curious. He set his wine glass on the coffee table and steepled his fingers, as he was wont to do when considering a proposition.

"If you really want, I'll give Edgar a call tomorrow and let him know you're interested. I'm sure if you waited a few more days or even a couple weeks, we could drum up something more, I don't know, appropriate given your background," Kyle said.

"That's generous, but I don't want to put you and Jess out any longer than need be. With a little money, I could get the Manistique house fixed up and ready for sale. It's been empty since my mom moved out. My sister would be thrilled if we could unload it for a reasonable price." The Hirsch family home, an hour east in Manistique, sat vacant and moldering in the harsh UP weather. Hirsch's older sister, Rachel, lived in Marquette and wanted nothing to do with the decaying residence.

"I wouldn't put much hope in selling it," Jess said. "Unless it's on the lakefront and some downstater with money wants it for the view, you might have trouble giving a house away. Last I checked, Manistique's down to being a one-mill town with not much else to keep young people home. Like I said, I see it here too." Despite meeting her husband at college in Lansing, Jess came from an old Upper Peninsula family descended from Cornish miners. She knew the local ins-and-outs as well as anyone.

"You're telling me. The real estate market is so rotten we didn't receive a single offer when we listed it for sale. The strongest nibble was the fire department's invitation to burn it down for training purposes. We couldn't stomach the thought of our childhood home going up in smoke."

"Someone must want it. Hell, I'd buy the place and live there myself if it weren't such a long drive to work," Kyle said.

"Make me a reasonable offer and it's yours. I'm sure Schoolcraft County could use a decent prosecutor."

Kyle laughed. "Forget about that, I've got a good thing going here. Besides, the kids enjoy living near their grandparents. I couldn't uproot them from school and their friends."

Hirsch drained the final dregs of the earthy, tannic wine from his glass. "Well, someone should enjoy it, at any rate. My dad saw the writing on the wall and took the early retirement buyout they offered. Figured he'd made enough off of the company and could spend the rest of his time fishing and hiking. Then he up and died three years later. I think he maybe got out on the lake once or twice after his last day at work. It's a shame really."

Kyle and Jess both sat mute, holding their wineglasses and avoiding eye contact. The specter of death killed the otherwise buoyant mood. Kyle broke the silence.

"I imagine you're worn out from your long drive up here. How about we show you to the guest room and give you some time to yourself?"

"That sounds fine to me. I'll try to stay out of your hair while I'm here."

Jess, who'd gotten up and collected the wineglasses, touched Hirsch on his upper arm with her free hand and said, "You're not 'in our hair,' Ben, you know that. Consider yourself part of the family." She walked into the kitchen to dispose of the dirty glasses. Hirsch cast one final glance at the sway of her hips as she disappeared around the corner.

"I know you've stayed here before, so make yourself at home." Kyle led Hirsch through the living room and to the ground-floor guestroom. "Jess had Maddie put fresh sheets on the bed before you arrived. I hope she did a good job."

"Hey, Kyle, I didn't want to mention it in front of Jess, but I thought about your offer—I'm in. I don't know how much help I can be, but I'll do what I can. It's about damn time I did something useful for a change."

"Good, I'm glad to hear that. I need to gather a file on these clowns, but when the time is right, I'll call you and let you know what I need you to do."

"Thanks, man. I can't tell you how much I appreciate this. I'll make it up to you someday," Hirsch replied.

"Don't mention it. If your friends can't be there for you, what good are they? Besides, I think it might do us both a benefit. You sleep well tonight," Kyle said, then switched off the hallway light and disappeared.

Hirsch shut the door. Alone again, the tumult of the day left him fatigued. It hit him for the first time how exhausting it was trying to hold himself together in front of others. Shedding all but his boxers and a white T-shirt, Hirsch pulled back the quilt and the top sheet and crawled into bed. As he lay waiting for sleep to take over, the faint stirrings of an erection demanded his attention. Thoughts of running his hands all over Jess's firm ass and hips while planting kisses on the nape of her neck gushed through his mind. Midway through his fantasy, shame washed over him as he remembered how this sort of behavior landed him in trouble in the first place.

This is a new beginning. Don't squander it. Striving for a disciplined lifestyle, Hirsch rolled onto his side and drifted off to sleep, ready to usher in a new chapter of his life.

THE SCREECH OF A SNOW shovel scraping against a concrete sidewalk woke Hirsch from a deep sleep. Its harsh sound indicated the arrival of snow overnight. The grating noise amplified the ache in his head, reminding him of the wine he had drunk the night before. The gray light of morning sliced in through the Venetian blinds, painting the room with its cold winter light.

As his eyes adjusted to daylight, the red figures on the bedside table alarm clock caught Hirsch's attention. Damn, it was already nine in the morning. He hadn't slept much in recent weeks, and his body decided it needed a break. He threw the covers back and sat up in place. Hirsch stretched his arms and evaluated how to spend his first free day in many years. The bed's fitted sheet had worked loose from the corner during the night and rolled back to the mattress's midway point. Maddie's bed-making skills evidently needed more practice.

Hirsch cracked the guest-room door open and listened to the rest of the house. The sole sound was the grandfather clock ticking away in the living room. The family had long since gone to work and school. He walked across the hall into the bathroom, undressed, and hopped into the shower, lingering under the nozzle longer than normal as a defense against the morning chill. After turning off the water, he drew back the shower curtain and liner, revealing himself to the mirror affixed over the sink opposite him. Unlike many of his friends and colleagues of a similar age, Hirsch had thus far avoided the curse of baldness. Only a few gray hairs stood out amidst the dark mass atop his head. While never of more than average height, Hirsch maintained his college weight and took pride in his still-trim figure. He had his mother's dark brown eyes but his father's angular jaw and chiseled nose. Only the bags around his eyes and crinkled crow's feet betrayed his age. Their lines stood as a fitting punishment for the chemical excess of his past two decades.

Hirsch wrapped a towel around his hips and walked back across the hallway into the guest room. He put on boxers, thick wool socks, a well-worn pair of tan corduroy trousers, and a red knit sweater over a thin gray T-shirt. Brushing his hair to one side with his fingers, Hirsch figured he looked as ready as needed for a day of unemployment. Although he had nothing planned for the day, there was no point in sitting around the house while the world awaited him. My new life is out there, he thought. Let's go find it.

The view from the window heralded another day of brutal cold in the Upper Peninsula. The overnight dusting of snow left the town frozen in a white gauze. A frigid gale ripping off the lake shook the bare tree branches overhead. Hirsch donned his flannel-lined jacket and zipped it up to his neck before stepping outside into the midmorning day. The wind stung his face and Hirsch flipped up his collar for added protection. Despite growing up a mere hour away, Hirsch's family rarely made the trip to Escanaba unless they needed provisions unavailable in Manistique. If he was going to be here for a while, he should at least get to know the area.

Hirsch worked his way down Lake Shore Drive, creeping along the northern edge of Ludington Park toward the lakeshore. He paused to stare out at the violent waters of Lake Michigan. While the lake's winter ice was mostly gone, the choppy surf remained menacing and foreboding. Hirsch recalled his youth and learning how to swim amidst the lake's endless blue depths. *"Rip current be damned, son. If you can't swim in the lake, it won't do you a lick of good to learn in the pool."* In his father's mind, capsizing miles from shore was an all-too-real possibility. Hirsch learned how to swim the hard way, but he never came to enjoy it.

Hirsch continued west along Ludington Street. The tidy residential neighborhood gave way to Escanaba's commercial thoroughfare. A scattering of brewpubs and taverns promised a future evening's escape from reality. As he strolled along in solitude, Hirsch reflected on the suddenness with which disgrace leaves its accomplice alone in the world. It was only months ago that he spent nearly every minute of his day in the company of others. From his ex-wife's warm presence in bed next to him—her rear snuggled up against his hips and his arm thrown over her midsection, cupping the soft flesh of her breast in his palm—to his waking hours engaged in an endless parade of clients, co-workers, attorneys, and others who kept the wheels of justice creaking along. He passed his so-called free time at a Lansing cocktail lounge frequented by other professionals. Most days, he could count on two hands the number of minutes of solitude. Now, disgrace left him alone—a being thrown into the world, struggling amidst an indifferent humanity.

Lost in his meditations as he walked past the local newspaper office, the vibration of his phone in his pocket alerted him to a call. Hirsch didn't recognize the number but answered after noticing the local 906 area code.

"Hello, this is Ben."

"Ah, Ben, how you doing? This is Edgar Trehearne. Your buddy Kyle asked me to give you a call."

"Oh, hey, Mr. Trehearne. I didn't expect you to get back to me so quickly."

"Please, call me Edgar or just plain Ed. Mr. Trehearne makes me sound old." Hirsch figured Edgar was in his mid-seventies at best from the hoarse straining in his voice. "Kyle tells me you're looking for work. I'm glad he called. You see, I keep in touch with my old fellas at the gas company pretty regular. We go and have coffee once a week, I suppose. Well, a young manager there—real nice fella but hasn't learned all the ropes yet, if you know what I mean—he says to me they're having a heck of a time finding folks to walk the gas lines and check for leaks. Folks that don't mind being outside all day and can pass a piss test." Hirsch got the impression that having coffee with Edgar would turn into a drawn-out affair.

"Anyway," Trehearne continued, "I says to the young manager, 'Well why the hell didn't you give old Edgar a call. I can find damn near anyone you need in these parts.' So he says to me, 'Edgar, if you could find me someone I could trust to do this job, coffee's on me for the rest of the month.' Far be it from me to refuse an offer like that, so I told him he had himself a deal. Here we are today."

"So, you're saying there's a position for me … with the gas company?" Hirsch asked, uncertain whether Trehearne's monologue was over.

"I sure am, Ben. If you want the job, you can have it. Long as you're not a dope smoker or hitting' that meth. Say, I forgot to ask Kyle—what kind of work have you done anyway?"

"I was a lawyer down in Lansing for a number of years," Hirsch replied, wondering if he'd scotched his chances at a new life. "But I did work on a road crew during college." He omitted that his sole purpose that summer between his sophomore and junior years was to rotate the "STOP/SLOW" sign an interminable number of times a day on a torn-up section of Highway 2 east of Gulliver.

Silence greeted Ben on the other end of the line until Trehearne replied, "Ah, well, we won't hold that shyster business against you, I suppose. As long as you don't mind getting your boots muddy and being out in the rain and cold, you can handle this. The pay's not much to write home about—fourteen dollars an hour, but it's better than nothing. Living's cheap in this neck of the woods, at least."

Hirsch winced at the salary. "So, what exactly does this job involve?" he asked.

"You'll be checking for gas leaks, you know, walking around with a leak detector. When one of those suckers blows, it makes a helluva mess. The gas company would just as soon not see that happen. Every year, they hire a few people, hand them a leak detector and a map, and turn 'em loose in the field searching for leaks. If you find one and pinpoint the spot, great—the company fixes it. If you don't find anything, then at least they can say they've covered their ass and checked."

Hirsch didn't think much of the work, but he had no other options. "I think this may be a good fit. When can I start?"

"Tell you what—why don't I go by your place tomorrow morning? I can take you over to meet with the powers that be at the gas company. I hear you're staying at the Seversons' old place. I know right where that's at. Me and old Judge Severson drank our share together back in the day. Let's see; tomorrow's Wednesday. How's ten a.m. sound to you?"

"That'll be fine, sir."

"Jesus, drop this 'sir' nonsense, won'tcha. Makes me feel like I'm back in the service. Say, Ben, is Mrs. Severson still living there? She was always one fine-looking dame."

Momentarily confused, Hirsch thought Trehearne was referring to Jess. He realized it was Eleanor Severson in question and replied, "Ah, yes, she is. She was out last night at some sort of club event, but I should see her soon."

"Lucky duck. I used to razz Judge Severson that I was going to woo his wife away from him if he didn't take good care of her. He didn't take it too seriously, I guess. There wasn't much danger of her leaving him for a yokel like me. We were still friends up until the day he died."

Hirsch chuckled and said, "Thanks for the opportunity. I'll be seeing you tomorrow." He ended the call and returned the phone to his pocket. He gazed down the street at the midday traffic, struggling to contemplate a future so different from his office-bound past.

Chapter 3

"YOU'LL NEED A GOOD PAIR of shoes, Ben. Hell, make 'em Red Wings if you can afford 'em," Edgar said as they rumbled through downtown Escanaba the next morning. They were headed to the gas company's office on the edge of town. The frosts of winter left the road in dismal shape, and Edgar's twenty-plus-year-old Chevy pickup truck absorbed every heave and cavity along the way. Discarded fast-food wrappers littered the floor around Hirsch's feet. The pungent stench of discarded banana peels mingled with stale sweat permeated the cabin. Edgar's cavalier disregard for the local speed limit made Hirsch clutch the armrest on the door for safety.

"I spent my fair share of time out in the woods of these parts. Back then, we were laying the gas line itself," Edgar said, continuing his sermon on suitable footwear. "You never know what you might land your foot in. Plenty of abandoned traps, that's for sure." Hirsch refrained from asking whether his Cole Haan chukka boots would suffice.

The man occupying the driver's seat glanced over at Hirsch and smiled, displaying a line of chipped and yellowing teeth. Edgar Trehearne certainly looked as though he'd weathered a lifetime of UP life. He had an unruly mop of stark white hair, a creased and lined face camouflaged by a graying mustache and patchy stubble, and a rotund belly that peeked out from underneath a ragged T-shirt. Hirsch had trouble believing this ossified figure of a man once hobnobbed with the likes of Judge and Mrs. Severson. Their social affiliations spoke to the lack of pretension amongst the area's residents.

"Damn, it's raining harder than a cow pissing on a flat rock," Edgar said while squinting through the driving rain blanketing the town.

Hirsch nodded. "Do you know who we'll be meeting with today?"

"It'll be that young fella at the gas company I told you about over the phone. Goes by the name Milo Feeney. He moved out here from Minnesota a few years back after the company transferred him. Not a local, but he seems like a decent enough guy. At least he laughs at my jokes, you know. He's expecting us."

Edgar turned right off Ludington onto Highway 2. They traveled north toward Gladstone before stopping at a parking lot on the highway's west side. The blue-lettered sign on the non-descript cinderblock building read "Peninsula Energy Company." Edgar brought the truck to a stop with a jolt, and they exited Edgar's truck and headed inside. Hirsch followed while Edgar waddled to lead the way. A scowling receptionist at a desk inside looked up from her computer to size up the visitors. Her scowl deepened at the sight of Edgar.

"I thought you were retired, Ed? Don't tell me you're already bored with fishing," she said.

"Aw, Virginia, you know you can't get rid of me that easy. But I'll tell you this much, you dodged a bullet here today."

"Is that so?" Virginia asked, raising an eyebrow.

"Believe it or not, I'm here for my friend," Edgar said as he elbowed Hirsch in the side. "Ben here wants to work for the gas company."

Virginia peered at him over her glasses as though she was unsure whether Hirsch was lineman material. "I'll let Milo know you're here," she said.

She pivoted at her desk to pick up the phone. They watched her gray-headed profile as she said, "Milo, I've got old Edgar and another guy here to see you. Uhm. All right … I'll tell them." She hung up the phone and jerked her head toward the hallway. "You can go on back."

"Thank you, Ginny," Edgar said as he led Hirsch to Milo Feeney's office.

"Don't call me that, Trehearne!" she replied.

Absorbed in a street map spread across his desk, it took Milo Feeney a moment to acknowledge the two visitors standing in his doorway. The tired man sitting before them looked to be in his mid-forties at best. His hair was prematurely gray and a pair of dollar-store reading glasses hung from a band around his neck. Milo Feeney was most assuredly not the "young fella" Hirsch expected from Edgar's description.

Milo sprung up and exchanged a rapid handshake with Edgar and Hirsch. He sat back down and said, "Gentlemen, make yourselves comfortable. Can I get either of you a cup of coffee?"

"Ah, Milo, you know we'd be here all morning if I took you up on that," Edgar said.

"Suit yourself," Milo replied, not bothering to wait for Hirsch's answer. "I was just going over the map of the territory we need to cover. Until Edgar here called, I thought I might end up doing it myself. Wouldn't be the first time. So, Edgar tells me you're interested in working with us here at the gas company."

"That's right—if the job's still open."

"It certainly is. I was prepared to transfer one of our Wisconsin crewmen over here. Truth is, though, I'd much rather hire a native who knows the area and the locals. Am I correct you grew up around here?"

"I did, yes, right over the county line in Manistique. My parents are both from the UP as well."

"Ben here's a good friend of Kyle Severson with the prosecutor's office," Edgar cut in. "You know, Judge Severson's kid."

"Judge Severson was before my time, I'm afraid. But I am well acquainted with Kyle. He's helped us out of a jam a time or two before. I owe him one." Hirsch wasn't clear why a county prosecutor would have much of anything to do with a private utility company. Milo didn't elaborate.

"Edgar's told me a little about the job, but I'd love to hear the details if you have time," Hirsch said.

Milo leaned back in his chair and steepled his fingers. "The long and short of it is we provide natural-gas transmission and residential heating services to most areas in the western and central Upper Peninsula. Natural gas does a helluva job of heating home and business alike but, as you likely know, it's incredibly volatile if it leaks. Check the news and, from time to time, you'll hear a horror story about a gas explosion wiping out an entire city block. We'd as soon avoid disaster at all costs, and so far, we have. I'm not keen on breaking that streak on my watch.

"Here's the deal—the only way to ensure the lines are intact is if we inspect every single foot by hand. That's where you come in. What I need is a gas-line safety technician who'll walk along the lines and check for any leaks." Milo paused to retrieve a device next to his desk. It resembled a metal detector with a plunger-like rubber nozzle on the end. "This right here is the instrument you'll be using. If you take the job, I'll show you how to use it in the field. If you detect a gas leak, then you'll need to take that tool over there and barhole the line to pinpoint the source." Milo pointed to a three-foot-tall narrow cylinder resting in a corner of the room.

"The most important thing is if you do find a leak, you report it immediately. We'll give you a cell phone for that purpose. No funny stuff now—we know it has service most anywhere in the greater UP. I fired a guy last summer who snoozed a couple hours after lunch claiming he was in a dead zone."

"All right, I'm curious how folks might react if they see me wandering through their property checking for leaks. People can be suspicious," Hirsch said.

"I'm glad you asked. When you're out in the field, you'll wear a blue vest identifying you as a Peninsula Energy employee. Most people seeing you wearing the vest won't think anything of it. They're used to us and know that the utility companies periodically need to check our equipment. A few will say 'hi' at most, though you do get a talker now and then—older folks by and large. I've had a couple try and talk my ear off about hellfire and damnation. That said, on rare occasions, you'll run into individuals who will not welcome your presence in the least. They're liable to scream at you about trespassing and private property rights and such. Mind you, we have every damn right to go onto their land and check our equipment. Let's say the concept of an easement is lost on these types. If that happens or, God forbid, one of them pulls a gun or threatens you, get yourself out as fast as you can. We'll deal with the legalities later. I like that you're a local. These are proud people living in a place unlike anywhere else in America. You know them. Honestly, the biggest threat you'll have to worry about is dogs."

"Lord knows I've been nipped a time or two in my day," Edgar commented.

"Take an umbrella," Milo said.

"An umbrella?" Hirsch asked.

"You heard me right. Open it up if the dog comes after you. Nine times out of ten, it'll scare them away. Say, I forgot to ask, are you a dope smoker, Mr. Hirsch?"

"No, I can't say I am."

"Crank? Heroin? Oxy?"

"Negative," Hirsch said.

"I didn't think so, but I had to ask. I personally don't give a shit, but it's company policy. Not even medicinal use, I'm afraid.

"You want the details, right?" Milo continued. "Pay's fourteen-fifty an hour, no benefits to speak of, but we do reimburse you for mileage on your vehicle. You have your own wheels, right?" Hirsch nodded. "Good. We don't work during wintertime, so this gig will only last until mid-summer. Maybe longer if the tightwads in corporate loosen the purse strings. If you want it, I can get you started tomorrow. I'll show you the ropes the first day but after that, we'll give you a map of the coverage area and you'll be on your own. The one requirement I must emphasize is that you cannot cut any corners with this job. We need you to be thorough and do it right. Take a day and think it over if you want, but I need an answer soon."

Hirsch's head swam at the realization that his new life would be a significant downgrade from his halcyon days as an attorney. At this point, what other reasonable option did he have? He barely had gas money, and no self-respecting business would hire a disbarred attorney.

"I can give you an answer now. Tomorrow's fine to start," Hirsch replied, accepting the cold, hard reality of what had become of his life.

"Good. Be here at nine a.m., and we'll hit the pavement. Make sure you bring all your paperwork so Virginia out front can get you on the books. That'll save us all extra time. She'll give you the address of a lab that'll piss-test you for drugs today. Remember, you're not a regular employee. Saves us some headache, but we still need to make sure you're not a murderer or rapist. Wear warm clothes and a sturdy pair of shoes or boots. Trust me, you'll need them out there." Feeney rose from his chair, signaling the interview was over. "Thanks again, Ed. I owe you one."

"Milo, you don't just owe me one, you owe me coffee for the rest of the month, remember?"

"That I do," Milo conceded. "Downtown coffeehouse at the usual time this Friday?"

"I'll be seeing you there, friend. Who knows, maybe this fella right here might join us before too long."

"Consider that an invitation to our weekly bullshit session," Milo said.

Hirsch and Edgar exited Feeney's office and returned to the reception area. Virginia held a canary-yellow slip of paper aloft but kept her gaze fixed on her computer screen.

"Thanks," Hirsch mumbled as he accepted the slip from

her. Hirsch decided to avoid getting on her bad side if at all possible.

Edgar dropped Hirsch off at the Seversons' house. As Hirsch opened the door to escape the fetid cab, Edgar said, "Looks like you're on your own tomorrow, partner. You'll either sink or swim in this business, but be sure to call me if you have any questions. Oh, and if anyone gives you shit out there like Milo mentioned, you let me know. Lord knows I've come across most folks in these parts."

"I'll keep that in mind. I can't tell you how much I appreciate all your help," Hirsch said.

"Ah, don't mention it, Benny," Edgar replied with a dismissive wave of his hand. "Least I could do for a friend."

"Milo's not the only person who owes you one."

"I'll remember that. Never know when I might need a favor from a young fella like you. Just ask Milo or Kyle."

Hirsch shut the door and Edgar sped away from the curb. Hirsch watched Edgar's truck recede into the distance. A faded "Superior State" bumper sticker clung to the tailgate.

"Welcome to your new life," Hirsch muttered. He stood on the empty sidewalk, a blue vest dangling in his hand.

"*YOUR FATHER'S DYING YOU KNOW*," Hirsch's mother, Justine, had whispered to him in the kitchen of the family home during his last visit to Manistique before his father's passing. Out of earshot, Murray Hirsch coughed and struggled to rise from his recliner. The squeaking of two small wheels rolling along the hardwood floor followed by the clatter of the screen door told them Murray had gone outside for another cigarette, oxygen tank in tow.

"How the hell is he still smoking?" Hirsch asked.

"Watch the language, Ben," his mother admonished him.

"I'm surprised he hasn't blown the whole house up yet." Justine only shrugged in response. A month earlier, his mother called Hirsch with the news—small cell lung cancer, inoperable to boot.

That Murray would not recover from the diagnosis was all too apparent. After all, Justine had seen it far too many times first-hand as a nurse at the county hospital. She looked at Hirsch with dark eyes inherited from her Ojibwe ancestors.

"You know no one could ever tell your father what to do. It served him well as a foreman at the mill, but here at home …" his mother paused before continuing, "well, it's not like I need to explain it to you."

Hirsch understood. While he revered his father for being a brilliant man of action who taught him much about life and how to survive in the north, his stubbornness and need for control exasperated all members of the household. Murray's bullheadedness drove Hirsch's sister, Rachel, out of the house in early adulthood. Hirsch himself limited his visits in the years before his father fell ill.

"I understand, Ma, but I can't believe the doctors didn't order him to stop. It's a miracle he can still breathe with lung cancer *and* emphysema."

"Two different types of emphysema," she added.

"I didn't even know there was more than one."

"Oh, they told him to quit all right in no uncertain terms, Ben. Doctor Korhonen said if he kept it up, he'd have no more than six months to live. If he quit," she shrugged, "who knows, maybe five years or longer. You can guess how that conversation went. You can't tell a man who's smoked for fifty-plus years to all of a sudden quit like that. Besides, he defends it by saying someone needs to keep Cromley company out there." Justine was referring to their neighbor across the street, a cantankerous former journalist whose primary pastimes since retirement appeared to be chain-smoking and complaining about the decline of journalistic integrity to whoever would listen.

"How are you handling it, Ma?" Hirsch asked, not knowing what else to say. He'd interacted with several bereaved clients in the course of his practice and knew how to empathize with their struggles. With his own family, though, he struggled.

"As well as a person can, I suppose. I told him not to smoke all those damn cigarettes years ago. He never listened. Said it gave him a way to bond with the crew at work. Made him one of the guys. Retired three years ago, but he never did cut back. And the guys never visited once."

The screen door clattered again, and Murray shuffled back into the living room toward his favorite recliner. He collapsed into the seat with a wheezing intake of air.

True to Dr. Korhonen's warning, Murray died five months later. Hirsch found himself standing with Rachel and their mother, overlooking Murray's fresh grave in Lakeview Cemetery on a bleak fall morning. It was the last time the four were together.

HIRSCH'S FATHER WAS OFTEN IN his thoughts after returning home. The morning of his first day of work, he walked into the Seversons' kitchen to scrounge up breakfast. A cereal box atop the refrigerator caught Hirsch's attention. Relieved, he grabbed it and, after searching several cupboards and drawers, also located a bowl and spoon. He considered brewing a cup of coffee but decided against it after inspecting their coffeemaker and realizing he didn't want to take the time to figure out how to operate it. Instead, he recovered a carton of milk from the Seversons' refrigerator and sat at the table. Against his better judgment, he indulged a favorite vice and gulped the milk straight from the carton. As he lowered it from his lips with a satisfied gasp, the Seversons' white-and-black cat leaped up onto the countertop near him. The cat stared straight at Hirsch with half-open, unblinking green eyes as if trying to decide what to make of this intruder.

"Are you supposed to be up there on the counter?" Hirsch asked the cat.

"No, she's not, but it's not like anyone here does a damn thing about it," a voice behind him said.

Hirsch started in surprise and jerked his head around toward the source.

Kyle's mother, Eleanor Severson, stood at the kitchen entrance. She wore her light-blue nightgown and clutched a white ceramic mug filled with coffee. Had she seen him guzzling milk from their carton?

"Oh, good morning, Mrs. Severson. I didn't know you were home." Remembering his manners, Hirsch rose as she walked into the kitchen.

"I stay in my apartment most of the day, but I thought I would come out to say hello," she said as she offered Hirsch her cheek. He kissed it after a moment of awkwardness, and she settled down on the chair next to his. "My apologies for missing dinner the other night. The Eastern Star meeting ran late as usual. Our Worthy Matron, Gladys, is a doll but lord can that woman talk. Kyle told me you'd be staying with us; he didn't say for how long."

"Only a couple of days, I imagine, ma'am. Kyle's lined up work for me. Today's my first day, actually. I should be out of your hair soon."

"Ah, yes, I heard what happened with your practice," she said while staring him down with steely blue eyes.

Hirsch swallowed hard. "Kyle told you about that, eh?"

"Oh, no, Mr. Hirsch, I read it myself. I take the Detroit paper, you see." Hirsch quit following the news after his suspension, but he was unsurprised by the media coverage. He could picture the headline in print—*Lansing Attorney Disbarred for Sexual Relationship with Client.*

"I suppose you don't think much of me in that case," Hirsch replied, not knowing what else to say to this intimidating matriarch.

"Oh, dear, I'm long past judging. You should have heard the stories Thomas brought home from his days in practice. None of them, and I mean none," she said, raising a finger for emphasis, "were all that innocent." Eleanor's late husband, Thomas Severson, a local legend in the UP's legal community, had passed away a couple of years earlier.

"It's a shame the state didn't see it your way."

"I suppose they didn't have much choice, Mr. Hirsch. All I can say is I hope you've learned your lesson. My father's old classmate at Saint Paul Academy, Mr. Fitzgerald, once claimed there were no second acts in American life. By and large, I haven't found that to be the case. Kyle's sung your praises since you first met in law school. I'd like to believe you still have plenty to offer the world."

Hirsch pondered her words. "Well, that's what brought me here, I suppose. I've been away from home for several years, but

I'd like to think I can make a difference. I hope I won't be written off as some downstater who abandoned his community and came back with his tail between his legs. Say, since I've been gone so long, do you have any advice?"

Eleanor sighed and glanced out the window at the gray morning sky. "I'm afraid it's not the same place you remember from childhood, Mr. Hirsch. Ever since the mines shut down, people have been desperate for work. There's simply not enough to go around. Those who had another opportunity headed south. Even the ones with good degrees who want to stay can't find jobs."

"It's funny, Jess mentioned that the other night as well."

"Lord knows she's seen it firsthand. The smart kids going through high school leave for college and never bother to come back. The ones that don't or can't afford it, well, you'll see what I mean if you look around." Eleanor fixed her gaze on Hirsch. "What I'm trying to say is don't be in the least bit surprised if folks you run into seem desperate. Goodness knows they're not all bad people, but many of them have nothing left and won't hesitate to take advantage of you. Consider yourself warned."

Hirsch opened his mouth to reply, nonplussed by the situation's gravity, but Eleanor rose from her chair.

"I best be letting you get back to your breakfast," she said. "I'd hate to make you late for your first day of work. Besides, I have a Rotary meeting in a couple hours, and I can't go looking like this. I can't have word spread that Mrs. Eleanor Severson's let herself go."

Hirsch stood as well. "I appreciate the advice," he said as he took her delicate hand into his. "Will you be joining us for dinner this evening?"

"Good gracious, I hope so. I think another evening of service organization hot air would about do me in." With a wave of her hand, Eleanor Severson shuffled out of the kitchen in her slippers and back into her private world.

TWO DAYS INTO HIS NEW JOB, Hirsch grew wary of imposing on the Seversons' goodwill. While they continued to welcome him as a member of the family, he feared their hospitality would soon grow thin. Besides, the sight of Jess Severson began to torment him, and, given his past proclivities, Hirsch no longer trusted himself to do the right thing. A glimpse of her the day before—prancing off to a tennis match in a sleeveless top and a skirt—damn near set him over the edge. Besides, he had a rent-free residence an hour away. Since work took him all over the peninsula, Hirsch figured it was just as well there as in the city. Thus, when Saturday morning rolled around, Hirsch loaded his truck with his handful of possessions. Since Jess had to take the girls to a gymnastics competition in Green Bay for the weekend, Kyle saw him off.

"Ben, I can't tell you what a pleasure it's been having you stay with us. I understand you want to move on to your own place. You're welcome here anytime you want to come back."

"You know I can't even begin to thank you enough. The two of you have been so good to me over the years. I'm sorry I've missed seeing your kids grow up," Hirsch said.

"The girls and Jess all loved having you around. You're really good with kids. It's a shame you and Allison never had any." At the mention of his ex-wife and the life he threw away, Hirsch's eyes darted to the ground. Kyle hastened to change the subject. "Look, I don't know what you're getting into with the house being empty for so long. If you need another pair of hands to help fix it up, give me a call."

"I'll keep that in mind, buddy. Thank you. Tell you what, once I have the place in decent shape, I'll have you over for a beer."

"Glad to see you've landed on your feet. Keep on fighting, okay? Oh, and I hope to be in touch soon about the Shaw brothers," Kyle said.

Hirsch nodded. Kyle hadn't mentioned his surveillance project since their meeting at the park days earlier, and Hirsch avoided resurrecting the subject. He shook Kyle's hand in farewell before getting into his truck to drive east to Manistique. The weather front that greeted him with clouds and snow when he arrived earlier in the week blew through, leaving the UP awash in the nourishing glow of spring. As he drove north along Highway 2, the sun bounced off the gentle ripples of the Little Bay de Noc and flooded his truck with a golden glow that mirrored his improved mood. While he still had reservations about returning home, the anxious anguish that choked him a week earlier was absent.

Hirsch reached Manistique within an hour. He crossed the Manistique River and took a left on Arbutus Avenue, bringing him back into the town's turn-of-the-century neighborhood. He hung a right onto Michigan Avenue and brought his truck to a stop in front of his once-and-future home. The old house faced him for the first time since his father's funeral. Hirsch's parents purchased the residence in the mid-seventies, shortly before his sister's birth. They'd outgrown their one-bedroom apartment atop a downtown store and longed for a permanent abode. It remained their home until Murray's death nearly forty years later.

The years of vacancy had not been kind. While it retained the graceful appearance typical of most early-twentieth-century Victorian homes, faded and peeling teal paint clung to the two-story building's exterior walls. Decades of lashing rain and snow morphed the white trim into a dirty beige. The red shingles covering the roof were warped in places, and several lay scattered about the yard below, casualties of fierce winds blowing off the bay. On the plus side, most of the windows appeared intact, and the porch spanning the length of the facade retained the intricate gingerbread woodwork his mother took great pride in maintaining.

Not knowing what to expect inside, Hirsch shuffled up the weed-strewn walkway and fumbled in his pocket for his keys. His housekey remained unused for many years. After all, his parents left the house unlocked unless they left town. Hirsch eyed the bowed and warped front steps and advanced with caution. The porch decking, while weathered and buckled in places, held firm. He unlocked the front door and nudged it forward, anticipating the worst.

The door swung open, and Hirsch reached in to flip the light switch on the inner wall to the left. It issued a dry click, but the light fixture overhead remained darkened.

Damn, it didn't occur to him that they'd shut the power off.

Hirsch needed to call the utility company to restore service. In the meantime, he added a trip to the hardware store for flashlights and lanterns to his to-do list. The home's air was stale, but nothing suggested a squirrel or other animal had crawled in and died during the vacancy. Hirsch walked from room to room, assessing the situation. A veneer of grime coated most surfaces, but it was otherwise in fair shape. The original hardwood peeked through bare patches in the garish shag carpet installed decades earlier. Fortunately, a smattering of furnishings remained in the house, meaning he wouldn't have to scavenge for used furniture in town.

Hirsch ascended the creaky wooden staircase and advanced down the hall toward his childhood room. He pushed the door open and found the contents frozen in time from when he left for college. Although stripped of its sheets, his twin bed sat in the corner opposite his old desk, while his dresser supported several youth sports trophies—participation awards, he figured. Faded Detroit Tigers pennants covered the wall, competing with the Aerosmith and Led Zeppelin posters he added during his teenage years. Overwhelmed by fatigue, Hirsch laid down on the bare mattress and cradled his head in his interlaced hands. Hairline cracks fanned out across the plaster ceiling.

Your life's really come full circle, hasn't it, Ben? he realized. Right back where you started and just as broke. Alone with his thoughts, Hirsch succumbed to a dreamless sleep.

Chapter 4

A WEEK OF WALKING THE GAS lines convinced Hirsch he had made the right decision to return north. The days were long, and he spent many an hour trudging through wind and rain that left his boots and clothes dripping wet. Nonetheless, the work was rewarding and cathartic. The solitude gave him ample time to reflect and untangle the hazy morass of his recent life. Out in the field, his mind wandered, and he relished the added time for introspection after years of triaging crisis after crisis in his practice. Hirsch walked eight to ten miles a day and soon lost weight and regained his youthful vigor. His 2006 Toyota Tundra pickup—now adorned with a royal blue-lettered Peninsula Energy Company decal on each door—became a familiar site throughout the neighboring counties.

Spring reigned throughout the Upper Peninsula. A warm southerly wind carried off the lingering remnants of snow, and the aspens and sugar maples began leafing out. The budding flowers and trees perfumed the air with a sweet aroma, competing with undertones of fertile decay from the decomposing leaves and other vegetation. Buried under the snow for several months, they now rotted under the sun, nourishing another season of life. The names of trees and other vegetation came back to Hirsch one-by-one after a decade spent trapped in various offices, alienated from nature. He ambled along, quizzing himself on their common and scientific names and making mental notes to research the unfamiliar ones during his evenings off. Alone in his silent house, he had no television and few distractions. Moreover, he avoided drinking and steered clear of the area taverns. Instead, Hirsch rediscovered the pleasures of reading. He spent his evenings enveloped in the warm glow of a battery-powered lantern, armed with a selection of natural-history books and well-worn field guides recovered from a box stashed in his sister's old bedroom.

After the initial days of familiarizing himself with his equipment and the art of walking the lines, the task became second nature. He dutifully reported the first potential gas leak he detected to Milo Feeney at the Escanaba office. Milo then dispatched a crew to investigate and implement any remedies needed. Knowing his work tangibly benefited people filled him with an unexpected sense of pride.

As Milo warned, the biggest threat to Hirsch's well-being proved to be the dogs, either roaming at large or penned up in homeowners' yards. They eyed him with suspicion, sizing up whether the intruder presented a threat. After a couple of nips to his pantlegs, Hirsch recalled Edgar's advice and took to carrying an umbrella while out walking. It had the desired deterrent effect when he brandished it in the snarling face of a charging Rottweiler while surveying a neighborhood in Munising later that week.

Only once did an actual human threaten Hirsch. One morning, he was outside of Seney checking a gas line leading to a residential address. Hirsch ignored the "No Trespassing" and "Do Not Enter" signs plastered near the entrance. After all, the gas line easement granted him the right of ingress as an agent of Peninsula Energy. He proceeded down a driveway bracketed on either side by dense stands of pine trees. Absorbed in his work, Hirsch didn't see the figure planted in front of him until it was too late. Hirsch froze in his tracks. The lanky man had a scraggly, graying beard and an unkempt mop of chin-length hair. A filth-streaked bathrobe loosely knotted around the man's waist revealed boxer shorts and a gray T-shirt underneath. More alarming was the invisible hand jammed stiff into the right pocket of the man's bathrobe. From the crazed look in the man's eyes, Hirsch didn't feel much like picking a fight with him.

"What the hell do you think you're doing out here? Do I know you?" the man demanded in an unhinged drawl.

"I'm with the gas company, sir—Peninsula Energy," Hirsch said in a measured tone of voice. "I've come to check and make sure your natural gas line's safe and leak-free."

"Safe, eh? I'll bet that's what you're here for, asshole. They told me they'd be back, but I didn't think they'd be this stupid. You think you could waltz right in and take it?"

"I'm not here to take anything. Like I said, I work for the gas company. I can show you my ID."

A look of disgust contorted the man's face. It was plain he didn't believe a single word from Hirsch. The man withdrew his hand from the bathrobe, revealing a sawed-off double-barreled shotgun in his grip. He pointed it at Hirsch and said, "Lemme ask you a question, boy. Do you feel safe now?" The shotgun clicked as the man cocked a hammer.

Hirsch raised his hands, one of which still clutched his leak detector.

"Easy now. No harm intended, sir," Hirsch said. "I'm going to walk back the way I came and leave you be, all right? I won't bother you anymore."

Hirsch shuffled backward, step-by-step, down the driveway. The deafening roar of blood pounding in his ears obscured all rational thought. He never took his eyes off the man but strove to avoid any direct eye contact at the same time.

"That's right. You get your ass off here right this minute and don't come back. I only warn once."

Hirsch wholeheartedly believed him and retreated down the driveway at a steady pace. When the deranged lunatic vanished from sight, Hirsch spun on one heel and ran the rest of the way. He was out of breath and quaking in fear by the time he reached the sanctuary of his truck. With trembling hands, Hirsch dialed Milo's number to report the incident.

"Milo, Ben here. Look, some lunatic just stuck a shotgun in my face while I was checking his line."

"Yeah, I warned you about those types," Milo said. "Had a few of them do that to me out in the field. The guy could be guarding a meth lab. Probably took you for an undercover cop. Hell, a leak might do the community a favor by blowing the god-damn place up. I'm only half kidding. We'll look into it, Ben. Thanks for the alert."

After this incident, Hirsch pondered carrying his late father's .38 Special in his truck. He decided packing a weapon would only escalate an already tense standoff. Instead, he relied on his instincts and hoped no one wanted to go to prison over shooting a lowly gas-line inspector. That encounter aside, he took his orders, followed them, and did his best to deliver without complaint. Other than the occasional leak or damaged equipment, nothing appeared out of the ordinary.

All that changed one morning on the outskirts of Nahma.

It only took Hirsch a few hours to cover the street grid of the small town situated at the terminus of the Big Bay de Noc. With time to spare, he plowed ahead, inspecting a scattering of residential lines on the northern edge of town. A cold drizzle fell across the peninsula as he hurried to finish the remaining territory. Hirsch wore his jacket zipped tight against the chill of the air. He looked forward to the warmth of home and a bowl of steaming hot split pea soup leftover from the previous evening. Hirsch glanced at the ground every few moments as he bounced the detector along the line's subterranean path.

A freshly dug trench running perpendicular to Peninsula Energy's gas line caught his attention. A smattering of leaves strove to mask the confluence—meaningless to the untrained eye. Hirsch brushed away the leaf camouflage with the toe of his boot, revealing loose-tamped earth a foot in diameter beneath. Hirsch yanked his service map out of his pocket and unfolded it with fingers trembling from the cold. Sure enough, the map confirmed an absence of service at the overgrown parcel. A run-down manufactured home peeked out from behind the overgrowth of vegetation at the end of the driveway.

Company procedure directed Hirsch to report any anomalies to the home office. He glanced around to see if anyone was watching, then fumbled in his jacket for a pocketknife. He flicked the blade open, drove it into the ground at an angle, and scooped the waterlogged soil away, mindful of the gas line eighteen inches below. After several minutes of digging, the blade clunked against a solid surface, and Hirsch withdrew the knife. He dove his bare hands into the earth, drawing forth handfuls of rich soil and casting them aside. He brushed the remaining loose dirt away and peered into the clearing.

"What the hell is this setup?" he said.

A yellow plastic pipe ran into a brass T valve spliced straight into the company's line below him. Hirsch stood and wiped the cold soil from his hands along his jeans. One thing was for certain—whoever did this knew what they were doing. He passed the leak detector over the entirety of the junction—not a single leak.

Fearful the landowner might discover him, Hirsch kicked the dirt back into the hole with his boots and spread leaves over the spot, restoring the scene. He made note of the address, finished his remaining inspections, and returned to his truck to radio in his find.

"Milo, this is Ben. I have another situation here I thought I should report."

"Sure Ben, go for it. Don't tell me another yokel out there pulled his piece on you."

"Not this time, but the week's still young. I was walking north of Nahma and stumbled upon something that didn't feel right to me. Do we have any record of service at 15105 GG Road by chance?"

"Give me a minute." The clicking of Milo's computer keyboard punctuated the lapse in conversation before Milo continued, "Nope, doesn't look like it. Nothing at that address now or in the past. Why, what'd you find?"

"Okay, this will sound bizarre, but it looks like someone tapped the gas line and ran service out to that address. I'm no expert by any means, but I'd say it's a recent job,"

The line on Milo's end fell silent. "Milo, you still there?" Hirsch asked, wondering if the call got dropped.

"Yeah, I'm here." Milo sighed and said, "Look, if what you say is true, we need to investigate this. I'll send a crew over—hell, I might even go myself. A few years ago, this was unheard of. Do you have time to come into the main office later this week? We should chat."

"Sure … is it really that serious?" He noted the marked distinction between Milo's response to this incident and his borderline-flippant reaction to Hirsch being held at gunpoint by a deranged recluse.

"I'm not going to lie, Ben, I'm concerned. I can't share everything over the phone, but this may be bigger than you think. Look, I gotta run, but do come in later this week—check that, make it tomorrow, all right?"

"Yeah, that's fine. I'll see you tomorrow."

While apprehensive over his discovery, Hirsch tried to put the incident out of his mind that evening. A double helping of split pea soup left him languid, and he nodded off on the couch only a handful of pages into a survey of pre-Columbian archeology in the Midwest. The ringing of his phone yanked Hirsch out of a pleasant dream about his ex-wife. He answered the call after seeing it was Kyle.

"Hey Kyle, what's going on?" he croaked out.

Kyle sidestepped his usual small talk. "Hey, Ben. Look, I just got off the phone with Milo Feeney. He mentioned you found something interesting on the job today."

"Uh, yeah, that's right. Looks like someone tapped the gas line over by Nahma. Milo said he'd follow-up on it."

"He did—that's why I'm calling you. Remember everything I told you about those two pain-in-my-ass brothers?"

"Yeah, the Shaw brothers, right? And their sister who married one of the Winslows," Hirsch said.

"Yes, exactly. I told you they'd been stealing left and right from folks. Well, there's more to the story. This whole charade started around a year ago with propane theft. They'd boost the whole tank. At first, we thought they were isolated incidents—meth cooks needing gas for their lab operation. Eventually, they started siphoning off the gas, which isn't easy. They leave enough in the tank to avoid discovery until they're long gone. They've moved on to natural gas theft. For a while, they'd bypass the meter. Judging from what you discovered, they're tapping the main lines now. I asked Milo to let me know if he came across anything suspicious."

"That right?" Hirsch said. That Milo was in on this as well and never bothered to mention it annoyed him.

"The long and short of it is, this is go time. We can't have this kind of nonsense going on in the county. I need your help nailing these guys. I know you said you're in—will you give us a hand now?" Kyle asked.

"Like I said, I can give it a shot. I don't know how much help I'll be."

"Okay, good. I'm glad you're willing to at least take a look. Here's what I have in mind: I'm pulling together some documents on the brothers for your review—criminal records, prison reports, and the like. I'll leave them in an envelope at the front desk of the office. If you want to stop by next time you're in town, they'll be waiting for you. Review them and then see what else you can find out about the boys. Maybe check around Lionel's place or drop by the old tavern they like."

"You know I have no clue what I'm doing here, right?"

"Don't worry about that. You're doing the right thing. The community needs your help. This is your big chance to make a difference. I gotta run now, but call me after you've had a chance to review the file; we'll talk next steps."

Hirsch ended the call. He wasn't keen on the whole matter, but he owed it to Kyle to make an effort. Besides, what harm could come from reading through a few files?

THE MORNING AFTER HIS CONVERSATION with Kyle, Hirsch dropped by the county building. As promised, the receptionist had a sealed manila envelope with his name scrawled across the front in red ink waiting for him behind the counter. He retrieved it and returned to his truck to review the records in relative privacy. Kyle's envelope gave Hirsch a starting point.

"No going back now," Hirsch said as he ripped open the sealed lip and extracted the contents. He leaned back and thumbed through the stack of stapled copies inside.

He began his investigation the same way he approached a case—by gathering as many background facts as possible. He knew how to follow a paper trail. Hirsch's first job as an associate attorney fresh out of law school involved a protracted lawsuit concerning an entire subdivision. Hirsch's firm represented the plaintiffs, and the case required identifying and joining every single owner in the subdivision as a defendant to the lawsuit. For over a month, Hirsch spent entire workdays sequestered in the Ingham County Courthouse analyzing deed records, compiling spreadsheets of the current owners, and noting any liens or encumbrances affecting the property. Hirsch became a fixture at the clerk's office, and he learned how to ask the right questions and endear himself to the staff. While he left that firm after only a year for another position, he never forgot the research skills and tactics honed while hovering over brittle plat books and microfilm machines.

As expected, the documents recounted the sordid criminal history of one Marcus Rodney Shaw, DOB: January 23, 1970. Kyle did Hirsch the favor of arranging the documents in chronological order, providing a narrative of the rise of a small-time criminal and public menace. The type was all too familiar from Hirsch's years growing up. The name on the document could have been any of a number of his classmates. Shaw's criminal history began at the age of seventeen with a minor-in-possession charge. A criminal trespass complaint followed two years later, hot on the heels of a DUI conviction. The next record from 1993 concerned felony assault charges filed against Shaw in Delta County. The charging document recounted how Shaw brandished a rifle at his estranged spouse and clubbed her with the butt of the stock, inflicting a deep gash on her scalp and requiring the victim's hospitalization. Shaw pleaded guilty to one count of aggravated domestic assault in exchange for prosecutors dropping the more serious felony charge. The court sentenced him to ninety days in the county jail and ordered him to have no contact with his former spouse. At the bottom of the order, Hirsch scrawled a note reminding him to obtain copies of the divorce proceedings.

Marcus Shaw's criminal record was quiet for the next seven years until after his thirtieth birthday. Either the stint in lockup scared him straight for a spell, or Shaw became more adept at concealing his crimes. Whatever kept Shaw on the straight and narrow for those seven years vanished when authorities charged him with a second DUI in Schoolcraft County and possession of a controlled substance with intent to distribute in Delta. The former resulted in the suspension of his license and another stint in the county jail, while the possession charge netted him a suspended sentence. Shaw couldn't avoid the urge to reoffend. Alger County jailed him the following year on a felony larceny charge. He stood accused of stealing a backhoe from a construction site outside of Munising and concealing it on his brother's property on the Garden Peninsula.

Shaw's luck had run out at this point. After he took the larceny case to a jury trial and lost, the judge sentenced Shaw to five years for the backhoe theft and reinstated the three-year suspended sentence on the older possession with intent conviction. This meant eight years of total prison time. Whereas a public defender represented Shaw for the crimes in his teens and twenties, the pleadings revealed that private counsel out of Marquette represented Shaw on all the charges in the 2000s. Hirsch figured this was when Catherine Shaw married Herbert, the Winslow family scion, and stepped up to the plate to defend her jailbird brother. Hirsch googled Catherine and located a picture of her with her husband. Catherine Shaw Winslow resembled her brother Marcus, albeit a healthier and more robust member of the family. Although in her fifties, a halo of golden hair framed her oval face, and she wore a well-tailored skirt and blazer. She could pass for forty with ease, Hirsch reasoned.

Kyle included a summary from the Michigan Department of Corrections indicating Shaw entered the Alger Correctional Facility in November 2002. His prison record disclosed several demerits and portrayed him as a defiant inmate, unwilling to conform to the rules of confinement. Nonetheless, the state granted his parole request after only four years. Shaw became a free man on December 3, 2006, when the state released him into the supervision of the Delta County Probation Office. Miraculously, he avoided any further arrests, and the court discharged him from probation in 2010. Another DUI followed in 2012, but the final batch of stapled documents concerned the most recent charge—a 2014 arrest for felony assault of a police officer in Luce County.

Hirsch didn't need to research the statute. This was a serious, serious crime carrying guaranteed jail time—especially for an ex-con with an extensive criminal record. He read on. A state police officer stopped a vehicle belonging to Shaw east of Seney on Highway 28 for speeding and expired tags. The officer ordered Shaw out of his vehicle after discovering he had an outstanding warrant. As the officer attempted to cuff him, Shaw managed to get ahold of the officer's service weapon and pistol-whipped him into unconsciousness. He left the gravely injured patrolman on the side of the road and sped away. So extensive were the injuries that the officer remained on medical leave for over a year recovering from head trauma and neurological damage.

A manhunt followed, resulting in Shaw's arrest at a tavern outside Rudyard three days later. Given the crime's severity, the court ordered him held without bail and arraigned him on multiple counts, including felony assault of a police officer. Shaw faced decades in prison on these charges. Once again, the same Marquette criminal defense firm, Lucas & Stevens, filed a notice of representation on Shaw's behalf. In Hirsch's dozen years of practice, he'd seen almost every pleading one could imagine, and he'd been lied to more times than he could count. Nothing surprised him.

The final pages in Kyle's envelope shocked him.

In a terse order, the court granted Shaw's motion to suppress a dashcam video of the incident and—more unusually—ordered the case dismissed for insufficiency of evidence. Using his phone, Hirsch found an article detailing the case's dismissal. The article stated the prosecutors were not interested in refiling the charges and declined to pursue the matter any further. While a smattering of commenters expressed outrage over the dismissal, the law enforcement community was conspicuously silent. The article hinted at the victim's reluctance to testify. It concluded by noting that authorities released Shaw from jail on March 11, 2015, and that he planned to live with his older brother outside of Garden in Delta County.

Blown away by how Shaw managed to get such charges dismissed, Hirsch began to understand and appreciate the county's discretion and hesitation in going after either of the Shaw brothers. Powerful forces played a hand here—forces that could disrupt an otherwise air-tight case and obliterate those who dared to intervene. Hirsch needed to tread with the utmost caution, lest he meet a similar fate.

Before closing Marcus Shaw's criminal file, Hirsch flipped between two photographs of Shaw and marveled at the difference. The chubby-faced, smirking nineteen-year-old with a fringe of a beard in his DUI mugshot was all but unrecognizable from the man in the 2014 photo taken after Marcus's police-officer assault arrest. In the latter, Marcus stared with vacant, malevolent eyes straight into the camera, his head tilted as if challenging the viewer to pick a fight with him. Leaner now, his parted lips revealed a line of yellowing, rotted teeth, and a scraggy beard covered a portion of his weathered face. A mess of unkempt blonde hair fringing his ears completed the look of a degenerate monster with little regard for humanity. What a contrast he made with his sister, Catherine. The seeming absence of empathy or concern in Marcus's squinting gaze rattled Hirsch to his core.

With his required reading completed, Hirsch paid a visit to the Delta County Courthouse in Escanaba. In comparison to Marcus's extensive criminal paper trail, the case file for his divorce proceedings comprised fewer documents. In short, his estranged wife, Sheryl Hermann Shaw, filed for dissolution of their marriage in early 1994 citing irreconcilable differences. Apart from a brief reference to the domestic abuse charges filed against Marcus, the pleadings lacked much in the way of gossip. Six months later, the court granted the unopposed petition. The sole fact of note was a reference to a fifteen-acre parcel of pre-marital property located on Summer Island awarded to Marcus Shaw. Kyle wasn't bullshitting him about Shaw's hunting camp.

In contrast, Lionel Shaw's divorce proceedings provided Hirsch with ample information relevant to his nascent investigation. At the age of twenty-two, Lionel married nineteen-year-old Melissa Ann Suomi at the Finnish Lutheran Church up in Houghton on the Keweenaw Peninsula. Lionel and Melissa had two children—Erika, born in 1989, and Thomas Jarkko, born in 1998. The Finnish heritage in Melissa's surname and the kids'

given names was unsurprising given the large Yooper population of Finnish descent. She later managed to earn a degree in
accounting from Michigan Tech. Melissa stayed home to raise
the kids during most of their marriage and managed the books
for Lionel's HVAC business.

Melissa claimed that throughout the marriage, Shaw Brothers Heating made ample money, but Lionel had a habit of diminishing the family assets through profligate spending and
gambling at several downstate casinos. Heavy credit card debt
resulted, and they financed a second mortgage on the house.
Hirsch underlined an allegation suggesting Lionel drank to excess and aided and abetted his younger brother Marcus in the
latter's suspected criminal activities. In light of Lionel's diminu-
tion of the family's assets and the financial sacrifices Melissa
made to raise their children, she asked to be awarded the family
home, as well as the complete interest in Shaw Brothers Heating.

The divorce proceedings lasted well in excess of a year. The
file contained numerous affidavits, financial statements, and
declarations, many of which remained sealed by order of the
court. Nonetheless, an October 2014 order awarded Melissa the
family home in Escanaba, a one-hundred-percent interest in
Shaw Brothers Heating and all its assets, as well as spousal support in the amount of $1,200 per month payable until Melissa's
death or remarriage. The court also assigned a significant portion of the martial debt to Lionel upon finding his gambling
habit represented the vast majority. The only asset of signifi-
cance the court awarded to Lionel was a mortgaged three-bed-
room, one-bath farmhouse on twenty acres in Garden.

Lionel's desperation laid itself bare in the divorce proceedings. Stripped of his livelihood of the past twenty-plus years and

owing a significant amount to his ex-spouse every month, Lionel was in dire need of cash. He had the ideal partner if crime was his only option left.

After a couple hours of research, Hirsch exited the courthouse with a stack of annotated photocopies. Shielding them under his coat against the spitting rain, he raced across the parking lot and entered the dry cab of his truck. Hirsch tossed the stack of papers face-down on the passenger seat and pulled out his cell phone. He knew one person who might be able to give him the inside scoop on the Shaw brothers—Edgar Trehearne. Edgar answered after a few rings.

"Edgar, this is Ben. Do you have a minute?"

"Oh, hiya, Ben. I was wondering how you been. I haven't heard much from you for a while now. If it wasn't for Milo telling me you've been busy with the company, I'd have thought you'd run off back downstate."

"Nah, I'm still here, Ed. Work's kept me plenty busy. I've had my hands full with the Manistique house too."

"Good, good. Well at least we haven't scared you off yet. I'll go by your place here soon. So, what can I help you with?" Edgar asked.

"I was wondering if you know anything about Lionel or Marcus Shaw. I understand they're an old-time Delta County family."

Edgar fell silent for a moment. "Ah, what on earth would you want with those two? Don't tell me they're drinking buddies of yours."

"No, no, nothing like that," Hirsch assured him. "Their names came up a couple of times while working for the gas company. Probably nothing, but I said I'd look into it. I was curious if you knew anything about them."

"All right. Well, I can't say I know the boys all too well personally. Jesus, I shouldn't call them boys; they're both grown men. Anyway, their grandfather, Doctor Shaw, was a decent enough sort. Hell, he was my doctor when I was younger. His son Jimmy—he's the boys' father, you see—well, Jimmy Shaw never amounted to much. He was a year or two behind me in school, but we weren't friends or anything like that. He sold insurance here in town and did well enough for himself. Can't say people had much respect for him, though."

"Why's that, Ed?"

"Look, Jimmy Shaw was married for years. His wife, Lucy, was a fine lady, really decent given all she had to put up with from her husband. Let's say Jimmy had a taste for young women."

"What, like fooling around with his secretaries?"

"No, no—it was more like no father in his right mind would let his teenage daughter alone with Jimmy Shaw. I have it on good authority that he paid for two high schoolers to go downstate and get abortions where no one knew them. It was an open secret around town. You know what, though, he got away with it. I raised a couple daughters and back when they were young, sleepovers were common enough. All the kids did it. No one gave it a second thought. That is, except when it came to the Shaws. I reckon there wasn't a parent in town who'd let their daughter stay over at Shaw's house. Poor Catherine, I'll bet it was hard on her. No wonder she ran off as soon as she could."

"Is Jimmy Shaw still around?" Hirsch asked. "I'm surprised someone hasn't gone to the authorities by now." The rain outside intensified, and Hirsch plugged one ear with his finger to deaden the sound of the rain pounding against the truck's metal roof.

"Nah, old Jimmy passed away ten years ago. Cirrhosis, I heard. Not too surprising, I guess, given how he lived. Explains where Marcus got it from. Last I heard, Lucy remarried a few years ago and retired down in Arizona with her new husband. Like I told you, a decent lady. I hope she's enjoying her retirement."

"What do you know about the boys?" Hirsch asked.

Edgar sighed. "Like I said, I don't know them all too well myself. The older boy, Lionel, was a businessman here. Did mighty fine for himself with this HVAC company he started. Lionel pretends to be rough around the edges and fancies himself a redneck. Truth is, he's too smart for his own good and everyone knows it. No clue where that came from—certainly not his folks. Made a filthy amount of money owing to the good work he did. Problem is, he's cursed by the poker bug. Gambles like a devil. His wife had enough and divorced him. Craziest part is, she may not know a damn thing about HVAC systems but she won the whole business in the divorce. She sold it for a bundle to a local contractor, took the money, and ran off downstate herself. Can't blame her much. I'm surprised she lasted as long as she did."

"What's Lionel been up to since the divorce?"

"I don't keep too close of tabs on him, but I heard through the coffee gossip he's living in this rundown old farmhouse on the Garden Peninsula. It's the old family place where his people settled in the late 1800s. No clue what he's doing out there, but I suppose he could still pick up his share of work if he wanted it. Mighty odd way of living for one of them prodigy types," Edgar said.

"I'm sorry, what was that?" Had he misheard Edgar refer to Lionel Shaw as a prodigy?

"Oh, you didn't know about the piano thing?"

"No …" Hirsch replied. "I guess I'm not in the loop on much of anything."

Edgar laughed. "Well, I haven't thought about it much for years, but Lionel played mighty swell at the piano. You wouldn't think so by looking at him. That's the truth. He performed at recitals here in town when he was young. Now I don't know the first thing about classical music, and my girls never made it much beyond Chopsticks themselves, but I'll tell you, he could've made a living out of it. He chose to learn a trade instead. Pays better, I suppose."

"Okay, so what about Marcus?"

Edgar's good-natured tone shifted to disdain in an instant. "Marcus Shaw is rotten to the core. I'm hard-pressed to think of a bigger waste of flesh in my entire life. The kid's a lying, thieving, little loser prick. I wouldn't trust the little bastard for one minute." This was the first time Hirsch had heard Edgar genuinely angry. "Let me put it this way, Ben—if someone had their mailbox smashed or their pet went missing when Marcus was young, odds were he was behind it. Look, my oldest was a year or two behind Marcus in school. She knew the type of boy he was. Tried to get fresh with her once, you know. We taught her to stand up for herself, and she kicked him right where it counts. He never messed with her again, probably too humiliated. The only thing you can do with a drunk loser like him is stand up to them. The best years this County had was when that little creep sat in jail. The reason he's not spending the rest of his life behind bars is because his big sis keeps bailing him out."

"Why?" Hirsch asked.

"Your guess is as good as mine. Lord knows I love my daughters, but if one of them did a number like he did on that poor cop, well, you know."

"I learned a bit about Catherine and the Winslows. How's she get along with her brothers?"

"Lionel was the middle child and, for whatever reason, he and his sister mixed like oil and water. I don't think they're all too close these days. What I can tell you is that Cathy dotes on her brother. Marcus. Just loves the little bastard." Hirsch had trouble picturing the steely Winslow matriarch as a "Cathy." "She's always gone out of her way to look after him, maybe because he's the baby of the family. She's the only reason he's not sitting in Jackson State Prison right now. Hell, I imagine he'd be dead if it weren't for her." Edgar paused. "That's all I know about those two derelicts. I'd as soon keep it that way. I suggest you do the same."

"Well Edgar, I can't thank you enough. You've been helpful as usual. I'll pass this information along, and they'll do what they can with it."

"One more thing, Ben. In case you weren't listening, steer clear of those Shaw boys. They're bad eggs. You're a good kid; you don't need to get mixed up with them. Whatever it is you've come here to do, be careful. Will you do that for me?"

"I'll do what I can, Ed. I appreciate your help on this one."

"Oh, anytime. Say, if you're in town this afternoon, stop by the diner. I'll be having coffee with a few of the guys from the gas company around one. You should meet them."

"Yeah, I should be able to make that work. Thanks for letting me know. You take care."

Hirsch hung up. The rain tapered off to a drizzle during their conversation, leaving the town gray and damp. Hirsch put his truck in gear and crept out of the courthouse parking lot and headed to Powers for his assigned work. Reason told him he should heed Edgar's warning, call Kyle, and tell him he was out. He could walk away and rebuild his life walking the lines. But all the mystery surrounding the Shaw family piqued his curiosity. How could a family this indoctrinated in evil, manipulation, and greed escape judgment for this long? Hirsch aimed to uncover the truth. Doing so without becoming the Shaw family's latest victim was the challenge.

THAT AFTERNOON, HIRSCH JOINED THE gas company regulars for their weekly coffee at a humble diner in downtown Escanaba. The group of men surrounded a table where Edgar held court, reveling in his role as host. Hirsch bought a cup of black coffee and settled into the remaining chair, catching Edgar mid-story.

"So, there we were, a good five miles from shore without a lick of gas in the tank and nothing but empty beer cans in the hull. A gale's blowing in out of the north, and it won't be more than an hour before the swells could capsize an ore ship. Ol' Charlie Crothers is sitting up front holding a broken paddle no more than two foot long, and I says to him, 'Charlie, you look like you've never rowed a boat in your life.' Charlie's got the paddle cradled in his hands like it's a goddamn fiddle, and all he says is, 'Ed, I told you one case of beer wasn't enough.'"

Hirsch guffawed along with the others, even though he didn't see much humor in the story.

"Say, Benny," Edgar said, acknowledging Hirsch's presence. "Glad you could finally join us. I've been telling the crew we hired a new guy, but they didn't believe me."

"Where'd you find him?" said a sour-faced man wearing a flannel shirt and clutching a cup of coffee with claw-like hands.

"Oh, Benny here just moved back from Lansing. A good friend of mine—Kyle Severson with the PA's office—said he was looking for work. Old Edgar sorted him out."

"Some government shyster, I suppose," the malcontent muttered.

"Kyle's a decent enough fella," Edgar offered in defense of their prosecutor.

"I meant this one," the man replied. "Lansing, eh?" he continued while looking Hirsch over. "Not enough jobs for you downstate or something?"

Hirsch opened his mouth to reply, but Edgar preempted him. "Easy now, Ned. Ben grew up right over in Manistique. He's come home is all."

"Could've fooled me," Ned replied with a sigh and a glance toward the door.

"Don't mind Ned," the fourth member at their table said. "He comes off a little gruff, but damned if you'll find a better TIG welder this side of Milwaukee. Tom Maki," the man said as he offered Hirsch an outstretched hand. Tom was younger than the other two and sported an unruly mop of blonde hair.

"Ben Hirsch," he replied, accepting Tom's firm handshake. Hirsch offered Ned his hand as well. Ned eyed Hirsch's hand with suspicion before giving it a limp grasp.

"Ned Caperton," he said.

Ben was well acquainted with Ned's type. Ned viewed him as a traitor to the U.P. and could barely conceal his disdain. Hirsch strived to ignore the hostility as best he could.

"What'd your folks do in Manistique?" Tom asked.

"My mom worked as a nurse for the county hospital, and my dad put in his career at the mill."

"Ah, I heard the mill had fallen on hard times. How's the town holding up these days?" Tom asked.

"I'd be lying if I said it's A-Okay. People manage as best they can—or they leave," Hirsch said.

"I suppose kids like you were too good for the mill. Small wonder it went under," Ned spat out without looking at Hirsch.

Hirsch suppressed the urge to fling his coffee right into Ned's sallow face.

"You run into any trouble out in the field yet, Ben?" Edgar interrupted.

"Other than the stray dogs you mentioned, only once. A guy last week went and pulled a shotgun on me while I was checking his line."

"That right?" Tom said. "How'd you get out of that one?"

"I backed out as slow as can be. He talked like I was there to case the joint and rob him."

"You can't be too careful these days," Ned said.

"Oh, and what, I suppose you'd have shot me, right?" Hirsch said.

"Mr. Hirsch, chill out. Can't you take a joke?" Ned said. He cast an expression of mock victimhood at his friends.

Unwilling to tolerate much more of Ned's aggression, Hirsch drained the remnants of his steaming-hot coffee and clattered the mug on the table. "Gentlemen, it's been a pleasure, but duty calls in Powers."

He stood and flipped a couple dollars on the table before heading out the door. Moments later, the doorbell jangled behind him.

"Ben, wait up!" Hirsch turned to see Edgar lumbering toward him. Edgar caught his breath and continued, "My apologies for Ned back there. I should've warned you about him. He's not usually this ornery."

"It's not your fault. My folks and I've been hearing that horseshit all our lives. Comes with the territory, I guess."

"Ned didn't used to be so bad, but ever since his wife passed away last year, he's just looking for someone to pick a fight with. Don't take it personally."

"It's fine," Hirsch said. "Let me know next time he's around though. I'll make myself scarce."

"You're one of us, Ben. Consider yourself welcome anytime."

"It'd be nice if I felt like it. I gotta get moving. I'll call you soon."

Hirsch walked down the block toward his parked truck. Halfway there, he spotted a battered Ford Explorer festooned with obnoxious bumper stickers that screamed Ned Caperton. Revenge got the better of Hirsch, and he ducked alongside the vehicle on the abandoned sidewalk. He popped the caps and bled the air out of two tires until the rims lay flat on the ground.

That'll keep the obnoxious old codger busy for a few hours, Hirsch reasoned.

Satisfied with his juvenile act of revenge against Ned Caperton, Hirsch drove north on Highway 35, expecting a long day ahead of him in Powers. As he rolled through the dense forest, Hirsch mused on his encounter with Ned. While infrequent, what troubled him most about these interactions was how they darkened his overall experience of the community. Growing up, most neighbors would move heaven and earth to help you. All it took was one malignancy like Ned or that shotgun-toting land-owner to poison an otherwise symbiotic hamlet. Hirsch contemplated the grim prospect of the Ned Capertons of the world taking over and leaving his hometown as little more than every man for himself.

God help us all if it comes to that.

Chapter 5

HIRSCH AWOKE WITH A START to a crow's caw piercing the afternoon silence. He'd returned home after finishing his inspection in Powers early and crashed fully clothed on his bed in exhaustion. The lone bird perched on a tree branch outside his window. It regarded Hirsch with an inquisitive gaze through a grime-streaked windowpane. The gauzy light outside heralded dusk's approach. Hirsch glanced at his wristwatch, confirming he'd fallen asleep for several hours. Sticky sweat coated much of his body. All the walking sapped his energy more than he realized. He needed to shake off the fatigue and had no shortage of projects around the house demanding his attention.

With the snow melted, Hirsch resolved to tackle the home's derelict yard. During the long vacancy, unraked maple and ash leaves had plastered the yard autumn after autumn. They remained there to rot under the snow for months on end. After finding most of the yard equipment in the detached garage rusty and unserviceable, Hirsch purchased a new rake and a pair of work gloves. Long years of office work left his hands soft and blister prone. It took most of the remaining afternoon, but he managed to corral the sludge-like mass of leaves into heaping piles throughout the yard. The grass beneath had a fighting chance at growing this year. While admiring his handiwork, Hirsch paused to wipe his brow. He looked up to see an aged man across the street standing on his porch wearing a yellow-stained wife beater and a gray robe tied around his waist. A cigarette dangled from his lips. It was their longtime neighbor, Mr. Cromley.

"Ben! I see you're back in town. I was wondering when you were going to stop by," Cromley said, tapping away the ash trail of his cigarette against the porch's wooden railing.

"Sorry I didn't get over sooner, Mr. Cromley," Hirsch replied as he reluctantly made his way across the street. "Work's kept me busy these past few weeks."

"Smoke?" Cromley asked, shaking a couple Winstons out and proffering the pack to Hirsch.

"Sure, why not." Hirsch didn't smoke but decided having one out of politeness couldn't hurt. He extracted a cylinder from the pack and placed it between his lips. Leaning forward, he cupped his hands over the weak flame of the cheap plastic lighter Cromley held forth. The blast of nicotine from the first drag went straight to Hirsch's head, leaving him woozy.

"So, how's life?" Hirsch asked.

"Oh, health could be better, I suppose, but I'm still alive." Never an altogether hale man in his younger days, Cromley stood hunched over with his left arm fastened against his chest as though lame. White hair fringed his otherwise bald head, but his walrus-like mustache was unchanged. Cromley fixed his gaze on Hirsch, his eyes suspicious but scanning for every detail, no matter how imperceptible. Cromley and his family lived across the street for as long as Hirsch could remember. Even after thirty-plus years, his intensity unsettled Hirsch.

"Are you retired, sir?" Hirsch asked, almost certain he knew the answer. Anything to take Cromley's focus off him.

"Shit Ben, I've been out of work for ten years. Enjoying my 'golden years' as they say." Before retirement, Cromley edited and reported for the local paper. Local officials dreaded whenever Cromley caught a whiff of a story that might lead him to their doorstep. He still authored the occasional editorial for the region's newspapers, raising the ire of many pillars of the community. In short, he was a thorn in everyone's side and reveled in it.

"You ever miss it?" Hirsch asked.

Cromley exhaled and ejected two streams of smoke through his nostrils before replying, "Sure, most of the time. To tell you the truth, what I miss most is being at the center of the action. In my time, we had a real opportunity to run an article that might actually change a mind or two. It kept the commissioners and the sheriff's office honest, I'll say that much. Hell, these days we're lucky if the local news runs a story as hard-hitting as a 4-H meeting. Apart from that, it's all drugs and guys beating the shit out of their families … probably high on drugs. Jesus."

A shrill scream tore through the air from behind Cromley's house. As long as Hirsch could remember, Cromley's peafowl were the bane of the neighborhood. At one point in the nineties, the ostentation numbered seven birds. Their throaty shrieks terrified Hirsch as a child. He'd often cross the street when passing Cromley's house, eyeing them out of the corner of his eye as they strutted behind the chicken-wire fence. The abrupt racket sent a chill down Hirsch's spine.

"How are Joey and Sam?" Hirsch asked regarding Cromley's two grown sons. Hirsch never much liked the Cromley boys.

They were mean-spirited bullies most of the time. He hadn't seen them in years and couldn't care if he ever did again.

"Ah, not too good, I suppose. Joey's still down at Jackson State. Has another eighteen months left on that damn drug charge. Fucking meth ruined this community, I'll tell you." Cromley paused and spat before continuing, "Sam's okay. His second wife left him, but he's in Battle Creek working as an investment advisor. Don't hear from him all too often since Mom passed away." Cromley didn't strike Hirsch as being the easiest person to have for a father.

"Sorry to hear about Mrs. Cromley. She was always nice to us," Hirsch said. Moira Cromley died a year after Ben's father—from lung cancer as well. As quiet and unassuming as Cromley was brash and abrasive, she and Murray enjoyed trading neighborhood gossip over a smoke.

"Thanks, Ben, you know how it is."

"Yeah, I certainly do."

"I'm gonna head back inside. Too cold out here for me these days," Cromley said, flicking his cigarette out into the yard. Cromley's bare and gnarled feet were blue-tinged, his vascular system ravaged by years of smoking. "Don't be a stranger. It's nice to see a familiar face from the good old days."

"I won't. You stop by too if you need anything," Hirsch said as the old man shuffled back inside through the screen door.

Hirsch alighted from Cromley's porch and made his way back across the street to his house. Already intoxicated from the nicotine, Hirsch dropped the half-smoked Winston in the middle of the road and ground it out under the heel of his shoe.

He walked into his living room. Kyle's envelope confronted him on the coffee table, but he lacked the slightest initiative to continue his review. What he needed more than anything was a drink. His encounter with the hillbilly lunatic, his discovery of a possible criminal syndicate, and Ned Caperton's unabashed bigotry left his nerves ragged and screaming for relief. After the month he'd had, a glass or two of whiskey couldn't hurt. He knew full well the perils of this temptation. Hirsch got in his truck and drove across the river to a familiar liquor store on Deer Street. He parked along the street front and entered the dimly lit store. A bell jangled.

"Anything I can help you with?" the bearded clerk asked without looking up from his smartphone.

"A fifth of VO, if you have it." While his years of high-living as a plaintiff's attorney left Hirsch with a taste for top-shelf Scotch and Rye, Manistique wasn't the type of town to stock pretentious booze.

"Be fifteen dollars and ninety cents," the clerk said as he plucked a bottle from behind the counter and slipped it into a paper bag. As he reached forward to accept the twenty Hirsch slid across the counter, the clerk finally examined his customer and paused. "Say, you wouldn't happen to be Murray Hirsch's kid, would you?"

"Ah, yeah … that's right. How'd you know?"

"I worked at the papermill. Murray was our foreman. Honest guy, I'll tell you. Most managers there wouldn't give it to us straight. Your dad would, and he always worked alongside us when needed. I remember seeing you with him at the company ballgames. Name's Keith Davies," the clerk said as he smiled and reached out to shake Hirsch's hand.

Hirsch was accustomed to hearing accolades heaped upon his father. In addition to his years of service at the mill, Murray

Hirsch was a volunteer firefighter, served as president of the local Lion's Club, and coached youth hockey in his spare time. Schoolcraft County needed leaders like Murray more than ever.

"Pleasure to meet you, Mr. Davies. I'm Ben. So how long were you with the company anyway?"

Davies sighed. "Started there when I was twenty-two years old, fresh out of a stint with the Navy. I worked there, oh, until about three years ago. Wasn't my choice to leave, but they downsized. I was one of the first to go. Early retirement, they called it. Truth is, us old codgers cost the company more than they care to spend. Had to take this gig here at the liquor store to make ends meet. I wouldn't mind retiring for real, but I have a couple kids I need to get through college." Davies bore the full evidence of his decades of labor. His crumpled denim shirt, scarred hands, and hollowed-out eyes led Hirsch to believe what he said.

"I hear you. It's a real shame what happened at the mill. I wonder what'll happen to this town when it's gone for good," Hirsch said.

"Beats me. I've lived here all my life. Truth is, I'd be out and hauling my ass to Arizona if I had the money. This past winter damn near destroyed my back shoveling all the snow. I already ache every day from thirty-odd years of heaving those boards. You try to convince the missus to leave, though," Davies concluded, shaking his head.

"Does she have family here?" Hirsch asked.

"Nah, her folks are long gone. Says she'd miss her girlfriends. I keep telling her I betcha one or two of them and their husbands would move south with us if we mentioned it."

"It's hard for folks to leave behind what they know."

"Well, you got that right, I suppose," Davies replied. "You in town visiting family?"

"The way things look, I may be here awhile." The tinkling of the doorbell heralded another customer's arrival, and Hirsch moved to leave. "It's good to run into a friendly face, Mr. Davies. I'm sure I'll see you around."

"I hope so, bud. You come here whenever you like. Oh, and if you need anything, don't be afraid to look me up. Any child of Murray Hirsch is a friend of mine."

Hirsch snatched up the paper sack and slipped it into his pocket. Taking his purchase, he bid Davies farewell and headed home. Hirsch found a dust-coated glass in a kitchen cupboard. He opened the sink faucet. The pipes squealed and clanked but rewarded him with a flow of rust-tinted water that soon ran clear. Hirsch rinsed the dust out of the glass and dried it with an untucked shirttail. Lacking any ice, he broke the golden plastic cap from the fresh whiskey bottle and poured a couple fingers of the amber liquid into the glass. Hirsch took a sip. The uncut burn of the whiskey's creamy, caramel flavor coated his taste buds and slid down his throat. Within minutes, the familiar flush of warmth emanating from his stomach washed over him. The lingering anxiety that had been gnawing at him over the course of the day ebbed away.

Thumbing his nose at better judgment, Hirsch grabbed the bottle and migrated into the living room. His cheap lamp cast a pallid glow across the spartan furnishings. Dark squares on the walls spoke as ghosts of the paintings and family photos that once graced the room. Hirsch flopped into his mother's thirty-plus-year-old floral print couch. The barren entertainment center across from him highlighted the dearth of amusements.

I'll at least need a radio if I'm going to be here for a while, Hirsch thought. He poured another portion of whiskey into the glass. He gobbled down a leftover pastrami sandwich, washing it down with the liquor. Soon feeling like the king of Manistique, Hirsch leaned back into the couch and gave himself over to his intoxicated revelry. This is your world, old boy. Anything you want is yours for the taking.

"Fuck Ned Caperton and fuck the mill," Hirsch shouted into the empty room. "They just wait until I'm back on my feet."

Two generous glasses later, confidence surged through Hirsch, unexperienced since his last successful jury trial. Beyond reason, and with his head abuzz from the spirits, Hirsch pulled out his phone, pleased to discover a couple bars of service. Throwing caution to the wind, he brought up his contacts and dialed the first name on his list.

The phone rang three times before his ex-wife answered with her gentle voice, "Hello, Ben."

"Hiya, Allison. It's been a while, right? I thought I'd check in on you. How's life?"

"I'm fine …" she said. His inebriation blinded him to the hesitation in her voice. "It's late, you know. Are you all right?"

"Yeah, sweetie, everything's good with me. I'm back home."

"Where? Your apartment?"

"Home, home, Allie. Not only that, I'm sitting right here in my parents' living room, soaking up the memories, if you know what I mean," Hirsch slurred.

"Ben, I have to ask you a question, and I need you to be honest with me. Have you been drinking again?" Allison asked.

"Oh, I had a couple to celebrate my homecoming. See, there's no TV or radio here at the house, so I needed a friend to keep me company. Old VO's never let me down yet. It's back to work for me on Monday out walking the lines."

"Walking the lines? I'm sorry, what? What are you doing up there anyway?"

"Oh, remember Kyle? My buddy from law school." Hirsch replied.

"Of course, I remember Kyle. We went to his house for Thanksgiving a few years back."

"Right, right. Like you'd forget the time we screwed in the Seversons' guest bathroom. I'm surprised I didn't knock you up that night." Hearing radio silence in response, Hirsch continued, "Anyway, I'd been staying with them for a few days after I got out of Lansing—I was facing eviction—and Kyle hooked me up with a guy who works for the gas company up here. They found me a job walking the gas lines—checking for leaks, reading meters, stuff like that."

"Wow, that … sounds interesting, Ben. Couldn't Kyle find you something with a firm if you wanted to move back home?" She sounded skeptical that such an intelligent and ambitious person like Hirsch could be satisfied with menial labor. Allison evidently didn't know about Hirsch's disbarment.

"Allie, they took my license. I can't practice anymore," Hirsch drawled out.

"Oh dear, I didn't know, honestly. What happened?"

Hirsch exhaled. "Let's say they didn't take kindly to what I did."

"Jesus, Ben. I don't know what to say. I mean, Lord knows I was upset like you couldn't believe, but I never hoped they'd disbar you."

"I know, I know. I haven't been thinking clearly these past few years. Maybe if I tried harder or hired an attorney instead of doing it myself, who knows, maybe I could've copped a suspension. After we broke up, I guess I quit caring." Ben could hear Allison sniffling on the other end of the line. Despite the oblivion of intoxication, a pang of guilt shot through him at resurrecting these old wounds. He couldn't help himself. "Allie … do you think we could try and make it work again? We were so good together. God knows I learned my lesson."

"Please don't ask me that, Ben. Christ, leaving you was the hardest thing I ever had to do in my life, but I had no choice. I forgave you. It took all my willpower, but I did. And I could never trust you after what you did to us. You were—and are—the love of my life, but I can't be with you." Hirsch could hear Allison fighting tears on the other end of the line.

"Everything okay, Allie?" a male voice in the background called out. "Fine, just talking with an old friend," Allison replied.

"The fuck is that?" Hirsch demanded.

"Ben, we're divorced, remember? There are some parts of my life you don't need to know about anymore."

"But … Jesus, Allie, how long's this been going on, anyway? Who is this asshole?"

"Stop. I don't want to discuss this with you right now; hear me?"

"It's just—goddammit, I didn't think it'd happen so soon," Hirsch said.

Her voice grew muffled as though she'd cupped her hand over the receiver. "Look, I need to go. You know you can call me if you need to talk. We shared a life together, and I'll try to help you if I can. But please don't call me when you've been drinking, okay? And for heaven's sake, stop asking me if we can get back together. Please, Ben. I'm asking you as a friend and your soulmate."

Reality crashed through his whiskey high, and Hirsch choked up. "I know, sweetie. I'm sorry, I really am," he replied.

"You don't have to apologize. But please, please consider my feelings. I don't want to hold onto this pain forever. Get some rest tonight and take care of yourself."

"I will, Allie. You do the same, okay?" Hirsch said before ending the call. He let the phone flop out of his hand and onto the floor where it clattered and came to rest. Stunned into sobriety, Hirsch instantly regretted his behavior. He curled up on his side, scalding tears of shame forming in his eyes. As the alcohol pulled him into a drunken, nightmare-ridden sleep, Hirsch pleaded for strength to not screw up again.

HIRSCH RAISED HIS EYELIDS TO a blinding beam of sunlight shining squarely in his face. A handful of hypodermic needles stabbed into his brain before he slammed his eyes shut. Moaning, he rolled over and burrowed his face into the crevasse between the couch cushion and seatback. The pain receded, but the tattered fabric reeked of a stomach-churning mixture of dust and cigarette smoke. Overcome by an intense urge to vomit, he lurched to his feet and stumbled into the small bathroom off the hallway, still woozy from the alcohol. Hirsch fell to his knees before the toilet, lifted the faux-wood seat, and disgorged the contents of his stomach into the rust-and-lime scaled bowl. Propelled by waves of nausea, he continued to retch until there was nothing left. A dry croak emitted from his throat. Exhausted, Hirsch slumped sideways against the bathroom wall, smacking his head against the towel bar in the process. He grimaced in pain and remorse as memories of the previous night surfaced in snippets of abject shame.

Hirsch lacked so much as a scintilla of energy to move. He sprawled on the floor for fifteen minutes, regarding the way the peach-hued plastic strip at the base of the wall had bubbled and peeled away, revealing wavy streaks of yellowing adhesive beneath. He figured he was the first person to use this bathroom in over five years and resolved to fix it up once he no longer felt as though his head would shatter at the slightest movement. Hirsch took a deep breath and rose to his feet, grasping the loose towel bar for support. He shuffled into the living room with shallow, measured steps, girding himself to survey the damage. The fifth of VO stood next to the couch, drained of two-thirds of its contents. With his remaining energy, he bent over, gripped the bottle by its neck, and marched into the kitchen. He undid the gold-colored cap, which he tossed into a corner, and poured the remaining liquor down the sink.

"No more," he said as the remnants swirled around the metal drain and vanished from view. The fumes wafting up from the sink sent him into another spasm of nausea, and he fought to keep from vomiting again. His appetite for breakfast was non-existent. As the kitchen lacked a trashcan, Hirsch propped the bottle on the counter as a monument to his folly.

He staggered back to the couch and collapsed, shielding his eyes against the sun. While he figured another hour of sleep could restore his well-being, the likelihood of that happening was slim to none. For the past ten years, he had struggled to sustain more than five or six hours of sleep on a good night.

Why do I keep doing this to myself? Hirsch wondered. Here I felt good for the first time in months and even have an honest job I don't deserve.

Hirsch took inventory of his life. It was alcohol that kept him out of the top tier of his law school class. Alcohol cost him a shot at a federal clerkship or placement with a high-profile national law firm. Alcohol spoiled multiple relationships with friends and lovers. Those weeknight happy hours, with their promise of good times and maybe an encore of drunk, clumsy sex with a classmate, were too hard to pass up. Instead, his weakness led to a regional, two-partner law firm, and he toiled for long hours as an associate before mustering the sense and courage to start his own practice. Jesus, Ben, think of all you missed out on, he reflected, sickened at the walking disgrace he'd made of his life.

Hirsch rolled to one side, catching a glimpse of his phone on the floor in the process. This brought forth a whole new round of self-recrimination as he groaned in agony at the memory of his conversation with Allison. Christ, what the fuck had he said to her, anyway? He'd worked hard after their divorce to maintain a positive relationship, though he spared her the details of his disciplinary proceedings. No good could come out of drunk dialing her from an abandoned house in the hinterlands of Michigan.

After half an hour of lying motionless with his head gripped between his hands, Hirsch accepted that sleep would not revisit him this morning. He propped himself up and assessed the day. Outside, the sky was partly cloudy. Ribbons of sun danced between the ash trees and on the street front. Early morning made old Manistique quieter than usual. Hirsch dragged himself off the couch and retrieved his heavy jacket from a blackened hook on the wall. He cracked the door, inviting the crisp, cool air of a

March morning into the stale house. The contrast between the outside air and the interior's oily stench reminded him how much his father's cigarette smoke permeated every surface inside. Tearing out the plaster and lathe walling and starting over again was the only way to eviscerate the lingering aroma. No wonder no one made an offer when they listed the house for sale.

Hirsch stepped out onto the front porch. He fumbled in his right-hand jacket pocket and extracted a pair of Wayfarer sunglasses, pleased to find he hadn't misplaced them in his drunken stupor. The daylight would have been agonizing without them. He refrained from swallowing any painkillers, hoping the punishment of a throbbing headache would cure him of any desire to repeat last night's misadventure. Getting his feet beneath him, Hirsch paced through town, heading south and west until he reached Highway 2. Minimal traffic crisscrossed the highway, and he crossed the road and entered Lakeview Park without incident. Lake Michigan lay spread out before him. While a recent warm snap had melted the ice, the frigid water churned away, menacing the handful of small vessels offshore. Hirsch's destination was the fire-engine-red lighthouse stationed at the end of the breakwater that jutted into the harbor.

Whipped with wind ripping off the lake, Hirsch navigated the wooden boardwalk that traced a narrow route along the shore. He reached the boulder-lined pathway to the breakwater extending from the tan sands of the beachfront. At one time, thousands of pounds of sawdust littered Manistique's beaches near the mouth of the river, tailings of the hulking giants of the vast white pine forests converted into lumber by the sawmills. That wood, in turn, built countless homes in lower Michigan and

Wisconsin and engendered fortunes for the timber baron families lucky enough to own a piece of the action. Much as this wanton destruction distressed Hirsch to his core, he couldn't escape culpability. After all, the last of the mills employed his father for years and served as the conduit for their survival and Hirsch's means of ascent in the world.

The rolling waves crashed against the solid concrete of the breakwater. Several landed with enough force to thrust the water into the air and splash the walking surface in front of him with a thin veneer of moisture. During a winter storm, these waves threatened any person foolish enough to venture out onto the breakwater. They risked being knocked onto the sharp rocks below or, worse, caught on the breakwater's lakeward side and swept out into the lake's vast depths by the rip current.

The deep-red lighthouse beckoned two hundred feet ahead, its automated beacon flashing at regular intervals. Relieved to find no one else in sight as he rounded the breakwater's dogleg, Hirsch approached the hundred-year-old landmark eager to rest in its shadow. The metabolizing sugar from the alcohol left him roasting hot, and he unzipped his jacket to ventilate the heat. He tiptoed alongside the lighthouse's concrete base and settled into a comfortable nook on the rocks below. Hirsch leaned back against the cool concrete. Spread out in front of him, the choppy blue water faded into the horizon beyond. To his right, the green forests of the Garden Peninsula stretched on for mile-after-mile, terminating in the shallow finger of Barque Point at his farthest field of view.

Hirsch clutched the back of his head in his fingers, digging his nails into his scalp. He resolved never to let this catastrophe of a life he'd created carry him further down the path of blight and dissolution. He'd known too many people in his professional and personal life who couldn't hold it together and sooner or later succumbed. Surrendered before the beauty and raw energy of the lake's magnificent power, his desire to drink withered. A renewed sense of purpose filled his soul. This is where you belong, Ben. Your home and your community's taken its share of lumps but it's not too late. This right here is your final act. Take advantage of it and save yourself.

Alone with his thoughts, Hirsch fell into oblivion, hypnotized by the pounding of the surf against the rocks and the whistle of the wind through the dark forests beyond.

PART II

Chapter 6

Reeling from his self-inflicted humiliation, Hirsch retreated into his Manistique home and did his best to start anew. He needed space to gather his thoughts, and the aging mausoleum was nothing if not good for contemplation. Early Sunday morning, he greeted the day as the light of dawn crept into the east-facing guest bedroom. His first week home, he camped out in his childhood bedroom, wedged into a cramped twin bed. Too many memories lurked in the other rooms, and he cloistered himself in the familiar haunt of his youth. After waking one too many mornings with a stiff neck, Hirsch relocated into their guestroom, which featured a queen-sized mattress with an elegant quarter-sawn white oak headboard. Comfortable at last, he relished his first pain-free night of sleep in weeks.

Armed with ample information on the Shaw brothers, Hirsch could no longer postpone a confrontation. Kyle had mentioned that Marcus Shaw liked to frequent a dive bar in Garden Corners. Hirsch knew the location well, if only by reputation. Lily's Tavern was a rundown watering hole on Highway 2 located between Escanaba and Manistique. Its owner and namesake doubled as hostess-in-chief for over forty years. Gruff and unsmiling, Lily Brannon did not suffer fools gladly. On multiple occasions, she brandished a double-barreled twelve-gauge shotgun stowed beneath the bar to break up a fight. That said, her stoic fortitude encouraged many a lush to unburden their souls to her. She arguably saved more lives than any licensed psychologist in the entire UP.

Lily's was once a popular dive for millwrights, fishermen, and other blue-collar workers seeking a shot with a beer chaser and honest company. Even Hirsch's father liked to drop by with his crew and trade gossip free from upper management's prying eyes. As industry faded and the old guard died off or moved south, Lily's deteriorated to little more than a hideout for hopeless alcoholics and petty criminals. A gang of bikers commandeered it from time-to-time, raising hell until they grew bored and roared off to terrorize another town. Paradoxically, tourists motoring through the UP on Highway 2 frequented Lily's as well. The tavern's derelict appearance conjured up a promise of authentic Yooper culture, replete with an *Anatomy of a Murder* vibe. If Marcus was a regular at Lily's, this was Hirsch's best shot at encountering him on neutral turf.

Hirsch faced a dilemma in accosting Marcus. Since his bender the previous month, Hirsch hadn't touched a drop of alcohol and had no desire to do so now. At the same time, anyone entering a place like Lily's and ordering a pop would immediately raise suspicion amongst the habitual drunks rotting away at the bar. Hirsch couldn't remember if they served food—not that he'd want to eat it if they did. If need be, he could sit in a corner, watch the ballgame, and keep to himself.

After completing a water-logged Friday walking the Menominee gas lines, Hirsch returned home and enjoyed a hot shower. He lingered under the steaming water, chilled to the bone by the humidity that saturated every stitch of his clothes. After nightfall, he changed into his least conspicuous outfit. He scrounged up a pair of worn-out, paint-spattered jeans, pairing them with dirty tennis shoes long past their expiration date. He settled for a faded gray sweatshirt and his hooded jacket, broken in by days spent out in the field. To complete the look, he rummaged in his childhood bedroom and recovered a vintage Detroit Tigers baseball cap, unworn for twenty-plus years. Despite its age, it fit his head and complemented the two-day growth of stubble he'd cultivated since resolving to embark on Kyle's mission. He stood before the bathroom mirror. A nondescript, hardworking townie ready to blow off some steam stared back at him.

Hirsch drove twenty minutes west from his house to Lily's. Anxiety gripped his chest as he drew closer to his planned rendezvous with a man capable of unpredictable mayhem. Despite being Friday evening, the parking lot was only half-full. Owing to the Peninsula Energy decals plastered on his truck, Hirsch drove around the back of the tavern and parked out of sight. The last complication he needed was Marcus catching a glimpse of Hirsch's truck.

Hirsch yanked the tavern door open. A wall of fetid air assaulted him with a bouquet of stale beer, cigarette smoke, sweat, and rancid fry grease. Hirsch scanned the room as the door clattered shut behind him. Four strident couples surrounded by empty pitchers of beer occupied a pair of booths on the far wall. Elsewhere, a trio of ragged men loitered over a beat-up pool table, clutching cues while carrying on an animated conversation revolving around the word "fuck." To his right, a handful of solitary drinkers populated the long wooden bar. Country music blared from a jukebox while the muted TV above the bar broadcasted the baseball game. He scanned the patrons seated at the bar and froze.

The profile of a brooding, hunched-over figure caught his eye. Even from a distance, the man's wiry frame resembled Marcus Shaw. *It's now or never.* Hirsch approached the bar and mounted a stool two down from the man. He focused his attention on the ballgame overhead.

"What'll you have?" a voice called out to him.

Hirsch's head snapped toward the source. His eyes settled on a young woman drying glasses at the far end of the bar. She was far from the type one normally encountered in a dive like Lily's. As she approached to take his order, he gave her the once-over. Slim waisted, she stood around five feet three and wore a pair of dark skinny jeans coupled with a chunky-knitted, oatmeal-colored sweater that hugged her perky breasts. A plastic tortoiseshell clip gathered her golden-brown hair up in the back. The woman evaluated her customer with keen, walnut-hued eyes. Hirsch guessed she was in her late twenties or early thirties. Her demeanor was pleasant, but a hardness around her eyes spoke of uncertain travails. She tapped her French-manicured nails on the counter, awaiting his reply. His old bachelorhood habit of glancing at her left hand confirmed she wore no ring.

"Uh, Miller Lite, please," Hirsch said. *One beer, Ben. One beer won't hurt. Nurse it over the next hour and go on home when you get what you need.*

The young woman fished a freshly dried glass from the counter and filled it from the tap, gazing into the distance as she mechanically performed the act. The frothy liquid formed a head as she tapered the pour and set the glass in front of him. A splash of foam slipped over the lip of the glass and pooled around the rim against the bar.

"Four dollars," she said.

Hirsch pushed a five-dollar bill across the bar and said, "No change." She picked it up, gave him a half-smile, and hurried to pick up an order from the kitchen counter. Hirsch glued his eyes to her denim-clad rear. After weeks of near anhedonia, the sight flooded him with desire. God, what he wouldn't give to watch her shimmy out of those jeans and take her against the wall. Confronted with a beautiful girl, the extent of his isolation became palpable. Months of self-imposed solitude left him thirsting for the most basic of needs—the lust-fueled coupling with another. He raised the glass to his lips and took a long sip to cool himself down.

"Verlander hasn't thrown anything worth shit since his injury," the man two stools down exclaimed, tearing Hirsch out of his half-baked fantasy over the bar maid. On the muted TV, the Tigers battled the Kansas City Royals at home. Runners were on second and third with one out and two balls. Although Hirsch was a diehard Tigers fan in his youth, excessive work and a gradual amelioration of his hobbies diminished his interest in the game. Even with a gun to his head, he'd struggle to remember more than an active player or two.

"Hard to believe they were in the series a couple years ago, ain't it?" Hirsch replied, concentrating on the TV screen. Play it cool, Ben, he told himself.

The man grunted in response and sipped his drink. Hirsch took the opportunity to glance over at his profile. The split-second look confirmed his fears—his fellow patron was none other than Marcus Shaw. The raw, coarse man clad in a camouflage jacket and a trucker hat was unmistakably the perp Hirsch studied in the mugshot. The last few years had not been kind to Shaw. What little weight he carried in 2014 had vanished, leaving him a skeleton with sinewy flesh stretched across it. Veins bulged from his neck. His bony, tattoo-riddled hands gripped a tumbler of vodka. The man's eyes protruded from his head and flitted back and forth between the TV screen and the door. With an animal-like visage, Shaw looked borderline unhinged. His weight loss and overall dishevelment suggested a recent, if not ongoing, struggle with hard drugs.

Hirsch had Shaw right where he wanted him. The only problem was he had no fucking clue what to do with him. This was uncharted territory. Under normal circumstances, he could take a witness's deposition, sit for eight hours or longer, and ask each and every question tangentially related to the case at hand. Hirsch's interrogations often frustrated opposing counsel, leading to objections that he was on a fishing expedition. Here, apart from a series of wild tales spun by Kyle, he had no hard evidence Shaw was guilty of anything other than being an ex-con. Once again, he pondered why Kyle had set him up for this charade in the first place. Hirsch was no private eye and everyone knew it.

Hirsch refrained from striking up further conversation with Shaw, concentrating instead on the ballgame and his beer. *He'll grow suspicious if I start questioning him.* Hirsch thought. Hirsch discovered the bottom of the glass much sooner than he anticipated.

Shit, I haven't accomplished a damn thing, and I'm already out one beer, Hirsch realized. *One more won't hurt, I suppose. Hell, it's a lager, so draining two is like drinking one regular beer, right? Two and then we're done and out of here.*

Hirsch raised two fingers to get the fetching server's attention and ordered a refill. A translucent bin of $2 pull tabs on the counter behind the bar caught his eye. If I'm in a dive bar, I might as well get the full experience, he reasoned.

"Could I have ten dollars' worth of those pull tabs as well?"

She scrutinized him for a moment. "Sure," she replied, with a shrug before snatching a handful from the bin. She deposited them on the bar in front of Hirsch next to his beer and swept up his cash. "Good luck," she said.

Hirsch ripped the paper tabs away from the first card—a loser as expected.

"I didn't know anyone still played those fucking things," Shaw said, breaking his fixation on the ballgame.

Seeing an opportunity, Hirsch selected an un-played card and slid it down the bar toward Shaw. "Try your luck on me."

Shaw regarded him for a moment with his pinhole eyes before he picked up the card. "Why the hell not." Shaw's tobacco-stained fingers tore away the tabs. His mouth extended into a twisted smile, revealing a gold cap over one molar.

"Well, whaddaya know. Ten bucks for doing not a goddamn thing." Shaw tossed the winner in the well of the bar and said to the server, "How about another round for me and my new friend here, tits. Looks like these are on you." She glared at Shaw but did as he asked. She planted another glass of vodka in front of him. Although Hirsch was only a few sips into his second beer, a third materialized.

"Drink up, buddy. Looks like you have work to do," Shaw said.

"Can't say I've seen you here before. You a local or passing though?" Shaw asked as they drank.

Shaw's question exposed Hirsch's abject failure to concoct a cover story ahead of time. "I live over in Naubinway," Hirsch said, thinking on his feet. "Been out of work and was down in Escanaba seeing about a job. Didn't pan out, so I thought I'd have a drink on the way home."

"Well, you picked a fine place to do your drinking. Local talent's not bad," Shaw said, gesturing with his glass at the young woman, now balancing four platefuls of burgers on her way to the rear of the bar. "What sort of work you in anyway?"

"Production worker at the mill most of my life. I got laid off, though, when they downsized the plant. Been looking for six months now. Nothing much else to do but drink and watch the ballgame."

Shaw nodded. "I hear you, man. Fucking goddamn liberals had to run all the hardworking folks out of business to save some stupid river trout or endangered bird. But no, we gotta send all our money to a bunch of crack whores down in Detroit who got nothing better to do than get knocked up by different guys—all unemployed. Don't get me started on the fucking Indians 'round here—they can do whatever they want. But I go out shooting one day and bag some threatened duck, they slap me with a thousand dollar fine. I tell you, friend, you wanna talk about endangered species, us white men are the most endangered species on the planet."

Christ, not another of these idiots. This asshole could be Ned Caperton's son. Half-tempted to stroll over and knock Shaw's teeth out, Hirsch took a long draw off his beer to regain composure.

"Well, shit. I'll be happy to do anything for work at this point. What about you? What do *you* do?" he asked Shaw, engaging him directly in the eye.

Shaw scoffed and flashed his rotten teeth at Hirsch. "Whatever the fuck I want, that's what I do. Why the hell work myself to death when I can sit in a place like this and stare at a lovely piece of ass like we have in front of us," Shaw said, pointing again with his glass at the pretty server's rear facing them. Hirsch didn't disagree with Shaw but wanted to beat the shit out of him for his casual misogyny. "Nah, man. I'm my own boss. I do contracting work here and there. I work when I feel like, drink when I need one, fuck when I want it."

"Here's to that." Hirsch raised his glass to Shaw.

"Damn right," Shaw replied before draining his glass. He pulled a pack of Parliaments out of his shirt pocket. "Smoke? Lauren here won't let me smoke inside, but I'll stand you one out front. I'm Marcus, by the way."

"Ken," Hirsch replied, as they stood and headed for the front door. At least he knew the young woman's name now.

"Keep an eye on our drinks, babe. I'll be needing another," Shaw called out to Lauren as he led Hirsch out into the chill of the Michigan evening.

Hirsch accepted Shaw's proffered cigarette and leaned in to ignite it over the orange flame of Shaw's Zippo. *Jesus, I've smoked more in the past month than in the last twenty years.* They puffed away in silence for a minute, watching the cars cruise by on the highway.

"You're not a fucking cop, are you?" Shaw asked, glaring at Hirsch, dead serious.

"Fuck no. My old man would've shot me a long time ago if I were. Never trusted them one bit."

"You had many run-ins with them assholes?"

Hirsch shrugged. "They pulled me over plenty—broken tail-lights, expired tags, speeding. Spent a couple nights in jail here and there, raising too much hell. Most of the time, I stay the fuck away and try not to get caught."

"Right on."

"You a cop?" Hirsch asked, looking at Shaw while blowing a plume of smoke from the corner of his mouth.

"Fuck you, man," Shaw said, laughing as he tapped the ash from his cigarette. "They've been on my case since I was a kid. And once you're in their fucking crosshairs, there's no getting away. I ain't even done nothing worse than what other folks be doing every day. Only difference is the law's on my ass."

"I hear you, man. Sounds like a raw deal. Fucking pricks."

Shaw nodded. "You like to party, man? Crank? Ice? I have some shit that'll blow the roof of your head off." Even with his white-collar background, Hirsch had no trouble understanding Shaw's proposition.

Hirsch nursed his Parliament, running his tongue around the edge of the recessed filter while considering the offer. "Maybe. How much?"

"Twenty-five for a quarter. Two hundred for an 8-ball. Your choice, bud. I know you ain't looking for work too hard. I've seen your type a mile away."

"You sure it's good shit, man?"

"No fucking doubt it is, cowboy. I should know, I made it myself." Shaw grinned in obvious pride.

Hirsch nodded. "You gonna be around tomorrow night? I need to scrounge up enough cash, but I'm liking the sound of this 8-ball."

His reticence spooked the dealer. Shaw dropped his cigarette into the gravel and ground it under the heel of his shoe.

"I may be, or I may not be, bud. If I'm here and you've got the money, we'll see what we can do. I'm warning you, though, if this is a set-up, I will hunt you down and break every fucking bone in your body. Naubinway ain't far enough to hide, hombre. You wouldn't be the first asshole to make the wrong decision, you hear me? Now let's get back inside and see how badly the Tigers are going to lose this fucking ballgame."

Hirsch flicked his smoldering cigarette into a puddle and followed Shaw back into the bar. They had little to say to each other the rest of the evening, apart from casual obscenities directed at the Tigers' poor performance. Hirsch finished his second beer and worked his way through the unwanted third. His remaining pull tabs were all losers, and he itched for an excuse to leave. He got what he needed out of Shaw, and further conversation could only risk exacerbating Shaw's suspicions.

Between the eighth and ninth innings, Shaw slid off the barstool and stumbled to the restroom to take a piss. Hirsch seized the opportunity to drain the remnants of his third beer and form an exit strategy.

"Can I get you another one, hon?" Lauren said, observing his empty glass.

"No, I think that's it for me tonight," Hirsch said as he slid the glass forward. "Mind if I ask you a question?"

"I suppose …" she replied, obviously anticipating another loser asking her lewd or inappropriate questions in this hellhole.

"You ever get sick of dealing with assholes like him?" Hirsch asked, jerking his thumb toward Shaw's empty barstool.

"Sure, who wouldn't?" Lauren smoothed a fallen lock of golden-brown hair back over her ear. "But if every woman working in a bar or restaurant took it personally and quit, there wouldn't be a place to work anymore."

"May not be the end of the world," Hirsch said. "Couldn't you work anyplace other than this dive?"

"I could—I mean, I do. But I have my reasons for working here too."

"And those would be?" Hirsch asked, eyebrows raised and smiling at her. The three beers fueled his loquacity.

"Tell you what—you seem like a decent enough guy. I help out here a couple nights a week. Why don't you stop by another time when it's not busy? If you're lucky, I'll be here and can explain it to you," Lauren replied with a smile and a subtle bit of her lower lip between her teeth. "It'd be better than dealing with the usual round of assholes and drunks who come through this place."

"I may do that," Hirsch said as he stood to leave. "I best be getting on home. Here's for having to put up with our friend." Hirsch flipped a twenty-dollar bill onto the bar. "You take care, all right."

"I do what I can," she whispered as Hirsch walked away from the bar. Before exiting, he glanced back and caught her gaze as she cleared the dirty glasses away from the bar and wiped down the counter. She smiled in farewell and turned around, allowing Hirsch to savor the sight of her taut behind as she walked back into the kitchen.

Groggy and with his bladder full from the three beers, Hirsch meandered back to his truck and backed it out of the parking lot. While reasonably sure he wasn't over the limit,

Hirsch drove with extra caution. The pressure on his bladder swelled to near-bursting, and he stopped halfway home to relieve himself in the darkened parking lot of a church. *Dammit, Ben. You had to go and hit the bottle again, didn't you?*

Hirsch expelled a forceful stream of urine over the church's well-manicured lawn. Relieved, he zipped up and resolved to call Kyle tomorrow and apprise him of his findings. Hirsch couldn't deny he was onto a scheme even bigger than natural gas theft. With luck, it would be enough to nail Marcus Shaw and maybe his older brother. With his undercover work complete, Hirsch could return to walking the gas lines and repairing the wreckage of his life.

Unfortunately, that evening at Lily's Tavern was only the beginning of his entanglement with the Shaw brothers.

Chapter 7

"He did what?"

"He outright offered to sell me meth." Hirsch had called Kyle the day following his encounter with Shaw with an update on his ripening investigation. "If I weren't there, I wouldn't believe it either. Even better, when I asked if his 'ice' was any good, he told me he made it himself."

"Jesus, he must be one of the dumbest criminals I've come across in quite a while—and I've met plenty. What if you were an undercover cop?"

"He did threaten to kick the shit out of me if it were a setup. Still, he seemed to trust a guy he'd known for, like, fifteen minutes. I shouldn't be too surprised, given the length of his rap sheet."

Kyle chuckled. "Well, at any rate, thank you. It sounds like we may have more to work with than garden-variety larceny charges, especially if he's running a lab himself. Hell, we might even bring the DEA in on this one and get some resources up here. Opioids downstate suck up most of the bandwidth. I'll run it up the flagpole and see what we can do."

"Sounds good, bud. Now I can get back to my normal job." Fun as it was playing PI, Hirsch preferred to let the pros run with the case from here on out. Rubbing elbows with hardened criminals like Marcus Shaw made him feel like a degenerate himself.

"Actually, there is one more thing we could use your help with, Ben."

Hirsch grimaced. "What do you have in mind this time?"

"Someone stole a two-hundred-and-fifty-gallon propane tank outside Iron Mountain yesterday. Brand new equipment. They cut it right off the base with a torch. Whoever lifted it moved quick and had their shit together. This heist has the Shaws' fingerprints all over it. Can you go by Lionel's place on the Garden Peninsula and see if there's anything suspicious? Even better if you haven't walked that area yet and have a plausible cover."

Hirsch equivocated over Kyle's request. He had already gone too far. But after all, Kyle had done to get him back on his feet, and he couldn't well refuse.

"It's true, I haven't checked out that area yet," he replied, resigned. "I suppose I could drop by later this week and take a peek. We've got one problem, though."

"What's that?"

"Our boy Marcus already knows me from sight. If he's hanging out at his brother's and spots me working for the gas company after I told him I was unemployed and looking to score crystal meth, well, I hate to think what he might do."

"Fuck, I see your point. I tell you what—how about checking the lines running to Shaw's home? You won't need to spend much time there. If you wanna go the extra mile, you could return at night. I doubt they'd see you."

His old friend's lack of regard for his well-being concerned Hirsch. Maybe he caught me staring at Jess's ass one too many times and decided to get revenge by flinging me into the path of a deranged criminal, Hirsch reasoned.

"You remember I'm not a cop or PI, right? You seem to be drawing me deeper and deeper into this mess. It's one thing to haunt the courthouse and pull property records—that I don't mind doing. Hell, I'm as good as anyone when it comes to following a paper trail. At any rate, no one's going to pistol whip me over it. Staking out a guy's house at night seems like a whole different level of dangerous."

Kyle sighed. "I know, I know. I hear what you're saying, Ben. Like I said, though, I can't formally bring the police into this on a fishing expedition until we have cold, hard evidence on these clowns. Remember that stack of documents I gave you? Did you read all those?"

"Sure, every page. Marcus Shaw should be sitting in jail for the rest of his life."

"That's exactly right. The reason he's not is because we have corruption here like you wouldn't believe. It hurts me to say that, being part of the system and all. The trouble is, none of this shit is in the least way illegal. Money talks, and right now, it's screaming that we can't touch the Winslow family—and by extension, the Shaw brothers—unless we have a damn good reason to do so. Goddammit, Ben, I'm trying to change things! I've spent my whole life here. It kills me to watch one family get fat off the land and game the system while hardworking families can't even put food on the table. It's no wonder so many folks turn to meth and oxy. It's a break from their misery. I'm fucking sick of it. Thing is, if I launch an investigation here in the office or raise it with the chief of police, you can bet your ass I'd be prosecuting traffic offenses. More likely, they'd find a pretext to fire me. I need your help. If we can blow this case open and jail these two, God only knows how that could set us up for next year."

Kyle's soliloquy gave away the whole scheme. "You want to be chief prosecutor, don't you? I'm guessing you know Hal Clark will retire next year and you want it for yourself."

"You're damn right I do! Look, I've wanted this job since we graduated from law school. It's the whole fucking reason I moved back up here! Hell, I turned down an offer from the State AG's office just so I could be a deputy prosecutor in lowly Delta County. How many people do that? Don't go thinking for a minute this is an ego trip. Get off your high horse. Hal's a good ol' boy. He's been with the office thirty-plus years and chief for the last twelve. Nothing's going to change so long as he's around. Believe me, I'm not the preferred candidate up here. They'd rather have a predictable puppet who won't rock the boat. That's not me. I figured if anyone would get it, it'd be you.

"I've never told you this, but they pushed my old man off the bench because he wouldn't put up with anyone's shit. Told him they'd find a candidate to run against him and make his life a living hell. Sure enough, he lost reelection and died a couple years later. They killed him, Ben. They killed him as if they'd gunned him down in the street. I need to bring home a couple big convictions to make this work. I need to show the people we can change. You didn't leave Lansing to get away from the temptations there; you came home for a reason. Now, do you want to be part of this change or not?"

Hirsch was torn between admiration for Kyle's crusade and a desire to tell him to go fuck himself and leave him alone. Before he had a chance to respond, Kyle added, "Look, I know you're hurting for money. I can make this worth your while."

"Wait a minute. I thought you couldn't have the PA's office paying off informants for their help, Kyle?"

"That's right, and I'm not suggesting the county pay anyone. I'll pay you out of my own pocket for your help. Cash, building materials, you name it. I'm ready to do whatever it takes to make this work."

Kyle's offer made him feel like a hired gun, and Hirsch didn't like it. Being Kyle's mercenary would irrevocably change their relationship. If Hirsch decided to help, it would be out of friendship and, moreover, out of duty to his community.

"I don't want your money. Tell you what, I'll run down there later this week and have a look," Hirsch said, against his better judgment. "If Lionel and Marcus are as much of a cancer as you and everyone else say, I suppose I should do my part to take them down."

"I'm glad to hear that. We could make a real difference this way. Who knows, if you help blow this case open, it'd be great PR for you as well. The bar might even look kindly on reinstating your law license."

Hirsch scoffed. "Judging from the tone of their last letter, I don't think they'll be in any hurry. I could save a sinking boat of schoolkids from drowning and they'd say I wasn't rehabilitated."

"All the same, I know you could use a break after this past year. Jess and I could see it on your face when you visited last month. Speaking of which, you should come on over in the next week or two for dinner. I'll talk to Jess and see what works for her."

"That sounds fine. As for the Shaws, I'll ask to walk that territory on Thursday if that works. No promises, but I'll let you know if I come across anything useful."

"Thursday sounds great, Ben. I cannot thank you enough for doing this."

"You sure as hell better nail these assholes, that's all I'm going to say," Hirsch said before ending the call. He settled back into the couch and buried his face in his hands. *Why on earth did you let Kyle coerce you into this foolishness? Too late to stop now.*

The mailman had come and gone during Hirsch's call with Kyle, and he walked onto the porch to check the mailbox. Amidst the usual flyers from the supermarket and credit card applications addressed to his deceased father, Hirsch came across an envelope with his ex-wife's name on the return address label. He walked into the house and plopped down on the couch, dreading what she had to say after his last drunk dial.

Hirsch tore down the edge of the cream-colored envelope with his fingernail and extracted the tri-folded single sheet of paper within. He unfolded the letter to reveal Allison's neat handwriting:

Dear Ben,

It's taken me days to write this letter since we last spoke. I started it three times and tore the first two up. Part of me wanted to never speak to you again, delete you from my contacts, and block you. Truth is, I did that twice, only to add you back the next day. What I've come to realize is that I can't bring myself to purge you from my life. You were my first true love and we shared too much for me to whitewash the past and start over.

I feel the least I can do is be honest with you, Ben. I've met someone from work and we've moved in together. I've explained to him that while we're divorced, you're still my friend and I care deeply about you. That said, I can't have you calling me at all hours of the night, drunk, and talking about us getting back together again. I've had to move on. It was the hardest thing I've ever done, harder than even that first year of residency and those long nights apart. I knew I could never bring myself to completely trust you again if we stayed together. It pains me to admit this but it's the hard truth.

In short, Ben, despite everything that's happened, I want you in my life. I know you've made mistakes but at your core, you're a good, well-meaning person. If you can accept me as a friend, even your best friend, consider it a gift we can share for the rest of our lives. All I ask is that you not tear open old wounds. It took me a long time to heal them and I'm not going to relive that nightmare. If you can live with that, my heart is and always will be open to you.

I'm glad you're back home. I hope the solitude gives you time to clear your head. Lansing wasn't good for you. Call me if you need to talk. I'll be there.

Love,

Allison

Hirsch allowed the letter to fall into his lap as he leaned back into the couch. He stared overhead at the peeling paint on the ceiling as he processed her words. Allison's letter was honest, heartfelt, and entirely justified. But goddamn it if it didn't piss him off knowing she'd replaced him so soon.

"None of my damn business," he muttered as he kicked back on the couch and tore into another paperback. Escapism was the only panacea he knew for heartbreak.

HIRSCH WOKE EARLY THURSDAY MORNING to the dulcet tones of Dale Cromley coughing and wheezing from his smoking porch across the street. Warm weather settled over the peninsula the day before, and Hirsch left the window open overnight to air out the stuffy room. He glanced over at his bedside alarm clock. Dammit, not even six yet. He hauled himself out of bed, shuffled over to the window, and slammed it shut to further spare him the sound of Cromley hacking up a lung. Hirsch flopped down on the bed with his arms over his eyes. With his mind racing, falling back asleep was a pipe dream. He saw little point in delaying the inevitable.

"This is the day," Hirsch said as he rolled back out of bed.

On Monday, he'd called Milo and requested the Garden Peninsula assignment. Hirsch explained that he had a doctor's appointment in town and needed time to get there. Milo voiced no objections, so Hirsch pulled the maps for the territory north of the town of Garden—a swath of land that included Lionel Shaw's property. Hirsch wasn't too concerned about casing Shaw's place during the day. He figured a gas company representative walking around in broad daylight wouldn't raise much suspicion. It was Kyle's suggestion that he creep up at night that worried him.

Since Marcus Shaw got a good look at him when they met at Lily's, Hirsch took pains to alter his appearance. Gone was the scruffy townie look, replaced by the costume of an aspiring mid-level professional. He shaved and swept his dark hair across his forehead. Hirsch put on a pair of dark blue slacks, black ankle-high work boots, and a brown button-up shirt. He slipped into the blue vest with the words "Peninsula Energy" emblazoned across the back and donned a matching ball cap featuring the company's logo. But for the vest and hat, Hirsch stood ready to walk into his law office at a moment's notice.

"Where the hell have you been?" he asked the familiar reflection staring back at him.

Hirsch took the back road to Garden, thus avoiding the summer traffic of Highway 2 and State Route 183. He liked the rustic splendor of this unpaved alternate route. One could avoid passing another car for miles and be surrounded by tall stands of trees on either side. At the village of Thompson, he took the southbound cutoff onto Little Harbor Road, opposite the road to the Thompson State Fish Hatchery. He cruised along the first several miles of paved road before the surface gave way to gravel. The familiar crunch of loose stone churning beneath his wheels rang out. The pine and beech trees rolled past on either side as he continued south. He veered west as the road rounded Barque Point and, moments later, traversed the invisible line bisecting the peninsula into Delta from Schoolcraft County. At one point, Hirsch brought his truck to a stop to allow a turkey hen and her flock of poults to cross the road.

Little Harbor Road intersected with State Route 183. The blue expanse of the Big Bay de Noc lay beyond. With time to spare, Hirsch turned left and made a quick pass through the small town of Garden. How many years had it been since he last came down this way? In grade school, his class took a field trip to Fayette State Park to explore the ruins of the old iron smelter. Long abandoned, the state rehabilitated the townsite for tourists, making it a popular destination on the peninsula. At other times, Hirsch rode with his father down to the boat launch at Fairport. There they would un-winch Murray's dented but sturdy fourteen-foot Lund boat into the lake and troll the waters around the islands to the south for whitefish. Twenty years had flown by since the two had last ventured out together.

Hirsch crawled through Garden, passing the Catholic church and its retreat center on the right and twinned by the white spire of the Lutheran Church on his left. The whole town was quiet as a Sunday morning. Several dilapidated houses stood vacant, long abandoned with yards overgrown by vegetation. A beyond-decrepit elderly woman pushing a walker crept her way up to the squat, brick post office building. The small town had succumbed to the fate of so many similar communities in the UP—decimation by job loss and families moving south in search of opportunities.

Hirsch turned around in front of the town's historical society museum. He'd seen enough. Lingering would only sow sorrow for the loss of yet another charming village to the ravages of so-called progress. The hamlet's natural beauty was its strongest asset and path to survival. That and the stark-white wind turbines towering across the skyline. Their blades whooshed in concentric arcs through the air. The behemoths appeared in the previous few years and caused no small amount of strife amongst the remaining inhabitants. Some landowners relished the profits guaranteed by the ground leasing fees, while others lamented the intrusion into the otherwise bucolic surroundings. He could appreciate both perspectives.

He stopped at a small gas station on the southern edge of town. A bell tinkled as Hirsch walked in the door. The woman in her mid-fifties sitting behind the counter appeared bored out of her mind.

"Can I help you with anything?" she hollered out.

"Just gonna grab a cup of coffee. Thanks." The woman grunted in response.

Hirsch walked to a counter along the back wall where a dispenser stood. He grabbed a Styrofoam cup and filled it with the acrid dark liquid. He breathed deep as the coffee's vapors wafted up toward his face, invigorating his groggy mind.

"I made it fresh near half an hour ago," the clerk continued. "It should still be hot, I hope."

"It looks fine to me," Hirsch said as he secured a plastic lid around the lip of the cup and returned to the counter. He handed the woman two dollars.

"That be everything or do you need any gas?" she asked.

"It should do it today, though I may be back later if I run low out on the job."

The clerk placed his change on the counter and fixed him with a piercing gaze through her mascara-caked eyes. "You work for the gas company?"

"Yeah. I'm from Manistique, but they assigned me to check this territory around here. We do it every year to make sure all the equipment's in good working order."

"That right, eh? Well, best be safe out there. I know a few dogs 'round here who'd give their right arm to bite a stranger like you. So would a couple of their owners, come to think of it," she added with a cackle.

"I'll keep that in mind," Hirsch said. He hurried through the door to escape.

"Enjoy your coffee. You never know who you might run into out there," she called after him in a deadpan voice. The note of menace in her demeanor spooked him, and a mile out of town, he dumped the coffee out the window, concerned the attendant might be an aspiring serial killer.

ONCE OUT AND ABOUT ON his route, Hirsch's sense of foreboding dissipated as he fell into his familiar pattern of scanning the lines for leaks. It allowed him ample time to daydream. Since his early days walking the lines, self-recrimination over his actions as an attorney dominated his thoughts. What troubled him most was not getting busted for even more egregious behavior. After all, who could forget all the extra hours buried in his clients' bills? At first, it was a sixth of an hour slipped in here and there on an email or call. Soon, he plastered the invoices with additional time for writing or "hearing prep." With fee awards in the tens of thousands of dollars, no one paid attention to an extra grand or two. An early mentor taught him to take a two-hour status meeting at which they'd discuss all their cases and bill a full two hours to each client. Hundreds—no, thousands of dollars for nothing. How many times had he lied to clients, let alone opposing counsel? How often had he deluded himself?

At three in the afternoon, Hirsch's route brought him to Lionel Shaw's property. The dread suffocating him earlier in the day came roaring back as he rounded the corner of Shaw's driveway. He peered down the two-hundred-yard gravel driveway toward the house at the end. His stomach tightened, and a rush of adrenaline surged through his chest. Swallowing hard, he inched his way along. He kept the rubber cup of his leak detector bouncing along the ground as his sunglass-shielded eyes scanned the property for any abnormalities. Hirsch soon reached a clearing where Shaw's modest home stood before him.

The house itself was inconspicuous. The single-level residence featured faded and grime-spattered white clapboard siding, a medium-pitched roof, and a door and two windows on the front of the home. A broken satellite dish dangled from the roof's edge. A thin gravel sidewalk connected the concrete steps of the front porch to the driveway. A rusty mailbox hung beside the door. The remaining letters imprinted across it read "SH W." An early 2000s-vintage Ford F-150 pickup truck sat parked alongside the house. Stenciled on the side of one door was the faded outline of the words "Shaw Brothers Heating." This evidence obliterated any doubt in Hirsch's mind that he had the right place. Hirsch headed for the natural gas meter on the side of the house. As Hirsch approached, the large barn in the backyard of the house caught his attention. It stood bereft of windows with its twin doors shut tight. The barn was the ideal place for the brothers to conceal any criminal operation. He squinted at the building. What could those two be hiding in there?

"Looking for something?" a gruff voice called out behind him.

Hirsch jolted at the abrupt sound and dropped the leak detector to the ground. It bounced twice before landing on its side.

Christ, not even five minutes here and I've made a damn fool of myself, he thought. Hirsch fumbled for the detector, then turned to face the voice addressing him. His eyes settled on the man who he assumed to be the elder Shaw brother, Lionel.

Lionel stood around six feet tall, with reddish blonde hair fringing the balding crown of his head. Although only in his early fifties, years spent exposed to the wind and sun left him with a lined face and crow's feet bracketing his eyes. Lionel sported a short red beard mottled with gray. He wore a pair of jeans, scuffed and stained work boots, and a faded blue T-shirt covered by a light jacket. Although lean like his brother Marcus, he lacked the latter's emaciated, drug-ravaged appearance. Lionel glared at Hirsch with guarded distrust. Hirsch could tell Lionel was the brains of the operation just by looking at him.

Afternoon," Hirsch greeted him. "I'm with the gas company. I'm out checking the neighborhood for leaks today."

"That so?" Lionel spat sideways at the ground to punctuate his remark. "Well, tell me, partner—did you find any?"

"Nope. I checked the whole line, and you're good to go. Solid equipment you have here. Give us a call if you notice any problems," Hirsch said and motioned to head back down the driveway.

Lionel raised his hand and extended two fingers commanding Hirsch to stop. "Trust me, bud. I'd be the first to know if we sprung a leak. I'd also take care of it before any of you fools could bumble your way through fixing it. I reckon you'd know that already if you was from 'round these parts." Lionel paused before continuing, "I do have one question for you though if you have a moment." Lionel's tone indicated Hirsch had little choice.

"Sure, shoot."

"You know I don't have any gas service beyond the house, right?"

"So far as the charts go, I can't see any," Hirsch said.

"All right, then. Any reason for you to be checking out my back yard? You seemed awfully interested in something."

"Oh, ah … no. Everything looks good to me. I needed to stretch and take a quick break. Lovely place you have out here though," Hirsch said.

"You sure about that? You sure I can't help you with something? You seem a touch jumpy."

"Ah, no sir. I don't run into many people out during the day. Guess I didn't hear you coming is all." There was zero chance of Shaw forgetting Hirsch now.

Lionel sighed and kicked at the gravel with the toe of his boot. "Let me give you a piece of advice. You seem like a decent sort, but folks around here don't take too kindly to strangers loitering on their property, even fellas like you who have as good an excuse as anyone. Mind you, I'm a reasonable man myself, so I get it. I really do, bud. Hell, you might even say we're brothers of the blue flame. You may have a right to be here, but I'm telling you, don't wear out your welcome. People usually find out when it's already too late."

"I understand. Thanks. I best be getting on my way," Hirsch said.

Seeing no use in prolonging this exchange, Hirsch started back to his truck, withering under Lionel's piercing gaze. Shaw's hand shot out and came to rest on Hirsch's chest, arresting the latter in his place.

"All I'm saying is do yourself a favor and watch it. Call me your guardian angel if you want." Lionel dropped his arm, allowing Hirsch to move forward. Hirsch could feel Lionel's gaze boring into the back of his head as he walked away. Hirsch was halfway to his truck smelling freedom when Lionel called out, "Say, do I know you from somewhere?"

Hirsch froze. Looking back over his shoulder toward Lionel, he replied, "I doubt it. I came here from downstate a couple months ago for work."

Lionel grunted. "That so? It's usually the other way around. Shit, must be hard times when folks are moving to the UP for work. I'd say I'll be seeing you, but I doubt you'll need to come 'round here again, right?"

"No, I don't suppose I will. You have a good day all the same," Hirsch said as he picked up the pace, leaving Shaw and his derelict spread behind.

He hustled down the driveway and soon reached the comfort of his truck. Safe inside, Hirsch gripped the steering wheel and breathed deep several times as he struggled to make sense of the encounter. The smart move would be to give up and quit this silly quest right this minute. He could fire up his truck, hightail it back home to Manistique, and call Kyle to tell him to shove it. Hirsch stood to gain nothing by poking his nose into the affairs of two unrepentant degenerates. Christ, he finally had a job that didn't try to kill him and felt better about life than in recent memory. Best go home and forget this entire mess.

Yet he couldn't shake one argument Kyle made during their last phone call. Decay, crime, and drug addiction were tearing his hometown apart. Hirsch could have stayed in Lansing and continued to indulge his freewheeling, out-of-control life. There was a reason he came back home; he just hadn't realized it when he left. On the surface, he made the move to save himself from flaming out in a morass of booze and overindulgence. For all his delusions that his work as a plaintiff's attorney was in the selfless service of his clients, the last ten-plus years were little more than a quest for self-enrichment and gluttony. His breath grew ragged, and he struggled against tears as a tidal wave of shame crashed over him.

You victimized countless people for little more than fleeting moments of pleasure. You took, you took, and you took more from others all your life, Ben. You hurt those who cared for you the most, and what the hell do you have to show for it? Hirsch punched the dashboard several times as hard as he could, sending searing ripples of satisfying pain coursing through his body.

If I am not for myself, who will be for me? Near-forgotten words of his forsaken faith came back to him. Hirsch couldn't deny he'd been for himself all too often in recent years, albeit in a crude and appetitive fashion. *If I am only for myself, what am I?* What the hell had he even done for his fellow man in his entire adult life? *And if not now, when?* Though not given to religious paroxysms, this edict resonated with Hirsch's predicament. And so it came to pass, amidst the ecstasies and agony of enlightenment, that Hirsch accepted his path to salvation—selfless service to the people he'd shunned for all too many years.

Liberated by his confrontation with shame and guilt, Hirsch fixed a stony gaze on the road ahead of him. No more, Ben. It may be too late to save yourself, but you can still rehabilitate your community. Redemption had to begin somewhere. It might as well start with taking down a pair of cancers on humanity. If Kyle was right, Hirsch needed to know what the hell Lionel and

Marcus were up to in Lionel's barn. There was only one way to do it, and the time was now.

Thus began Hirsch's career as the self-appointed savior of the Upper Peninsula.

Chapter 8

DARKNESS SWEPT ACROSS THE GARDEN Peninsula as Hirsch lay prone behind a thin row of elderberry shrubs. The aroma of damp soil and clover emanated from the cool earth beneath him. Three hundred yards ahead lay Shaw's property. The last remnants of daylight shriveling away in the west highlighted the gray outline of Shaw's barn. The house sat behind it, partially obscured from view by the barn. A thin light shone through the windows of the house. Hirsch tightened the collar of his jacket as the chill of night swept through the air. As the last embers of the sun extinguished into the Big Bay de Noc, fingerlings of fog rolled in off the bay. They merged into a hazy gray wall of darkness that lent a quality of menace to the evening. Crickets chirped their evening song, competing with the low hum and whoosh of a wind turbine behind him. The nocturnal concerto of twenty-first-century Delta County rang out around him.

After his fateful moment of revelation earlier that afternoon, Hirsch had no choice but to confront the Shaw brothers on their own turf. He went home and changed into the darkest clothes he could find. Too nervous to eat, he laid on his couch and stared at the water-stained ceiling tiles overhead, wondering if he'd ever set eyes on his childhood home again. With nightfall imminent, he returned to the peninsula and parked his truck on a dirt county road one section north of Shaw's property. He picked his way through an empty field bracketed by a pair of churning wind turbines. Alone, he faced the epicenter of the Shaws' putative criminal headquarters.

The temperature plummeted as the full grip of darkness fell across the peninsula. With the stars and the slim crescent moon as Hirsch's sole illumination, it was now or never to advance. A ribbon of fog drifted across as cover, and he rose to a crouch. Advancing, he brushed his way through the shrubs, hurtling step-by-step toward the barn. The hoot of an owl pierced the evening's silence. At the sound, Hirsch dropped to the ground in a spread-eagle position a hundred feet from the barn. His cheek pressed into the cool soil as he listened for the slightest echo of human activity. With a pounding heart and shallow breath, he crawled back to his feet and crept closer to his target.

The barn's aged wood was warped and devoid of all but a scattered scrape of yellow paint. A faint glow pierced the gaps in the siding. As he reached the barn, Hirsch sank to his knees and peered through a half-inch gap between the weathered pine slats. Several commercial-grade propane tanks lay scattered throughout the barn alongside dozens of gauges, hoses, and brass valves of varying complexity. The menagerie appeared valuable even to Hirsch's untrained eye. A decrepit tanker truck sat parked to one side of the barn. Hirsch had little doubt the tank served to transport purloined fuels or gases.

"What the hell have you boys got yourselves into?" he muttered into the night.

As Hirsch scanned the barn for any more clues to the Shaw brothers' activities, a new sound froze him in place. The faint tinkling of a piano echoed across the fogbound farm. Drawn to the siren-like call of the gentle notes, Hirsch stood. He inched his way along the side of the barn, homing in on the source. The adagio tempo of the notes intensified as he approached the corner. He came to a stop and listened with care. The music originated from Shaw's house.

The hair on the back of his neck rose as he recognized the piece—Chopin's Nocturne in D-flat major, played by the hands of a master.

For Hirsch, no other composition provoked such a visceral reaction. After all, it was the same nocturne floating through the music school at Michigan State when he first set eyes on his future wife sitting behind a piano. Hirsch was running late for his 1L contracts class when he cut through the music building to shave a couple minutes off his journey. He didn't expect to be waylaid by a copper-haired waif perched on a piano bench with the rehearsal room to herself. She wore her long mane pulled back into a ponytail that brushed between her shoulders as she swayed to the music. Her strong, nimble fingers glided across the keyboard as she navigated the nocturne's ending. Her eyes were closed in pensive concentration. As the haunting final notes lingered in the air, she opened her eyes. Hirsch stood paralyzed in the doorway.

She fixed her bright green gaze on Hirsch. "You're a Chopin admirer, I see," she said, lifting her hands from the keyboard.

"Chopin. Yeah, who doesn't?" Hirsch shifted his casebook from one hand to the other, straining to recall anything about the Polish composer.

"Most people prefer the mazurkas or the concertos, but I find the nocturnes more—demure, I guess."

"I mean, really, who wouldn't love the nocturnes?" Hirsch said. His ignorance of classical music had to be palpable.

"It's nice to find someone who appreciates Chopin," she continued. "Not many students here do," she added with a nervous giggle.

"What can I say? He's a classic for a reason." Hirsch felt like an idiot but couldn't think of what else to say. He plotted a trip to the library to learn every shred of information he could about Chopin and nocturnes in case he encountered this angel again.

"I'm Allison. I'm playing a recital this weekend, and I'm *terrified* of blowing it. I keep rushing the cadenza. My instructor thinks I'll be fine but thank heavens for this practice room." Allison pivoted toward him with her hands clasped in her lap.

"I'm Ben. It sounded pretty good to me. Are you studying to be a concert pianist or something?"

Allison laughed and said, "Oh lord, no. I'm just an amateur. Jeez, I'm not even a music major. Biology. I start med school here next fall. I've played piano since I was five. I just do it to stay sane."

"A doctor, wow. Puts me to shame. I'm late for class," he said, noticing the clock on the wall behind her. "I should get going." He didn't make the slightest motion to move.

"Well don't let me keep you," she said, returning her delicate hands to the keyboard. "Say, Ben, I'm sure a guy like you has a crazy social life, but if you're free Friday evening, stop by the recital hall. It'd be nice to have a real classical music fan there."

"Sure, I'll try to make it," he said, striving to play it cool. Hirsch lingered for a few moments as the petite nymph thundered into a Bach sinfonia. Spellbound, he pulled himself away and stumbled into class five minutes late, to his contracts professor's overt disdain.

Hirsch attended Allison's recital that Friday night and asked her out to dinner during the sparsely attended reception afterward. Years later, Hirsch would watch her sit at their piano stark naked and rehearse the nocturne as moonlight streamed through the window, basking her pearly skin in iridescent splendor. Hirsch would wait until the last glimmer of notes dissipated into silence, then sweep her off the bench to make love on the floor of their den.

As he stood alone in a fallow field on an Upper Peninsula night, shivering, those halcyon days felt like an eternity ago. Waves of emotion swept over Hirsch as he craned his neck to catch the languid notes and soft arpeggios dancing through the night air. The player approached the thundering cadenza, and Hirsch lost all cognizance of his mission. He held his breath, focusing his full attention on the notes pouring forth from an open window. The pianist drew the ghostly nocturne to a close, and Hirsch stood transfixed, unable to move a muscle in the presence of absolute beauty.

Then the world went black.

"BIND HIM UP REAL GOOD, you hear me."

As Hirsch came to and raised his eyelids, a piercing pain penetrated his brain. He slammed his eyes closed to extinguish the light. He moaned in agony as a throbbing ache radiated across the back of his skull. He tried to reach and assess the source of the pain but couldn't budge his hands so much as a single inch. Nylon ropes bound his hands and feet. The rough cords cut into his bare skin. He lingered half-conscious in a fugue state. A torrent of frigid water smashing into his face gave Hirsch an appreciation for the situation's gravity. The chill knocked the wind out of his chest and left him gasping as his eyes flew open. Wide awake, he looked up from the filthy floor on which he lay. The coarse murmur of surrounding voices told Hirsch he was the captive of none other than Lionel and Marcus Shaw.

"Well, looky who decided to wake up," Marcus said behind him. "Did the little snoop have a long enough nap?"

Hirsch tried to turn his head to explore the world around him but a searing ache snapped his neck forward. Hirsch surveyed the room, venturing only to shift his eyes. Sawdust, crumpled paper, and metal shavings littered the stained concrete floor beneath him. An unpainted slate-gray stone wall stood in front of him. He stretched his gaze to the right. A rickety wooden staircase rose to what he took to be the ground level of the house. He shuddered, terror-stricken at the realization he was tied up in a basement.

Marcus Shaw returned, carrying an empty bucket that Hirsch assumed held the gallon of cold water dripping down his face and onto his shirt. The coppery flavor of blood filled his mouth. He ran his tongue around the perimeter of his teeth and gums. A jagged gap replaced half an incisor. Lionel dragged a metal chair screeching across the floor and brought it to a stop in front of where Hirsch lay. The brothers each grabbed Hirsch by an armpit and dumped him onto the chair. The stage was set for Hirsch's interrogation.

"Who the fuck do you think you are prowling around here?" Marcus asked.

"I work for the gas company," Hirsch garbled out. "My job is to go out and check for leaks. I was following up on an incident I flagged earlier today." It was the only plausible story that came to his mind.

"Oh, is that right? You expect me to believe that horseshit, buddy? I may not be a genius like my brother here, but I ain't come across too many gasmen gallivanting at night all dressed in black, snooping on other people."

"He's not making that up," Lionel said as he walked across the room to join his younger brother. "At least not the gas company part. This asshole's name is Ben Hirsch. You care to argue with me on that?" Lionel asked as he flipped Hirsch's Peninsula Energy identification card onto the ground in front of him. The laminated card landed face-up with Hirsch's mugshot-like picture staring back at him. Confronted with the evidence, Hirsch shook his head.

"Let me add to that you're former attorney Benjamin J. Hirsch, late of Felton and Hirsch in Lansing, and recently disbarred for screwing a client. Is that right as well?" Lionel added, crouching in front of Hirsch to address him at eye level. Lionel's cold but calculating gaze rested inches from Hirsch's face.

"How on earth did you know that?" Hirsch asked.

Lionel stood and said, "Do you think I don't know how to use the internet? While you were laying there out cold, I googled you on the off-hand chance I might learn something about you. Much more than I expected as it turned out. Hell, I figured you were an oxy-slave searching for a place to rob. Come to think of it, you may well be."

Before Hirsch could respond, Marcus shoved his brother out of the way. He squinted at Hirsch, scrutinizing him.

"Wait a minute, I know this son of a bitch. Only he told me his name was Ken and wanted me to sell him some crystal. What the hell is going on here?"

Marcus reared back and struck Hirsch's jaw with a vicious backhand. Hirsch winced in misery at the sharp snap of his neck. He stretched his mouth open to work out the tingling soreness.

Lionel laid his hand on Marcus's upper arm. "Let me handle the questions for now, all right, Marc?"

Marcus grunted in response but acquiesced and stepped away. He leaned against a cluttered table next to the wall but kept his eyes glued on Hirsch. The latter expected Marcus to leap at the slightest opportunity to rough him up again.

"Now what's a disbarred downstate attorney doing in the UP working for the gas company and trying to score meth in his free time? Why are you really here?" Lionel asked.

"Look, I lost my law license a few months back, and I needed a job. I'm from around these parts so it seemed like a good fit to come on home. The gas company was the only place that would take me. That's the honest truth."

"All right, all right, I already know you're from Manistique so don't try to play me. I may look like a dumb hick to you but I can hold my own, especially when it comes to the gas business. Something didn't smell right when I caught you here earlier in the day. But I says to myself, 'Nah, ol' Lionel, you're being paranoid's all.' I should've trusted my instincts. You didn't look like you belonged there, clutching that leak detector and wearing a blue vest. So let me ask you again, Mr. Hirsch, who is it you're working for?"

Hirsch hesitated for a minute, his eyes shuttling between the two glaring brothers. "I told you, I work for the gas company. I needed to follow-up on a potential leak. I got the impression you weren't keen on having me around earlier."

Lionel looked straight at Hirsch and snorted. "Fine, have it your way."

Lionel gave his brother a brisk nod and stepped out of the way. Marcus took a pull off a half-empty bottle of Wild Turkey before passing the bottle to his brother, who did the same. Fortified, Marcus lifted a two-inch-thick Chilton auto repair manual off the workbench. Crouching before Hirsch like a catcher awaiting a fast ball, he swung the manual with both hands across Hirsch's face. A torrent of pain exploded through Hirsch's skull as his head snapped to the right. The whole left side of his face went numb before searing ripples of torment coursed through his flesh. He had but a moment to recover before Marcus reversed direction and bashed the manual across the opposite side of his face.

"Who the fuck are you working for?" Lionel repeated.

"I told you, I'm with the fucking gas company," Hirsch bleated through swollen lips. The reward for his intransigence was two additional swats with the repair manual. Each landed with greater force than the last. Hirsch's brain exploded in a supernova of agony, and pin-like stars danced beneath his closed eyelids. This was pain beyond pain, the only benefit being he expected to reach a maximum threshold and soon pass out.

"I'm going to give you one more chance, asshole. If you want to walk out of here alive, I'd suggest you start talking." Lionel spoke in quiet, measured tones and stood with arms crossed. He watched with near disinterest as his brother clobbered Hirsch about the head with the manual.

"Look, I don't know what I else I can tell you," Hirsch said between heaving breaths. "I'm not on anyone else's payroll. You gotta believe me on this." A lie of omission perhaps, but true nonetheless.

Rage swept through Marcus as he flung the blood and saliva-smeared manual into a corner. "That's it, I've about had it with this lying little motherfucker," he screamed. Marcus reared back with his right hand and delivered a swift hook that connected with Hirsch's left eye socket. The force of the impact tipped Hirsch back in the chair, slamming the back of his head into the cold concrete behind him. Half conscious, the room spun as the voices of Marcus and Lionel swirled about him. Marcus reached down, grabbed Hirsch by the shirt collar, and yanked him back to a seated position. By the time he was upright, his left eye had already swollen shut.

Amidst the white noise echoing in his mind, Hirsch heard Lionel say, "I don't think this little bastard is quite ready to talk. You still have that ol' welding torch down here, Marc?"

"Sure do, brother!" Through his one good eye, Hirsch watched Marcus walk into the shadows of a far corner of the basement. Moments later, he returned holding an acetylene torch in one hand and wheeling the appurtenant tanks and regulator in the other.

Hirsch widened his terror-stricken eye as Marcus approached him. A gleeful menace permeated the sociopath's face. At that moment, Hirsch accepted he may not walk out of this basement alive. Marcus would undoubtedly take great pleasure in torturing him to death. All that stood between him and that fate was the dubious reasonableness of the elder Shaw brother.

That hope faded as Lionel called out, "Light 'er up!"

Marcus opened the torch's valve, unleashing the hiss of gas throughout the room. He extracted a metal flint lighter from his pocket and stroked the metal bar several times across the flint while holding it near the torch's tip. A spark caught and ignited the oxy-fuel. It blazed before Hirsch's eyes as a sinister dark red-orange flame oozing oily black smoke. Marcus adjusted a knob at the base of the torch until the flame shifted to a scorching-hot blue. Marcus waved the flame in arches inches from Hirsch's face. The ambient heat seared his flesh, and he yanked his head away as far back as he could to avoid being burned. Hirsch hy-perventilated and near passed out as he witnessed the back-lit menacing glee written across Marcus's face.

"Where do you want me to start, bro?" he asked Lionel.

"Well, I've found the bottom of the feet to be a good place. Might be a challenge with him tied up like this. How about I rip his shirt open and see what he cares to share with us?"

"I'll bet he doesn't have a hair on that pasty little chest of his. Let's find out," Marcus replied.

Lionel stepped forward and leaned down in front of Hirsch, preparing to rip his shirt open with his hands. Hirsch gagged at the odor of Lionel's chewing tobacco and stench of rotting teeth. He couldn't hold out any longer.

"Okay, okay. Turn that fucking thing off and I'll tell you everything," he said.

"Ah, so the little shitheel can talk," Marcus said. "Whad-daya think? Should I run this over him a few times for wasting our time?"

Lionel waved his hand palm down at his brother. "Let's see what he has to say first. I've had these goons on my case since Melissa ran off, and I'd like to know what he has to do with this. I wanna know which casino the little bastard is with."

Casino? Who do they think I am? Hirsch wondered.

"So, Mr. Hirsch, you best get to talking," Lionel said.

Hirsch caught his breath as Marcus twisted the knob to cut off the gas, suffocating the blue flame. Hirsch expectorated a clot of slimy blood onto the floor and replied, "All right, here's the deal. I *do* work for the gas company and I was checking this neighborhood for leaks earlier—but that's not why I came back tonight. The county thinks y'all are stealing natural gas. They suspect you stole a propane tank or two recently. I came out here tonight take a peek at what's in your old barn out back. That's all."

"So what, you're snitching on the county's payroll as well?" Lionel said. "Jesus, don't tell me they're desperate enough to start hiring disbarred shysters to do their dirty work. Mind you, I'm no man of the law myself but common sense tells me that wouldn't look too hot in court."

"No, I'm not working for the county. I doubt they know a damn thing about my involvement in all this."

"Then who the hell are you working for?" Lionel demanded.

"No one. I did it as a favor."

"A favor! A favor for whom?"

Hirsch paused, reluctant to throw his friend under the bus. Still, this wasn't the Hanoi Hilton or Guantanamo, and Kyle hadn't sworn him to secrecy. Defeated, he replied, "Kyle Severson, the deputy prosecuting attorney."

Lionel and Marcus exchanged a glance of disbelief. "And why the hell would the Delta County deputy PA ask a disgraced scumbag like you for help?" Lionel asked.

"Kyle's an old friend of mine. We went to law school together. He knew with me working for the gas company, I'd have the perfect cover to snoop around on the company's dime. I didn't much want to do it, but I couldn't say no to him—he's been a good friend over the years. One of the few left."

"Like father, like son," Marcus interjected. "You know he's Judge Severson's kid, right?"

"He is … what about it?" Hirsch replied.

"That old bastard was always busting my balls when I was younger. I was making out all right until that self-righteous prick decided I needed to go to jail. Total bullshit charges. He gave our daddy a hard time too," Marcus continued, addressing his brother.

"Now it looks like his boy wants his pound of flesh as well from us Shaws," Lionel said. "Leave it to Kyle to fuck with our arrangement. Won't cure his shame," he added.

Hirsch hadn't the foggiest clue what they were talking about.

"Okay, so what do you say we strangle this motherfucker and dump his body out in the bay as a message to that pissant Severson and anyone else who wants to mess with us. After I work him over with this here torch, of course," Marcus said.

Marcus moved to grab his flint striker and strike the torch up again. Hirsch's bowels turned to water. This wasn't how he hoped his life would end, but here he was.

"Hold on, hold on," Lionel said as he waved Marcus off from commencing his torture of Hirsch. "Much as I'd love to, Severson knows his boy is snooping on us. If he goes missing or they find a body, guess who'll be the first people they come after. They don't have shit on us for now. Otherwise, he wouldn't send this bumbling dipshit out prancing around other people's yards like he's Sam fucking Spade."

"Sam who?" Marcus asked.

"Never mind. Point is, we can't kill him. Not yet anyway."

"Well, what the fuck are we going to do with him—cut him loose until he comes back again?" Marcus demanded of his brother.

"I think Mr. Hirsch's career as a private investigator is over." Addressing Hirsch, Lionel continued, "I know for a fact you saw nothing here on the property 'cause I have nothing to hide. You wouldn't know what you're looking for in any case. Just because you work for the gas company doesn't mean you know shit about the business.

"Here's what's gonna happen. We'll turn you loose and you'll call your buddy, mister prosecutor, first thing tomorrow. You'll tell him you didn't find nothing and that you're done with this investigation. Second, neither of us want to see you ever again. In fact, I'd suggest you quit this damn job of yours and head back south to Lansing where you belong. Fuck, make it Mexico for all I care. If I so much as catch you on this property again, I'll put a round through your head, no questions asked. With my 30-30, you'd be dead before you even hear the shot. Far be it from me to say what might happen if Marcus gets ahold of you first."

Hirsch nodded. Disgusted and disappointed at the turn of events, Marcus flung the acetylene torch on the bench next to the wall and dropped the striker, which clattered to the floor. He took another generous gulp off the Wild Turkey, his eyes burning with hatred for Hirsch. Nonetheless, he refused to countermand his brother's plan.

Lionel moved behind where Hirsch sat. "We're taking you out of here," he said as a slipped a rough burlap sack over Hirsch's head, eclipsing any source of light.

"Gimme a hand with this, Marc," Lionel said as the two brothers untied Hirsch from the chair before jerking him to a standing position. He had but a fleeting relief from bondage before they bound his hands and feet again, tighter this time. Lionel ordered Marcus to grab Hirsch's legs. Hirsch went horizontal, and they carried their burden across the basement floor. The distinct sound of their footsteps clomping up the wooden staircase echoed through the basement. The air grew cold as they exited into the night air.

"Toss him in the back and grab that old tarp by the shed," Lionel commanded.

Hirsch had but a split second to brace himself as the brothers swung him twice and heaved him through the air. He landed with a thud against the truck bed. His throbbing head banged against the steel, sending a fresh wave of pain radiating through his skull and down his spine. Stray gravel dug into his side and arms, and moving so much as a muscle exacerbated his discomfort. The plastic tarp crinkled as it unfolded over him while the brothers worked to secure its corners with heavy stones.

"Let's do this," Marcus called out as he climbed into the Ford and slammed the door. The engine fired up, and the truck shifted into reverse.

Over the ensuing fifteen minutes, Hirsch had no clue where they might be taking him. The sound penetrating the truck bed told him they were travelling along a gravel road and—in all likelihood—moving away from town. Space and time lost all meaning in captivity. Bound up and concealed beneath a tarp in the back of a reprobate's pickup truck, Hirsch could only laugh. This was all wildly unnecessary on their part. After all, Hirsch knew where they lived. He concluded this whole charade was little more than theatre designed to intimidate him. Admittedly, it worked.

After the longest quarter hour of Hirsch's life, the truck pulled to the roadside and ground to an abrupt stop. Both doors flew open and the gravel crunched under the brothers' feet as they moved to either side of the truck bed. The frigid night air assaulted him as the brothers yanked the plastic tarp away. The tailgate clattered open and one brother grabbed Hirsch about the ankles, dragging him out of the truck bed. The loose stones and rocks littering the truck bed sliced and tore into Hirsch's exposed flesh as he slid along the rough metal. They each grabbed Hirsch by an arm and brought him to a standing position.

The three men stood in the silence of a Michigan night. Lionel spoke up. "All right boy, here's how this works. We're gonna leave you here. You can figure your way out of this mess. Marc here's got a pistol pointed right at your head, so don't try anything funny." The distinct click of a pistol hammer being cocked told Hirsch Lionel wasn't bluffing. "You feel me?" Lionel asked. Hirsch offered a deliberate nod in response.

Without a word of warning, they shoved him into a ditch. He landed facedown against the slimy muck at its base. Moisture oozed through the hood, filling Hirsch's nostrils with the stench of decay.

"Here's your pocketknife back, asshole. Looks like you'll need it," Lionel said and laughed. The object clattered against the rocks lining the ditch before sliding to rest against Hirsch's side.

A deafening roar assaulted Hirsch's ears as Marcus unleashed five rounds of ammunition in Hirsch's direction. The slugs battered the embankment above him and a mélange of dirt, grass, and pebbles rained over Hirsch. Marcus let loose a howl that echoed through the night air. With ears ringing, Hirsch listened as the brothers reentered the truck. The engine revved up, and he paid attention when the truck made a U-turn and sped away back the way they came. At least he had an idea of how to find his vehicle.

Paralyzed with fear, Hirsch waited a solid minute after the din of Shaw's truck faded in the distance. The discomfort of laying in the ditch aspirating swamp water grew to be too much to handle. With fingers numb from cold, he recovered his Swiss Army knife and managed to pry open the blade. It took several minutes, but he sawed through his bounds, liberating his wrists and ankles. Hirsch struggled to his knees and ripped the hood away from his head. The pitch-black night revealed few clues about his whereabouts. He crawled out of the ditch and sat on the side of the road with his head clasped between his hands. The throbbing and ringing inside his brain died down enough to gather his thoughts.

Hirsch's jacket offered scant protection against the chill of the night. The cold set his teeth chattering, exacerbating his already menacing headache. The clinging damp from the ditch threatened to rob him of his remaining body heat. Hirsch steadied himself with one hand and rose to his feet, with knees shaking and head swimming with nausea. He'd left his phone in his truck—wisely, in retrospect—and had no source of light to guide him to safety. Thus, with only a foot or two of visibility at most, Hirsch shuffled step-by-step along the deserted gravel road. Searing pain flooded through every inch of his body as the shock wore off and the full magnitude of the attack took hold.

Hirsch crept along the dark abandoned road one pace at a time. His footfalls echoed in the lonesome silence of the night. He recognized the path he trod was Garden Grade Road, an access route bisecting the heart of the peninsula and lined with foreboding swamps on either side. An icy wind blowing off the bay chilled Hirsch even further as he entered the second hour of his odyssey. At one point, he slipped on the gravel and fell to his knees. The sharp stones sent additional needles of pain coursing through his already exhausted body. Nonetheless, he rose to his feet and within an hour reached a fork in the road leading him to his vehicle.

The faint outline of his Toyota parked off the side of the road manifested itself in the thin moonlight peeking through a break in the clouds. Never had Hirsch been so glad to see his vehicle. With heaving breath, he stumbled forward through the final steps on sheer willpower. Hirsch fell against the side of his truck with a thud and wrenched the door open. Fishing his keys from his pocket, he started the engine, desperate for any heat that would soon flow from the dash.

Paralyzed with sheer exhaustion, Hirsch's head landed against the steering wheel. A trickle of tears flowed from his eyes and down his face. He'd survived kidnapping and would-be torture by a couple deranged hillbillies, but what did he have to show for it?

Only after hours of reflection would he have an honest answer for himself. By then, the events he set in motion that dreadful night on the Garden Peninsula spiraled well out of his control.

Chapter 9

Late the following morning, Hirsch lay convalescing on the couch in his Manistique home. His sister, Rachel, sat beside him on a chair, dabbing at the swollen cuts on his face with a damp washcloth. By the time he struggled home in the twilight hours of dawn and collapsed in sheer exhaustion, he had no idea who to call for help. One look in the mirror told him a long recovery awaited.

Hirsch first instinct was to reach out to Kyle, but Kyle would know the Shaw brothers did this to him. Kyle would be obligated to arrest them, which in no way would guarantee Hirsch's safety once Catherine Winslow secured their inevitable release on bail. Instead, Hirsch dialed the sister he hadn't seen since their father's funeral. To his luck, she took the day off from teaching and drove down from Marquette.

"Who did this to you, Ben?" Rachel asked, her voice laced with concern over her foolish younger brother's appearance.

"I'm not sure I'm ready to talk about it. I don't even know where to begin."

"You've been home for two months and I didn't even know it. I'm not surprised; I suppose you haven't told Mom yet either."

"I guess I was waiting until I had the place spruced up. Thought I'd surprise everyone. We talked about putting it back on the market," Hirsch said.

Rachel surveyed the living room and gazed out the front window. "Well, I noticed the yard looked much cleaner when I pulled up. It was like a haunted house before. You've clearly made yourself useful."

"The three of us should decide what we want to do with it. I don't see you or Mom ever moving back here—ouch!" Rachel had hit a tender spot on Hirsch's forehead with her washcloth.

"Sorry, Ben. Some of these cuts are deep. I'd say you should go to the hospital, but I have a feeling you'll say no. Be prepared for a few scars. As for this place, I wouldn't worry yourself over it. The money would be nice, but it's more important my little brother has a roof over his head."

Grimacing, Hirsch pulled himself into a seated position on the couch. Under the harsh light of day, he examined the collection of gashes and bruises decorating his body. He'd already called Milo and spun a story about falling from the roof of his house while replacing missing shingles. He estimated he'd be out of commission until Monday at the earliest. Milo told him not to worry and stay home as long as he needed. Since Hirsch worked by the hour, it wasn't like the company had to pay him for time missed.

Rachel regarded him with tired eyes. She had her long brown, gray-flecked hair pulled back into a ponytail and wore a loose-fitting, light-red sweater with blue jeans. Hirsch gathered she must have jumped in her truck and drove right down after talking with him on the phone. Rachel taught English literature at the university and normally took a great deal of care with her appearance.

"Are you safe, Ben, or is there something you need to tell me? This isn't normal," she said, gesturing at his injuries.

"I'm assuming I can tell you this in confidence?"

Rachel smiled. "Of course you can. Always the lawyer."

"After I lost my law license, a friend of mine from law school, Kyle—he's a prosecutor over in Escanaba—well, he put me in touch with a guy at the gas company. They had a temporary gig. My job is to go out and check the gas lines for leaks. I didn't expect much of it, but the truth is, I enjoy it. Lots of exercise and it doesn't require much thought. So, a week ago I caught wind someone might be stealing natural gas, which I didn't know could be done. I did what I thought was the right thing and reported it to my supervisor.

"Lo-and-behold, the law's been onto these guys for a while now—two local brothers. Kyle suspects they're running a whole criminal empire of sorts. Problem is, these two clowns come from a well-connected family so the police can't touch them. Trust me, they've tried. Since I work for the gas company, Kyle asked for a favor—keep my eyes open, and see what these two were up to. Looks as though I got too close instead."

"Jesus, Ben. At least tell me they can lock them up for what they did to you."

"Sis, no one can know about this. No one. Especially not Kyle or anyone connected with law enforcement. These brothers swore they'd hunt me down and murder me if I breathed a word to anyone. After this," Hirsch said, gesturing in a circle around his face, "I believe them."

"Well in that case, you need to quit right this minute. Whatever crime the police are too scared or lazy to investigate, it isn't worth losing your life. Please tell me you're done."

"Yeah, yeah, I know. I've learned my lesson. I don't know what I was doing out there pretending I'm a detective. I don't know a thing about this business."

"All right, all right. Here, put this over your eye," she said, handing him a bag of frozen peas. "So out of curiosity, you mentioned these criminals were well connected, right?"

"Yeah, why?" Hirsch lowered the frost-coated bag onto his throbbing eye socket. The shock of the chill gave way to relief as the inflamed tissue grew numb.

"Are you saying there's some sort of mafia running around the UP I didn't know about?"

Hirsch began to laugh but winced in pain. The area where Marcus kicked him in the chest felt like a red-hot dagger being jabbed into his ribs. Recovering, he replied, "Nah, no mafia I know of. More like they have a sister who married well and has half the UP politicians in her pocket."

"I see. Anyone I've heard of or is it better I don't know?"

Hirsch pondered her question. "I don't see how it matters much either way. Their sister's a woman named Catherine Winslow. She married into this well-to-do family up around your parts. I suppose you've heard of them."

"Wait. Catherine Winslow, *the* Catherine Winslow?"

"Yeah, one and the same, unfortunately."

"Ben, Catherine Winslow's only the most powerful woman in the community. She's on the university's board of trustees.

Folks even want her to run for congress, though I doubt she'd go through with it. How on earth did a person from a lowlife family like hers get mixed up with the Winslows?"

"Your guess is as good as mine. From what I've gathered, she's done well for herself but still looks out for her brothers. The youngest one was caught on camera pistol-whipping a state police officer at a traffic stop, but she managed to get the charges dropped. Hard to imagine that level of influence, isn't it?"

"I understand why you want to steer clear of the Winslows. I don't get how you got pulled into this in the first place," she said.

"Let's say I didn't want to disappoint an old friend. I was down on my luck; I owed him one. Seemed like a good way to redeem myself. Strange to think what guilt and shame will encourage you to do." Hirsch sunk back into the couch, fatigued from revisiting the past few weeks.

"What's your plan, Ben? I can stay a couple more days. Travis is out this weekend, and Ethan is at a sleepover at a friend's house. I have to be back at work by Monday." Hirsch assumed his brother-in-law, Travis, was out fishing or hunting like he did most weekends. Their few stilted interactions over the years consisted of sipping beers and chatting about the Lions or Packers. Travis liked to believe they had a friendly rivalry over the two teams. In reality, Hirsch had scant interest in football. He had little in common with his gritty, outdoorsman brother-in-law and often wondered how he and Rachel ended up together in the first place. Perhaps the time they spent apart was the secret to their success. Hirsch last saw Ethan—Rachel and Travis's twelve-year-old son—with his face buried in a portable gaming console. He barely acknowledged his uncle's existence the entire evening.

"I appreciate that, sis, I mean it. This place isn't much for accommodations, but you can have the guestroom. This couch will suit me fine."

"And then what? What comes next?" Rachel asked.

"I'm not sure what my plan is. For now, I'll go back to walking lines for the gas company and try to keep my nose clean this time around. After that, who knows. It's a seasonal job so I'm only on through August at the latest. I may end up slinging burgers at Clyde's. I'm not qualified to do much else of any worth and value."

"How about getting your law license back? Could they reconsider their decision?"

"Rachel, I think I have a snowball's chance in hell of ever practicing law again. Once they throw you out, well, I can count on one hand the number of times they've reinstated an attorney."

"Well—maybe you could be one of them."

Ben threw up his free hand. "Honesty, I don't know if I even want to. My life was an absolute mess. I worked like crazy, and what do I have to show for it? I'd likely find my way back into trouble. It's time to try a new career. If nothing else, I could go back to school and learn a useful trade."

"You're always welcome in my English lit class, brother," Rachel responded with a smile. "Reading a little Hardy could do you wonders."

"I was thinking more along the lines of welding, but I'll bear that in mind." Hirsch doubted *Tess of the d'Urbervilles* could cure his maladies.

TRUE TO HER WORD, RACHEL stayed with her brother through the weekend. After a fitful bout of sleep Friday night, he woke in sheer agony but took heart he was hitting bottom in terms of pain. At least he could stagger under his own power to the bathroom. He slept on the couch to avoid navigating the stairs. Rachel rounded up a secondhand television, and they installed it in the living room. While Hirsch lacked cable or even basic internet service, an antenna isolated a pair of broadcast signals. They spent Saturday evening watching the Tigers battle the Indians. The last time Hirsch caught a baseball game was the evening of his reconnaissance at Lily's—the night he encountered Marcus Shaw. Even that evening was a fond memory as he recalled flirting with the pretty server, Lauren. The reflection of his battered mug in the mirror Saturday morning told Hirsch it would be weeks before he looked well enough to show his face at Lily's, or anywhere else for that matter. He shuddered to think what Marcus might do if he caught Hirsch prowling around his watering hole again.

Rachel announced she had to leave Sunday afternoon to return to her life in Marquette. She delighted him by spending most of Sunday morning cooking. Although Hirsch could muddle his way through a casserole or grill a steak, it was plain as day Rachel inherited their mother's culinary skills. The result left his refrigerator stocked full of spaghetti, chicken noodle soup, chili, and other delicacies that would nourish him for several days to come. That afternoon, Hirsch hobbled out of his house to see her off. He hadn't set foot outside since staggering home from the Shaw's early Friday morning. Rachel's Dodge Ram pickup sat parked behind his Toyota. He shielded his eyes against the bright morning sun piercing the fragile cortex of his wounded brain.

"Drive safe, sis," he said as he hugged her goodbye.

"Why don't you come up and stay with us now that you're living here again. Ethan would love to see you. Travis could use a hunting or fishing partner too."

The thought of spending part of the day wandering through the woods or captive in a boat with his brother-in-law filled Hirsch with incipient boredom. Nonetheless, he responded, "I'll do that. I don't know the last time I visited Marquette. I'd love to see everyone again."

"Sounds good. Stay out of trouble, you hear me? Or I'll have to go after these creeps myself." Rachel laid a hand along Hirsch's cheek. He nodded, hoping he could keep the promise.

Rachel jumped into her truck and fired up the engine. She did a U-turn on Michigan Avenue and headed up Steuben on her way out of town. Her journey home would take her through the heart of the Hiawatha Forest before emerging to face the turbulent waters of Lake Superior at Munising. As her taillights faded into the distance, Hirsch caught Cromley's penetrating stare out of the corner of his eye. No doubt the wheels were turning in the old journalist's mind as he assessed Hirsch's injuries. Not feeling in the least like discussing it, Hirsch did the minimum by raising two fingers in greeting before retreating up the front porch steps and into the solitude of his own home. Cromley would have to wait another day for a good glimpse at Hirsch.

HIRSCH COULD NO LONGER DELAY the inevitable. He picked up the phone and dialed his benefactor. Kyle answered after a couple of rings with a hearty greeting for his longtime friend.

"So, did you have any luck checking out Lionel's place?" Kyle asked after they exchanged pleasantries.

"I did. I went by the place twice. The first was to check the line for any actual leaks. I snuck back later that night for a closer look."

"And? ..." The cloying eagerness in Kyle's voice incensed Hirsch.

"Nothing. Absolutely nothing at all," Hirsch lied. "They're either squeaky clean or they've done a one hell of a job covering their tracks."

"How close did you get? Maybe there's a shed you might have missed on the land." Kyle's desperation to nail these two bordered on obsessive.

"Dude, trust me. There was nothing. I spent close to an hour there in the middle of the night. I even snuck up to the barn and took a good look inside. Nothing but a bunch of old farm equipment and junk that didn't look as though it'd been touched in years. Unless they stole a broke-down tractor, we're out of luck. Sorry to disappoint you."

"Well, that *is* disappointing. Not with you, of course," Kyle rushed to add. "I thought we'd find hard evidence this time."

"They may well be up to no good—just not there. Like I told you earlier, Marcus is cooking meth. Where? Hell if I know. It may take old-fashioned police work to go any further with this."

"Yeah, I suppose so. I still have to thank you, Ben. You took a colossal risk on this and did everything we asked. It's not your fault you didn't find anything." Kyle's words notwithstanding, his disappointment stung.

"They'll screw up again, just give them time."

"At any rate, we need to have you over for dinner. Maybe sometime soon." Kyle's invitation came with less enthusiasm than in previous calls.

"Sure thing, buddy. I'll be out of town for a little while but I'd love to visit after I get back."

"Is that right? Where you off to?" Kyle asked.

"I figured it's time to visit my family now that I'm home. I can rig it with the gas company to check those areas. I'll be gone a week or two at most."

"All right, Ben. Be sure and give me a holler when you're back in town, okay?"

"Will do," Hirsch said and hung up.

Hirsch had no intention of visiting his family. Hell, he didn't even plan to leave town if he could help it. But he was finished playing Kyle's personal PI. What he wanted more than anything else was a few days to himself to escape this latest round of madness. In a corner of his mind, though, the Shaw brothers' actions rankled. This was the UP after all, not Detroit or Lansing. That two reprobates could steal, con, and terrorize his home with impunity appalled Hirsch. He couldn't imagine his father's generation putting up with this. But Murray was gone and most of his kind were too. Who the hell would take their place? he wondered. Someone with more fortitude than Hirsch, he knew that much.

OVER THE NEXT SEVERAL DAYS, Hirsch rarely left the house. While the paucity of his paycheck stung, recovering from his injuries seemed the better way. Hirsch filled his time with reading and performing minor home repairs as light-duty exercise. Rachel's secondhand television proved to be a bigger distraction than Hirsch anticipated. Despite only receiving the two channels, Hirsch tuned into the local news and daily programming all too often. Days later, he caught himself sprawled on the couch with an empty bowl of chili balanced on his stomach while an insipid afternoon talk show blared from the TV. Overwhelmed with self-loathing, he stood up, snapped off the TV, and stretched in preparation for his first walk in several days. He slipped into a light jacket, and the energy to confront the world surged through him for the first time since the beating. It was Thursday afternoon.

Hirsch walked out his front door with no direction in mind and headed down the crumbling walkway to the street. The late-April day welcomed him with overcast skies but warming weather. For once, Cromley was absent from his front porch and couldn't waylay Hirsch into an interrogation. He headed north on Steuben. Along the way, he passed older homes occupied by an ever-aging population. Hirsch worried his hometown would sink into a downward spiral of dotage and exodus without new jobs to replace those lost by the mill and other industries. Hirsch's face still bore the stigmata of healing cuts and bruises. These drew the concerned attention of several onlookers as he passed by them. He acknowledged each person with a half-raised wave of the hand but otherwise kept to himself and es-chewed eye contact.

Steuben's grade rose in elevation as Hirsch proceeded north. Upon cresting the hill, he reached the red-brick walls and wrought-iron gates of Lakeview Cemetery. He last set foot in the cemetery when his father passed away, and he flushed with shame at his dereliction of filial duty. Hirsch walked through the gates and bore a left at the first driveway, heading toward the cemetery's newer section. His father lay buried next to the graves of Murray's parents, Mordecai and Rosa Hirsch—Canadian Jewish immigrants who came to Manistique in the 1930s and established a delicatessen on Cedar Street. Though it closed long before Hirsch's birth, several older residents he encountered had fond memories of Hirsch's Deli.

He came to a stop before his father's stone. The marker lay flush with the ground and read "Murray Abraham Hirsch" with the dates 1941–2016 and the corresponding Hebrew years 5701–5776 chiseled beneath his name. While never particularly devout, Murray made this token nod to his heritage. Hirsch had to think the three individuals buried before him were amongst the few Jews in town, let alone in the cemetery.

Murray Hirsch was decisive and blunt in his assessment. Though he could be off-putting at first, crews working under him came to appreciate his gruff exactitude. Although it bothered him as a child, Hirsch likewise grew to admire his father's unflinching integrity. What would Murray do in his son's shoes? His wary father would never agree to the scheme Kyle Severson concocted. That said, he likewise wouldn't tolerate the abuse by two miscreants like Marcus and Lionel Shaw. Murray had little patience for self-indulgent ne'er-do-wells. He more than once put a cocky young mill worker in his place.

Hirsch gave himself over to another couple minutes of respectful silence. He stepped back to the gravel driveway and gathered three small pebbles. Per custom, he distributed one apiece atop his three ancestors' headstones. Another stone rested on each. Had Rachel visited without telling him? Ceremony complete, Hirsch left the graveyard. He headed downtown, passing the old hospital and the combined middle and high school he and his sister attended years before. He loathed school and never returned to visit after graduation.

Reaching the main business drag along Cedar Street, Hirsch walked past the small storefronts and businesses. Several stood abandoned with dusty For Sale signs plastered in the windows, but it heartened him to find a handful of restaurants and small shops doing strong business. Halfway down the street, the dull ache gnawing in his left leg since he left the cemetery grew more distracting. It was time to take a break. Cozy dive bars populated Cedar and welcomed him with promises of cheap drinks and hearty pub food. After taking a beating and enduring a couple alcohol-free weeks, he figured he'd earned a beer or two. Moderation, Hirsch told himself. Avoid the binge and you'll be fine.

He ducked into a tavern favored by his father's mill workers back in the day. Only a handful of regulars occupied the lounge at this early hour, none of whom looked familiar. The honey-hued wood paneling of the walls and yellowing acoustic tiles of the drop ceiling welcomed him. Hirsch commandeered a stool at the end of the bar nearest the door. An unsmiling bartender clad in a muscle shirt approached.

"What'll it be?" he asked.

"Miller Lite, please. And a menu if you have one." Without response, the bartender grabbed a single-sided menu from beneath the bar and slid it in front of Hirsch. He snatched a clean glass and headed for the tap. Less than a minute later, the bartender placed the full glass before Hirsch.

"Three dollars. You want anything to eat?"

The menu featured limited options, but seeing a cheeseburger as the safest bet, Hirsch ordered one with a side of fries. Hirsch brought the chilled glass to his lips, savoring his first sip of beer in weeks. Within minutes, he drained half of the glass and already felt better, physically and mentally.

Ten minutes later, the bartender returned with the burger and fries in a red plastic basket. He set it down in from of Hirsch and paused.

"Jesus man, what the hell happened to your face?" he asked.

Hirsch laughed. "You should see the other guy." He'd always wanted to use that line but never had the opportunity until now.

"Like I haven't heard that one before," the bartender responded, shaking his head as he walked away. He slapped a washcloth down on the other end of the bar and said, "Serves me right for asking I guess."

"Ask me no secrets, I'll tell you no lies." Hirsch was on a roll with hackneyed phrases.

"They don't pay me enough to listen to this shit." To the bartender, Hirsch was yet another day-drunk screwball wasting his time.

The burger wasn't bad, and it cut through the swelling hunger generated by the long walk. Halfway through, he raised his fingers to grab the bartender's attention and asked for another beer. The second one tasted better than the first and the confidence that had all but evaporated in the past two months trickled through his brain. The more he drank, the more anger and boldness replaced his fear and self-doubt. Thoughts broke through like weeds in the cracked pavement.

Who the hell were the Shaw brothers to run around the County unfettered, beating people up and acting like they owned the place? What gave them the right to freeload off the already impoverished, hardworking people up here? And who the fuck does Marcus Shaw think he is peddling out homemade meth to anyone who wants it? Knowing him, it's shitty product, anyway. Really, who gives a damn about propane or gas?

The answer was obvious—they needed to go after the drugs.

Fuck this, if nobody else will do a damn thing about these assholes, then by God I will, Hirsch swore. When he sat in his truck after confronting Lionel Shaw for the first time, Hirsch realized the only way to save himself was by saving the community. He didn't know how to go about it the right way and ended up with a royal ass whooping. Hirsch raised the glass to his lips and emptied the remaining contents down his throat. Full of liquid courage, he stood—the barstool screeching behind him as it pushed away—and reached into his pocket to extract a twenty-dollar bill. He slapped it on the bar, told the bartender to keep the change, and slammed the tavern door open with one hand, emerging into the bright light of day. As a man with a mission, Hirsch looked out upon the world—his world—with a new sense of purpose.

Hirsch yanked his phone out of his pocket and hunted through his contacts for the one person he felt he could trust with his scheme.

"Hiya Ben. It's been a while, eh?" the hearty voice answered.

"Hey Edgar. Wanna go fishing?"

Chapter 10

"You sure you want to go through with this, Ben?" Edgar Trehearne asked as they launched Edgar's seventeen-foot Boston Whaler Montauk boat at the Fairport harbor. "We could load her back up and high tail it home if you're not feeling up to it."

"I've made my peace with our decision. I'm not turning back now." Hirsch cranked the winch handle on the boat trailer, inching the fiberglass-hulled craft into the water. Edgar sat in the cab of his truck with the window rolled down, monitoring Hirsch in the rear-view mirror. "Are *you* having second thoughts?" Hirsch called out over the rumble of the idling truck.

"Nah, I said I'd help, and I'm a man of my word. Let's try not to get us both killed if we can help it."

"Easier said than done given who we're dealing with," Hirsch muttered.

The previous day, Hirsch had joined his newfound mentor in the kitchen of Edgar's ramshackle Escanaba home. Edgar lived alone since his wife, Margaret, had passed away two years earlier. Their three children all moved out of town years earlier, leaving Edgar as the sole remaining member of his family. It was little wonder he clung to the cadre of friends left in the only community he ever called home. It also explained his outreach to newcomers like Hirsch. They had gone fly fishing for brook trout on the Whitefish River twice at Edgar's invitation after Hirsch started with the gas company. Hirsch swallowed his pride and even joined the coffee crew on multiple occasions. Edgar proved to be a font of wisdom and regional knowledge, and Hirsch grew to trust the old man's candor and guidance.

Edgar greeted him at the door wearing a raggedy, undersized T-shirt and a pair of worn-out jeans. His unkempt hair sprung forth in awkward gray tufts. Edgar made a pot of coffee while Hirsch sat at a square, enamel-surfaced table dusted with crumbs from Edgar's breakfast. Edgar divided the brew between two ceramic mugs. and carried them to the table, setting one down in front of Hirsch before taking a seat.

"So, Ben, what'd you want to talk with me about? Something tells me this is more than fishing. You having trouble at the gas company, eh? Don't tell me Milo's busting your balls now."

"Work's fine," Hirsch said. "You're right though—I am in a bit of a fix." Hirsch paused. "Look, I know we haven't known each other long, but can I trust you with something serious?"

"Yeah, you can. I know I clown around a lot, but if you need my help, I'm all ears."

"Okay, thank you. Unfortunately, it's the Shaw brothers again."

Edgar groaned. "Didn't I warn you to stay the hell away from those boys? I told you they're no good. Ten bucks says they have something to do with your face too." Edgar hadn't mentioned Hirsch's wounds until then.

Hirsch sighed and looked down before responding, "I'm in

too deep to stop, Ed. I owe you an explanation." Over the next half-hour, Hirsch relayed the story of his involvement with the Shaw brothers, starting from the time he discovered the tapped gas line weeks earlier and Kyle's entreaty to snoop on the brothers. His story concluded with Lionel and Marcus dumping his battered body out on Garden Grade Road the prior week. His confession delivered, Hirsch awaited Edgar's judgment.

"Jesus, I can't believe Kyle Severson of all people would rope you into a mess like this. I know the old judge didn't think much of the Shaw family, but he'd never stoop to dragging his friends into a cockamamie scheme. I guess I owe you an apology too for mixing you up in this whole gas business in the first place."

"You have nothing to apologize for," Hirsch said. "I owe you one for reaching out to me. The job's the best thing that's happened to me in a while. If work was all I had to do, we *would* be going fishing. Who on earth could have known I'd get the piss beaten out of me?"

"All right, so what now? They may well kill you for meddling with them again. Maybe you best forget about all this. I hate to say it, but they're not worth dying over."

Hirsch pointed at the healing cuts and bruises on his face. "You see this? Nothing justifies this. The first day or two after the beating, I considered quitting and heading downstate. Sooner or later, I could find a decent-paying job in Lansing if I wanted one. Thing is, the more I thought about what Lionel and Marcus are doing to our home, the more it pissed me off. Sure, they beat the hell out of me, but they've been terrorizing folks around here in one form or another for years. When's it going to stop, Ed? What's it going to take to kick these assholes to the curb? I guess what I'm saying is this—If I don't try, I doubt if anyone else will."

Edgar blew through his lips in exasperation but nodded. Finally, he said, "All right, so whaddaya have in mind, anyway?"

"Okay, here's the deal," Hirsch said, setting down his coffee mug and looking straight at Edgar. "Remember I told you Marcus offered to sell me meth outside of Lily's Tavern?" Edgar nodded. "Well, when they had me down in Lionel's basement, I got a good look at the surroundings and didn't see any makings of a meth lab. Granted, I only know what I've seen on TV, but the place sure looked clean. Same goes for the barn. As far as I know, Marcus is living there with his brother. How long, I couldn't say. Thing is, when I reviewed the court records, I found Marcus owned land out on Big Summer Island. You know where that is, right?"

"Sure do. We took the girls camping there a couple times and fished the waters plenty."

"I thought you might know the place—that's one reason I called. It's a longshot, but I did some research and the land's still in Marcus's name. From the satellite images, there's a cabin or other structure on the property. If Marcus isn't bullshitting us and he's cooking meth, I'd put money on him doing it at his place on Summer Island."

"What are you suggesting we do about it?" Edgar asked.

"Here's my idea—if we could get close enough and take pictures or video of a meth operation, that's solid evidence we can take to the police or the PA's office. I know his sister has considerable political pull, but they'd be hard pressed to ignore a full-blown cookhouse. Getting Marcus behind bars would be a good start. Chances are he won't be home, and we'll get a good look at the property."

"And if he is? I can't imagine Marcus Shaw would let a couple fellas wander around shooting pictures," Edgar said. "Especially since he's warned you already and we've had our differences."

"If it looks bad, we'll abort the mission and go on home. Seriously, Ed, if you want nothing to do with this, I'll leave right now and never mention it again. I can rent a boat and do it myself. I won't guilt trip you like Kyle did with me." Hirsch pushed his chair back in preparation to leave. What kind of mamzer was he to even think of involving Edgar in his scheme?

"No, no, sit and stay a minute," Edgar said, motioning for Hirsch to stay seated. "I want to see those boys get their comeuppance as much you do. It's just who I am to think of all that could go wrong, I guess. Happens when you have kids. I never told you this but my nephew, Stephen, OD'd on meth and died last year. Smart kid, a hard worker, but he fell into it and couldn't find his way back out. I don't have a clue if Marcus sold it to him or not, but I guess it don't matter much." Edgar paused. "I might be a seventy-three-year-old man, but if I can help you, I will. If nothing else, I have a boat we can use," he said, pointing to the seventeen-foot vessel parked outside on a trailer in his yard. A sun-bleached blue tarp masked the windshield and control deck. "She's not much to look at anymore, but she'll do."

"I think she'll work fine," Hirsch said. "When was the last time you had her out on the water?"

"Oh, last summer, I suppose. I don't get out there much these days. Ever since Maggie passed, I've stuck to fishing lakes and streams like we did. Not as much fun to go out on the lake by your lonesome. It'll be good to be back out there."

"All right. I have to go back to work Monday. Milo gave me the past week off to recover. I shouldn't press my luck though. You free tomorrow afternoon to give this a shot?"

"Shit, Ben, all I've got is time. Let's do it."

THE FOLLOWING AFTERNOON, HIRSCH AND Edgar stood at the southern tip of the Garden Peninsula preparing to dive headfirst into the secret dealings of Marcus Shaw. They met up earlier in the day at Edgar's home in Escanaba. Edgar had done his part to prepare for the journey. Hirsch found the trailer already hitched to Edgar's beat-up GMC Sierra truck and ready for departure. Edgar made this look like the real deal by stocking the Boston Whaler with fishing tackle and equipment. A chill hung over the late April day. Hirsch bundled up against the cold and eyed the ominous gray sky as they journeyed down the highway. When they stopped at a gas station to top off the tank, the attendant noticed their boat.

"It'll be a choppy one out there today," the attendant said as he handed Hirsch his change. "A front's moving in out of the southwest. Should have the lake to yourselves."

That news suited Hirsch—the fewer witnesses on the water the better.

Drizzle peppered the peninsula, and the wind blowing off the bay confirmed miserable conditions awaited them out on the lake. The temperature plunged into the low forties as they traveled down Highway 483 toward Fairport. Chilled even with the heater of Edgar's truck blowing on him, Hirsch tightened his heavy jacket. The lump pressing into his side reminded him this was no ordinary excursion. Before he left for Edgar's, Hirsch shoved his father's nickel-plated .38 Special into the right-hand pocket of his jacket. He decided to take it after the Shaw brothers made it clear he wouldn't get a second chance. Hirsch never cared for guns in particular. Though he grew up around firearms, and Murray saw to it both he and Rachel learned how to load and safely operate one, he never showed much interest in them as an adult. He only came to own one after his father passed away and his mother insisted Hirsch take Murray's pistol. She worried about his safety living downstate. Hirsch admittedly felt a fraction safer knowing the cold steel pressed into his side could be the difference between stopping Marcus Shaw in his tracks or meeting death at his hands.

At the Fairport boat launch, the Montauk slid into the water and Hirsch ceased cranking the winch as it became buoyant. He grabbed ahold of a nylon painter affixed to the bow and gave Edgar the thumbs up signal. Edgar inched the truck forward until the trailer cleared the water. Hirsch minded the ship while Edgar parked a hundred feet away—the only vehicle in the normally active parking lot—and ambled back to where Hirsch stood. Both wore their swampers, and Hirsch allowed Edgar to climb in first before following him into the boat. Edgar shoved them away from shore using a weathered oar. With the skiff bobbing in the shallow water, he leaned over the side and paddled them around to face open water.

"Fire her up!" Edgar called out. Hirsch manned the controls and cranked the ignition. After several tries, the long-dormant motor turned over, coughed, and rumbled to life. Angling the ship southeast, Hirsch surveyed the water ahead. While low clouds obscured the horizon and a persistent drizzle limited visibility, the flat, tree-lined shoal of Little Summer Island loomed to their right. The faintest outline of their destination—Big Summer Island—lay in the distance. They cleared the shallow waters surrounding the harbor and Hirsch eased the throttle forward. The motor rewarded him with a low growl and their speed increased. Edgar finished organizing their supplies in the aft and joined Hirsch in the passenger seat.

"You ever been out this way before, Ben?" Edgar said over the roar of the four-stroke engine and the slap of the surf against the ship's prow.

"Yeah, long time ago. My Dad and I came out fishing this way now and then. Been about twenty years, I suppose. Can't say we ever set foot on Big Summer, but we built a campfire and fried fish for lunch once on Saint Martin."

"Your old man sounds like a decent type. Real Yooper I'll bet. I wish I could've met him."

"You'd have gotten along with him. I wish we'd had more time together. I was in too big a goddamn hurry to get out of here, I guess. My Dad could be intimidating. By the time I realized what I was missing, it was too late."

"I hear you, Ben. I tried telling my kids the same thing, but it's hard. They have their own lives and have to find their own way in the world. That's how it is, you know. If your old man was like me, he didn't hold it against you."

Hirsch nodded. Edgar's words gave him comfort he wasn't a total disappointment as a child. As they neared Big Summer Island, he pulled a plastic freezer bag out of his pocket containing two photocopies. The first was a record from the clerk's office in Escanaba depicting Shaw's parcel on the island's southeast side. As the island was largely uninhabited, Hirsch didn't expect too much trouble finding Shaw's shanty. The second document was a satellite image printout. Although a dense canopy of trees ran right up to the shore, the faintest hint of a structure emerged in a clearing.

"What do you know about this place?" Hirsch asked as they approached the island's northern tip. He angled the boat southeast, tracing their way around the circumference of the atoll. A series of modest cabins lined the island's mist-shrouded north shore.

"Not a lot, truth be told. Years ago—long before my parents' time or, hell, even my grandparents' time—fishermen and loggers lived out there. They even had a townsite there along Summer Harbor," Edgar said as he pointed out an indentation in the shoreline. "I suppose life was mighty harsh. Wild country in those days. Think of it—you're stuck on an island, miles from any civilization. In the winter the storms and snows would blow so hard you couldn't see your hand held out in front of your face. The rest of the year, you never know when a forty-knot gale might blow up and leave you stranded for God only knows how long. No sir, island life may sound like a dream these days. It certainly wasn't for those pioneers. 'Course the Indians lived here for years before any white folks showed up. They excavated one or two settlements awhile back." Hirsch hadn't mentioned his heritage to Edgar yet. To his credit, Edgar eschewed the downright derogatory language often directed toward natives by white men of Edgar's generation.

"You ever spend much time on the island yourself?" Hirsch asked.

"Oh sure, plenty of times camping and such. I had a buddy who lived out in Garden and owned a sliver of land on the north side. He let us camp there. We'd spend a weekend fishing, hiking through the woods, and having a good time. See, most of the island's owned by the government, and no one gave a damn what you did out there. There sure as shit weren't any meth labs. My buddy sold out long ago and moved to Texas. Probably been thirty years or more since I last came here."

"Ever think you'd come back?"

Edgar scoffed. "Well, I sure as hell didn't expect to do it like this."

As Hirsch and Edgar rounded the northeastern edge of Summer Harbor, they came face-to-face with the great expanse of Lake Michigan and its churning gray waters. From where they sat, near a hundred miles of turbid open water separated them from the western shore of the Lower Peninsula. Only a smattering of isolated islands lay in between. The magnitude of the lake's sheer volume and the vast, oceanlike depths sent chills through Hirsch. A boat could lose power midway across and be lost for days, if not forever. Many a forlorn ship lay beneath the unrelenting waves that lapped the shore now and for all eternity.

As they traveled south along the eastern shore, the wind howled with increased vigor. Hirsch reduced power as the ride grew rough. Angry waves slapped at the skiff, sending spumes of white foam into the air. Shaw's property lay ahead. Hirsch wanted to make the most of the remaining daylight, and he steered the bow toward a level beach. Edgar nodded in approbation at the suggested landing point. Hirsch killed the engine and swapped places with Edgar. Using the remaining momentum, Edgar beached the ship. Upon hearing the sounds of stones and pebbles grinding beneath the hull, Hirsch leapt over the side, splashing into a few inches of shallow water. He ran aground and grabbed the painter attached to the bow. Edgar sprang out as well, spry for his age, and together they harnessed the boat's inertia with their combined strength to pull the ship well out of the water. Looking back at their work, Hirsch felt confident the vessel would sit unmolested while they made their way inland. A dense forest of pine and cedar began where the beach ended.

"Come look at this, Ed," Hirsch said as he brandished the maps he'd brought along. "Looks like we'll need to walk southwest through these here trees to reach the cabin. You want to wait here while I check it out?"

"Nah, I didn't come this far to babysit the boat while you do the dirty work. I told you I'm in," Edgar replied.

"All right, then. Let's do this."

Hirsch shoved the papers back in his pocket and with a nod to Edgar, they advanced into the maze of towering cedar, birch, and hemlock trees. A dense morass of vegetation and looming branches soon swallowed them. It was all too easy to get lost in such a forest and die trying to find a way out. As a teen, he'd learned his lesson to always carry a compass and a map following an ill-prepared hiking trip with a pair of friends. They were scared shitless after becoming disoriented in the Hiawatha National Forest. While they eventually found their way back to his friend's car, the trip involved several extra hours of aimless wandering and misgivings over mirage-like landmarks. Nervous laughter and a shared cigarette masked the terror each felt at their close brush with death. Here on the island, the metronomic crashing of the waves against the stony beach offered a beacon should they become turned around at any point.

It took the pair half an hour to reach what Hirsch believed to be the Shaw property. A slippery moss lining the forest floor and a multitude of branches and shrubs slowed their journey. Soon though, they reached a clearing, and the unmistakable outline of a dwelling emerged in the distance. Seeing the shack, Edgar put his hand on Hirsch's shoulder.

"Get down. What if someone's home and sees us?" Edgar said. They both crouched while assessing the landscape.

The cabin was not built to impress. Perhaps fifteen by twenty feet in size, it featured weathered gray slats and a rusty tin roof. South of the dwelling, the clearing narrowed and trailed off toward the waterfront. A half-collapsed lean-to and an outhouse rounded out the remaining structures on the property. Two windows and a door with battered red paint adorned the front of the cabin while another window looked out from the side closest to them. Tinfoil blanketed the insides of each window, sealing off the cabin from the outside world's gaze.

With their target identified, Hirsch began to document his sleuthing. He dropped to a prone position, feeling the coolness of the moss-covered ground against his body. Using the camera on his phone, he snapped a series of pictures of the cabin. The looming mature evergreens cast long shadows over the property from the fading late afternoon light in the west. Between the gathering darkness and the intensifying rain, they had little time to get a good look at the place.

Hirsch stood and glanced at Edgar as if to say this was the point of no return. They could either move forward or turn around and go home. Undaunted, they set foot out into the clearing and advanced one step at a time until they reached the side of the cabin with the single blacked-out window. Pressed against the wall, Hirsch peered around the corner and encountered a smaller backdoor. Hirsch tiptoed to it and pressed his ear to the crack between the weathered door and the jamb for half a minute, listening for the faintest rustling or movement inside. Hearing nothing, he raised a gloved hand to try the knob. The knob turned freely, and he gave it a full twist, cracking the door open an inch.

An overpowering smell of ammonia and sulfur mixed with the acrid stench of chemical smoke poured forth from the cabin. Edgar and Hirsch both gasped as their lungs caught the full spectrum of toxic odors emanating from inside. Hirsch flung the door open, flooding the dimly lit interior with the cold, gray light of afternoon. The only illumination inside came from a battery-powered lantern propped on a table. The cabin consisted of a single room, and a rapid glance inside revealed not a soul was home.

Hirsch stepped onto the threshold and into the cabin. Edgar followed, brandishing a twelve-inch Maglite that he shined across the disturbing contents. While Hirsch was no expert on drug production, he knew in an instant he was standing in an honest-to-God methamphetamine laboratory for the first time in his life.

A collection of plastic jugs—some empty, others full—cluttered the room. Three smoldering burners and a selection of plastic funnels peppered a low table to the right of the backdoor. Hirsch paused as his eyes settled on an active Bunsen burner flaring beneath a glass beaker. The bright blue flame smashing into the beaker's base gave Hirsch flashbacks to his captivity in Lionel Shaw's basement, terror-stricken as Marcus Shaw menaced him with a welding torch as an instrument of torture. A fifty-gallon propane tank stood near the front of the cabin while an assortment of hoses, trays, and empty pharmaceutical boxes and blister packs littered the floor. Shelving lined one wall, laden down with jugs of assorted chemicals with labels reading acetone, muriatic acid, and starter fluid amongst others. The fumes wafting through the cabin made Hirsch nauseous, and he yanked the neck of his sweater over his mouth and breathed through it after witnessing Edgar doing the same. Neither thought to bring a gas mask.

Edgar raised his flashlight to illuminate the upper section of one wall. Numerous pornographic images cut from glossy magazines lined the wall, all varieties of the same shot—head-on photographs of women with their legs spread and vulvas on display. Isolated out of context, each was so clinical it could have come from a gynecological textbook. The pictures were uniformly devoid of any eroticism or passion and aroused not the slightest glimmer of desire. Hirsch and Edgar exchanged a baffled glance, confronted with the specter before them amidst the chaos of the lab.

"Beats the hell out of me," Hirsch said.

The pictures did serve to remind Hirsch of their purpose in coming here. He pulled out his phone and snapped away at their surroundings. Edgar illuminated different segments of the cabin with a flashlight beam while Hirsch took several pictures. They worked in tandem to capture the circumference of the room, focusing on the ample paraphernalia littering every surface. A tray of a cloudy, fractured substance resembling peanut brittle sat next to a burner. Finished crystal meth, Hirsch concluded as he photographed it. A gnawing fear gripped him in the pit of his stomach.

"How on earth did we wander into an unattended cook-house?" Hirsch asked. The operation was unmistakably active and the longer they remained inside, the greater their risk of encountering the operator.

"Maybe we shouldn't press our luck," Edgar said. "Let's have a look over here and skedaddle."

Blinded by the elation that he had what he needed to put one or both of the Shaw brothers away for years, Hirsch followed Edgar into the front of the cabin. A narrow cot and primitive living space lay carved out amongst the ruin and malevolency strewn about the dwelling. Edgar gestured for Hirsch to inspect a pile of papers and trash next to the cot. Hirsch leaned over next to Edgar to get a closer look at the nest, picking up a spiral-bound notebook in the process. Hirsch began to read the handwritten contents, struggling to digest the musings of Shaw's deranged mind.

"What the hell do you think you're doing?" a voice behind them demanded.

Stricken with fear, Hirsch looked at Edgar. Each recognized this could be their final moments left on earth.

"I picked one hell of a time to have a smoke down at the beach. Otherwise, you'd both be dead," the voice continued. "Now raise your hands and turn around, real slow like. I got a round chambered so don't try anything funny, you hear."

Hirsch and Edgar did as instructed. Dropping his phone to the floor, Hirsch incrementally extended his hands and arms, before twisting to face Marcus Shaw. Despite the cold, Shaw wore only jeans and a ragged undershirt. He gripped a semi-automatic Glock pistol pointed in their direction. His eyes bulged with malice while his lips stretched wide across his mouth revealing twin rows of yellowing and rotting teeth.

"Well, looky what we have here," Shaw said as he recognized his trespasser. "Funny you know. Best as I can recall, my brother and I told you to stay the fuck away from us. Figured we made that clear clobbering you half to death. Guess I should've expected this from a shit-for-brains dimwit like you. I gotta say I'm surprised to find you here—I figured I'd run into you down at Lily's and have to kick your ass out back when that waitress with the nice tits wasn't looking. Tell me, boy—how'd you know I was out here?"

Hirsch swallowed hard. Finding his voice, he said, "Your divorce records said you owned this piece of land. Figured I'd take a chance on finding you here alone."

"Divorce records? Sweet Jesus, that was twenty-odd years ago, man. Leave it to that fucking bitch Sheryl to screw me over one more time. Well nice work, lawyer boy. I gotta hand it to you on this one," Shaw said with a mock nod of approval. "You're actually lucky in a way, you know that?"

"How's that?" Hirsch asked.

"If you'd come around when I was in here working, we wouldn't even be having this conversation. I'd have shot you before you had the chance to get through the door. I keep this here piece loaded for just that reason." Shaw paused for a moment to let that sink in and swiveled toward Edgar. "Now who the hell are you, old man? You related to this jackass?"

"My name's Edgar Trehearne. I'm a friend of Ben's, Marcus."

Perplexation rippled across Shaw's face, soon replaced by insight. "Trehearne? Well shit, wait a minute. I've known a Trehearne or two. You wouldn't happen to be Stacey Trehearne's father, would you?"

"Yeah, that's right," Edgar said through clenched teeth.

"Well Christ man, Stacey was the nicest piece of ass at Escanaba Senior. She was a few years behind me and all, but she sucked my cock all the same. Shoulda seen her on her knees, pop." Shaw grinned in enjoyment at tormenting the old man he held at gunpoint.

"Why you son of a bitch!" Edgar screamed as he reared back and let fly the Maglite held aloft in his right hand.

The solid-black flashlight cartwheeled end over end, missing Shaw's skull by an inch. The flashlight harmlessly flew out the open backdoor behind Shaw, landing in the waterlogged grass beyond. Thrown off balance as he dodged the projectile, Shaw jerked the trigger on the Glock, sending the slug of a .45 ACP round straight into Edgar's upper left shoulder. The shot's velocity catapulted the old man backwards. He collapsed over the cot behind him and banged his head against the front door. A deafening report filled the small cabin, and the acrid smell of gunpowder added to the menagerie of odors already plaguing the doomed space.

Hirsch took the split-second opportunity to dive between the propane tank and a table, offering him limited cover. As he fell, he thrust his hand into his pocket, grabbed ahold of the .38 Special inside, and yanked the trigger twice. Two lead slugs ripped through the front pocket of his heavy jacket as another bullet from Shaw's pistol whizzed over Hirsch's head. A quarter-second earlier and he'd be dead.

Hirsch's first slug struck Shaw's left arm, thrusting him backwards. He crashed against the shelving that supported dozens of chemical jars and canisters. Several shattered, dousing Shaw and the surrounding floor with their contents. The second slug vaporized a half-gallon glass bottle of toluene perched atop a shelf. The volatile liquid exploded into a sooty, yellow fireball that plumed several feet out into the room and scorched the ceiling. The sweet smell of the burning fluid invaded Hirsch's nostrils. Shaw unleashed a howl and crashed to the floor as the toxic cocktail of chemicals soaking his clothes burst into flames. Dancing ribbons of fire leapt forth from his writhing body. With the limited control remaining over his body, Shaw squeezed off three aimless shots. Two penetrated the roof while another shattered the window above Hirsch, shredding the tinfoil covering. The remnants of the dying daylight streamed into the room.

Hirsch lay paralyzed on the floor, confronted with the horrifying spectacle of Shaw being burned alive by his own meth supplies. Though his ears rang from the fired shots, moans from where Edgar lay against the door broke him out of his trance. Hirsch snapped his head over. Blood soaked through the shoulder of Edgar's jacket.

If I lay here any longer, all three of us could die in this godforsaken cabin, Hirsch realized.

He rolled onto his knees and crawled to where Edgar lay. Along the way, he recovered his phone from the floor. Hirsch summoned his remaining strength and heaved Edgar's body over his back with one arm. As the chemical conflagration rendered passage through the open backdoor impossible, he fumbled with the lock on the front door. He wasted precious seconds but soon had the door open. Hirsch gasped for fresh air as he launched himself forward with Edgar across his bent back. They crashed with a thud on a muddy front walk coated with a thinning layer of sharp gravel. He clawed at the ground and pulled them away from the growing flames before rolling Edgar off his back to lay supine on the damp grass and moss.

Panting with exhaustion, Hirsch craned his heck to view the cabin. He jerked his head down as one final round discharged from Shaw's Glock sailed out the door well above them. Amidst the roar of the fire, a hoarse scream of blinding pain and rage emanated from inside. Moments later, the remaining accelerants and chemicals inside the cabin combusted with an earsplitting boom, blowing out the remaining windows. An undulating ball of fire streamed forth from each, mingling in an acrid black cloud that ascended into the sky. Hirsch could no longer detect any movement through the miasma of toxic smoke and roiling flames. The conflagration's intensity suggested only minutes remained before flames consumed the whole structure.

Hirsch rolled onto his side to face Edgar. The old man lay with his mouth agape and wide eyes staring aloft. While pale and in obvious pain, he didn't appear to be in imminent danger of dying.

"Look Edgar, we're gonna get you out of here and back to the mainland, okay? You took one in the shoulder, but you're not going to die. We can't stay here any longer though," he said, glancing back at the growing inferno behind them. "We don't want to be anywhere near that shit inside as it burns. You think you can walk if I help you?"

"Marcus," Edgar replied. "Is he …?" Confusion and pain left him unable to finish his question.

"He's gone, Ed. We don't have to worry about him any-more. Now let me help you up." The old man writhed in anguish as Hirsch helped him sit up. He let Edgar catch his breath while Hirsch assessed the situation. The temperature hovered in the upper thirties, and the dwindling daylight suggested they had an hour left at best before nightfall. If they had any chance of returning to Fairport before dark, they needed to leave.

"I know it hurts like crazy but we need to high tail it out of here. Boating on a cloudy night seems like a good way to end up at the bottom of the lake."

Hirsch gingerly helped Edgar to his feet.

"Ah, Benny, this is nothing. A good dose of the shingles for a month makes a gunshot feel like a bee sting."

Hirsch wrapped Edgar's good arm over his shoulder and led them one step at a time in an arc away from the immolated cabin that continued to belch black smoke through the doors and shattered windows. A shower of sparks heralded the roof's total collapse. Amidst a swirling firestorm of methamphetamine, chemicals, and porn, Marcus Shaw met his end.

Chapter 11

BY THE DYING LIGHT OF DAY, Hirsch guided them down the narrow clearing running from Shaw's cabin to the beach. They halted near the water's edge. Shaw's derelict skiff rested on the shore.

"We're a good fifteen, twenty-minute walk to your boat, Edgar," Hirsch said. "It'll be pitch-black by then. This'll have to do." The thought of the old man bleeding to death from the exertion galvanized him with fear.

"Wait—you suggesting we hightail it home in this rust bucket?" Edgar said between gasps as he cast a wary eye over Shaw's craft.

Shaw's diminutive Starcraft was even more battered than Murray Hirsch's old Lund boat from Ben's childhood. Banged up, scratched, and dented, the skiff's only concession toward comfort were two weathered wooden benches. A jumble of fishing line, shredded food wrappers, and empty Coors Light cans littered the hull. Did this asshole take care of anything? Hirsch wondered. A rusty twenty-five-horsepower Evinrude outboard motor with faded seafoam-green paint anchored the stern. The cracked and blurry fuel gauge offered no clue whether they had enough gas to reach home.

"It's this or we bed down here for the night," Hirsch said. "Can't say I want to risk it with that wound of yours."

"Sleeping near a burning meth lab doesn't sounds too hot. Give me a hand."

Hirsch helped Edgar into the Starcraft and eased him onto the front bench. He then summoned all his strength to shove the boat out into the water until it floated clear of the shore. The crash of a wave flooded his swampers with frigid lake water. No time to worry about that, he concluded as he hopped into the rear of the boat and took a seat on the aft-bench adjacent to the motor.

"It'll be a miracle if this piece of shit gets us anywhere close to home," Hirsch said while examining the ill-maintained and weather-scarred outboard motor. "Leave it to Marcus Shaw to screw us over one more time."

As they drifted in the rain-dappled water, Hirsch adjusted the throttle control arm to the "start" position. He yanked the starter rope. The battered engine only coughed and sputtered in response. Three more attempts met the same fate. Hirsch made to pull the starter rope a fourth time.

"Jesus, Ben, give her a rest or you'll flood the engine."

Chastised, Hirsch backed off and waited the longest thirty seconds of his life. Edgar sat hunched over and panting. The wooden benches were anything but comfortable to a man in his seventies suffering from a gunshot wound. He glanced toward Shaw's cabin. Thick coils of oily black smoke billowed forth above the trees. A strong whiff would likely kill a person, considering the panoply of chemicals stashed inside.

"All right, open her wide and give it a good yank," Edgar said.

Hirsch grasped the starter rope and pulled with all his might. A cloud of exhaust burst forth as the motor roared to life.

"Let's go home!" Hirsch shouted over the din of the motor. They had no time to waste, and Hirsch opened the throttle wide and steered them out of the cove and north in the direction of Fairport harbor. At a high speed, they would cover the distance in minutes. Menacing whitecaps replaced the gentle reticulation of the waves on their voyage out. Ice-cold wind and rain lashed at Hirsch's face, and he squinted to chart their escape. What appeared to be a bank of fog loomed dead ahead.

It was only when they hit the white wall that Hirsch realized his error. In an instant, the spitting rain that haunted them the entire afternoon morphed into a mass of driving snow. In sheer whiteout conditions, a cloud of swirling, wet snowflakes enveloped them. To Hirsch's horror, Edgar vanished into the white haze. *Did we escape Shaw's meth lab only to die like this?* he wondered. The wind-whipped crystals lashed into Hirsch's eyes, and he cut the throttle to keep his wits about him. He flipped his hood up to afford a brief respite from the onslaught.

The wicked weather was unsurprising—late-season snowstorms often menaced the lakes. The fiendish lake-effect snow wreaked havoc with many a sailor's transit over the years. Countless shipwrecks littered the lakebed, and Hirsch had scant desire to join the ranks of drowned sailors. Admittedly, they'd be the first to drown while fleeing a burning meth lab. He could as easily plow the craft into the island and kill them both from sheer disorientation.

"I can't see a goddamn thing, Ed!" Hirsch shouted at the invisible figure before him.

"I've seen this before. We can't outrun it," Edgar said, resigned to their fate. "It'll be a good mile inland before it lets up."

Hirsch had no choice but to reverse course. Dripping wet, he shivered as the snow pelted them without mercy. He jerked the control arm hard-right and brought the skiff around to his best guess at a 180-degree position from their heading. Cranking the throttle open, he squeezed his eyes shut and hoped for the best. They plowed ahead, blind to the world, and placed themselves in fate's hands.

"Deliver us from this goddamn mess and I'll never try this again," Hirsch said, imploring the spirits to rescue them from this nightmare.

He strained through ice-rimmed eyes every few seconds, searching for any point of reference to guide them to safety. Instead, white upon masses of white confronted them. Hirsch felt like a pilot lost in the clouds—alone, disoriented, forsaken. After a minute that crept by like an eternity, the stinging globules of snow turned to wet splotches upon his face, and Hirsch opened his eyes.

The snowstorm lay behind them, but the looming pines of Summer Island stood straight ahead. Goddammit, I overcorrected and now I'll kill us both, Hirsch realized as he screamed. They risked plowing into the rocky shoreline at full power. Death by blunt force trauma as a substitute for drowning held slim appeal.

Summoning his dwindling strength, Hirsch forced a hard-left turn that sent him and his ailing passenger sliding in their seats and slamming into the hullside. The skiff skirted along the shore in shallow water. The crunch and pop of rocks and pebbles pinging off the hull rang out as they skated along the coastline. Hirsch guided them into deeper waters with zero room to spare.

Hirsch's first instinct was to retreat to shore and seek shelter by the smoldering husk of Shaw's cabin. Sitting in open water only risked encountering another blinding band of snow. As Edgar noted, camping alongside a burning meth lab all night might be worse than dying of exposure out on the lake. Hirsch wracked his brain for any alternatives as Edgar coughed and moaned in pain.

Then it hit him—Poverty Island.

Less than a mile south lay a miniscule atoll bisecting the channel between Summer Island and St. Martin Island. In Hirsch's youth, Murray would take him and Rachel out fishing amidst these islands. Devoid of any improvements save for an abandoned lighthouse on the southern shore, Poverty Island lived up to its name. They stopped once to picnic on the island and romped about the lighthouse grounds that, even then, had fallen into grave disrepair. Murray refused to let them explore the lighthouse keeper's residence for fear they would fall through the floor or impale a foot on a rusty nail. The passage of thirty-years' time could only have wrought further deterioration. Still, the lighthouse represented a chance—albeit remote— at finding shelter. Hirsch decided to risk it.

"Hang with me, Edgar. We're going for Poverty Island."

"The lighthouse, eh?" Edgar said, recognizing the plan at once. "Sad day when that's our best shot."

Motivated by fear the temperature would plummet even further, Hirsch drove the boat as fast as the derelict old motor could handle and steered them south. The final minutes of daylight offered the faintest illumination through the slate-gray clouds overhead. They reached the island's northernmost tip, and Hirsch eased the control arm left, gliding them along the eastern shore. They neared their salvation. The tattered remnants of light from the setting sun in the west backlit the decapitated spire of Poverty Island Lighthouse. With no remaining options, Hirsch killed the motor and grounded the boat ashore in the elongated shadow of the lighthouse tower.

"You hanging in there, Edgar?" Hirsch asked as he crawled forward to check on his friend. The howling southwest wind rendered the evening air downright glacial.

Edgar peered at him through glassy eyes. "I've been better. Feels like the morning after an all-nighter at the Elks. Good work getting us out of that fix back on the water. I've had friends caught like that—they never came back."

Hirsch recoiled in alarm at the sight of Edgar's shoulder. Thick blood had soaked through the heavy denim and trickled down his left sleeve, leaving a shiny mauve splotch against his navy jacket. If he lost much more blood, they'd have little chance of getting out alive together.

"Here's the deal, Edgar, I don't see us getting back home tonight. Weather's too damn nasty. Best we can do is bed down here in the lighthouse—what's left of it anyway, get a bandage on your arm, and hope for the best."

Edgar nodded, resigned, and looked toward the decaying lighthouse and the attached keeper's residence. It was obvious much of the roof had already collapsed and offered little in the way of shelter.

"You got a lighter on you?" Edgar asked. "I quit smoking years ago. Good chance we'll freeze to death if it gets much colder out here."

Fuck, of course he neglected to bring any survival equipment, Hirsch realized. Sure, he had a pair of Ray-Ban sunglasses in his pocket but a lighter, nah. If his father were alive, there'd be hell to pay. But wait—wasn't Marcus Shaw was a smoker?

Remembering the nest of detritus strewn about the hull of Shaw's skiff, Hirsch knelt and pawed through the agglomeration of junk. Hirsch lacked the time or desire to investigate most of the decaying filth. He struck gold though when he clawed under a pile of soiled and frayed rope in the bow. A translucent, neon-green Bic lighter floated in a film of oily water. Hirsch picked it up and shook the water off.

"Bingo." Hirsch brandished the lighter at Edgar. Pleased to find it contained a trace amount of lighter fluid, he jammed it in his pocket. "Let's get out of this damn boat and into the lighthouse before the snow hits," Hirsch said.

He wrapped Edgar's good arm around his shoulders, and they inched their way up a weathered set of stone steps toward the forlorn structure. Overgrown vegetation and scattered rocks littered their path, forcing them to go slow and search every step for a solid foothold. Hirsch illuminated their path forward using his cellphone's dwindling power. Edgar heaved and wheezed his way there but managed to cover the ground without collapsing.

The building's condition confirmed Hirsch's worst fears—the lighthouse-keeper's residence stood in absolute ruin. The wooden roof lay in tatters—collapsed and rotten in all but one corner. The "floor" was little more than a mound of decaying roof fragments and gray shingles piled over bare concrete webbed with numerous cracks. Nonetheless, the four walls endured, and peeling white paint clung to the faded red brick. The chimney likewise stood proud, and the spire of the lighthouse loomed over them, casting an ominous shadow in the cloud-shrouded ascending moonlight. The ruined building represented their only hope of survival.

"Wait here by the door, Ed. I'm going to see if I can find us a place inside to camp for the night." Hirsch eased Edgar down onto a concrete step against the wall.

He stepped into the dank structure through a busted-out doorway. The mixture of ferruginous metal and nails scattered across the floor made Hirsch grateful for the tetanus booster he'd received months earlier. Amidst all the garbage and filth layered on the collapsed floor, he found precious little of use. Cold beads of water dripped off the intact portions of the roof suspended overhead. Hirsch ducked into a corner of the building that offered a modicum of shelter from the elements. He grabbed a half-rotten board and swept the debris away from the foundation, fashioning a primitive clearing for them to rest. This is as good as it's going to get, Hirsch concluded, as he returned outside to fetch Edgar.

"It's not a pretty sight in there, but it's better than dying of exposure," Hirsch said as he helped the glassy-eyed old man to his feet. "Come in and we'll see about getting a fire going."

He led Edgar into the room and sat him against the stone wall of the century-plus-old structure. The sturdy fireplace proved to be an unexpected gift. Using his bare hands, Hirsch wasted no time in scooping out the muck coating the firebox. Tiptoeing around the room, he gathered the driest pieces of wood from the ample mess littering the floor. The wood was damp and moldy at best, but he prayed he could get a small blaze going and offer them a scintilla of warmth. He rummaged through his pockets for any tissues, receipts, or other miscellaneous paper he could find. This included his two printed maps that led him to Shaw's cabin in the first place.

"We needed to get rid of these anyway," Hirsch said, waiving the maps at Edgar before ripping them into fragments and adding them to the pile. Hirsch sat back and took the near-empty lighter into his hand. He took a deep breath. Edgar's fear-glazed eyes shone from a distance as he observed Hirsch.

"Come on baby, catch," he said as he flicked the lighter and coaxed a weak flame from its tip. He waved a gas-station receipt over the flame and watched as the flimsy slip of paper turned a golden brown and caught fire. Hirsch eased the receipt forward into the firebox, brushing it against the other paper and small bits of wood until the flames singed his fingers. Hirsch dropped the scrap amongst the tinder and waited. The shallow golden flames rippled along the other paper debris before evaporating into a wisp of smoke and soon diminishing into nothing.

"Ah, for fuck's sake," Hirsch muttered as he clawed in his pockets for another slip of paper.

"Here. Try spreading a few pieces throughout the wood," Edgar croaked. Edgar's trembling hand held forth several scraps of paper. Hirsch shuffled over and accepted the papers from him. The slim stack included Edgar's fishing license. He raised his eyebrows at Edgar who said, "Don't worry, Ben. You owe me for another one when we get home." At least Edgar retained his sense of humor.

"Put it on my tab," Hirsch replied. "Hang in there with me, okay?" Edgar nodded, though his hands and heavy eyelids fell in exhaustion.

Hirsch scampered back to the fireplace. Following Edgar's advice, he folded and inserted the scraps of paper and cards at various points betwixt the driest specimens of kindling. The lighter only had a few more seconds of life at best. He flicked it alight and hurried to ignite the sturdy fishing license held aloft in his left hand. Using the burning card, he spread the flame to the interwoven slips of paper. A pale-yellow flame took hold of each as a faint glow illuminated the room. With his work done and the dry paper spent, Hirsch sat back and hoped for the best. They would live or die depending on the outcome of this moment.

Hirsch held his breath as the drier wood smoldered. A whiff of woodsmoke wafted across his nostrils. Soon, a stronger flame rippled across the kindling and a narrow spool of smoke coiled up the chimney.

With Edgar's condition deteriorating, Hirsch couldn't afford to waste any time celebrating this minor victory. He hastened to scour the room for any remaining wood to feed the fire. He piled it forth near the hearth to let it dry, then turned his attention to where Edgar lay regarding him with silent approval.

"I need to see that wound, Ed." Edgar winced as Hirsch slipped his blood-soaked coat off his shoulders. Hirsch leaned Edgar forward and rolled his tattered T-shirt up over the pale, dry flesh to evaluate the full extent of the damage. What he wouldn't give to have Allison here. Congealed blood surrounded the yellow-and-purple-bruised entry wound positioned left of Edgar's breast. A fresh trickle seeped from the ragged hole and oozed down his chest. Hirsch shifted to check the other side. A clear exit wound on Edgar's upper back spelled relief.

"I have good news for you, friend. Looks like the bullet passed clean through. Saves us the grief of trying to pry it out with a pocketknife." Edgar grunted in response between wheezing breaths.

Recognizing the biggest risk to Edgar's survival was death by exsanguination, Hirsch stripped off his own T-shirt and cinched it tightly around Edgar's shoulder, fashioning a makeshift bandage to staunch the blood flow.

"That's the best I can do. It's not much, but it'll keep you from bleeding out." At this point, Hirsch's own survival took a back seat. If Edgar died, it'd be on his head for getting him into this mess.

"Jeez, Ben, I took the shirt off your back."

Hirsch helped Edgar lie down near the fire and draped the man's jacket over him. Edgar would need all the extra warmth he could get with the temperature set to plummet overnight. Amidst his fussing over Edgar, the freezing dampness in Hirsch's swampers screamed for attention. Each issued a loud slurp as he yanked them from his feet. He then stripped off his soaked socks, wrung cloudy fluid from each, and laid them on the hearth in hopes they would dry out by morning. Shivering from the chill of the early spring night, Hirsch slipped his own heavy jacket—complete with its two powder-singed bullet holes piercing the right pocket—over his naked flesh. He laid down alongside Edgar to begin their long journey through the frigid Michigan night. Despite the warmth emanating from the flickering fire, clouds of mist rose from their breath before dissipating in the air.

"Your old friend Charlie Crothers was right," Hirsch said.

"Eh?"

"That story you told not long after we first met. About you and Charlie stuck out in a boat. He said one case of beer wasn't enough."

"If Ol' Charlie was here, he'd be more worried about having a beer in his hands than any of this mess," Edgar said.

Hirsch laughed. "Like I said, maybe he had the right idea." Hirsch fell silent. The only sounds were the crackle of the fire, the wet plop of the sleet falling on the cratered roof, and the ragged heave and wheeze of Edgar next to him. Hours remained before the first light of day.

"When did this world start going to hell?" Edgar asked between heaving breaths, breaking the cadence of the settled sounds in the ruin.

Hirsch had no good answer. "I think it's been going that way for a long while, unfortunately. Some days it seems worse than others. Call it a slow burn if you want."

"Maybe I notice it more now that I'm old. More time on my hands to take it all in. Mind you, I've never been the type to shit on the younger folks and blames them for all our troubles. I know there's more to it than that. Hell, look at Marcus back there and the way he talks. Here's a grown fella who should be working a steady job and raising a family. Instead, he's running a meth lab in the middle of the woods so he can pass out vile poison to anyone he sees fit. A criminal record a mile-long to boot. And those pictures, Jesus, Ben! I couldn't handle it once he started talking about Stacey like that—I couldn't stand it any longer. Like I told you, I know Marcus was a bad egg and all, but good lord."

"It's like we've gone insane somewhere along the line," Hirsch said.

"Eh. The guys at the coffee shop all have their explanations. Most blame the economy going to hell, what with all the mills and the mines shutting down and business fleeing south. Others like our friend Ned stick it to the foreigners—the Arabs downstate, the Mexicans, what have you—for taking our jobs. There's always someone to blame for our problems other than ourselves. It's all a bunch of horseshit if you ask me."

"Well, what's your theory?" Hirsch asked.

"Damned if I know, Ben. Somewhere along the line, I lost touch with the world too. There's plenty of folks I oughta reach out to, but I'm too gosh darn lazy most of the time."

"Only connect, right?" Hirsch said.

"Say what?"

"Oh, just a line from one of my sister's books."

"You mind me asking what you did to get yourself in trouble downstate?" Edgar asked. "I mean, I know Kyle said you had some problems with your license, but I didn't want to be nosy."

"Nah, it's fine to ask. I should've told you about it long ago. My fuck-up is the reason you're in this mess to begin with. What happened is, I had a relationship with one of my clients."

"Wait, you mean to tell me that'll get you disbarred? I figured that sort of nonsense happened all the time," Edgar said.

"Well, maybe so, but it's a big no-no regardless. I knew that, and the truth is, I should've known better."

Hirsch took a deep breath and continued, "At first, Alice Martens was the blessing I'd had been waiting for my whole career. Me and my law partner, Greg, were schlepping along doing okay with slip and falls, fender benders and the like, but we needed a big case to make our names. Alice, her husband Todd, and their son and daughter were headed home to Lansing after visiting family in St. Joseph. Todd was driving the family minivan and their two young kids sat in the backseat. It was late at night and the roads were terrible. Todd was going slow and taking his time to get them home in one piece. Problem was, the snowplow driver in front of them wasn't doing the same. He failed to check his blind spot and merged right over into the Martenses' van. Todd didn't have time to slow down. The snowplow clipped the Martenses' front-left fender and sent them smashing through a guard rail. They rolled a good thirty feet down the embankment. Alice lived, but Todd died instantly. Their nine-year-old son, Brandon, died in an ambulance on the way to the hospital. The daughter, Olivia, survived, but she spent several months in and out of the hospital with broken bones and a lacerated liver. Turns out, the snowplow driver was drunk at the time of the accident."

"Jesus," Edgar said between wheezing breaths.

"Yeah, it was beyond tragic. And based on what she'd told me—lucrative as all hell. The liability seemed open and shut. I figured we could finagle a settlement in the range of ten million. Maybe more if the state refused to settle and went to trial. We'd clear over three-million dollars in fees.

"Later that week, Alice and Olivia came into the office. The girl was still in pretty rough shape—a couple wretched scars on her face and a cast on one arm. Alice Martens was beautiful, let me tell you. She was slim and stood around five feet two. She had this auburn hair that fell in long soft curls about her shoulders. Just lovely all things considered, and she looked at me with these deep blue eyes. Alice had a hard time talking about the crash, but I did my best to set her at ease. Long story short, she agreed to hire us to handle their case."

"You worry about having feelings for her?" Edgar asked.

"No, I didn't. I mean, my marriage was good and all. I hadn't fooled around with another woman since I met Allison. It surprised me as much as anyone."

"All right. So, what happened?"

"Over the next several months, I devoted most of his energy and working hours to the Martenses' case. Greg took on the lion's share of our other matters, which left me free to dig through the mountain of documents the state kept handing over. Pretty soon, I was meeting with Alice on a weekly basis to prep for trial. I don't think either of us realizing it, but we started flirting. The gestures were innocent enough—the way she playfully slapped my forearm when I made a joke, my palm on the small of her back while guiding her to the courtroom during a pretrial hearing, or the hugs we began to exchange months into preparation. By the time I recognized we'd gone far enough, it was already too late.

"The state eventually subpoenaed Alice to take her deposition. We needed to nail it, and I suggested she come in over the weekend when she didn't have to work. It was late, and we'd spent a couple of hours working through the questions before I realized I'd forgotten a stack of photos in my office. I brought them back to the conference room, but as I leaned over to put the pictures in front of her, I put my left hand on her shoulder without thinking. Alice glanced up at me. Then I did it—I leaned in and kissed her. We kissed like that for a while, and soon enough, she turned around in her chair to face me. I looked at her, and she gave me the faintest hint of a nod. Next thing you know, I'd lifted her up on the conference room table, and we went at it right then and there. After it was over, Alice went to the restroom. I got dressed, confused as all hell by what just happened. She was quiet after that, but we both felt pretty damn awkward. Either way, we finished our prep session and she went on home."

"I suppose that was the end of the case for you," Edgar said.

"Well, that's the thing. At first, it seemed like I'd gotten away with it, like nothing had happened. Alice continued to come to my office for meetings, and we spoke over the phone on a regular basis about the case. I put it out of my mind and plunged ahead with trial prep over the next several weeks. That all came to an end the month before the trial. I was editing a motion in my office when I caught sight of Greg escorting Alice into his office. Alice only looked at me for a split second, but it told me everything I needed to know. Greg took over the case and saw it through trial. The jury ended up awarding her fifteen million. A week after the jury verdict, the Discipline Board served me with Alice's professional-misconduct complaint. Not one client walked through my door after that day."

Hirsch fell silent for a moment.

"My point is, what you're talking about with the world going to hell and all, I feel it too," Hirsch continued. "It got so bad working down south that I hurt a great number of people who cared for me. I drank way more than I should. Still do. My wife loved me; I drove her away. I only trusted myself, and that grows to be a pretty goddamn lonely way to live. It came to be I wanted to be alone so bad, I sabotaged every relationship. Truth is, I wasn't much good to myself or anyone before long.

"You get to the point where all you can think about it every horrible thing you've said or done to another person. It makes you want to die of shame. You're literally sick with it. I hope you never know that sort of self-loathing. I got my wish in the end—

I was alone and had nothing to show for myself."

"So, how's it feel now, Ben?"

Hirsch paused to consider Edgar's question. "Better than it should. I mean, most people look at a guy who fumbled away his career and consider me a failure. I feel like I have a purpose now though. People need me. Sure, folks relied on me plenty before back when I was lawyering but, to be honest, I was only in it for the money. Bad as this all went down today, I feel like we tried to do something for our community. I worry it's all going to fall apart any minute. Fact is, I expect it to."

"What do you aim to do about it?" Edgar asked.

"Hell if I know. Make the right decisions, if I can. Fat chance. Seems I've added the title 'killer' to my list of attributes. What troubles me is it may take years for the consequences of our actions to catch up with us. I imagine I still have to pay for all the wrong I've done."

They lay in silence for several minutes as Edgar rested. "I'm sorry for what happened back there, Ben. I wish I hadn't lost my cool—you didn't need that. Maybe Marcus would still be alive."

"He'd have shot us both and left us for dead, that's what would've happened," Hirsch said. "You think a crazed meth head like Marcus Shaw was ever going to sit down and hash it over with us? Flinging your flashlight gave me a chance to take a shot and make our escape. We didn't have much choice at that point."

"Eh, that was a fine Maglite too. I at least could've hit him with the damn thing," Edgar said before launching into a coughing fit.

"Take it easy there, friend." Hirsch laid his hand on Edgar's good shoulder to calm him. "We've got all night in this icebox. You need to conserve your energy as best you can."

Edgar caught his breath with a harsh wheeze. "I will, I will. All this aside, it's been good having a fella like you back in town. I know you screwed up something mighty. Don't get me wrong, you sure as hell needed to pay for it. Doesn't make you a bad person, though. We need more like you up here. Sad to say, I doubt it'll happen the way the world's headed. At times I come to feel we're the last of our kind."

"Look, there's one more point we need to discuss before we get back to civilization," Hirsch said. "We have to get our stories straight when we make it out of this—and we will make it out, Edgar. I'm not giving up on you. Ever been questioned by the cops?"

"Nah, just speeding tickets and the like." Edgar groaned, then said, "A busted taillight once."

"Then you're in for a real treat. There's no sugarcoating what happened. Your boat's on Summer Island. Between that, the fingerprints on your Maglite, and the two slugs from the barrel of my gun, the police will put us there in no time flat. As soon as that happens, they'll be asking questions about why the hell we were out there and how a meth lab just so happened to burn down. Here's the rub—no one knows we were looking for Marcus or his place in particular. Well, I suppose this was all Kyle's idea in the first place, but he can *and will* deny he's ever had a thing to do with it. I can't prove otherwise," Hirsch said.

"I think I see where you're going with this. Marcus shot at me and you returned fire. No escaping that. I mean, I know he's burnt to a crisp and all in that mess, but I betcha they can still tell you hit him, right?" Edgar asked.

"As far as I know, you're one hundred percent correct. Here's what I think happened—we were out fishing on the lake. We had a late start to our day but so what. Thank heavens you loaded us up with that tackle. Anyway, we were trolling alongside Summer Island enjoying ourselves when the temperature cratered and that snowstorm hit. We were so afraid of being lost out there that we beached your boat on the island. We needed shelter and headed inland. We came upon a cabin, not knowing it was an active meth-lab operation. Turns out, we showed up and startled its occupant. Being an experienced outdoorsman, I had a firearm on me. We'd never seen the guy before. Once the man shot you for no apparent cause, I had no choice but to return fire. Textbook case of self-defense. The man had a ton of dangerous chemicals strewn all over the place. They blew up. Seems like a reasonable risk of business if you ask me."

"That's more or less the way it went down. I wonder, though, what'll they make of us being in the damn cabin?" Edgar asked.

Hirsch shrugged. "With all the damage, I'm not sure they can. Maybe we stepped inside before the man realized we were there. We didn't know anyone was home. Sure, it's trespassing, but we did it to survive. I doubt there's a prosecutor alive that'll charge us for that."

"I hope you're right. I wanted to spend my retirement bullshitting with the boys down at the coffee shop, not wasting away in prison. I'm too old for that nonsense."

"That won't happen; I won't let it happen. Hang in there for me and we'll get you back to bullshitting soon enough. I'll gladly join you if we make it out of this alive. I won't even tell Ned to fuck off. Truth be told, I doubt the police will be all too brokenhearted to see a meth lab go up in flames. It's Lionel and Catherine Winslow that have me worried."

"Jesus, one disaster at a time, all right?"

"Fair enough."

"One last thing," Hirsch said while extracting his phone from his pocket. "Those pictures I took won't help matters. They need to go." Hirsch went through and deleted every last photo of Shaw's cabin and its contents.

"Good call," Edgar said.

"Try to sleep, Edgar. It's a long, cold night ahead of us. Who knows what tomorrow will bring to get us back home."

After Edgar murmured in assent, Hirsch piled a final load of wood on the fire for the night. He laid down and observed the flickering flames consume the fresh wood. The full weight of fatigue from the day's activity soon overwhelmed him. He drifted off to the gentle drum of dripping rain and the hiss and pop of immolating timber.

THE CAW OF A RAVEN circling overhead roused Hirsch from a dreamless sleep. The lingering aroma of woodsmoke perfumed the air. Above him, the cool light of morning streamed through the tattered remnants of the fallen roof. Poverty Island indeed! The forlorn lighthouse measured up to the island's name.

Hirsch sat up and assessed the situation. After a night prostrate on the cold cement floor, every joint, bone, and muscle howled in protest. He could only imagine Edgar's agony. He breathed a sigh of relief—Edgar lay next to him softly snoring. Despite hollow cheeks and pale flesh, he'd survived the most tortuous night of his life. They had a chance to make it out of this living nightmare together. Hirsch twisted his neck toward the fire. The dying embers of burned-down wood smoldered with a weak glow. They were lucky it lasted this long.

Hirsch struggled to his feet. He gasped in discomfort at the sharp pinch in his lower back radiating down the sciatic nerve of both legs. How on earth had he slept on a forest floor with no padding in his youth? he wondered. Stretching relieved a scintilla of the pain, but he had little doubt the boat ride home on choppy water would be excruciating. Hirsch tiptoed his way outside the decrepit lighthouse to assess the day. Last night's storm had blown through, leaving a brisk but calm morning on the lake. The first rays of sunlight cresting the horizon to the east highlighted the remaining white paint clinging to the lighthouse tower. Hirsch marveled at what a stately landmark this lighthouse would have been in its heyday. Passing sailors and ships making their way to and from Green Bay and Escanaba would slide past it, bidding them farewell into the untamed expanses of the ancient lake.

Hirsch warmed his stiff body in the sun, extending his arms far above his head and relishing the relief it offered. Loosened up, he paced down the broken-up stone path leading to the shore. Marcus Shaw's skiff rested safely on land. The sight filled Hirsch with relief. He had little time to waste in getting Edgar much-needed medical attention. He glanced at his phone—not a goddamn bar of service.

Since they took great pains to conceal this trip from others, it could be days before anyone thought to send forth a search party. Hirsch relieved himself against the embankment, then ambled back up the trail. He walked past the lighthouse to eye the waters to the west. He had a handful of options for getting Edgar to safety. At first blush, the most attractive was retracing their steps to Summer Island, swapping out Shaw's skiff for Edgar's well-maintained Boston Whaler, and cruising to Fairport where he could drive Edgar to the Schoolcraft Memorial Hospital. Hirsch dismissed it, realizing it'd be an hour-long drive to the hospital from Fairport. The chance of having cell phone service to hail an ambulance was likewise slim. Besides, he'd waste precious minutes transferring Edgar from vessel to vessel and then into his truck. The old man could bleed to death halfway there, and it'd be Hirsch's fault.

He gazed to the northwest, and his heart sank. The twenty-plus-mile direct route to Escanaba across open water and up the Little Bay de Noc represented Edgar's strongest opportunity for survival. *Lord knows if we have enough fuel*, Hirsch mused.

Hirsch ducked into their makeshift sanctuary and knelt next to Edgar. Finding him fast asleep, Hirsch tapped him on his good shoulder and said, "Edgar," to rouse him from sleep. The old man snored away.

"Edgar!" he repeated. Edgar shuddered and awoke with a start, followed by a howl of pain as the unvarnished reality of his shoulder wound hit him like a freight train.

"What is it? Jesus, where the hell am I?" the man moaned in confusion from pain, blood loss, and the disorientation of displacement. Edgar's confusion echoed Hirsch's bewilderment when he opened his eyes that morning to the ruined landscape.

"Edgar, it's me, Ben. We're stuck in the old lighthouse on Poverty Island. We had to camp and wait out last night's storm. It's better out there, but we need to get you to a hospital. I don't want to waste any more time." With a hand to Edgar's back, Hirsch raised him to a sitting position.

Edgar winced and nodded as he returned to consciousness. His rapid breathing calmed as he recalled the full magnitude of their situation. "Thanks for taking care of me last night. It's more than anyone asked you to do."

"I got you into this situation, and I'm going to get you out. It was my idea to go after Marcus Shaw. I'm responsible for you now," Hirsch said.

"I don't want to hear another word about this being your fault!" Edgar wheezed between breathes from diminished strength. "I told you before we left that we were in this together. Besides, I'm not going to pretend I miss Marcus or feel too broke up about what happened to him. Hell, even if I die out here, at least I know my golden years weren't spent in vain."

"You're not going to die. Sure, he shot you, but it could've been worse," Hirsch said, pretending he knew a damn thing about treatment and prognosis of gunshot wounds. "Now enough about yesterday. Let's get you out of here." Hirsch helped Edgar to his feet. "Fair warning—this won't be easy. I have no phone service so I can't call anyone, and we don't have time to return to Fairport and wait for an ambulance. I'm taking you straight across to Escanaba."

"In Marcus's piece-of-shit old skiff? That'll be a sight."

"She'll have to do. We've wasted enough time already fiddling around on these damn islands."

With Edgar's good arm slung over Hirsch's shoulders, the two men staggered into the streaming daylight of a UP morning. Aided by full visibility, they had a much easier time picking their way across the overgrown island to the stone beach where Shaw's Starcraft awaited. Hirsch tipped the boat on its side, draining excess water built up during the night's storm. He went through the now-familiar routine of situating Edgar before pushing off from shore and hopping in himself. As they bobbed in the shallow water, Hirsch undid the rust-streaked gas cap on the motor. A pool of fuel sloshed around the bottom of the tank. Here's hoping we'll reach Escanaba, he thought.

Hirsch jerked the starter cord. The engine sputtered to life on the third try. He kept an eye on Edgar in front of him while weaving their way amongst the rocks bracketing Poverty Island's southern shore. Once out in the passage between the island and neighboring St. Martin Island, Hirsch angled the skiff to the northwest, headed for the Peninsula Point Lighthouse and the Little Bay de Noc beyond. Throwing himself at fate's mercy, Hirsch opened the throttle as full as it could go. With the prow tilted ever so slightly up, they plunged into the vast depths of Lake Michigan.

The miles they traveled across the open water were one jumbled blur. The terrain receded behind them as they entered a no-man's land of hypnotic undulating waves that crashed against the prow at a menacing cadence. Overcome and panting from sheer exhaustion by the time they rounded the southern tip of Stonington Peninsula, it took all of Hirsch's remaining energy to reduce the throttle and extract his phone. His heart leapt at seeing the bars of service and he dialed 911.

"Nine-one-one, what's the address of your emergency?" the female operator asked.

"This is Ben Hirsch and Edgar Trehearne. We need an ambulance to meet our boat down at Municipal Beach. We should be ashore in a minute or two," Hirsch shouted over the motor's hum and water's roar.

"I'm sorry, sir. I didn't hear your location. Did you say you're coming in on a boat?"

"That's right—a fishing skiff. Look, my buddy Edgar's seventy-some years old and hurting bad. Gunshot wound to the shoulder. We're headed for Municipal Beach. We need to get him to the hospital as quick as possible."

"He's been shot? I'll dispatch an ambulance right away. They'll meet you down at the park, sir. You'd better hope this isn't a joke," she replied.

With his final duty completed, Hirsch ended the call and slipped his phone into his pocket. He leaned back, opened the throttle once again, and pointed them toward salvation. Escanaba awaited ahead.

His senses aflame with a preternatural vigilance, Hirsch grasped it all—the piercing cold borne aloft by the western wind, the pounding of the waves against the oxidized hull of their skiff, the lash of the lake's vaporized mist burnishing his sun-scoured flesh, the undulating green smudges of the aspen trees ahead afresh with the budding of spring. The last thing Hirsch remembered before consciousness surrendered to overwhelming fatigue was how gorgeous the flashing beacons of the approaching harbor appeared silhouetted against the lake's horizon.

Deliverance.

PART III

Chapter 12

"You can't go in there, sir. Doctor Lesch said he needs rest."

"Well, when can I, ma'am? I'm his friend—I promise he'll be glad to see me. Besides, he doesn't have family in town."

"I understand that, sir. It's up to the doctor on call, though. Is this for an investigation, Mr. Severson? There's protocol we need to follow for police investigations."

"No, no, nothing of the sort. I'm here on my own. Mr. Hirsch is an old pal of mine. We've helped each other over the years. It's my turn now."

A distant conversation rumbled in Hirsch's ear as he drifted in and out of consciousness. It was as though he were on a theatre stage and the voices he picked up were actors delivering their lines. He didn't yet know what part he played in this drama—no one bothered to explain it to him. Fighting against a fatigue like none he felt before in his life, Hirsch forced his eyelids open. The grid and tiles of a drop ceiling came into focus. He shifted his pupils about the room—aseptic décor, a wall-mounted television, and an unoccupied twin bed beside his.

A hospital room—I'm in the hospital. He'd survived the ordeal out on the water. He had no idea how long he lay there unconscious. And where the hell was Edgar?

"If you'd care to wait downstairs in the lobby or leave your number, I can send word when he's well enough to see you," the female voice recited from stage right. Hirsch gingerly rotated his head to find a severe-looking nurse guarding the doorway. Kyle Severson stood behind her. He wore a tan raincoat and had one arm akimbo while leaning against the door jamb with the other.

"It's okay, let him in," Hirsch said while raising a couple fingers, one of which had a pulse oximeter clipped to it. He drew them toward him ushering his visitor inside.

"Are you sure, Mr. Hirsch?" the nurse asked. "I could have the doctor examine you first if you'd like. I imagine you're still exhausted."

"That all right. The exam can wait."

"As you wish, sir." She lowered her voice and said to Kyle, "Don't wear him out or we'll have to ask you to leave."

"You have my word," Kyle replied.

The nurse vacated the doorway and Kyle entered. The heels of his black Oxfords clicked against the linoleum floor as he approached Hirsch's bed. He pulled a chair over and sat himself down alongside the bed, between Hirsch and the window. Kyle rested his elbows on his knees and cradled his face on clenched fists. He wore a grim expression and regarded Hirsch without saying a word. Afraid of the worst, Hirsch broke the silence.

"Edgar. Is he …?"

"Edgar is alive, Ben. They rushed him into surgery this morning. He lost a great deal of blood, but he's in the ICU. It'll be touch and go, but the doctors think he'll live. Quite an ordeal for a seventy-plus-year-old man, wouldn't you say?" Kyle allowed several seconds to pass by. Hirsch recognized the tactic—he'd employed it many a time with an uncomfortable witness. "A fishing trip, eh?"

"I never meant for this to happen—you know that," Hirsch said.

"I'm quite certain you didn't intend to get Edgar shot. What I don't understand is how you could be this reckless, *Ben*. If you'll recall, all I asked was you keep tabs on the Shaw brothers and see if they were thieving property and gas. I wanted your help in building a case. What I didn't anticipate was you getting into a shootout and blowing-up a goddamn meth lab!"

Hirsch's gaze narrowed. "How—"

"Edgar mentioned that part before he went under. Half the fucking sheriff's office is over there investigating. State police too. I expect the AG will be on the line with Hal before long. What the hell were you thinking getting Edgar involved in this, anyway? Didn't I tell you not to breathe a word to anyone?"

"Look, I made a mistake, no doubt. I was trying to—" Kyle cut Hirsch off midsentence with a raised hand.

"You need to get your story straight. I'd as soon you not tell me anything that could lead me to perjure myself. I'm a county prosecutor, Ben. We don't have attorney-client privilege in our communications, you know that."

"We were out fishing," Hirsch began with grave deliberation. "We hit a freak snowstorm and landed on Summer Island looking for shelter. Edgar knew a few folks had cabins out there. We came upon one that looked inhabited, hoping we could hunker down until the storm passed. We startled the occupant, he shot Edgar, I returned fire in self-defense, we escaped. That's the whole story. Edgar will tell you the same thing."

"You'd best hope he does—assuming he makes it. Needless to say, the police will be interested in both of your stories. Nine times out of ten, no one would care all that much about a deceased meth cook with a mile-long rap sheet. You and I know full well is a different situation. I can promise Catherine Winslow will put the screws on the department to throw all our resources at hunting down the shooter. You'll undoubtedly be interviewed. I'd suggest you retain counsel, but you don't have a pot to piss in. Besides, you'd probably refuse."

Hirsch's frustrations with Kyle boiled over. "For Christ sakes, isn't this what you wanted? You've been on my case to investigate these two assholes since the day I set foot in town. Hell, I'm beginning to think you invited me up here so you'd have some gullible shill to do your dirty work. Now one of the two biggest assholes in all the UP is dead and you're pissed. What gives?"

Kyle slammed his fist into his leg. "Goddamn it, Ben! There's a right way and a wrong way to do this. Okay, was asking you to do a little snooping the most honest or ethical thing I've ever done? Maybe not. I'll give you that. You'd better believe I won't make that mistake again. I'd hoped you could come up with eyeball testimony or pictures we could use to build a real case and prosecute them. I sure as hell didn't mean you should pull this amateur cowboy shit and kill one of them. What the hell were you thinking?"

"Well maybe you should've thought about getting me involved before they tied me to a chair and beat me senseless. That's what this nonsense earned me." Kyle furrowed his brow. "Didn't know about the beating, did you? I'm guessing that's never happened to you, mister clean-cut prosecutor. If I've learned one lesson since leaving practice, it's the world doesn't operate according to the same well-defined rules that guide our work. There's a wildness out there, an ugly brutality, one you don't know shit about and I sure as hell didn't before getting sucked into this whole mess. I know you well enough, Kyle. You're one smart guy and you mean well, but you're ambitious. You wanted that prosecution. You needed to avenge your father's downfall and guarantee yourself that PA job you've wanted as long as I've known you. I did this 'cause, well—who the hell knows why. It pissed me off seeing a couple losers terrorizing our community. So chill the fuck out. We're not all that different when you get right down to it. We just go about it our own ways."

Kyle's eyes flashed with anger, and he opened his mouth to respond. His jaw quivered, but he held his tongue. Each avoided the other's gaze.

"All right. I'm not going to sit here and judge you," Kyle eventually said. "We've known each other too long to piss it all away on a spat like this. I accept you did what you had to do. Understand you have to live with the consequences. So do I. This'll get ugly, you realize? I won't throw you under the bus, but I don't know how much I can protect you. Be careful, that's all I ask."

"I'll be fine, thank you. Right now, I just need to rest," Hirsch said. Their exchange left him drained. He laid back and shut his eyes, hoping Kyle would take the hint and leave him in peace.

Kyle glanced at his watch and stood. "Look, I need to get going. Let's get together once this all blows over, how's that sound?" Kyle placed his hand on Hirsch's gowned shoulder.

"I take it this means no spaghetti dinners for a while, right?"

Kyle snorted. "Hell, I forgot all about dinner. Jess wonders why I haven't had you over."

"Well give Jess my regards, friend. Heck, I may even call her myself. After all, we're old friends too, you know."

Kyle looked askance at Hirsch as he walked to the door. He paused at the threshold. "It's funny you know. For the longest time I wondered why Jess chose me over you. I don't think it's any secret she liked you. Now I understand."

Hirsch only stared in response before Kyle waved his hand dismissing his thought. Kyle disappeared down the hallway, leaving Hirsch alone with the dawning realization of the mess he'd made.

THE HOSPITAL DISCHARGED HIRSCH LATER that afternoon. Although trembling with fatigue, he was otherwise uninjured. The hospital had no reason to continue holding him. Before walking to Edgar's house to recover his truck, he first went to check on the old man. He located the intensive-care unit and presented himself at the reception desk. The ICU nurse manning the desk looked up long enough from her computer to scrutinize the visitor.

"I'm here to see Mr. Trehearne. Is he well enough for visitors?"

"Mr. Trehearne is out of surgery and is unconscious," she said, her gaze having reverted to her monitor. "You're welcome to go see him. Room 322. Try to let him rest. He needs his sleep."

"I'll make it quick, ma'am," Hirsch said as he opened the thick glass door to the unit.

"He has another visitor already, just so you know," she called out after him. He raised his hand in acknowledgment as he shut the door behind him.

Hirsch proceeded down the ICU hallway to room 322. A temporary placard to the right of the door jamb bore Edgar's name scrawled in magic marker. He glanced inside, unsurprised to find Milo Feeney occupying one of the two available chairs. Hirsch nodded to Milo as he took the remaining seat. Edgar's pale figure lay motionless in the hospital bed. A bevy of tubes, multicolored wires, and other medical paraphernalia crisscrossed his body. A regular beep emitted from an EKG machine in the corner of the room. The arc of Edgar's vitals traced along the green LCD display screen in parabolic waves.

What the hell have I done here? Hirsch wondered.

"Word is you saved his life," Milo said without looking at Hirsch. "The doctor said if another hour or two had gone by, he'd be dead from blood loss."

"I feel like I cut it too close as is. We hit a damn snowstorm out on the lake. I couldn't bust us out. We bedded down for the night on Poverty Island."

"Good lord, where at? Don't tell me you stayed in that abandoned lighthouse," Milo said with a sideways glance at Hirsch.

"No other choice, I'm afraid. That place saved our lives. If it weren't for the fireplace in there, we'd have died of exposure."

"Well, I have to say we all owe you one, Ben." Pangs of guilt flooded through him upon hearing this. "Everyone at the gas company loves Edgar. He's like our dad. A few of the other guys plan to stop by later today."

"Has anyone told his family yet?"

"The hospital reached out to his youngest daughter. She

lives down south in Texas but caught the next flight up here. Should be here tonight. It'll be good for him to have family around. 'Course I know any of his friends would move heaven and earth to help him."

"I can understand why," Hirsch said. Both men paused their conversation and looked in solemn silence upon Edgar's prostrate figure laying before them. The sedated man breathed softly with his mouth agape. "Sorry about missing my shift today. I haven't been the most reliable employee these past couple weeks."

Milo waved a hand in dismissal. "Don't mention it, Ben. The gas lines will still be there tomorrow. This fella here," he said, gesturing at Edgar, "this is all that matters right now. You call me when you're good and ready to come back. We'll get you out on the road. Go ahead and take the rest of the week off if you need it."

"Thanks Milo. I hope I'll only miss a couple more days. The police will want to visit about this. I'd as soon get that out of the way and move on with life."

"I can't say I envy you there. Being questioned is no picnic in the park, even if you did nothing wrong."

"Trust me, you have no idea," Hirsch said, recalling the dozens, if not hundreds, of depositions and interviews he'd conducted or defended over his career. The fear and apprehension written across their faces haunted him even years later. Now it was his opportunity to feel the heat.

"Say, Milo, I need to go see about my truck. Would you mind letting me know when Edgar wakes up? I'll come back as quick as I can."

"Sure, sure, you've got it. I'll stick around for a while longer. If I hear anything, you'll be the first to know. Lord knows he'll be glad to see you."

Hirsch chortled. "I hope he feels that way."

He stood and shook Milo's hand, then exited the confines of the ICU. Hirsch navigated the hospital's labyrinthine hallways until he reached the front entrance. Stepping outside, he basked in the radiant sunshine of a beautiful spring day. What a difference a day makes, Hirsch thought, recalling the rain and blinding snow pelting them only twenty-four hours earlier. Illuminated by the sun, the orange band on his left wrist memorializing his hospital stay caught his attention. He ripped it off and tossed it in a nearby trashcan to celebrate his freedom.

The sunlight and warmth pouring down across Escanaba proved to be a blessing. It soothed Hirsch's aching muscles and joints and nourished him on his journey to Edgar's. He prayed to all things holy that he'd never spend another night in such straits again. The walk from the hospital to Edgar's home on the edge of an older neighborhood in town took fifteen minutes. Relieved to find his truck parked where he left it, Hirsch unlocked the door and climbed into the toasty cab. A wave of fatigue hit him and he leaned back into the seat with his eyes shut to savor a moment of rest. Within seconds, the call of sleep tugged at him.

Naturally, his phone rang moments later, snapping him wide awake. The caller ID displayed a restricted number. No sense in delaying this any longer, he reasoned, answering the call.

"This is Ben."

"Mr. Hirsch, this is Detective Mark Springer with the Delta County Sheriff's Office. I understand you're out of the hospital."

"That's right."

"I'd like to visit with you about what happened on Summer Island." The detective's booming voice rattled Hirsch, and he lowered the volume on his phone.

"All right. What can I help clear up for you?" Hirsch said. He couldn't see any viable path out of this.

"We could use your help in making sense of all this. It's a discussion I'd prefer to have in person. It's getting late in the day so how about coming down to the station tomorrow morning, say ten a.m. Will that work for you?"

"I can make ten work," Hirsch conceded.

"Very well, we'll see you at ten. Oh, and Mr. Hirsch?"

"Yes?"

"I understand you are, or at least were, an attorney. This is merely an interview but do you plan on having counsel present?" Detective Springer asked.

"Ah, well, no, I hadn't thought much about it to tell you the truth. Probably not." Despite his decade-plus-long career in practice, his last exposure to criminal law came back in his second year of law school. "Are you suggesting I need one?" he asked.

"Your choice, Mr. Hirsch, as you know. I'll plan on seeing you at the office down here by the harbor tomorrow morning. I'm looking forward to visiting with you and getting more clarity on this matter. It's not every day we find a burned-out meth house with a dead body inside it." The detective's casual tone confirmed Hirsch's suspicion this was no "interview."

"Well, in that case, I hope I can help."

"So do I. So do I." After another moment of uncomfortable dead air, the detective added, "Well, good day to you, Mr. Hirsch."

Sleep was out of the question. The last thing he wanted to do was sit through a high-pressure police interrogation. However, dodging an interview would only worsen matters for him and Edgar. Besides, if he didn't go voluntarily, he soon enough find himself at the station courtesy of an arrest warrant.

Hirsch drove home along Highway 2. Tourist season was closing in on the UP. Traffic had picked up significantly since he arrived a couple months earlier. Many of the cars and SUVs he passed bore out-of-state plates. Several towed boats or had kayaks and mountain bikes strapped to the roofs. Conditions out on the lake would be a much different experience from that of yesterday.

Several miles west of Manistique, a ravenous hunger overtook Hirsch. The hospital didn't bother to feed him and his last meal was lunch the day before. There was only one solution for a hunger this pressing, Hirsch concluded. He made a beeline for Clyde's Drive-In on the west side. At the counter, he ordered a Big C burger with fries, a basket of chicken tenders, and a large strawberry shake to wash it all down.

Taking his order to go, he returned home and fell at once to gorging himself on the grease-saturated meal. The burger took but a minute to eat, and he made quick work of the fries. He took his time with the chicken tenders but soon felt almost normal for the first time since yesterday. Sated, Hirsch sank back into the cushions of his couch. He took a long pull off the shake, draining the pink liquid down until it responded with the gurgling sound of reaching bottom. Only when he'd sucked out every appreciable drop did he pitch the cup amongst the other refuse. He considered flipping on the television to catch part of a baseball game, but he lacked the energy to follow the action.

With the sun setting across the lake and western shore, Hirsch felt zero motivation to do anything productive. Without bothering to discard the fast-food waste in the trash, Hirsch stretched out along the couch. He spent the rest of the evening reading a worn and foxed Penguin-edition of Saul Bellow's *Seize the Day* his sister had left behind after college. Hirsch could relate to Tommy Wilhelm's tragicomic plight and loss of everything dear to him. He could only hope he'd learned from his mistakes and could rebuild his life, long before it was too late like it was for Tommy. Hirsch finished the short novel in one sitting as darkness filled the room and shadows grew across the walls. With too much on his mind, he cast the book aside and hauled himself upstairs to bed. Though stricken with sheer exhaustion, he nonetheless had trouble falling asleep. The specter of tomorrow's interview with Detective Springer haunted his waking thoughts.

Alone in his decaying world, he knew neither quiet nor peace.

Chapter 13

"Why don't we take this from the beginning, how about that? Tell me what you know."

Hirsch sat across a plain conference room table from Delta County Sheriff's Office Detective Mark Springer. In his mid-fifties, with graying hair swept over his scalp, a prodigious mustache, and dark eyes, Springer embodied a character out of central casting for the role of police detective. He wore a white dress shirt with blue pinstripes, a solid red tie, and black suspenders. A leather shoulder holster held a small caliber revolver, likely a .32 ACP or .38 Special based on Hirsch's limited knowledge. Despite his best efforts, Hirsch's eyes darted to the weapon from time-to-time—a nervous tic he was positive the detective noticed.

Hirsch occupied an uncomfortable metal chair, and he kept his interlocked hands on the table. A passerby could mistake him for a visiting attorney in his charcoal-gray suit paired with neatly polished Oxfords and silk tie, rather than the subject of an investigatory interview. It was the first time he'd worn a suit since his disbarment. He tugged at his stiff shirt collar where the crease cut into his neck. At Detective Springer's prompting, Hirsch recounted his story. He explained how he returned to the Upper Peninsula from his home in Lansing, how Deputy Prosecutor Kyle Severson steered him into a temporary position with the gas company, and how by virtue of that job he came to know Edgar Trehearne.

"Were you acquainted him before you came to Escanaba, Mr. Hirsch?"

"Uh, no. I first met Mr. Trehearne a day or two after I got to town. From what I've gathered, he told Kyle about the job. After Kyle said I was interested, Edgar picked me up at Kyle's house and drove me to an interview down at the gas company office—out on Highway 2. I guess Edgar's friends with quite a few folks there."

"You didn't know him beforehand; I understand that now. What I'm struggling with is how the two of you came to be good enough buddies to go out fishing here after only a couple months. Did you socialize with Mr. Trehearne extensively since you met him?"

"Well, 'extensively' might be a tad generous."

"Okay, so how would you describe it?" Springer sat back in his chair and shot Hirsch a look that said, cut the goddamn lawyer horseshit. "I'm not here to put words in your mouth."

"I mean, we'd get together for coffee every couple weeks. Or at least Edgar—Mr. Trehearne, that is—would join me and the other guys downtown. We'd drink coffee and bullshit in the morning before we setting out to work. We went fly fishing together a couple times on the Whitefish. Apart from that, he knew the job as well as anyone. I'd call him up for advice when needed."

"What sort of advice?"

"Oh gosh," Hirsch began, glancing toward the ceiling with his hands raised. "Let me put it this way. Even though I was born and raised in Manistique, I've been gone twenty-plus years. Ever since I went away to college. From the get go, I could tell Mr. Trehearne knew this area like the back of his hand. I'd ask him for suggestions on which roads to take, where I should eat lunch, who to watch out for. Useful things you might say."

"Wait, what do you mean 'who to watch out for?' Could you elaborate for me?" Springer asked.

"Certainly. He'd tell me who I could trust and who I'd need to watch my back around at the gas company. I can't say it's a cutthroat business, not compared to my old line of work, but still—Edgar knew who might be good to get to know. For my career that is," Hirsch rambled. "Also, just in the general sense of who to watch out for in the community. This can be danger-ous work—I had a gun pulled on me once."

"Woah, woah, okay. Let's pause there," Detective Springer said, thrusting his palm out at Hirsch. "I'll be candid with you, Mr. Hirsch, I checked our database for your name. Doesn't sur-prise you, does it? I found nothing referencing you filing a re-port. Did you ever notify law enforcement someone had bran-dished a firearm at you?"

Bringing up that incident was a mistake. In attempting to defect from his suspicion over the Shaw brothers, he'd made a bigger mess for himself. Seeing no other option once he'd opened the door, Hirsch replied, "Ah, no, detective, I didn't report it. Not to the police anyway. Since it involved a potential safety issue for our crews, I called in and notified the boss what happened. I assumed if the gas company felt it were a problem, they'd take it to the police. I can't say if they ever did anything with it. It's a job hazard, I suppose. Folks don't like strangers coming onto their property, no matter the reason. The guy struck me as a kook. Thing is, if I'd called the police on it and you tried to interview or arrest him, lord knows what he might do the next time one of us wandered over."

"So, you decided to do nothing?"

"Best to let sleeping dogs lie, I guess."

"Is that right?" Detective Springer stared at Hirsch over a pair of horn-rimmed reading glasses he'd slipped on while Hirsch spoke.

The detective scrawled away in a looping script on a yellow legal pad placed on the table in front of him. After a half-minute pause to jot down his thoughts, Detective Springer returned his attention to Hirsch. "Let me ask you this, did you discuss Marcus Shaw—or any member of the Shaw family, for that matter— with Mr. Trehearne before Saturday night?"

Hirsch opened his mouth but Detective Springer interjected, "Actually, wait. I have another question before you answer. Did you ever meet Marcus Shaw before yesterday?"

"Well, yes, it so happens I did," Hirsch conceded.

Detective Springer set his pen down, sat back in his chair, and steepled his fingers. He squared his gaze at Hirsch. "All right. Why not tell me about that."

"Very well." He couldn't bluff his way out of disclosing he met Marcus Shaw at Lily's. There was an eyeball witness placing the two of them together—Lauren the server. "I met Marcus Shaw once at a bar, maybe three, four weeks ago."

"And what bar would that be?"

"Lily's Tavern. It's on Highway 2 about halfway between

Nahma and Manistique, if you know the area."

"I'm well familiar with Lily's," Springer growled. "Tell me though—are you a regular there? I'd never peg you as the type for that sort of establishment. You pop in there dressed like that?" Springer asked, pointing at Hirsch's suit with his pen.

"I wouldn't say I'm a regular," Hirsch replied, ignoring the detective's dig at his polished appearance. "I can count on one hand the number of times I've been there. My old man enjoyed it back in his day. I was headed home from a team meeting in Escanaba and felt like having a beer and catching part of the baseball game. Tigers fan."

"Brewers fan myself, but I won't hold it against you. How'd you go about meeting Marcus Shaw in a place you dropped in for a beer and a ballgame, as you put it?"

"That's the rub, sir—Mr. Shaw was watching the game too. We were the only two patrons at the bar—I mean, sitting at the actual bar itself. Other folks were in the building. I only drank a couple beers, well, maybe three, the whole time I was there," Hirsch said.

"I'm not a state patrolman, Mr. Hirsch. Forgive me if I don't care how many drinks you had. Now, about Mr. Shaw, you were saying—"

"Yeah, he sat a couple barstools down from me. Best as I can recall, we chitchatted about the ballgame and the chances for the Tigers' season. Verlander was on the mound that night. I bought a handful of pull tabs and tossed one Shaw's way."

"Can anyone corroborate your being there that day?" Detective Springer asked.

"Good question. I mean, there were maybe a dozen other people throughout the bar that evening. No one I recognized."

Hirsch mimicked wracking his brain before adding, "Gosh, I really couldn't say."

"You sure about that? Anyone working there that night?"

"You could check with the staff, I guess. I don't know why they'd remember me, though."

The detective scratched a note on his legal pad and said, "I'll look into that." Returning to Hirsch, he continued, "So how'd you know it was Mr. Shaw sitting with you at the bar?"

"He told me his name right before he offered me a cigarette," Hirsch said.

"You a smoker?"

"No, but if someone's offering, I'll smoke one. I burned one of his out in the parking lot."

"Getting back to Mr. Trehearne and his involvement in this whole mess, did you ever talk with him about Marcus Shaw?" Detective Springer asked.

"I did. Not long after."

"And why might that be?"

"Oh, he tried to sell me drugs. Shaw, I mean," Hirsch said, deadpan and staring straight at Detective Springer.

"Say what?" Springer peered at Hirsch again over his reading glasses.

"When we were out front of the bar having a cigarette, he pitched me on buying drugs. Asked if I liked to party. Offered me something called an 8-ball, if I remember right. I don't know a whole lot about drugs, but I think it was meth. Makes sense in retrospect."

"Let me make sure I understand this, Mr. Hirsch," Springer said, raising his voice. "A guy you just met at a dive bar who didn't know you from Adam offers to sell a complete stranger an illegal and highly dangerous drug. Is that what you're telling me?"

"That's the long and short of it, sir."

"This is the second time I've having to ask this question—did you ever tell anyone in law enforcement about Mr. Shaw's offer? Anyone at all?"

"I didn't think it would do much good," Hirsch said.

"And why's that?"

Hirsch snorted. "You know why."

"What the hell is that supposed to mean?" Springer tossed his pen on the desk. Hirsch remained silent. Detective Springer continued, "You know, Mr. Hirsch, for an officer of the court—or a former one, I should say—you seem to have a real disregard for the rule of law. Or at least the institutions. You seem to think you get to decide what is and isn't worth investigating. I feel there's more to the story than you're letting on to. This attitude will get you in real trouble someday."

Silence fell across the room as the detective let his sermon sink in. After an interminable delay, Springer cracked a smile. "Really? He tried to sell you meth? Who in God's name would be so stupid? I mean, seriously." The detective erupted in laughter.

"I had the same thought," Hirsch said. "To Shaw's credit, he *did* ask if I were a cop. I could truthfully answer him no, I wasn't. The whole encounter was odd, though, which is why I asked Edgar about him. Like I said, Edgar knows lots of folks around here."

"And what did Mr. Trehearne say about your mutual acquaintance?" the detective asked, snapping back to his sober demeanor.

"He didn't know Marcus all too well. That said, my story didn't surprise him. He told me Marcus had a reputation for a wild streak here in town. Said he had an older brother too. Warned me to stay away from Marcus for my own good."

"Did he tell you anything else about Mr. Shaw's family?"

"He said Marcus came from a wealthy family or, at least they were well connected."

"I see. That's one way of putting it," Detective Springer responded. He turned to a fresh page on his legal pad with a rustle. "Did you ever see Mr. Shaw again after that time at Lily's bar? That is, before Saturday night."

Hirsch faced a crisis of conscience at this juncture. If he told Springer about the incident at Lionel Shaw's farm, he'd spoon-feed the police a direct motive for targeting Marcus Shaw's cabin. This could place him, not to mention Edgar, in jeopardy of prosecution. On the other hand, the only living witness to his night in the basement was Lionel Shaw. Lionel wouldn't admit to clobbering a stranger solely to prove he knew Hirsch. Besides, if Hirsch ever got caught in a misstatement, what were they going to do—disbar him again? The lesser evil lay in an evasive answer.

"I may have seen him around, but I can't remember any particulars," Hirsch replied.

"Really? You can't recall whether you ever saw or talked with a guy who offered you drugs? Is that what you're telling me here, Mr. Hirsch?"

"Yeah, well, that's about it. Lots of middle-aged guys around these parts look like him. It's a small town, you know."

Detective Springer stared at Hirsch for what felt like an eternity. He clearly didn't believe Hirsch but had no way of proving his doubt. The hum emanating from the florescent lights overhead grew deafening. Having no choice, he moved on with his interrogation.

"All right, let's circle back to yesterday. What made you decide to go fishing with Mr. Trehearne?"

"Well, I'd been thinking about going ever since I came home a couple months ago. My dad took me and my sister out fishing from time-to-time on the lake. Not all too often, but enough we have fond memories. It's gotta be like eighteen or twenty years since we last went. He passed away a few years ago."

"My condolences," Detective Springer offered.

"Thank you. Like I said, I'd been thinking about it since I came back home, but I don't have a boat. Casting from the shore isn't the same. But then I remembered Edgar telling me he had himself a fishing boat. His kids are all grown up and gone so he doesn't get much chance to use it. I thought it might be fun for both of us. So I called him on, oh, Friday or Saturday, I suppose. I asked him if he wanted to go fishing. He liked the idea, and that was that."

"Why Sunday though? Didn't either of you know the weather would be terrible that day?" Springer asked.

"Well, yeah, we understood it might rain a little. We figured there'd be fewer people out on the water. Less competition, I suppose. Besides, they say the fish bite better when it's raining."

"I've heard that one too many goddamn times. I'm not sure it's true. Let's work with this for a moment. I understand you and Edgar decided to go fishing. The timing's odd, but I'll let it slide for now. Walk me through how the hell you landed on Summer Island and, more precisely, at Marcus Shaw's cabin." Detective Springer sat back in his chair with eyebrows raised, ready to hear out the critical part of Hirsch's story.

"Edgar and I set out from Fairport Sunday afternoon. We intended to troll the waters for whitefish and lake trout. I'd had some luck in years past in the shallows around Summer and St. Martin Islands—even as far south as Washington Island. We were chatting about local history and characters Edgar knew over the years when a freak snowstorm blew up off the coast of Big Summer Island. I tell you, we had near zero visibility out there. It was a stroke of luck we were already near the island when the snow hit. We didn't have any other choice. It was beach it on Summer Island or drown on the lake," Hirsch concluded.

"I understand you ended up on Summer Island," Detective Springer cut in. "We located Mr. Trehearne's Boston Whaler yesterday afternoon as part of our investigation. What I can't wrap my head around is how you two ended up a half-mile away from the boat at Mr. Shaw's front door. Think you could clear that up for me?"

"Ah, sure," Hirsch said. "See, Edgar knew Summer Island pretty well. From fishing and camping all those years. He shared its history when we were out trolling before the snow hit. He knew folks had summer cabins on the island, but he wasn't sure where. After beaching the ship, we were so hell bent on getting away from the snow we headed inland. It was damn cold and wet there on the shore. If nothing else, we figured we could shelter in the trees.

"Maybe we got turned around, I don't know. All I can tell you is, when we came upon that clearing, we were freezing our asses off and soaked through and through. It hit me we had a real risk of dying of exposure. I'd never been so glad to see a cabin in my life."

"Did you know if anyone was home?" Detective Springer asked.

"No, not at the time. We figured that might be the case since I saw a little smoke coming out of the rooftop stovepipe. We walked up and knocked on the door, but no one answered. So we tried the door and found it unlocked. Was it wrong? Maybe. I don't ordinarily go in for trespassing. It was a matter of life and death."

"Did you try to get the attention of any person who might've been inside?"

"Oh, I suppose we called out 'is there anyone home?' when we first opened the door," Hirsch said.

"What happened once you opened the door? Did you go inside?"

"We knew as soon as we opened the door that something wasn't right. This terrible smell came from the cabin, like a chemical stench, you know. Anyway, we walked in. Once I saw all the chemicals and the lab equipment, I knew we were in the wrong place. I looked at Edgar and, from his expression, I could tell we both realized we were standing smack dab in the middle of a meth lab."

"Wait a minute—how'd you know it was a meth lab?" Detective Springer asked.

"From watching TV shows and the news, I sorta knew what to look for—the blacked-out windows, the odor, all the canisters of acetone and other chemicals, the burners. Honestly, what the hell else could it be? Canning preserves? Anyway, it wasn't a place we could stay long term, which was a real shame since we were freezing cold. I guess I'd rather die from exposure than meth poisoning," Hirsch said.

"How long were you in there, anyway?"

"Only a couple of minutes at most. We looked to see if anyone was home. Mr. Trehearne had a flashlight, so we gave the place a good once-over. Figured we'd need to report it to the sheriff once we got back to civilization, you know."

Detective Springer scrutinized Hirsch. "Based on your track record, I highly doubt you'd do it. All right, what happened next?"

"Well, next we know, a man's standing behind us, telling us he has a gun and to raise our arms real slow like. We both turned, and I see it's Mr. Shaw holding a pistol on us. He'd come in through the backdoor. I don't know if he recognized me or not. Whatever the case, he didn't care why we were there. He shot Edgar right in the shoulder. I had barely enough time to return fire. Twice. I don't know if I hit him or not, but the chemicals on a shelf next to him caught fire. He did too. I'd never seen a man burned alive, and I hope to hell I never do again. After that, there's not much to tell. My chief concern was getting Edgar out of there and to safety."

"Let me get this straight—you had a gun on you, correct?" Springer asked.

"Yes, that's right, sir."

"Where was it?"

"What do you mean?" Hirsch asked.

"Where'd you keep the gun? Holstered? In a pocket?"

"I had it in my coat pocket. That's the only reason I got a clean shot off without Shaw noticing. Blew a couple holes in my coat, unfortunately," Hirsch said.

"Do you ordinarily take a gun to go fishing?"

Hirsch shrugged. "Well, sure, most of the time. I mean, my dad always kept one on him, in case we ran into wildlife or the wrong person. I suppose I was taking after him,"

"Okay," Detective Springer continued. "I want to make sure I have all the facts correct here. Let me summarize this for us. You chose to go fishing on a day with terrible weather with a guy you only knew a couple of months. You had a concealed firearm on your person. You hit a patch of rough weather, made landfall on an island, and wandered into a cabin that happened to be owned by a man you met only a couple weeks earlier. A guy who offered to sell you drugs. You shot that same lowlife during a firefight and, in the process, burned his cabin down. And you're telling me all this was a matter of pure coincidence?"

Hirsch held his hands up. "What can I say other than that I wouldn't believe it myself if it didn't happen that way. Truth is, though, the UP's a small place. You never know who you might run into out there."

Detective Springer assumed an even-toned voice. "Mr. Hirsch, I want you to listen to me carefully. I'm not a fool. I've done my homework, and I know about your background. It takes effort to get disbarred in this state, I must say. God knows far worse attorneys out there are still practicing. So, forgive me if I have trouble believing everything you've told me. I think there's more to the story than what you're letting on to. I do believe you knew Mr. Shaw before Sunday's incident, but I have a feeling it goes beyond a chance meeting in a bar. The problem is, there were only three witnesses to what went down on Summer Island—you, Mr. Trehearne, and Mr. Shaw. Now one of those three is dead. Given his body's condition, I doubt we'll get much out of him other than a bullet from your pistol."

Detective Springer raised his voice and continued, "I'll be honest with you, Mr. Hirsch. I don't buy your story. The problem is, I can't prove it—yet. Suffice it to say, you'd better damn well hope Mr. Trehearne backs you up, or it'll be your ass on the line. Marcus Shaw was no angel, believe me. I'd be lying if I didn't say he's one less meth dealer we have to put up with in this county. But we can't have folks running around on some vigilante justice kick. Don't think for a moment I won't charge you if I found out this was premeditated or that you shot first. Hell, I'll even nail you on murder by accountability if Mr. Trehearne doesn't make it. I don't know what your beef was with Mr. Shaw, but if and when I do find out, I can promise I'll have you in bracelets quicker than you know it. Are we clear?"

Looking straight at Detective Springer, Hirsch nodded. The lawyer in him reared its head. "Am I free to leave, detective?" he asked.

Detective Springer dropped his pen and smiled. "Mr. Hirsch, this was and is a voluntary interview. You're free to leave anytime. But I presume you already knew that."

Detective Springer stood. It was obvious nothing further would come of this discussion. Springer passed Hirsch a business card. "If you remember anything else that could be pertinent to our investigation, please let me know. I'm warning you one more time, Mr. Hirsch—if I learn you haven't been candid with me today, I won't hesitate to bring you back in again. Next time, it won't be a voluntary interview. Understood?"

Hirsch nodded as he accepted the card. The detective held the door open, and Hirsch left the conference room and walked down the hallway to the front entrance. Emerging into the light of midday, he gulped the fresh air with relief. He'd dodged a bullet this time. What foolishness to get involved with this mess in the first place. His first inclination was to blame Kyle. If not for him, Hirsch would be going about his business trying to rebuild his life. In the final analysis, though, there came a point when this fiasco turned personal, and Hirsch made it his mission to rid the world of Marcus Shaw.

Mission accomplished, Hirsch hoped he'd have the wisdom and restraint to keep his nose clean going forward. He had no way of knowing his troubles were far from over.

Chapter 14

Hirsch recommitted to his job over the ensuing weeks. In atonement for his extended absence, he surrendered his days to the yoke of the leak detector and the subterranean spiderweb of gas lines fanning out across the UP. Freed from the burden of running a clandestine investigation, Hirsch spent his time outdoors in the regenerative warmth of late spring. The long hours provided a much-needed distraction. Images of a flame-enshrouded Marcus Shaw haunted Hirsch's dreams. Most nights, he bolted awake sheathed in a cold sweat as Shaw's dying screams reverberated through the corners of his mind. His waking hours were hardly better—their final encounter with Shaw replayed in an unending loop. It felt as though he could will another outcome, if only he might remember it differently.

Well before eight o'clock, he was in his truck and tracing his way on forest-lined highways and narrow gravel roads deep into the UP. He took short lunch breaks and preferred to eat a homemade sandwich or a piece of fruit while perched on the open tailgate of his Toyota. He'd allow his legs to swing free over the ground while spotting cedar waxwings, pileated woodpeckers, and jack pine warblers in the forest canopy overhead. Having grown disillusioned with most human company, Hirsch embraced the vast wilderness and the cacophony of nature for companionship.

While his workdays varied in length, Hirsch often returned home by six p.m. Evenings found him cloistered in his living room and renewing his acquaintance with the dormant pleasure of following baseball. His days concluded on the couch, clawing his way through his sister's innumerable cast-off books. The lack of material distractions helped with his enlightenment. By early June, he'd polished off volumes by Tolstoy, Hemingway, Hardy, O'Connor, and Flaubert. While never a pleasure reader in school or college, Hirsch appreciated these storytellers' exploration of the human condition. They often featured ordinary protagonists thrust into extraordinary circumstances. A dogeared and tattered copy of Thomas Wolfe's *You Can't Go Home Again* resonated with his current predicament.

Edgar's recovery inched along. The hospital upgraded Edgar's condition to stable after three days in the ICU and transferred him to a less restrictive unit. Hirsch paid Edgar a visit prior to his discharge. He walked into Edgar's room to find a woman a handful of years older than himself occupying the visitor's chair with ramrod-straight posture. Edgar sat up in bed spooning yellow pudding into his mouth with his uninjured arm.

"Ben!" he hollered, wiping away a smear of pudding on his lower lip. "I want you to meet my daughter, Laurel. She flew in from Corpus Christi for a couple weeks. Laurel, this here's the man who saved my life."

Laurel Trehearne rose from the chair and offered Hirsch her

hand, palm down. Dressed in a denim romper and with mid-length chestnut hair fixed in tight curls, Laurel favored blue eye shadow and sported a pair of cat-eye glasses. With her lips set in a compressed line, her saturnine demeanor suggested she didn't hold Hirsch in the same regard as her father did.

"Pleasure to meet you, Laurel," Hirsch said, taking her hand. "Edgar's told me plenty about you."

"That's funny. Seems he never told me a thing about you—at least until he wound up in the hospital."

"Ah, well, I've only been here a couple months. Your dad's been the best pal a guy could ask for."

"Looks like Dad's been a little too helpful, as usual," she said.

"Ah, sweetie, I told you this could've happened to anyone," Edgar said from the bed.

"But did it need to happen to you?"

The sensation of an island shootout and immolation of a clandestine meth lab made for abnormal drama in the UP. Several regional papers picked up the story. While none mentioned Hirsch or Edgar by name, the mystery surrounding two fishermen stranded on an island amidst a late-spring snowstorm generated ample speculation in the public eye. Given the lacuna between the public narrative and Edgar's account, Laurel had ample grounds for distrust.

Laurel's single-word replies to Hirsch's remaining questions made for an awkward fifteen minutes, and he leapt at the opportunity to excuse himself when a doctor arrived to check Edgar's range of motion. Hirsch made himself scarce the remaining two weeks of Laurel's visit.

After the hospital discharged Edgar and Laurel returned to

Texas, Hirsch resumed visiting the old man twice a week. Edgar's recovery limited him more than he expected. Frustrated about missing his regular social commitments, he kvetched to whomever would listen. Hirsch's visits relieved him from the housebound boredom of daytime TV and physical-therapy exercises. Hirsch even endured an hour in Ned Caperton's company, replete with the latest conspiracy theories and casual bigotry. When alone, Edgar and Hirsch rehashed their interviews with Detective Springer. Hirsch breathed a sigh of relief to find the pertinent details harmonized. For the time being, the prosecution's sword of Damocles hanging over them held its place.

ON A MID-MORNING SUNDAY, HIRSCH received a call from the one person he should have reached out to long before.

"When were you going to tell me you were back in town?" the familiar voice of Hirsch's mother, Justine, asked.

"Hey Mom. I suppose Rachel told you?"

"No, she didn't. Say what you will about your sister's life choices, she can keep a secret." Despite all of Rachel's academic and career success, their mother never thought much of Rachel's husband. For reasons known only to her, it colored the perception of her only daughter.

"I called the county earlier this week about the property taxes. Imagine my surprise when I come to find out someone had restarted the utilities," Justine said. "I could only think of one person who might be squatting there. Mr. Cromley keeps an eye on the place for me. I called him. He told me you'd been living there since March. He figured I already knew. Said you weren't home too often."

"I'm sorry, Ma. I should've told you I was back home. Life's been a real mess lately, you know." What else might Cromley have shared with her? Hirsch wondered. He had little doubt Cromley's all-seeing eyes had catalogued his injuries.

Justine sighed. "I know, Ben. You don't need to explain it. I of all people would understand if you ever wanted to talk about it. You didn't need to hide from me."

"I wasn't hiding, Ma. It's just that … hell, I don't know what I'm trying to say." He had no real excuse for not calling her and she knew it.

"You're sounding like your father now. Speaking of Dad, have you been by to visit him?" Justine asked.

"Yes Ma, I visited him and his folks a few weeks ago. Their stones look good. It's peaceful out there."

"Good, Benny. I'm glad to hear that. Please go for me. I don't get out there as often as I'd like. I'd come over more if I knew my only son lived there, but oh well."

"Ma, look, I'm sorry. Spare me the guilt trip. I feel bad enough as is lately. How's the family over there in the Soo?" Hirsch asked, changing the subject.

"Oh, it's always one thing or another with this bunch. Your Aunt Margie's at my place most days. She complains about her arthritis and wonders why her kids moved away." Aunt Margie was the family hypochondriac. Well-meaning, but the victim of multiple poor life choices, Margie nonetheless endured—a survivor. "Half the time I wish I'd stayed in Manistique. But I couldn't live in that house with your dad's ghost in every corner. Besides, Margie needs me and, to tell you the truth, I need her too. She's the only sibling I have left other than Uncle Henry, you know."

"Ah, and, how *is* Uncle Henry?" His mother's younger

brother was a legendary self-promoter and social climber. Previously tribal chairman before a contentious election ended his reign, Henry Archambault leveraged his considerable influence to open the first tribal-run casino in the UP. He made decent money but threw it away time and again on "too good to fail" business schemes he concocted. Henry's relentless hucksterism fostered a tense relationship with his down-to-earth sisters.

"Uncle Henry's Uncle Henry. Hasn't changed since he was a young man and tried to wrestle control of the bingo hall. He's opening a restaurant here in the Soo, but he has his hands full with his new wife."

"What on earth does Uncle Henry know about running a restaurant?" Hirsch asked with laughter before sputtering, "Wait—Uncle Henry got married again? What is this, wife number three? What happened to Aunt Doris?"

"My word, Ben, you really have been gone too long. Aunt Doris passed away five years ago. Henry remarried last year. She's a good fifteen years younger than him and worked as a hostess in the lounge at the Ojibway. I suppose she put the whole restaurant idea in his head. Maybe you'd know this if you actually gave our family the time of day."

Confrontation with his mother's wisdom left Hirsch chastened and ashamed. "I'm sorry, Benny," she continued. "I'm not trying to make you feel bad or anything. I know you did what you had to do amongst the *wayaabishkiiwejig* in Lansing."

"Thanks, Ma. I know I screwed up plenty out there in the world. I'm trying to fix this—I just haven't figured out how yet. I promise I'll visit soon, okay? It was wrong of me to wait this long to tell you I'm back home."

"I won't hound you about visiting me. You will when the

time is right. You're always welcome here, and the family will be glad to see you again. You know how they feel when one of our own comes home."

"I do, I do," Hirsch said. "I'll try to be a better family member from now on. You brought us up to remember how important it is."

"Just be yourself. That's all I've ever wanted for you. Well, your Aunt Margie's on her way over to bend my ear about whatever latest mess her children got themselves into. I best prepare myself."

"In that case, I wish you luck, Ma. Too bad I couldn't be there to help. Love you." He hung up, ashamed at how he'd disappointed another person who cared for him.

THE ILLUMINATED SIGN FOR LILY'S Tavern beckoned Hirsch to stop. He was headed home following a long day of leak checks around Munising. The welcome respite of a cold beer proved irresistible. Besides, he needed to wash the stain of Marcus Shaw from his memory. Shaw's malevolent glare across the bar haunted him. Hell, maybe a new experience here will help, he thought as he parked his truck. Given the early hour by summertime standards, the parking lot was near empty.

Hirsch made his way inside. The derelict tavern was unchanged from his last visit. The same band of regulars held court around a table in the back of the bar. In loud voices, they debated a subject that escaped Hirsch's comprehension. At another table, a gaggle of women shrieked over a video displayed on one woman's phone. Two townies occupied barstools, their attention fixed on the ballgame playing on the overhead television screen. To Hirsch's pleasant surprise, Lauren stood behind the bar. She rested her hands on a counter behind her, looking bored but fetching. With her shoulders pulled back, her ample breasts strained against her thin rust-hued sweater. A pair of dark denim skinny jeans and tan leather boots completed her look. Dressed for an Ann Arbor or Madison wine bar, she once again looked out of place in this dive.

A pang of desire flooded through him. Lauren smiled upon seeing Hirsch approach the bar. He returned the smile as he sat, doing his best to take in each inch of her petite figure. She wore her golden-brown hair loose today. It brushed against her shoulders while a few teased strands framed her porcelain-toned face.

"I was wondering if I'd see you here again," Lauren said. "I thought our clientele might've scared you off for good."

Hirsch laughed. "It takes more than a few weirdoes to keep me away. I've known plenty. Besides, I enjoyed talking with you. I was worried you wouldn't be here."

"Slim chance of that happening," Lauren said while surveying the room. "What'll it be tonight?"

"Miller Lite's fine. Draft please."

"Coming right up," she said as she snatched a glass and filled it from the tap.

Hirsch's glances ping-ponged between the uneventful ballgame on the TV and Lauren's lithe figure as she went about her work. Her long, fragile fingers deposited the beer in front of him. Hirsch took a sip of the cold brew and pronounced his satisfaction with a slight nodding of his head.

"Ken, right?" she ventured. It reminded him that Ken was the name he gave during his bumbling attempt at investigating Marcus Shaw.

"Close. It's Ben."

"Well, I'm glad you came around again, Mr. Ben. I'm Lauren." Hirsch opened his mouth to reply, only to be interrupted when a burly lumberjack type several stools down slid his empty glass forward on the bar where it caught the lip of the rail and spun. The glass clattered to its side but avoided crashing to the floor.

"You know, Butch, you could holler for another one instead of pulling that crap," Lauren said.

"Ah sweetie, what can I say? I like to keep you on your toes," Butch slurred back at her. He wore a grease-smeared John Deere trucker hat with the bill elevated toward the air.

"Believe me, I have enough of that," she said. Hirsch watched her pour the man another beer. She held her glistening lips slightly open with the tip of her pink tongue pressed against the roof of her mouth. Her brown eyes focused on the beer as she swayed her hips back and forth to the Aerosmith song blaring from the jukebox. She delivered the beer to Butch, who flipped a few worn dollars on the bar in tribute. After taking his first sip, Butch emitted a drawn-out belch, punctuated by an enthusiastic "yeah!" in an endorsement of his performance.

"I should serve him in a goddamn sippy cup," she muttered as she passed Hirsch. Her banter suggested she'd much rather be talking to him than dealing with the ordinary scattering of drunks. He was more than happy to oblige.

"You never told me why you're working here," Hirsch said.

"And what makes you surprised I work here?" Lauren leaned in, planting her elbows down on the bar opposite him. She rested her face on her interlaced fingers inches from his face, her unblinking eyes demanding an answer.

"Well, it's just … I mean, there are …" Hirsch said, fumbling for words before blurting out, "Look, you're awfully classy to be working in a place like this." He worried he may have offended her. "Don't get me wrong, I love dive bars and all, but I'm—well—a little surprised."

"Don't worry. I'm just giving you a hard time. You're right though," she said as she stood up, "this isn't my normal day job. Like I said, I fill in here a day or two a week to help out."

"Oh yeah? You know the owners?" Hirsch asked. It'd be his luck if the bar turned out to be her boyfriend's business. It wouldn't be the first time Hirsch found an attractive, unmarried woman was nonetheless attached.

"It's my grandparents' place. I guess I should say my grandma's now ever since Granddad passed away a couple years ago. My Uncle Steve manages the business-side, but she still owns it."

"And would your grandma be the namesake of the bar?"

"The one and only Lily Brannon," she said as she labored to pour another pitcher of beer for the rowdy group at the back of the bar. "They bought the place in the sixties. Embarrassed the hell out of her when Granddad named it after her, but I guess the name stuck. She's in her eighties but tends bar a couple days a week."

"I suppose I ought to drop in when she's working. She might remember my dad," Hirsch said as Lauren brushed past him to deliver the pitcher to the rear table. An aroma of vanilla in her wake cut through the stench of stale beer and dried piss. Hirsch watched from the corner of his eye as she floated across the room.

She returned moments later. "Be on your best behavior in that case. Grandma doesn't put up with anyone's crap. Not many people can handle the type that likes to come in here. Lily Brannon can."

"Has the crowd always been this rough?"

Lauren's demeanor shifted. Nonplussed, she said, "No, the clientele's a new development. It sucks to be honest. Used to be, we'd get mostly guys from the mill, fishermen, foresters, maybe an occasional tourist. My Dad worked at the Thompson fish hatchery before I was born. People would drive from Garden and Rapid River too. Once the mills closed and people drifted south or died, it changed."

"I understand," Hirsch said with a grim nod. "My Dad worked at the mill too."

"Well, you'd know what I'm talking about, wouldn't you? Now it's a bunch of bikers, obnoxious drunks, and meth heads who need a drink when they're not high. One of our regulars— a real asshole—got himself killed a few weeks back. The TV said his meth lab exploded. Crazy, huh? You hear about that?" Hirsch blanched, dreading to broach the subject. His near-empty glass rescued him. "Another beer?" she asked.

"Sure, why not." He polished off the dregs in one swift gulp and slid the glass forward. Lauren snatched it up and rinsed it before pulling him another pint. "Apart from moonlighting here, what do you do?" he asked.

"I teach math at the high school in Gladstone," she said while returning the beer.

"That right?" She's a smart one too, he thought.

"What—that surprise you?" Lauren said with a toss of her head that scattered her hair and piled it on her left shoulder.

"No, no, not in the least. Truth be told, I wish I'd gone into teaching. Hard to pay the bills these days, unfortunately."

"Hence why I'm spending my time with this crew of derelicts—present company excepted. Well, you know my sob story, what is it you do?"

Hirsch anticipated this question sooner or later. Dishonesty dictated his life for far too many years. Building a new life would be meaningless if he perpetuated old habits. Hirsch chose candor with his newfound friend.

"I work for the gas company out of Escanaba. I practiced law down in Lansing, but it didn't work out. I grew up nearby and decided to come home."

"Well, are you glad you did?" Lauren traced a couple fingers through her hair.

Hirsch looked away for a moment and raised his eyebrows in thought before replying, "So far, yes. It's odd, you know. I've only been away twenty years, but it feels like there's no one left in town I remember. I mean, I see a few people I recognize and all, but they're like ghosts. Most of them are so old, they could be. After my dad died and my mother moved east, I never imagined coming back."

Lauren nodded as she grabbed a tub of clean glasses and set it on the bar. "I know you how feel. I grew up around here. I left too—for college. Madison. Graduated in 2011."

"What the hell brought you back, if you don't mind me asking?"

"I couldn't find work anywhere else. Not a real job anyway. My marriage wasn't great either, if you must know. Figured a change of scenery might help," she said as she unloaded the glasses.

"Well—did it?"

Lauren came to a full stop, arms akimbo and head tilted. "No, we're not together. We were married three years. He followed me here grudgingly. He left, I stayed."

"Sorry to hear that. Divorce sucks."

"Don't be, it's for the better. Besides," she added after a pause, "I doubt you're all that upset."

Hirsch gave a half-smile and said, "Not the easiest place to meet someone, is it?"

"You're telling me, especially working here." Lauren swept her hand across the bar's expanse. "Not to mention I have to fend off the advances of my very married principal at school."

"Jesus, couldn't they fire him for that?" It surprised him a supervisor could get away with blatant harassment in this day and age.

"Not when half his family is on the school board. Even thinking about his hairy, liver-spotted hand on my shoulder makes me shudder. I've toyed with leaving town, but I'm close to tenure and don't want to start all over again. Besides, I like seeing the kids learn and most of my family's still here."

Hirsch opened his mouth to ask her another question when the rumble of several motorcycle engines approached the tavern. Moments later, three leather-clad bikers breached the door with an orgy of whoops and shouting. They commandeered a table near the middle of the floor and looked at Lauren in expectation.

"I'd better go take care of this, hon," she said as she sauntered over to the table where they sat. She brushed her fingers against Hirsch's forearm as she passed by. The entrance of the rowdy bikers heralded a shift in the evening's mood. The peninsula's assorted lowlifes slouched into the bar seeking solace with the closest company to friends they knew. Lauren was near run off her feet over the next hour, mixing drinks and filling orders.

"Steve better damn well get here soon," she spat out as she flew by Hirsch cradling a tray of whiskey and colas. A moon-faced woman—her gut hanging out beneath her T-shirt—snatched one up with both hands and sucked at the amber liquid. Hirsch glanced at the clock, surprised to find it was already nine-thirty. He'd sworn himself to a three-beer limit and was midway through the third.

After dealing with a flurry of orders and drinks, Lauren caught a break. She paused behind the bar, near breathless from scurrying back and forth between tables. She took advantage of the lull to slip a hair tie out of her pocket and arranged her honey-brown hair in a casual ponytail. Doing so showed off her delicate ears. The silver hoop of a piercing adorned the helix of one. Hirsch shot her a sympathetic look.

"Is it like this every night?"

She laughed. "No, it gets worse."

Hirsch had to take the opportunity. "I'm afraid I gotta run after this beer. Look, I know you probably get sick of hearing this, but would you be up for having dinner with me next week?"

She regarded him with her lips slightly agape. "Most guys who hit on me here creep me the fuck out. I make Steve tell them to leave. But yeah, I think I'd enjoy dinner."

"Does Wednesday evening around seven work? Or are you here?"

"Wednesday's fine, Ben. I'm off that night."

"How about dinner in Escanaba. The Stonehouse Restaurant is near the best in town, I'm told."

"That sounds lovely to me. My ex was too cheap to take me there. Now I'm too poor. Here, what's your number?" she asked as she picked up her phone from behind the bar. Hirsch told her and she tapped at her screen. "Okay, I sent you a text so you'll have mine. Write me back and we'll sort out the details."

"Will do." He stood and put on his jacket to leave. "You hang in there tonight, all right? Hopefully your uncle will get here soon."

Lauren shook her head. "He'd better damn well, or I'm walking out at ten come hell or high water."

"Can't say I'd blame you," Hirsch responded as he wandered out into the darkened night. The silence of the evening and chill in the air cleared his head. Standing in the yellow glare of the roadhouse sign, Hirsch paused to gaze at the moonlit lake shimmering beyond the highway and contemplate his future. Maybe there was something—or someone—who could keep him here longer than he expected. Hirsch headed home, brimming with anticipation. Even his near-bursting bladder failed to derail his mood. For the first night in weeks, Marcus Shaw failed to haunt his dreams.

HIRSCH SAT ACROSS THE CANDLELIT table from Lauren. The sight of her luminescent eyes in the flickering radiance paralleled the warm glow within him. This was his first real date in ages—arguably since his marriage to Allison. His foray into Tinder before departing Lansing failed miserably. Most matches declined to respond, and his one booze-soaked hook-up with a curvy but dull New England transplant left him feeling hollow and cheap. After his disbarment, he deleted the app altogether.

They occupied a two-person booth seated beneath a Kincaid-esque painting of a cottage. Lauren dressed for the warmth of the early-summer UP night. Her coral-and-white-checked gingham dress fell a hand's width above her knee while a thin cashmere sweater shielded her shoulders and arms from the chill of the restaurant's air conditioning. Hirsch tried—but failed—to keep his eyes off the inch-and-a-half of cleavage revealed by the undone button at the top of her dress. She pretended not to notice.

The waiter came by to take their order. Lauren ordered the teriyaki salmon while Hirsch settled on the steak au poivre. Both opted for a salad of fresh greens with house-made vinaigrette to start. Minutes later, the waiter returned and uncorked a bottle of Sonoma County pinot noir and proceeded to pour each of the guests a glass. The earnest server praised the wine's mouthfeel before excusing himself. The burgundy liquid shimmered in the candlelight as Hirsch raised his glass aloft and smiled at Lauren.

"Here's to new adventures in old places," Hirsch said while she sipped from her glass.

"Isn't that the truth," she replied after savoring the first taste. "When I was younger, I always said I'd get out of here and start a new life in the city. Now look where I am."

"I hear you on that. This is the last place I thought I'd end up. I still don't know if I made the right choice. I'm curious—what made you go into teaching?"

Lauren sighed as she set her wine glass down. "Teaching was never part of my life plan, let's put it that way. After I graduated college, I wanted to work as a data analyst or statistician for a Fortune 500 company in Chicago or another big city. I'd never lived in one. I thought we'd go and have some adventures, travel, you name it. Truth is, this was during the recession and *no one* was hiring. Especially new grads without a lick of experience. Besides, I married young and had my husband to consider."

The waiter returned and deposited a tray of olives on the table. Lauren selected one, popped it into her mouth, and sucked the fragrant oil from her index finger. "Fortunately," she continued, "I had the sense to complete the teaching licensure program in math—just in case. After, like, a year of nothing, I was desperate, and my mom called and told me about a job that opened up over in the Gladstone school district. My ex worked in IT so he could find work most anywhere. Why the hell not? I figured. I applied and interviewed. I didn't think much would come of it, but a couple weeks later, they called and offered me the job. That was four years ago and here I am."

"And are you glad you took it?" Hirsch asked after another sip of the smooth wine.

"Well, it pays the bills … barely. I mean, I love seeing the kids actually learn useful skills, but it's hard to scrape by on a junior teacher's salary. The extra money and tips I get working at Lily's help. I guess it could be worse. At least I'm not working a pole out on Highway 35 or selling my panties online to make ends meet."

Hirsch laughed at the notion, though the thought of watching Lauren perform an erotic dance made his face burn in pleasant shame.

"I can't complain though," she continued, "I own my own house. That's more than most people my age can say. I have college friends who moved home with their parents after graduation. Five years later, a few are still there. Speaking of which, you've never told me where you live. I'd love to know a little bit more about a mysterious man like yourself."

"Well, I'm fortunate too in a way. I grew up in Manistique, and we still own our family home. My father passed away a few years ago and my mom moved to the Soo to be closer to her siblings. We tried selling the old place twice, but no one wanted it. It needs a good renovation, but I feel at home there."

"Are you all by your lonesome?" Lauren asked.

"Yeah, sure am. I didn't move back in with my parents so much as move into their empty home. It's awfully big for one person, I guess. Built around the turn of the last century and still has the original woodwork. Truth is, I don't spend a whole lot of time there what with work and all."

"Well, it sounds lovely to me. I love old houses. Maybe I'll get to see it someday."

Hirsch tipped his glass toward her and said, "I think that could be arranged."

Amidst the gentle din of conversation throughout the busy restaurant, Hirsch and Lauren enjoyed their salads and entrées paired with the wine. Lauren's cheeks grew rosy and, loosened by the spirits, they chatted away. They compared their childhoods growing up in the UP, shared highlights of their respective college experiences, and hinted at their utter loneliness since moving home. While they waited for dessert and coffee, Hirsch reached across the table and took her hand into his, caressing the crests of her knuckles with his thumb.

"Can I ask you a personal question, Lauren?"

"Sure, why not."

"You mentioned at Lily's that you were married when you moved here. Do you mind me asking what happened? I guess

I'm surprised any guy would let you go."

"It's okay to ask. There's really not a whole lot to it. My ex-husband and I met in college. He was a couple years older than me and a computer-science grad student. We only dated a year before we married. I was just twenty-one at the time and a junior in college. My Mom and Dad thought I was foolish for getting married so young, but I was head over heels in love with Tim. No one was going to tell me otherwise. His family lived in Evanston, Illinois. We got hitched there that summer at a park right on the lake. After graduation, I spent about a year in Madison hunting for work. Substitute teaching was the only paying gig I could find. If you think teaching's hard, give that substitute nonsense a try.

"Tim had plenty of job offers all over, but we decided we'd wait until I found something permanent. After a while, it pissed him off when I couldn't find anything. It was like I was holding him back. I eventually resigned myself to teaching until the economy improved. Like I told you, they offered me the job here in Gladstone. Then we had our first big fight. Tim didn't want to move to a podunk northern Michigan town, but my parents and grandparents were getting old, and I wanted to be closer to them. I suppose it was selfish of me, but I was young and didn't know any better, I guess. I told him we'd move or he could kiss me goodbye.

"Anyway, we came to Escanaba. Tim wasn't at all happy about it, but he found a good paying job as a systems administrator with the hospital. Problem was, it was below his talents and he knew it. That's when he really began to resent me. We went downhill in a hurry. I spent more time at school with my students and colleagues. Tim mostly hung out in Escanaba. I'd like to say it was his fault but, the truth is, we both started to see other people. After a year living here, we knew it was over. He moved to Chicago. With my share of the divorce settlement, I put a down payment on a little house in Gladstone. A couple years later, here I am."

"I have to admit, I was a little nervous about asking you out. Part of me worried you get hit on all the time at the bar and I'd be yet another creep looking to get in your pants," Hirsch said.

Lauren snorted. "Well, it does happen a fair amount. Comes with the job and being a woman, I suppose. You try to be friendly and make customers feel welcome. They take it as flirting. The main difference is most of the guys hitting on me are middle-aged, balding drunks who I wouldn't let get near me with a ten-foot pole. Like, I keep an honest-to-God baseball bat behind the bar. Trust me, decent-looking, well-spoken guys like you are hard to come by. It's been a year since I last went out on a date."

"That's a little surprising," Hirsch said. "There must be a few eligible bachelors out there, I'd hope."

"Maybe, but for obvious reasons I don't hang out much in bars—as a customer anyway. When your co-workers are your sole peer group and social circle, it's not much of a dating pool. Besides, most of them are married. My last boyfriend was the junior-high gym teacher. Stereotypical jock. We didn't have much to talk about. You work with what you got."

"Life brings about mysterious surprises," Hirsch said as the waiter placed their desserts in front of them.

"That it does." Lauren said, then licked a spoonful of chocolate mousse with the tip of her tongue.

HIRSCH DIDN'T SLEEP WITH LAUREN that night. He bid her fare-well with a kiss on her porch and a promise to call when they both had a free evening. On their third outing the following week, they spent the day hiking in the Seney National Wildlife Refuge northeast of Manistique. He brought a bird book, and they passed several hours identifying the wood ducks, mergan-sers, and sandhill cranes dotting the landscape. Warm weather graced their hike, and Lauren sported a sleeveless t-shirt and pair of spandex shorts. Hirsch took frequent opportunities to glance at her ass whenever she stared through a set of binoculars. Later that evening, they changed and drove to Escanaba for Italian food paired with ice-cold Peroni beer.

After driving to Lauren's home in a quiet neighborhood of Gladstone, Hirsch pulled into her driveway and put the vehicle in park with the engine idling. He leaned across the center con-sole of his truck to give her a goodnight kiss. She reciprocated his affection, and they soon found themselves gently kissing for the next fifteen minutes. Her nimble tongue darted across his, and he interlaced the fingers of his left hand through hers, feel-ing her delicate fingers warm against his hand. She broke the kiss long enough to rest her forehead against his. Her soft, warm breath pulsed against his mouth. She raised her long eyelashes, locking her eyes against his.

"Do you want to come in?" she asked. Hirsch nodded.

Lauren escorted him into her tidy cottage-style home. She decorated the house with muted floral tones and white-painted furniture. Hirsch had little interest in the décor at that moment. Once she shut the front door behind them and kicked her shoes off, Lauren fell into his arms. They exchanged deep kisses while running their hands over the other's body. Lauren slid a bare thigh up along Hirsch's leg, and he responded by wrapping his hand around the soft skin and hooking her leg over his hip. He stiffened as she ground against him, eliciting gentle moans of pleasure from her. The intensity made him glad he remembered to buy a pack of condoms from a gas-station restroom earlier that day.

After several minutes of frenzied embraces, Lauren guided Hirsch by hand into her bedroom. Hirsch kissed the nape of Lauren's neck while drawing the zipper of her dress down to its base at the small of her back. Her dress fell to the floor with the faintest rustle, and Hirsch kissed down her upper back and shoulders while undoing the clasp on her bra. She hunched her shoulders forward and let it slip off to join the dress. He stepped back and took in the sight of Lauren's trim figure clad only in a peach-hued thong that traced down the groove of her rear. Cupping his hands over her breasts, Hirsch resumed kissing Lauren's neck and nibbling on her ear. Her nipples hardened between his fingers, and she gasped as he stroked them. She turned to face him, and Hirsch embraced her as she hooked a finger in her panties and shimmied out of her thong. It coasted to the floor and she stepped away from it. Hirsch disrobed and joined her naked in her bedroom's faint light.

Lauren fell backwards onto the bed. Kneeling before her, Hirsch concentrated his affections on her with short licks, and her soft moans encouraged his efforts. Within minutes, she threw a hand over her mouth to stifle a cry as her entire body shuddered. The cool flesh of her thighs clenched alongside Hirsch's head, and he maintained a rhythmic pace as he brought down from her orgasm. Lauren spent a couple minutes panting and recovering from the burst of unadulterated euphoria percolating through her body. She ran her fingers through Hirsch's hair—his head resting alongside her inner thigh.

"Take me from behind," she said.

Not needing any more prompting, Hirsch rose to his knees and guided Lauren into place. They coupled, and a steady pace achieved over the ensuing minutes drew them into a synchronic rhythm. A second orgasm rippled through Lauren and Hirsch soon joined her. They collapsed on the bed with hearts racing and minds numb with gratification.

Flush in the post-coital stillness of the night, Hirsch and Lauren laid supine. The dull glow of the streetlight through the window bathed them in a cool light. For several minutes, they fostered the silence, savoring the indefinable feeling. Hirsch held Lauren's hand and, from time to time, shifted his gaze over at her, as if to confirm what he'd long hoped for was happening.

Lauren broke the silence. "It's been a long time since I've felt this way, Ben. I'm a little nervous at where this is going, but I'm really liking it."

He nodded. "Me too."

"Remember back at the restaurant when you asked me about my marriage and what happened?"

"Yeah, I do. Sounds like you did the right thing, hard as it must've been."

"Well, what about you? Have you ever been married?"

Hirsch nodded and looked over at Lauren. He rolled onto his side to face her, lowering an arm over her waist while draping his head on his other folded arm.

"I was married, yes. For ten years, to a wonderful woman. We divorced before I moved up here."

"So—what happened?"

"I fucked up big time. I had a great marriage, a wife who loved me, and a good paying job. Life was moving along well and fine, then I screwed up. I'm not sure where it all unraveled, but I lost control. I had an affair with a client. Maybe I drank too much, maybe I worked too hard. Truth is, I have no one to blame but myself."

"No offense, but, knowing lawyers, I'm surprised it doesn't happen all the time," Lauren said.

"It may well, but I got caught. The bar came down hard on me for it. I lost my practice, and they yanked my license. That wasn't the worst of it. In a way, getting tossed out of the profession was the best medicine. No, the biggest consequence was losing my wife. I hurt her something awful and she could never forgive me for it. Can't say I blame her. She couldn't see much point in us going on with it lingering in her mind. She told me she wanted out. I didn't fight it. It was my own damn fault, and I deserved everything that happened to me. Now here I am, right back where I started." Hirsch fell silent before adding, "I should've told you all this before. I understand if you don't want anything to do with me now."

"Well … do you still have feelings for her?"

"I care about her, but I've moved on. I'd still be in Lansing if I hadn't. But I'm here, and it's time I built a new life. I'm not the same man I was before."

Lauren rested a hand alongside Hirsch's cheek and stroked his face with her thumb. "I'd like to believe people can change." She paused and frowned as she looked away from him. "Look—

there's something else I should tell you about me too. I know I might seem like I have my shit together, but I made my share of bad decisions as a teen."

"Who didn't at that age?"

"Well, let's just say some are worse than others. When I was sixteen, maybe seventeen, I had an older boyfriend who got me into stuff I knew better to avoid. At first it was a big thrill having this hot guy in his twenties with a nice car and a real job showing interest in me. Before that, I'd dated high school boys and such but they were all so immature compared to Tony. Anyway, it started out innocently enough. I didn't want to tell my parents I was dating him—I knew they wouldn't approve—so I snuck out of the house whenever I could. He'd pick me up at the end of the block, and we'd drive off out of the way and have sex in his car. Other times, I'd tell my parents I was going over to a friend's house for the weekend. Instead, I spent the weekends with Tony at his place.

"It was all good clean fun for a while—then he introduced me to crystal meth. I didn't know any better. God, what a rush at first. You could take that and screw for hours, it was amazing. Pretty soon, though, I didn't care much about anything else. I fell out of touch with my friends. My grades tanked—hell, I didn't even go to school half the time. I looked like crap, and no one in my family had a clue what was happening to me. They assumed I was depressed and wanted me to see a counselor. I flipped my shit on them more than once." Lauren rolled over and buried her face in the pillow before continuing.

"It all fell apart when I got pregnant and couldn't hide it anymore from my parents. I was a wreck. I wanted to drown myself in Lake Michigan so no one would know. I confessed everything to them. They were horrified, not to mention hurt from being lied to for the past six months. Still, they were there for me. I had an abortion, and my folks sent me to a rehab clinic in Minnesota to get clean. I guess it worked—I never touched that shit again. Once I came home from the clinic and tried to put my life together, I was disgusted with myself. It's hard to face yourself in the cold glare of sobriety. It made me sick to think of what I'd done and what I'd said to my parents and friends. It's weird, but it was like this nightmare I hadn't actually lived through. Remembering it was like watching a movie. I damn near puked out of shame every time I thought about my past.

"After that, I did well enough in school and decided I wasn't going to spend another day throwing away my life. Truth is, most of the reason I came back is how good my mom and dad were to me through it all. They're getting older. I figure I owe it to them to be around when they need me."

Hirsch traced his thumb along Lauren's back. He refrained from speaking to let her get anything else she wanted off her chest.

"I guess what I'm trying to say is, I know we haven't known each other long, but I really like you. Before we get serious, promise you'll be honest with me. I'll do the same for you."

"I've learned my lesson," Hirsch said. "I know what you mean about not wanting to waste a single day, especially when you get a new lease on life. I'm done hurting people, especially ones I care about." Hirsch punctuated his statement by leaning in to kiss Lauren.

They exchanged soft kisses for several minutes. Lauren's hand found his groin, and she rolled onto her back to accommodate him. They enjoyed a gentle bout of lovemaking with

Hirsch cradling her head in his hand. Lauren came first with a shiver and sharp cry, then Hirsch followed moments later. It was well past midnight, and both lay exhausted. Hirsch watched her fall asleep with her hands clasped between her glistening thighs before he drifted into a deep slumber himself.

THE BRIGHT GLARE OF MORNING came all too soon. Hirsch sat in Lauren's living room, wearing yesterday's rumpled clothes. The stubble on his cheeks begged for a shave. He sipped from a mug of lukewarm, leftover coffee, struggling to clear his head after a brief night of sleep. The sounds of Lauren dressing and humming from her bedroom amused him while he surveyed the living room under the light of day.

Three books occupied her coffee table—*Eat, Pray, Love*, a glossy tome on rustic-chic décor, and something called *The Wine Merchant's Daughter*. Maybe literature wasn't her thing, he decided. He spent several minutes flipping through a photo album from her college days. He considered pocketing one snapshot of her and several friends at a Badgers' tailgate. The four svelte girls stood clad in red-and-white tube tops and yoga pants and posed for the camera with coquettish pursed lips. Lauren anchored one end and had her hip thrust out toward the camera. He figured she'd notice it missing and abandoned the idea.

Lauren stepped out of the bedroom, coiffed and dressed to begin another day of work. Hirsch smiled upon seeing her, amazed at his fortune in finding such a talented, lovely woman swooning for him. He stepped toward her and put his hands on her hips to pull her closer. He planted a gentle kiss on her lips.

"It goes without saying last night was wonderful," he said.

"It's been a while for me. Most of the guys here couldn't

hold a conversation if they wanted to. The creeps at the bar sure can't."

"Maybe I can have you over for dinner at my place soon. I'm no wizard in the kitchen, but I can put a meal together."

"Sounds lovely, Ben. I wouldn't mind getting out of town, even an hour away. Cabin fever hits me hard after a long winter."

"Well in that case, would a weekend out of town interest you?"

Lauren smiled. "I couldn't tell you the last time I did that. God, a weekend of sex and room service sounds like heaven."

"A trip to Marquette and a stay at the Landmark sounds like the ticket—if you have the time, of course."

Lauren bit her lower lip between her teeth and said, "Speaking of which, I bet we have time for one more thing." She dropped to her knees and unbuttoned Hirsch's pants. Taking him into her mouth, Lauren gave Hirsch a blowjob that left him weak in the knees and shuddering with pleasure. Finished, she buttoned up his trousers and stood to face him. Her crimson-flushed face made her look even prettier. They exchanged a long kiss as he cradled her slender waist in his hands. She feathered her hair back into place with her fingers and pulled a tube of lip gloss out of her purse to apply a veneer of lush sheen over her mouth.

"All right, I gotta run to work now. Call me when you're free and we can do this again," Lauren said, giving his cock a squeeze through his trousers before they headed out to their respective vehicles. She blew him a kiss as she pulled away. Hirsch watched her vehicle fade into the distance before putting his truck in gear and heading home to start a new day.

Resurrected, he looked upon his world through a different lens.

Chapter 15

THE LOW BUZZ OF HIRSCH'S phone woke him early the Saturday following his date with Lauren. Half asleep, he fumbled for the phone on his nightstand.

"You fucking prick!"

"What's the matter, Lauren? Are you okay?"

"Don't 'what's the matter me.' Guess who paid us a visit last night at the bar?" Hirsch could guess at any number of unwelcome guests. "A goddamn county detective, that's who."

"What—what did he want?"

"He wanted to know about that asshole meth-head who died a couple weeks ago. The cop pulled out a picture and asked if I knew you. Then I remember you were all buddy-buddy with him the first night we met. That was you they talked about on the news, you asshole!"

"Woah, woah, hold on. I can explain all this," Hirsch said.

"Save it. Jesus, I've never been so embarrassed. I have to tell the cop you're my new boyfriend, and he goes off asking me all these questions about you shooting a man and burning his cabin down. When the hell were you going to mention that, anyway?"

"Look, I didn't want to get you involved in that mess." Hirsch jumped out of bed and grabbed at clothes scattered on the floor to put on. "Besides, it was an accident. Let me come over and see you. We'll talk this over. I promise it'll make sense."

"You come anywhere near my house and I'm calling the cops. What was all that bullshit about you being honest with me? I suppose you were trying to get in my pants like every other jerk here. This is what I get for dating a guy I met in that shithole of a bar. I should've known better—" Lauren voice trailed off into a sob.

"No, no—that's not it at all, Lauren. Seriously, I just need to explain it to you."

"Oh, fuck off," she said and ended the call.

Jesus, how the hell did I manage to screw this up again? Hirsch wondered. He stood with the phone in his hand and his wrinkled trousers around his knees. He sank back onto the bed, clutching his head in his hands and digging his nails into his scalp. After fifteen minutes of self-recrimination, he stood and finished dressing. He needed fresh air and sustenance to sort through his latest catastrophe.

Hirsch walked downtown to a small restaurant known for serving a decent and hearty breakfast. He didn't feel like being seen but was damn hungry. Although he stuck to yogurt or fruit with coffee before his workdays, Hirsch allowed himself the luxury of a full breakfast one day per week. The dining room stood half-full at eight-thirty in the morning, and Hirsch secured his favorite table adjacent to the large floor-to-ceiling windows that formed the storefront. Sunlight poured over him, and Hirsch shielded his eyes as he peered out into the street.

"Can I move you to another table in the shade, hon?" the waitress asked, seeing him squinting.

"Nah, I'm okay here. I could use a little extra sunshine to-day."

"Suit yourself. I'll be by with coffee."

Most visits, he liked to gaze out across the streetscape and watch it come alive with weekend traffic and pedestrians pacing up and down the sideways. After the morning Hirsch had, he couldn't care less. A white Ford F-250 with an oversized muffler and rear window decorated with gun-rights decals obscured his view. This time of the year, tourists far outnumbered locals, though it was hard to tell who was who in many cases. A jocular group of young men in ball caps and auto-racing shirts seated at a neighboring table shouted at each other above the café's din of conversation.

When the waitress returned, Hirsch ordered a ham, mush-room, and Swiss omelette with a side of hash browns and rye toast. He settled back to enjoy the steaming cup of black coffee in front of him while contemplating how to move forward with life. Should he just pack it all in and return to Lansing? Clearly, he fucked up royally no matter where he lived.

The chair opposite him issued a loud screech as a calloused and grease-stained hand dragged it along the floor. A man took a seat in it and brought his elbows down on the table with a thud. For the third time in the past month, Hirsch looked straight into the face of Lionel Shaw. Hirsch held Shaw's gaze without expression, not wanting to betray a hint of surprise. Par-alyzed with fear, he waited for Shaw to make the first move.

"Good morning, Mr. Hirsch," Shaw said, breaking the si-lence. "Mind if I join you for a cup of coffee?"

Hirsch said nothing but continued to regard the elder Shaw brother with a stony, blank stare. Shaw raised a hand with his index finger extended to get the waitress's attention. She sauntered over to the table.

"One coffee, miss. With cream if you will. Nothing else today," he said. The waitress scribbled down his order and moved away.

"I didn't expect to see you again, Lionel," Hirsch said. "At least not under these circumstances. Are you following me?"

Shaw smiled as he removed his tattered ball cap and placed it on the table. He rubbed his hand over the gray-speckled red hair clipped short around his balding head. A half-inch-long reddish beard fringed his jaw. He continued to examine Hirsch with pale blue eyes that offered no hint at his mindset. Shaw wore weathered jeans and a red-and-yellow-checkered flannel shirt open at the collar. A pack of Marlboro Reds peeked out from the breast pocket of his paint-splattered shirt. Shaw's calm demeanor and the half-smile on his face sent a shiver down Hirsch's spine. Beneath Shaw's rough appearance was a man of high intelligence and education.

"Mr. Hirsch, you're not a difficult man to find, let's put it that way. Fact is, nowadays it's hard for anyone to fly under the radar. Besides, I already know what you drive and where you work. After all, you sought me out, not the other way around."

"Okay, so why are you here sitting in front of me today?"

"Let me cut to the chase," Shaw said before pausing when the waitress returned with his coffee. "I know what you and Edgar Trehearne did to my brother. I won't sugarcoat things—Marc was a drug dealer and all-around lowlife. He could be a hard man to love much of the time, believe me. I can't pretend the police will lift a finger to put you and Trehearne behind bars where you belong. Thing is, I didn't come here today to harangue you about prison and our so-called justice system."

"Then what the hell are you doing here, Lionel?"

"You're a lawyer, Mr. Hirsch. You like telling stories, right? I'm guessing you told a few real whoppers in your time. I need you to understand why I can't let my brother's death go unanswered. I thought I might share a story of my own if you care to listen."

"Do I have any choice in the matter?"

Shaw looked around the restaurant and issued a short laugh. "We're in a public place, aren't we? I'd say you're free to get up and leave any time you'd like. Besides, if you prefer, we could always continue this at that old house of yours on Michigan Avenue. Love what you've done with the yard, by the way. The place went to hell the past few years, didn't it?"

Panic slammed into Hirsch like a body-blow to the gut. How long had this creep been keeping an eye on him? Thank God he lived alone. Hirsch had little choice other than listening to his interlocutor.

"Go on," he said.

"Good choice," Shaw said. He settled back in his chair and slowly nodded. "Sitting here in front of you, I suppose I look like an ignorant hick, right? I'm used to that by now. Can't say I mind all too much. People find it disarming. Truth is, I want folks to underestimate me. I'm guessing that happened to you a time or two given your current predicament. Now who wants to hear a tale of woe from a divorced, unemployed, middle-aged man? No one, that's who. I want to tell you about a boy who grew up as an outsider.

"This boy came into the world in the summer of sixty-six. His family was solid middle-class, and fate could've dealt him a worse hand, all things considered. He had two parents like most folks. His father worked a professional job in town and made decent money. His mother could afford to stay home and take care of the kids. Not much like it is nowadays, eh? The boy had a grandfather—a physician and a well-respected member of the community. That boy loved his grandfather and, in time, he came to be his favorite person in the world. To round out this postcard-perfect family, the boy had an older sister, six years his senior. Three years later, a younger brother came along. A big, happy, all-American family of five you might say.

"That child didn't have much to worry himself about those first few years of life. No one beat him, and they fed him well-enough. It wasn't until he grew up a little that he started to feel different from the rest. First time he noticed, he must've been six or seven years old. It was Christmas time with the family all together in the den of their home. You can picture it, I imagine—tree all tinseled out, presents wrapped and stacked under the tree, Christmas music blaring from the stereo. The adults are already getting lit off the spiked eggnog, and those kids are tearing around the place giddy with excitement.

"Dad has the camera out like you'd expect. You'd seen him take a bunch of family pictures before, but you were too young to notice what was going on. That's when the boy hears Dad tell his sister, she's about ten now, 'hold you baby brother so I can snap a picture of the two of you in front of the tree.' The boy naturally thinks Dad wants a picture of all the kids together, so he crowds in alongside his sister, all smiles and eyes aglow. That's when he sees Pa swooshing him out of the way with his hand and telling him to scram. And what happens? Ol' Dad takes a cute picture of sis holding her baby brother and doesn't give one more thought to the son he's left sitting on the side-lines. He keeps waiting for Pa to call him over, but it never happens.

"And that's when it hits him for the first time—his folks treat him different than his siblings. He doesn't remember another single damn thing about that Christmas, but he'll never forget that moment for the rest of his life. From that day forward, he notices every little slight they make toward him. He catalogues them in his mind, one by one, though it'd be years before he figured out why. It's only when he's older, maybe eight, he receives a hint. The boy's done something foolish—broken one of his sister's tchotchkes while tossing a ball across the house.

"'You don't belong to us, you're not one of us!' his sister hurls at him in a fit of anger. The boy's confused and doesn't understand what she means. She won't tell him anything else, but he can see from the look on her face she's already said more than she should've. She makes it clear if he breathes a word of this to anyone, he'll pay for it. He believes her. His youth turns into a protracted hunt for clues about who in the hell he is.

"So, the boy gets older, grows up, and comes to find out he's smarter than most folks. I don't mean he makes good grades or anything—he's too busy horsing around in class most of the time. Surprising part is, he's off the charts on these aptitude tests all the kids have to take. This confounds damn near everyone since his folks are known for anything but their intellectual prowess. He's in third grade and the school wants to bump him up a class or two, maybe even send him to this goddamn gifted-student program. Truth is, the boy's embarrassed by the whole charade and wishes it would go away. His folks are indifferent and his sis teases him about it. In the end, he acts out in class, gets into fights on the playground, doesn't bother to do a lick of homework, mouths off to his teachers, the usual nonsense. The school does its best to forget he ever showed a speck of promise. Left to his own devices, he looks forward to a life of mediocrity and disappointment.

"Then the real calamity hits. The boy's nine years old and he's sitting in his weekly elementary school music class. He never showed much interest in music before—his sis told him to shut up every time he opened his mouth to sing. One day he's screwing around, banging away on whatever set of drums or xylophones they had sitting there in the classroom. A third-grade music class is one notch above sheer chaos. The teacher has enough of listening to all the racket and orders the boy to go sit on the piano bench off in a corner. I suppose she figured he'd be out of the way and could mind his own business. He's sitting there bored to tears, and he starts picking out the melody to a Bach fugue on the keys with his right hand. Now the kid may damn well not even know who Bach was, but there he is, playing from memory a two-hundred-plus-year-old organ piece he'd heard in church last Sunday. Never touched a piano before in his life, but he hammers out a simplified version from start to finish—at tempo even.

"Next he knows, the whole damn classroom's gone quiet and all the other kids are staring at him. Same goes for the teacher. He thinks he's fucked up real bad this time. Sure enough, when he's pulled out of class and sent to the office later that afternoon, he knows he's really in for it. Only he gets to the principal's office and sees his music teacher and a strange woman sitting next to the principal. Lord if she isn't a frumpy, mean-looking old hag. Well, that's that, he decides—she's come to haul him away to the reformatory. You can imagine his surprise when they tell him the old crone is a piano teacher. They want him to study with her for free.

"At this point, the kid's royally confused. He doesn't give a shit about classical music and never thought much about playing an instrument, let alone the godforsaken piano. If you put a gun to his head, he'd have chosen the drums just to piss everyone off. He warms to the idea though after his family finally shows an ounce of interest in him. The boy figures maybe he's made them proud for once in his life. He later comes to find out they were hoping he'd win a ton of prize money. Ma wanted a trip to West Palm Beach after all. The kid wasn't aware at the time, though, so he makes the best of it."

The waitress bearing Hirsch's omelette interrupted Shaw's story.

"Here you go, hon," she said as she placed the plate in front of Hirsch. He glanced at it and back at Shaw, who smirked at Hirsch.

"Well don't let me interrupt your breakfast," Shaw said. "All you need to do is listen."

Though Shaw killed Hirsch's appetite, he picked up his fork and cut into the warm omelette. A rivulet of Swiss cheese oozed from the incision and pooled on the plate.

"Here this child is, all of nine years old, and he's gone from being a lazy screw-off to a kid with a budding career as a concert pianist. Soon he finds himself excused from school early three times a week so he can walk four blocks to the home of spinster

Moira Adams. Miss Adams, as her students call her, is a Julliard graduate and taught piano lessons for years down in Madison for the university. Lord knows how she ended up in this dead-end town. She's retired and all, but resigned to taking on one last pupil based on the music teacher's excited call. Trouble is, the boy's scared shitless the first time he goes to her house. Miss Adams was what you might nowadays call a hoarder. Damn near every room inside was chock full of stacks of moldering papers, piles of ratty clothes, decaying boxes of junk, and God knows what else. He'd never seen anything like it before in his life. No wonder she stopped taking students. Anyway, I say the junk clogged 'near every' room because she had one corner cleared out for a baby grand piano. After that, whenever he comes over, he makes a beeline for the piano and tries to avoid the chaos all around him. He'd hold his breath against the stench of decay and mustiness at first, but he eventually gets used to it.

"The first time that child sat on the piano bench, he had no idea he'd be spending the next eight years doing the same thing—week after week. Old Miss Adams sits propped on a chair next to the piano where she can keep an eye on his fingers. Now bar none that boy must've been the most ignorant piano student ever to sit in her esteemed presence. He can't read a lick of music to save his life. He doesn't know the difference between a sharp or a flat. Hell, he couldn't even name a single note on the keyboard. He had to be the first student she needed to show where middle-C is. The pedals are a fucking mystery.

"She starts him off with Bach, seeing's how that's what he toyed with in the first place. Gets him to where he can play a Goldberg Variation or two. Soon enough, she has him working through Brahms, Mendelsohn, even a Rachmaninoff prelude.

The boy can't explain the sounds coming from his hands—though I suppose no one can. He never has to think about it. The notes flow from his fingertips. Good as he might've been, it was never quite enough for old Miss Adams. She pushed him and pushed him for more. They'd run at least an hour over most days. There were times he wanted to lean over, wrap his hands around her wrinkled old neck, and choke her to death. Fact was, that boy loved that tough old bird more than he did any member of his family. She actually gave a damn.

"The child gets older. He still does a piss-poor job in school, but it's only 'cause he doesn't give a shit about any of it. In junior high, they make all the kids take the SAT exam, for practice or some nonsense, and he outscores most of the high schoolers. Like a 1500 or higher. By this time, though, the only thing he cares about is playing the damn piano. While the other kids are throwing shit at each other in class or jerking off whenever they have a chance, his fingers are thundering away on his desk, practicing his Chopin. Most of his classmates decide he's a total oddball and avoid him.

"He starts off small time and plays these grade-school recitals, mostly for family. The other kids are bored out of their minds and show up because their parents made them. You wouldn't believe the number of halting Elton John covers that child had to listen to those early years. But here he is, hammering out a Mozart sonata that would befuddle even the most gifted student. The audience offers polite applause after most kids play. After he finishes, the church hall is silent. They don't know what to do with this. It's clear he's never going to go anywhere in a small town that couldn't give a shit about classical music. Miss

Adams calls in whatever favors she has left and convinces a conservatory in Chicago to take him on as a summer student—free room and board even. His parents are happy to get rid of him. They figure this is his only chance to make something of himself.

"Sure enough, he throws himself into practice even harder than before. Plays for twelve, fourteen hours a day. He comes down with an aching, awful case of tendonitis, but tries to hide it from his instructors. Ends up in howling pain one night and ties ice packs to his wrists to get through the day. The instructors there have to drag him away from the piano to eat or sleep. All his hard work pays off though. By the time he's thirteen years old, he's winning competitions across the Midwest—Chicago, Minneapolis, Madison, Cleveland. The Chicago Symphony invites him to play as a guest, and he holds up under the wilting glare of its venerable conductor. Hell, the boy even flies down to the Van Cliburn Competition in Dallas and comes close to winning it his first time. He romps his way through Schumann's *Kreisleriana*. Old Miss Adams will hardly leave her house, let alone set foot on a jet plane, so his sis of all people escorts him to Texas. He figures she came along to skip out on the recital and spend her time at Neiman Marcus.

"You'd think his hometown and family would be proud of him. Truth is, neither have a clue what to do with this freak of nature. Sure, the paper dutifully runs an article spotlighting his success, but it's clear they're as confused as his folks are. The kid rarely talks to anyone. Seems like he'd make the perfect target for bullies to beat up on at school, right? Turns out, they're all so intimidated by him, none will come near the boy. He notes their behavior. Each sideways look they cast at him is another stinging pinprick.

"By the time he's in high school, the boy knows the score. He's seen enough of the world to understand what his peers and community value. He's still playing the piano, but he does everything within his power to hide it from the world—like it's a shameful secret. At home, he'll only play when he has the house to himself. Desperate to fit in, the kid takes up smoking, stealing them when he has to. He buys a battered, used pickup truck with the prize money his parents didn't weasel away. He starts dressing like a millwright. Chases pretty girls from other towns who don't know a thing about him—the ones that don't consider him a freak. Smokes dope when he can get his hands on it. He even starts huffing paint and glue with his younger brother. Tells anyone who asks him what he wants to do after graduating that he'll probably go work at the papermill or some shit. Still, like clockwork, the boy's ass is on the bench at old Miss Adams's falling-down house four times a week, practicing like there's no tomorrow. She can tell something's deeply wrong with him, but he plays so beautifully, she keeps her mouth shut. At last, he can be himself around her. These practice sessions maintain his sanity more than any shrink or pill ever could. He can't give it up and he knows it.

"Then it happens. His senior year of high school, he's seventeen years old, going on eighteen. On a crisp October afternoon, he walks to his lesson and guess what he finds. Miss Adams is slumped over in her chair, dead as dead can be. She was there waiting for him like always. He can't control it; he cries like he's never cried before. He's lost the only person other than his brother who's ever loved or cared a damn thing for him. He slides to the floor with his head clenched in his hands, sobbing. An hour goes by before he can get his act together to call the police. There are times when he's sitting in class weeks or months afterward, he's so sick with grief it takes all he has not to howl. He'll run into the bathroom and slam his head and fists against the wall until he's bleeding and numb with pain.

"It's not a week after they bury her that he gets a letter in the mail. It's from Julliard Academy, offering a full-ride scholarship to study piano in New York. He never bothered to apply and figures Miss Adams must've pulled some strings. This is the most prestigious honor he could've received. You know what he does? Before anyone else can see that letter, he chucks it in the fireplace and watches it burn to ashes."

Shaw paused, staring at Hirsch to emphasize the magnitude of his sacrifice.

"That night, he swipes a bottle of hooch from his folks' liquor cabinet and proceeds to get roaring drunk. The boy decides it's as good a time as any to cruise on south to Marinette and visit this little freshman he'd been screwing off and on for a few weeks. Doesn't get more than ten minutes out of town when he wraps his truck around a tree. Spends a couple days wandering around the woods, half hoping he'd die of exposure before anyone finds him.

"He knows there's nothing left for him in this town. A month after Miss Adams dies, they bulldoze her house along with everything in it. Seems the place is too big a disaster to clean out and sell, and some developer wants it for the land. The boy stands across the street, horror-stricken, as the jaws of a Cat demolition excavator chew through a wall and impale her old piano in its iron fangs. His heart near stops and he swoons at the noise—strings snap and piano legs buckle as the bulldozer wrestles forth one last inharmonious chord from the old beast.

He sits motionless on the sidewalk the rest of the afternoon as his one sanctuary is reduced to a cluster of jagged rubble. Within a few days, it's like the place never even existed. After that trauma, he's numb to whatever pain the world can throw at him.

"The boy doesn't have any clue what to do with his life. His test scores are so good, Michigan Tech invites him to come study in Houghton for free. Rather than ply his trade as a concert pianist, he picks the most mundane vocation he can think of—heating and air conditioning engineering. Figures he'll wash out of the program and the school will throw him out once they realize what a bunch of goddamn fools they were to admit this clown in the first place. Problem is, the young man comes to find he's all right at the business. Hell, he even enjoys it. No one knows who he is up north, and he reinvents himself as a blue-collar townie. Grows a beard, shaves his full head of hair real short like, keeps a lip full of chew at all times, and drives a bigger, more obnoxious truck than any of his classmates. He sure as shit doesn't play the piano anymore. In fact, he doesn't touch one for years after the day he walked in and saw Miss Adams dead in her chair. He can't wash that image out of his mind.

"Despite all the partying, boozing, and general hellraising, the kid comes close to graduating college. He surprises even himself. So what happens? In his last year, he goes and knocks up a girl. She's a nineteen-year-old from the Keweenaw Peninsula—daughter of a Finnish Iron Range miner. She decides she's going to keep the baby, and he does what he thinks is the honorable thing and marries her at this Finnish Lutheran Church in Houghton. He can't understand a word the old pastor from the motherland says, but it all seems legit enough. His baby brother is the only member of his family who even bothers to show up.

The rest are either too embarrassed or gave up on him when he quit earning prize money. Since the girl doesn't have a job and will have her hands full with the baby, the boy—well, man by this point—quits school to earn an honest living. Fortunately, he paid close enough attention to what Tech taught him, and he hangs his own shingle for a heating and cooling outfit. Old Miss Adams left him a few dollars when she passed. He takes the last of it to buy a utility van and enough equipment to get himself started with the business. The fellow catches a break when a former instructor takes pity on him and throws a few leads his way.

"For the next twenty years, the man does his best to play white picket fence and provide. At first, he tries bringing his kid brother into the operation, seeing's how he's nineteen and already gliding down the primrose path of delinquency. It only takes the man a month to realize his brother has zero work ethic and couldn't care less about showing up on time, much less getting the job done. Most days he'll be screwing around or poking his nose where it don't belong in folks' homes. The man has enough when he catches his brother shoving a pair of teen-girl undies into his pocket from a home they're working in. They part ways, but on good enough terms.

"The man does well enough on his own that, within a couple of years, he frees them from their crummy one-bedroom apartment in Marquette. They move into a little bungalow with a yard for the kid to play. His wife turns out to be no slouch either. Between raising the kid and taking care of the house, she finishes school and gets herself an accounting degree. Pretty soon, she's keeping the books and running the day-to-day operation from home while he's out in the company van putting in seven-day weeks.

"That man tried for most of his life to leave his hometown behind, but what does he do but move his family there not long after he turns thirty. Still can't explain why to this day. He's raking in cash hand over fist, gaining a reputation for good work, and they can afford themselves a swell house in a new subdivision on the edge of town. He has enough work that he hires another couple guys to join his crew. Even though one child's enough for him, his wife cajoles him into having another and pretty soon she's got a bun in the oven. Before he knows what's happening, she's waddling around their house, heavily pregnant, and caressing her belly every chance she can get. She has him over a barrel and, like that, their whole dynamic changes overnight.

"Anyway, without even realizing it, the man knows he's locked into a life he never intended for himself. Pretty common story, I suppose, but everyone's midlife crisis is unique to them. Part of him has died inside, but nothing much happens for the next ten years. He works, they earn good money, improve the house, buy nice cars, and take family vacations to Disneyworld. Hell, to anyone on the outside, it sounds like the good life. And in a way, it was. It really was."

"What the hell happened?" Hirsch asked, interrupting Shaw's monologue for the first time. Hirsch gave up on eating his omelette. It sat in front of him, turning cold with the cheese congealing on the plate.

Shaw shot him an annoyed glance. "I'm getting to that, Hirsch." Composing himself, Shaw continued, "Two things happen to the man, I suppose you could say. First, his putative father dies in 2007. They weren't at all close, and the only time they saw each other was at Christmas when he and his wife hauled the kids over to see their grandparents. The man didn't expect so much as a kind word from him after he died. Imagine the surprise when he comes to find out the old man left him the family farm on the Garden Peninsula. It wasn't much to look at—forty acres with a run-down two-bedroom farmhouse and barn, but it was his land all the same. His grandfather, the old town doc, grew up on that farm and took the boy to visit before he passed. The sole person living in the farmhouse was his grandpa's spinster sister—the man's great aunt. When she broke her hip and moved into a convalescent home, the vacant house gathered dust. At first he thinks, hell, I'll sell the damn place and pocket the cash. It's not like he knows jack shit about farming.

"Anyway, he drives there one day to check the place out. Figures it's cluttered with junk he'll have to dispose of before he unloads it for what the land's worth. By and large, he's right. He paces from room to room, observing old furniture caked with dust and littered with mouse shit. I'll have trouble giving this hellhole away, he thinks. I'll have to pay someone to demolish it. Then he wanders into a small side room and stops dead in his tracks. Sitting in front of him is a dirty upright piano that looks as though it hasn't been played in ages. He recoils in shock. The first thought racing through his head is that he should light a match and torch the whole goddamn place right on the spot. He hasn't touched a piano in twenty-plus years, and he's paralyzed with sheer dread. The man's never suffered an anxiety attack before, but he's teetering on the brink of one right there. Blood's pounding in his ears and he knows he should turn and walk right out. His feet are like lead, but he plants one in front of the other until he's standing by the piano.

"Birds are chirping through a shattered window, but otherwise, it's just the sound of his stuttering breath in that room. With his index finger, he raises the fallboard and reveals a set of yellowing black and ivory keys. He tests the rickety bench to see if it'll support his weight, then eases himself down on it. It creaks under him but holds. He extends his shaking hands forward toward the keyboard. They steady as though soothed by magic, and he plays the *Moonlight Sonata* from start to finish. The piano's out of tune as hell, which he expected, but playing that piece ignites a passion in him he hasn't felt in years. It was like waking up after a coma and seeing the world for what it really is. When the reverberations of the final notes fade into the all-consuming silence, he rises from the bench a changed man.

"The man decides to keep the place. Doesn't tell anyone why. Whenever he can, he's sneaking off to the farm, often for eight, nine hours a day. He arranges for a crew to head out and do the real work, then he runs off in the other direction. Plays entirely from memory. All he does to get it right is conjure up Miss Adams sitting right there next to him. Lo-and-behold, it works. Pretty damn soon, she's correcting him and shouting like they were back at her house twenty-odd years earlier. He picks it up like he never quit back in high school. His family thinks he's working, and the business doesn't suffer one bit since he delegated his work to his contractors and trained them well. His wife and kids know something's wrong because he's more and more distant at home. She thinks he's having an affair and, in a manner of speaking, he is.

"His second misfortune is a trip to Detroit the following year for an HVAC conference. I say misfortune because the hosting venue is a large downtown hotel-casino. The man's never been much of a gambler but one evening after a few drinks with his colleagues in the industry, he thinks 'what the hell' and sits down at a video slot machine. Business is good and he's flush with cash, so he drops a hundred bucks into a five-dollar-a-pull machine. Doesn't think much of it and he's steadily losing his C-Note. Seventy dollars down, though, he hits three sevens and ends up walking out of the casino with over thirty grand in cash. Before he knows it, he's hooked. Goes back the next night and manages to give five grand back to the house. Who cares though when you're up over twenty-five large for the weekend.

"He finds any excuse he can to leave town over the next five years and hits the Indian casinos throughout the Great Lakes region. He wins now and then, he loses even more, but he's making good enough money it doesn't matter. Problem is, the economy tanks and work screeches to a halt. He knows he should call it quits. Lo and behold, he decides to give it one last hurrah on another HVAC conference trip—this time to Vegas in 2012. Over the course of four days, he manages to lose two-hundred-thousand dollars playing video poker. The casino takes him for a whale and puts him up in a deluxe suite for the night. They even send up a call girl on the sly to blow him two nights in a row. The man wipes out a savings account they'd set up for their kids' college tuition in a matter of hours. The night before he's scheduled to fly back home, he lays there without sleeping a wink, staring at the ceiling. He knows he's fucked up beyond repair. Even thinks about tossing a chair through the window of his twenty-third-story hotel room and leaping through the hole. Probably would've saved everyone a ton of grief.

"As expected, his wife flips her shit when she discovers all the money vanished. He knew it would happen sooner or later since she handled all the books anyway. She kicks him out, and he goes to live at his dilapidated farmhouse on the peninsula—the sole place he has left to call home. Playing piano is the only waking activity holding him together. He plays for hours on end to flush the bad memories from his mind. Surprise, surprise, the man's wife files for divorce. The court gives her damn near everything she asks for—the house, the business, what's left of their cash assets, you name it. He waves goodbye to twenty-plus years without a second thought. His sole saving grace is she can't get her hands on the farm seeing's how he inherited the property in his name only. She owns the business and keeps it running, like she had all along. No one notices he's gone.

"There the man is, sitting in his filth-strewn farmhouse with only a piano for company. He doesn't gamble anymore, not that he could. Most of the little income he receives goes to child support. He can't afford a pot to piss in so he spends his days practicing at his piano. It distracts him from hunger and loneliness. There are days when, without even realizing it, he plays well into the night until he keels over from exhaustion, prostrate on the floor. His life's a mess and—it's a bit of a stereotype, I suppose—but he takes to drinking. During the rare weeks he can scrape a few dollars together, he makes his way to a bar in Garden where he drains beers until he's roaring drunk. Once in a great while, he picks up a woman and they screw on the seat of his truck after closing time. Most of them are alcoholics themselves, divorcées looking for a shred of companionship. He's so blitzed out of his mind, he can't remember a thing of it most mornings. Besides, he's past the point of caring.

"What he feels most of all is shame. I'm talking about a shame that clings to you and haunts your every waking minute.

A shame so strong the longest, hottest shower of your life couldn't begin to wash it away. You could go on a bender until your blind drunk and can't see straight enough to walk. Even in those depths, the shame will burrow its way into the recesses of your mind and take root there. You could fall to your knees, puke your guts until there's not a drop left to disgorge—that dread-filled specter of shame will be all that remains.

"You'll ponder ending this disaster of life every day but hold short. The only way to atone for the monster you let yourself become is to parade your shame for all to see. Scorn is your antidote and only friend. You can't elude the shame because it's a part of you and oozes from your pores. Even worse, the harder you try to move on and forget it, the more you're reminded what an irredeemable screw-up you are. It eats away at you until there's nothing else left to think about. The biggest curse of having a mind like a steel trap is you remember every awful thing you've ever said or done to another person, and you're damn near sick with shame from all the destruction and grief you've brought onto the world. I'm willing to bet you know a thing or two about this type of shame, Mr. Hirsch."

With downcast eyes, Hirsch avoided the indictment of Shaw's gaze.

"The man's pushing fifty at this point and knows he has nothing left to offer the world. He figures he's screwed his life up so bad, it won't be long before he loses control of his truck driving home from the bar and annihilates himself. Hasn't seen his kids in months since his house is too much of a mess to bring them over. He's what you might call hitting bottom. It's in this pit of despair that the last person he'd expect to be his salvation comes along—his younger brother.

"The man's damn near a recluse by this time. He only goes out to eat or visit the tavern. Otherwise, he sits in his garbage-strewn home, plays piano, sleeps a fitful hour or two on the floor, and tries to ignore the outside world as best he can. That all changes when his brother comes stumbling back into his life. You see, the prodigal son is fresh out of jail for the umpteenth time. His family loved the crazy kid but his father's dead, his mother's long gone to the southwest, and his sister's turned into this bigshot who can't afford to have her jailbird brother around, much as she adores him. The brother has no choice but to seek out his equally disgraced older sibling. Without even asking permission, he moves himself right into the farmhouse.

"You'd think having two unhinged drunks with mental-health issues living together would be a recipe for disaster, right? Maybe so, but they bring out each other's strengths. The rest of the world might not see it that way, mind you, but that's what happened. The younger brother is an idiot, but he has this uncanny flare for criminal machinations. His older brother flirted with breaking the law—mostly stupid shit like speeding, driving drunk, cutting corners at work—but it'd never occurred to him to make a living outside the law. That is, until his younger brother convinces him that with his skills, they could make a ton of money stealing and fencing property. The older brother imposes a sense of discipline in his wayward sibling. He gets him to cut down on the drinking, the hellraising, and generally making an ass of himself. Tells him the only way this would work is if they both laid low and kept quiet. Lo-and-behold, the kid brother does. For the next two or three years, they both stay out of trouble and draw as little attention to themselves as possible. The neighbors assume they're a couple eccentric middle-aged men living in poverty on an old farm. People probably assume they're gay, who the hell knows.

"The man's still got the chops he learned in twenty-plus years of running a business. With the man's pickup truck, they start pulling small-time jobs. Stealing scrap metal, stripping copper wiring from vacant homes, boosting propane tanks and selling them out of state off the books, you name it. Most folks would get themselves blown up or even killed trying this tomfoolery. The man knows what he's doing, and it's often days before the real owner even catches on. The boys hit upon their grand scheme—tapping lines to run pilfered natural gas to other houses. Friends of his delinquent younger brother, mostly. Poof! No more expensive heating bills during the long winter. Now and then the gas company catches on and seals it off, but folks appreciate any small break they get. Makes them turn a blind eye to whatever else the brothers are doing. It's real Robin Hood shit when you think about it.

"It all hums along fine for a couple years until the younger one gets cocky. He's had drug problems most of his life—using and dealing alike. He can't resist the temptation of getting back into the game. Dealing's one thing and the man could ignore it so long as he wasn't involved, but the kid brother begins showing all the signs of using himself. Starts to become unreliable, misses 'work' more often than not, backslides into his old habits of spending late nights out at the tavern, and picking fights with the wrong folks. Soon enough, he vanishes for long stretches—days at a time. Then, when the man musters up the courage to confront him and help him get clean, his brother disappears. It'll be days before he finds out it was too late to do a damn thing. He's dead. Dead because a meddlesome little fool decides to stick his nose where it doesn't belong.

"At the end of the day, there the man is. He's destroyed his career, lost his family, blown through a small fortune, has little to call his own but an abandoned old farm in a dying part of the country. He's as much a forsaken bastard as the day he was born. The only person who ever showed him an ounce of loyalty is gone as well. If I said a man in that position could be dangerous, you will agree. A man like that could be desperate." Shaw cracked his knuckles. "What would you do if you had nothing left to lose?"

Shaw sat back, his monologue complete. He folded his arms across his chest and looked straight at Hirsch.

Hirsch returned his stare for a long moment. "That's one hell of a story, Lionel, but I don't really know why you're telling it to me. What exactly do you want from me?"

"There's two points I want to get across to you. First of all, it's best you know Mr. Severson hoodwinked you into this so-called investigation. In case you haven't already picked up on this, Mr. Severson's motivations were not all that pure."

"I get that. He wants to run for prosecuting attorney next year. He thinks getting tough on crime will help."

"Mr. Hirsch, I can assure you if Mr. Severson or any other cop in this county wanted to get tough on crime, there are more than enough criminals to round up. Hell, I could turn CI and haul in dozens. You and I both know this is all a personal vendetta against me and my family."

"Okay, and why's that?" Hirsch asked. Kyle did mention the Shaw family's attempt to discredit old Judge Severson for going too hard after Marcus Shaw in sentencing. Grudges die hard. But Hirsch wanted to hear firsthand.

Lionel Shaw laughed. "Surely you've figured it out by now—Kyle Severson is my half-brother."

What on earth was this nonsense? Hirsch wondered. He looked at Shaw with raised eyebrows, encouraging him to volunteer more information.

"If you need me to draw a picture," Shaw continued, "I'm happy to oblige. Judge Thomas Severson is my father. Our families ran in the same circles for years. Old Thomas had an affair with my mother fifty-odd years ago. I'm the result of that union. For the longest time, few folks knew about it, especially Eleanor Severson or the rest of the judge's family."

"Wait a minute," Hirsch interrupted. "I thought you said your sister sat you down when you were young and said you weren't one of them?"

"I wondered about that for the longest time myself. Truth is, I have no clue how she found out. Catherine is incredibly perceptive. If anyone could pick up on a clue, it's her."

"How in hell did the judge keep that so well under wraps?"

"Thomas and my father, Jimmy Shaw, struck a deal—if Jimmy agreed to raise the child as their own and never breathe a word about it to anyone, Thomas would keep money flowing to my folks like clockwork each month. In the end, they agreed and took responsibility for raising me. Granted they didn't put in much effort, but they did it. They had Tom Severson over a barrel and took full advantage of it."

"So, what happened?" Hirsch asked.

"To his credit, the old judge kept up his end of the bargain for many years. After my old man passed away, he made sure the money kept coming to Mom, even after she moved out of state. In his old age, though, he must've decided enough was enough. One day, the money dried up. The checks stopped arriving in the mail. Now mom didn't seem to complain much about this herself. She had enough from Dad's estate and the judge's money to live a cozy life in Arizona."

"Hold on," Hirsch said. "How'd you find out about these payments?"

"I didn't know for years. Even long after I realized Jimmy wasn't my dad, I still didn't know about the money. No, it was after Jimmy died and I spent time going through all his papers when we cleared out the house that I figured it out. He had a real mess of them up in his office. Seems Pa kept records of all his income over the years—both on and off the books. At first, I couldn't figure out why in Sam Hill Judge Thomas Severson of all people kept sending my parents hundreds of dollars every month. Then it clicked and all made sense. I even confronted my mom about it. She was upset, believe me, but finally came clean about my real father.

"I wasn't of the mind to do a whole lot about it. Figured he gave my folks more than their fair share, and, as for me, I saw little point in harassing an old man after forty-plus years of penance. I made the mistake of telling Marc though. We got good and liquored up one night at the farmhouse, and it slipped out. That boy may've done mighty stupid things in his life but damn, he knew an opportunity when he saw one. He concocted a whole scheme. The judge was famous for putting in long hours and late nights during trial. One dark and quiet evening, we accosted him in the courthouse parking lot. Scared him real good. Well, we drove him where we could be alone, and Marc went to work doing what he does best. We threatened to expose him to the paper and all his colleagues unless he kept the money flowing—only to us this time."

"You blackmailed him in other words."

"Call it what you want, Mr. Hirsch. All I can say is it turned out to be a godsend after my wife divorced me and cleaned me out of my business and every dime I made. Severson's cash was the only way I could keep the farm on the peninsula. We also made him promise to retire from the bench. I couldn't've cared less, honestly, but Marc had enough of his shit and wanted him gone."

"Okay, I get that, but there's one problem. Judge Severson died a couple years ago. Isn't this all over?"

"A setback, yes, but once again, Marc worked his magic. After Tom died, we put the squeeze on his squeaky-clean son, Kyle. We knew he had big plans in mind for his own career. In a small town like Escanaba, a scandal like that could taint the Severson name forever. Like I said, Eleanor Severson didn't have a clue about all this. From what I gathered, Kyle idolized his father and would do anything to keep us quiet. For two-plus years, he's held up his end of the bargain.

Hirsch swooned in his chair. The blood drained from his face and a sick feeling spread across the pit of his stomach. His closest friend had played him from the beginning. All the solicitude and attention foisted upon Hirsch was little but a ploy to lure Hirsch into his scheme. Set up the Shaws, put them behind bars, and stop the payments. Who'd believe a couple white-trash jailbirds?

As if reading Hirsch's mind, Shaw said, "And that's where you come into this whole damn mess. Kyle couldn't go after us himself, so he conscripted a goddamn fool to do his dirty work for him. It backfired on him though. After you spilled the beans that night about who sent you, we paid him a visit. Shook him down for double what he was sending us, and a promise that you'd leave us the fuck alone. Guess you ignored that last part."

"Wait, what? Kyle knew we'd met? Did he know you beat me senseless?"

"He knew every fucking detail, man. Of course, he had to play dumb with you to keep his secret. You know the old saying, 'with friends like these ...'" Shaw's voice trailed off, and he gazed out the window.

Hirsch needed to process this new information, but it was neither the time nor the place.

"All right, you said there were two things you wanted to tell me. What's the second?" Hirsch asked.

Shaw squared himself toward Hirsch and raised his index finger. "Let's not beat around the bush—you killed my brother. I know you had your reasons and, sure, they may seem noble to you. I consider you to be a pawn in all this. None of that matters to me. I'll level with you Hirsch—Marc was a genuine asshole. Hell, I'm no psychologist, but he could've even been a socio-path. But he was my brother, and he was the only member of my family who ever showed me an ounce of goodwill. I can't let that go unanswered. I won't even get into what my sister might do to you. God knows she loved the little brat too in her own way.

"I'm putting you on notice I'm coming after you. It may be tomorrow; it may be ten years from now. Mark my words, I am going to hunt you down and make you suffer and pay for what you've done to us. I want you to live with the fear and anguish I've felt the past few months since you started on my case.

Maybe I'll even pay that little schoolteacher sweetheart of yours a visit. It will not be pretty and, I can assure you, it won't be pleasant."

Shaw shoved his chair back with a screech of its feet against the floor. He flipped a twenty on the table. "Breakfast is on me. I hope you enjoyed it. You never know what your last meal might be." With a tip of his soiled ball cap, Shaw strolled out of the busy café and into the sundrenched light of a Saturday morning. Hirsch's gaze followed Shaw as he proceeded up Cedar Street until disappearing from view.

Hirsch's cold, uneaten omelette stared up at him. Shaw's pronouncement squelched his appetite, and nausea roiled his stomach. With his mind racing, Hirsch assessed their hour-long conversation. He had little doubt Shaw could make good on his pledge. Whether he intended to murder Hirsch or merely scare him into fleeing Schoolcraft County, he didn't know. The black dog of paranoia hovered over him, omnipresent and unshakeable.

Welcome to hell.

Chapter 16

Hirsch moved through the world a haunted man in the week following his encounter with Lionel Shaw. Shaw's specter loomed around every corner. The rustle of the brush out in the field left Hirsch's heart pounding. A strange car passing his house sent him peering through the blinds on trembling knees. He took to packing Murray's .38 Special around the clock despite lacking a concealed carry permit. The weight of its steel offered the security of a fighting chance. Loath to draw anyone else into danger, he retreated into himself. His truck and home became his cocoon. The outside world, his prison.

Paranoia is a feeling unlike any other. It's distinct from the emotion of fear and divorced from the unease of anxiety. Paranoia takes the most benign happenings and twists them into a malevolent howl of unrelenting anguish. Trusted friends and neighbors merit a second look, with suspicion replacing comfort. The unknown vanquishes the familiar. Hirsch fell headfirst into the vertigo of paranoia and never looked back. At night, he shoved his dresser against the bedroom door and laid awake with his loaded pistol beneath his pillow. A coiled rope adorned his windowsill in case Shaw resolved to roast him alive in his own home. On a good night, a couple hours of tormented sleep was his sole relief.

Shaw's opening salvo came in the early hours of a Tuesday morning after Hirsch drifted to sleep. Tamed by an expired Valium purloined from the medicine cabinet, he lingered in the bliss of dreamless respite. The crack of a rifle shot, followed by the tinkling of shattering glass roused him from his rest. Awake in a heartbeat, he bolted upright. Tires squealed outside as a vehicle hurtled south along Steuben Avenue. Reeling from the sedative, Hirsch wobbled his way downstairs to find his living-room window shot out. Shattered glass blanketed the couch and floor. A blackened hole now defaced the opposite wall above the television. With the blade of a Swiss Army Knife, Hirsch dislodged the bullet and held it before his eyes. He rotated the disfigured slug between his thumb and index finger, examining it in the gray morning light.

This was no assassination attempt. All the houselights were dark, and Shaw had no way of knowing whether Hirsch occupied the living room. Rather, it was Shaw's way of announcing his campaign against Hirsch—as promised, one of protracted terror. It had its intended effect—Hirsch's torment rivaled his night in Lionel's basement.

Logic told him he should get out. Quit his job, load his truck, and vanish in the dead of night. True, he'd be out of work and broke again within weeks, but remaining in the UP was a death sentence. If need be, he could beg his ex-wife for a few dollars to scrape by on. That humiliation was slightly preferable to execution by gunfire. Still, he couldn't bring himself to give up. The Shaws of this world held sway for too long. Vanishing would only hand them one more victory. After agonizing days of handwringing, Hirsch knew what he had to do. It was time to confront Kyle Severson. Kyle set this chain of events into motion and Kyle needed to end it.

Early Wednesday morning, he drove into Escanaba and parked near the Delta County Courthouse. A cool breeze blew off the bay, and Hirsch paused on the sidewalk for a moment's respite from the tumult and turmoil in his life. Paranoia snatched that moment away in an instant. Could Shaw be watching him from atop the Harbor Tower? The drab cylinder betrayed no hint of a lone man touting a 30-30 rifle, but Hirsch hurried through the courthouse door all the same. He found his way to the Prosecuting Attorney's office and presented himself at the front desk.

"I'm here to see Deputy Severson," Hirsch said.

"You have an appointment?" the clerk asked.

"No, but tell him Ben Hirsch is here to see him. He'll make time."

"One moment," she said before dialing an interoffice call to Severson.

"Mr. Severson, you have a Ben Hirsch to see you. He's not on the schedule," the clerk said. "Okay, I'll tell him," she continued after a pause.

"He'll be down in a few minutes. Wait here," she said to Hirsch.

As promised, Kyle emerged minutes later wearing a dark business suit and a tight smile on his face.

"Good to see you, buddy," he said with his hand extended. "You in town for work?"

"I thought we might have a word in private," Hirsch replied, ignoring Kyle's proffered hand. "About that matter we've been discussing, you know."

Kyle's smile remained fixed on his face, but the flinch in his eyes told Hirsch his friend had little desire to talk. "I'm afraid it's a rather busy day," he said. "I'm due in court soon. How about we get together for coffee or lunch later this week?"

"It can't wait, Kyle," Hirsch said, determined to not let his friend squirm out of this confrontation. "Let's have a word in your office. It should only take a few minutes."

Hirsch caught the clerk gazing at them askance. He had little doubt she listened in on the whole conversation. Kyle saw this as well, as he hesitated and threw a glance her way.

"Fine, Ben. I'm afraid I can only give you ten minutes at most. The last thing I need is a contempt of court fine."

"I think we can cover what we need to discuss."

Kyle buzzed them through the door with his badge, holding it open for Hirsch. It closed behind them with a click. They turned a corner and followed the utilitarian hallway before reaching Kyle's tidy office. His window looked out over the blue expanse of the Little Bay de Noc. A tranquil view for a troubled man.

Kyle slammed the door behind them. "What is it you needed to discuss with me so badly you had to interrupt me at work?" Kyle elbowed past him and walked behind his desk. He faced Hirsch with arms crossed.

"When were you planning on telling me Lionel Shaw is your brother?"

Kyle stared back at him with unblinking eyes and set jaw. "I didn't think it was relevant." Kyle paused. "Besides, he's my half-brother if you must know."

"Brother, half-brother, cousin, what the hell does it matter? I want to know why you lied to me and sent me on a wild-goose chase. What was all that nonsense about helping the community?" Hirsch asked, his voice rising and quivering in frustration.

"Woah now. Simmer down." Kyle held up his hands with his fingers extended. It couldn't look good for his colleagues to hear a screaming match in his office. "Listen, back when we first got in touch, I could tell you were in a bad way. I've known you long enough. You're the type of guy who needs a purpose in life. We were worried you might hurt yourself. We couldn't—"

"Oh, so getting me mixed up with a couple homicidal meth heads was for my benefit? Is that what you're telling me?" Hirsch shouted.

"Let me finish. And stop yelling, for Chrissake. I wanted to help you. I'm sure that's more than most of your so-called friends or former colleagues might have done. I could've ignored you and kicked you to the curb like the others. Need I point out you're the laughingstock of the bar? You know how embarrassing it is to get disbarred for screwing your client? Jesus, Ben.

"I took a chance. I took a chance on you. I invited you here, put a roof over your head until you pieced your life together, and found you a job. And what's more, I gave you an opportunity to be part of a real case again. Where you could make a difference for the community. Then you had to go and kill a man. Who the hell asked you to do that?"

"Let me remind you how this all came to pass," Hirsch said. He struggled to restrain himself from leaping across the desk and wringing Kyle's neck. "You recruited me to spy on a couple deadbeats running a crime ring. You kept the whole damn operation on the down low and begged me not to mention it to another soul. We met in secret, and you fed me a bunch of documents to review. You claimed it had to be this way because the county couldn't be seen as targeting the Shaw brothers. All hell would break loose if their sister found out, right? Truth is, the Shaw family's been blackmailing you and your dad for years. What frightens you more than anything is a scandal coming back and tarnishing your beloved father's reputation. You knew if you went after them yourself, they'd spill the beans on your family's dirty laundry. It'd all be over. No more PA job, and sure as hell no judgeship in your future. Besides, I'm not so sure it wasn't about the money all along. Word is, the Shaws shook down your old man for years. Now Lionel's doing the same to you. It'd be nice to not have to pay that any longer."

Kyle seethed across the desk. "I suppose you feel real proud of yourself coming in here and lecturing me like this. Amazing a fella like you thinks he can claim the moral high ground on anything. Let me explain something to you, Ben. I want to make sure you understand this. Do you think you can do that? Thomas Severson was a modern-day saint. He wholeheartedly gave his life to the people of Escanaba. He did damn well in law school and could've landed with a big-league firm in Chicago—or anywhere else for that matter—and made a boatload of money. Instead, you know what he did? He goes home and hangs his own shingle. He spends five years practicing law as a small-town, jack-of-all-trades lawyer. Handles divorces, trusts and estates, misdemeanors, you name it. People like him. They see he's honest, trustworthy, and knows what he's doing. Remember when qualities like that mattered? He gets himself elected Prosecuting

Attorney when he's only thirty years old—the youngest PA in the state. Ten years, *ten years* he spends slaving away to keep this county safe by locking up criminals. Defense attorneys appreciate him too since he's fair and will cut a deal. He knows it doesn't make sense to lock up a man who's the family's sole breadwinner. Based on their respect, the people elect him judge.

"My dad spends the next thirty years on the bench. He had plenty of opportunities to move on to bigger and better things, mind you. Twice the governor offers him a spot on the state Court of Appeals. And you know what, he turns them down. Why? Because he loves his hometown and can't tear himself away. You wanna know the most amazing part—this whole time he's also being a husband and raising a family. He worked his ass off all day long, but he came home in the evenings for dinner with us. He made sure he spent the weekends with his wife and kids too. Most nights he'd work another couple hours after we went to sleep. That's more than you can say for most dads who don't work half as hard as my father did. Don't even get me started on all the good he did for our town. He served on the school board, he volunteered for any organization that asked, did several stints as a Rotary Club officer. Hell, he was even a Boy Scout troop leader."

Of course he was, Hirsch thought. He resisted the urge to slow clap at Kyle's virtuoso display of filial piety. Kyle wasn't finished.

"All of this good he does for the world but, lo-and-behold, he makes one mistake. One *single* mistake that nearly destroys it all. I'm sure you can picture it well enough, Ben. It's the sixties, all the town's movers and shakers are spending Friday night out at the Elks Club. They're guzzling cocktails and swapping sea stories. Temptation can take down even the strongest of us. You know that as well as I do. My father has a one-night stand with the pretty wife of the town's biggest rascal. I'm not making excuses for what he did. It was wrong and I thank God my mom's never found out. I aim to keep it that way. Fact is, we all make mistakes, but we shouldn't be punished the rest of our lives."

Kyle pointed his finger at Hirsch and lowered his voice. "What Jimmy Shaw did to my dad and what his sons have done to me is unconscionable. Hell, it's blackmail, pure and simple. We paid the price for far too long, and I'm not going to let them keep destroying our lives. You wanted a purpose in life, I gave you one, Ben. You can't tell me it didn't feel good."

"Feel good? *Feel good?* What the hell are you saying? Are you trying to tell me it feels good to snoop around like the neighborhood creep? That it feels good to get tied to a chair and get the shit kicked out of you by a couple deranged hillbillies? That is feels good to ambush and kill a man, then spend the rest of the night praying that a seventy-three-year-old man you dragged into this whole mess doesn't die on you? That it feels good to have a homicidal lunatic out to murder you any chance he gets? Christ, I don't even know where to start with that."

"Wait, wait," Kyle interrupted. "What the hell are you talking about? Who on earth's trying to murder you?"

"Oh, come off it. You can put two and two together. Lionel Shaw knows I killed his brother. He knows where I live, he knows where I work, he knows everything he needs to about me. Last week, he tracked me down in Manistique and said he's coming after me. Yesterday, a bullet shattered my window in the middle of the night. For all we know, he's watching us as we speak. I'm a dead man walking, my friend."

"Holy shit. Why didn't you tell me earlier? Let me see what I can do from our end. I have connections over in Schoolcraft. We can have an officer keep an eye on your house. Would that work?"

"Kyle," Hirsch said, shaking his head, "I've had enough of your help. I'm done worrying at this point. It's liberating in a way. Facing death every waking minute does that."

"Well, if you don't want my help, what do you want? Why'd you come here?" Kyle said, near shouting. "Is it money? Are you trying to shake me down too like Shaw did?"

"Oh, please. Don't even start. And fuck you for even suggesting I'd do that. The whole reason I came here today is to paint a picture of what you've done. You've already killed one person and, in all likelihood, I'm going to die too in the next few weeks. When that happens, the blood is on your hands."

Motionless, Kyle avoided eye contact with Hirsch. The two stood silent for a full minute. The ringing of Kyle's desk phone interrupted the lull. Kyle hit the speaker button.

"Yes, Janelle."

"Your hearing before Judge Lundegaard in the Kirby case is in five minutes. Courtroom C."

"Thank you. I'm leaving now." Kyle hung up and returned his attention to Hirsch.

"You heard her. I have to go. I'm sad it came to this. Contrary to what you seem to believe, I had your best intentions at heart when I brought you here. I could waste more time defending myself, but why bother. Like I said, if you want police protection, I can make it happen. Otherwise, there's little I can do for you. Maybe it's best you leave for good. You made a mistake coming home."

Kyle gestured toward the door. Hirsch opened it halfway, preparing to leave the office ahead of Kyle but stopped.

"Humor me with one more question," Hirsch said. "Suppose this all played out like you planned it. I play detective and unravel the Shaw's big scheme. I turn the evidence over and the police arrest them. Lord knows they're going to make every excuse under the sun to beat the charges. What would've prevented them from exposing your father—or you, for that matter? Wouldn't they have every reason to squeal once they had nothing left?"

"Perhaps. But really, who's going to believe a couple cons trying to weasel their way out of a charge. Besides, I'm not dumb enough to write them personal checks in my name or anything. Give me a little credit."

Hirsch shrugged. Keep your damn mouth shut and walk on out of here, he told himself.

"I remember something, Kyle. Back in our law school days, Allison invited Jess over one evening for drinks. They'd had a few and probably didn't think I could hear them from the other room. This was right before the two of you married. I remember distinctly hearing Jess confide to Allison she'd always had a bit of a crush on me, ever since that Saturday morning you first showed up with her at the tailgate before the Spartans-Badgers game. The reason she planned to marry you was because she knew the life you'd have together. Her exact words were, 'Kyle might be dull, but he's an honest, decent guy. He'll make a good husband.' If only she knew what a lying, manipulative sack of shit you turned out to be."

Kyle's fist crushed into Hirsch's face before he had any chance to react. The impact slammed Hirsch into the door jamb.

His hand shot up to cover the searing pain in his cheekbone. Hirsch dissolved into laughter as he slid to the floor.

Jesus, Ben, you've been hit more in the last six months than the rest of your life combined, Hirsch realized.

"Oh, you think this is funny, do you?" Kyle said. "That's always been your problem—you think life's one big goddamn joke. Get out of here, Ben. Just get the fuck out. And don't let me catch you near my house or my family ever again, you hear me?"

Hirsch looked at Kyle through one eye. The prosecutor huffed in rage, his face scarlet, and his hair disheveled. Hirsch shook his head and gathered his wits to leave. With his head spinning, he crawled to his feet and navigated the long hallway to the front entrance. The knot swelling on his face drew curious stares from Kyle's colleagues. Hirsch could've made it ugly for Kyle and had him arrested. In reality, all he wanted was out.

Upon reaching the staircase, Hirsch hurried down the stairs and burst forth into the bright sunshine of a humid summer day. All around him, ordinary folks went about their lives. Tourists strolled along the sidewalk and laughed, enjoying a glorious morning in the UP. None worried about being trailed, hunted down, and executed at a moment's notice by a vindictive concert pianist. Trouble had come for Hirsch. With profound unease, he moved through the world haunted by a menace of his own creation.

Chapter 17

OVER THE FOLLOWING DAYS, HIRSCH never laid eyes on his nemesis. Shaw's presence nonetheless shadowed him everywhere. Shaw left a sprinkling of *memento mori* for Hirsch to discover. Several gestures struck Hirsch as cliché, like the dead sparrow left on his front porch with a gruesome twist in its neck, or finding the door of his truck smeared with dog feces. More disturbing was the manila envelope addressed to "Detective" Hirsch in his mailbox. An eight-by-ten black-and-white photograph of Hirsch exiting his house rested inside. The candid picture itself was unremarkable. The chilling part was the absence of Hirsch's eyes. Two hollow holes emitting an eerie glow stared back at him.

Hirsch distracted himself with work. He volunteered for assignments far and wide across the peninsula. He'd rise early and drive to Grand Marais in the predawn hours to begin a ten-hour shift, then head west the next day to Iron Mountain and the rolling hills of the Huron range. Where he once relished the sights, sounds, and smells of the land, he now shuffled through the day like a zombie. He often came home unable to recall a single event. The liberation of exercise mutated into a slow march to his inevitable violent death.

Hirsch tried calling Lauren a handful of times to plead his case. After not even reaching her voicemail, he concluded she blocked his number and gave up. Alone, Hirsch passed the evenings in his somber home. He moved the television to his bedroom and wasted hours enshrouded in gloom, illuminated only by the screen's flickering glow. He'd tried reading but lacked the concentration to do it justice. Letting that stimulation fall to the wayside, Hirsch retreated from shadows into darkness. His father's pistol was his closest companion. He practiced drawing it from beneath his pillow, releasing the cylinder with one hand, reloading, and aiming at the door while crouched behind his bedframe. Tormented by an invisible persecutor, he became a prisoner in his home. His jailor lurked beyond, scheming new means to taunt his captive.

THE ASSIGNMENT PIERCED HIRSCH WITH dread the moment he answered the call. Since his run-in with Lionel Shaw, he'd avoided the Garden Peninsula for any reason. It was Shaw's territory, and Hirsch had scant desire to bring the fight to his sworn enemy's front door. His control over the matter evaporated when the gas company dispatcher deployed him south of Garden to inspect a reported leak. As he drove down State Route 183, the symptoms of an anxiety attack had that plagued him in recent weeks struck anew. His heart rate spiked, waves of nauseous energy roiled his core, and sweat broke out across his entire body. Not even the air conditioner running full-blast could overcome the discomfort of mental anguish. The county road leading to Shaw's farm zoomed past on his left. Only a couple months earlier, he'd crouched outside the perimeter of Shaw's property to play detective and ferret out a supposed criminal syndicate. His life was never the same after that evening.

Hirsch's anxiety dissipated as he cleared the town of Garden and reached his destination. With the confidence of a seasoned veteran, he checked each line in the designated territory. The detector wand swung with an effortless flow across the ground. Rarely stumbling or missing a spot, he made efficient use of his time. Midway through the afternoon, he encountered a possible leak on a line bisecting a potato field. Needing to pinpoint the location, Hirsch retrieved the bar holer from his truck. He positioned the sounding rod over the line, grabbed the plunger, and plowed the rod several inches into the loam. The solitude of the lonely, windswept field forced him to consider his predicament.

"That one's for the years you wasted at work, not giving a shit about anything but yourself," he said. He thrust the rod deeper.

"That one's for Allison, Alice, and Lauren," he said, jabbing the rod to punctuate each of their names. He gripped the plunger handle with both hands and plumbed further into the soil.

"That one's for being foolish enough to fall for all this nonsense in the first place." Hirsch gave the rod one final jab, driving it well into the ground below.

"And that one's for you, Ben. God-willing you've learned something from this mess, you pathetic screw-up."

Panting from the exertion, he stumbled backwards with his hands on his knees. Once he recovered, Hirsch bored another couple test holes. Satisfied he'd zeroed in on the leak's source, he radioed-in the location meriting follow-up by the repair crew.

With the hour past six, Hirsch called it a day. Exhausted from de minimis sleep and the torment of living in fear every waking minute, Hirsch wanted nothing more than to return home and collapse in his sanctuary.

To avoid a second pass by Shaw's place, Hirsch took the cutoff along Little Harbor Road and back through the peninsula's eastern shore to Manistique. Within a mile, the pavement gave way to the crunch of the gravel surface. As the sun hung low in the west, the tall trees cast long shadows over the roadway. With the road to himself, Hirsch relaxed for the first time all day. He basked in the warm glow of sunset, and the accumulated tension flowed out of his enervated body.

The explosion of his rear window into a thousand glass shards shattered his calm. A smattering trickled down his back and lodged sharp against his flesh. A cracked spiderweb of jagged lines fanned out across his windshield. The unmistakable outline of a bullet hole stood at its epicenter.

Hirsch's eyes darted to his rearview mirror—Lionel Shaw's Ford F-150 followed a hundred feet behind. Shaw leaned out the window clutching a pistol while sizing up his prey for a second shot. Hirsch jerked the steering wheel to the left as Shaw pulled the trigger. A thunderous boom filled the air as the slug whizzed past Hirsch's truck.

Galvanized with a singular awareness, Hirsch floored the pedal. He tore down the road, raising a flurry of spun-out gravel and dust in his wake. Shaw drew closer, his truck materializing through the billowing beige cloud. The Toyota's overtaxed engine groaned as it labored to outpace Shaw's powerful Ford. Hirsch's only hope was to swerve and leverage as much roadway as possible while maintaining their dwindling separation. Trees whipped by on either side of the road with needles of sunlight slicing through each. Hirsch's speedometer crested seventy, and the narrow road ahead melted into a blur.

As the roadway curved northeast along Parent Bay, Shaw rammed Hirsch. A sickening crunch and whine of crumpling metal rang out. The Toyota twisted to the right, sending him careening toward the ditch. Hirsch gripped the wheel, fighting inertia to regain control and stay on the road. The truck fishtailed as it flirted with the lip of the ditch. A hair's breadth further would have sent him cartwheeling side-over-side to be pulverized by the forest. Recovering control, Hirsch jammed the gas and took his truck over eighty. Shaw followed close behind. Hirsch glanced back through the roiling dust cloud. A possessed gleam consumed his pursuer's face. He grimaced with eyes riveted on Hirsch and hands white-knuckled around the steering wheel.

Just ignore him, Ben. Keeping this rig upright is your only shot at survival.

The two engaged in a cat-and-mouse battle as they tore down the road. From the other direction, a blue SUV approached their direct path. Hirsch laid on the horn to warn the motorist. The driver swerved off the road and pancaked into the ditch at the last second. The Ford's bumper again ground against his. Shaw gave up on firing his gun at Hirsch—his truck served as a deadlier weapon. As they hurtled eastward, a lethal ninety-degree turn taking the road northward towards Thompson awaited.

You know this land as well as anyone, Ben. Use it.

With shaking hands, Hirsch gripped the wheel with all his strength and aimed his truck straight at the mouth of a private roadway. The dead-end dirt road was his one shot at outsmarting Shaw. From his time spent out on the lake, Hirsch knew the peninsula terminated in a ragged series of limestone cliffs. A sixteen-foot drop gave way to a narrow gravel beach and the lapping waves of Lake Michigan beating against the shore. Hirsch thundered down the winding dirt road, his truck bucking along the rutted trail. Shaw followed at his heels. The road emptied into an abandoned field, and Hirsch tore through the tall foliage with Shaw right behind him. The invisible cliffs lay straight ahead.

Resigned to fate, Hirsch squeezed his eyes shut and cranked the wheel with mere feet left to spare. He screamed as his mind went blank. His truck spun to the right, doing two three-sixties as it ripped through the overgrown clearing. A withered birch tree brought him to a dead stop when the truck slammed into it at full speed. The left side of Hirsch's body bashed against the door with a dull thud. Dazed and wounded, he'd survived. He opened his eyes.

Shaw's truck was nowhere to be seen, but a deafening crash roared across the area as Shaw's truck alighted off the cliff and slammed against the rocks and brush sixteen feet below.

An ooze of moisture coated Hirsch's brow and trickled over his eyelids. He reached a hand up to wipe it clean. His palm came away red. No sense in worrying about that now, he concluded as he brushed his bloody hand on his pantleg. Hirsch killed the engine and extracted himself from the driver's seat. Crawling out through the passenger door, he stepped into the abandoned field. His limbs ached and complained, but he shuffled to the cliff's edge and peered over.

Shaw's Ford lay in ruins. Though right-side up on the ground, the jagged limestone had pummeled, slashed, and crumpled the cabin's roof. Shattered glass blanketed the rocks. Ribbons of steam rose from the Ford's hissing engine while the stench of leaking gasoline perfumed the air. Despite pain coursing through his body, Hirsch picked his way down the cliffside, finding footholds that allowed him to ease down to the base. Once on level ground, Hirsch brandished his revolver and drew a bead on the Ford's mangled cabin and ruined windshield. Hirsch advanced one step at a time, creeping toward the vehicle and the body strapped into the driver's seat.

Shaw's blood-streaked visage turned to Hirsch. He appeared as little more than an undulating red mass of flesh filtered through a prism of shattered glass. Blood seeped from a deep cut on his forehead, and one eye had already swollen shut. Shaw gulped for air. His mouth moved in an attempt to speak, but no words formed through the stumps of his shattered teeth. Shaw elevated his right hand, displaying two crooked fingers. Scarlet-red flesh hung from them in ribbons. Shaw examined his hand in silence through his one good eye. Hirsch couldn't help but think that as Shaw lay there on the brink of death, the wounded man's sole concern was whether he would play piano again.

"I'll call for help," Hirsch said, at a loss for what else to do.

Shaw's bloodied hands fluttered in exasperation, and a low gurgle emitted from his throat. Hirsch retraced his steps up the jagged cliff until reaching his truck in the clearing. During the chase, his phone had dislodged from his pocket and skittered across the cabin floor. Hirsch crouched and peered through the open door before spotting it wedged beneath the passenger seat. He scrounged with one hand and recovered it. Though cracked along the display screen, it still operated. For the second time in a month, he dialed 911.

It took some effort convincing the dispatcher that Shaw's accident wasn't a hoax, but they agreed to dispatch a deputy and an ambulance. There was no explaining his way out of this, he realized. Delta County had him connected to Marcus Shaw's death. Even the most gullible cop wouldn't believe he came upon Lionel Shaw in a wrecked truck by pure coincidence. Though the accident took place in Schoolcraft County, Detective Springer would call him within days. Not wanting to be caught with a concealed weapon, he tossed his pistol in the glove compartment before hiking up the roadway to Little Harbor Road. He rested against a sugar maple and rubbed his palms into the sides of his head. The cut above his forehead throbbed with pain. He'd be sore as hell in the morning—a feeling he'd grown accustomed to over the past several months.

Within half an hour, flashing lights and a wailing siren heralded the arrival of an ambulance from the county hospital. A Schoolcraft County Sheriff's deputy followed soon after. The medics handed him a cold compress which he pressed against his head to slow the swelling. He led them down the road and through the clearing to Shaw's truck. The EMT crew worked with the deputy to pry the driver's door open on Shaw's truck. Once the door burst open, they extracted the broken spectacle of a man onto a gurney. The emergency crew labored to inch him up the cliff until they reached level ground. Amidst the noise and chaos of the scene, Lionel Shaw's high-pitched wail echoed through the clearing. A garbled snippet sounded to Hirsch like, "I can't feel 'em."

Shaw caught sight of Hirsch as the medics lifted the gurney into the ambulance. He yanked his oxygen mask aside with a mangled hand and said, "Just you wait, Hirsch. This isn't over yet! You hear me? This isn't—"

The twin doors of the ambulance slammed shut, cutting Shaw off. The ambulance pulled away, leaving a rising cloud of dust in its wake as it sped toward the county hospital. Hirsch spent the next twenty minutes giving a statement to the responding deputy. The young officer had his blond hair clipped high and tight and looked at Hirsch through clear blue eyes. Hirsch glanced at the deputy's nametag—Swanson. He jotted Hirsch's statement down in neat, precise ciphers into a black-bound notebook.

"You okay to drive home, or do we need a tow?" Deputy Swanson.

Hirsch's scratched, battered, and bullet-hole-ridden truck failed to inspire much confidence. Not exactly the best ad on wheels for Peninsula Energy.

"Well, she still runs. I think I'll be fine to drive it," he replied.

"Up to you, boss. She sure ain't pretty, but it's your call. I'd be more worried about your head if I were you. I can't force you, but try and have a doctor look at that. You're free to leave though. I need to run to town and get a wrecker out here for that mess," Deputy Swanson said, gesturing at the cliff where Shaw's Ford lay below.

The young deputy took one more look at the accident's carnage and whistled in sheer bewilderment. Hirsch nodded and thanked him. Deputy Swanson got into his patrol car and pulled away, leaving Hirsch alone on the windswept clearing.

Soon enough, the scars of their high-speed chase on the roadway would be all that remained of Shaw's pursuit. The evening sun faded away through the trees to the west, bathing the clearing in twilight. Hirsch saw no reason to linger. He crawled through the passenger door of his old companion truck and drove to Manistique in silence. Hirsch ignored the stares from passing motorists as he traveled along Little Harbor Road and onto Highway 2. He focused on nothing but getting home. The nightmare of a day couldn't come to a merciful close soon enough.

Upon arriving home, Hirsch parked in front of his house. As soon as he killed the engine, he regretted not pulling around back. True to character, Cromley stood perched on his porch with a Winston in hand.

"Jesus Ben, looks like you drove through a war zone. You out using it for target practice?" he said, canvassing the ruins of Hirsch's vehicle.

Hirsch didn't bother to look at his interrogator as he exited his truck. "I don't even know where to begin with this one. I'm not sure I'm ready either."

"I suppose I'll read about this in tomorrow's paper. Even our local coverage wouldn't pass up a story like this. Makes me wish I were still in the business."

"I don't doubt it, Mr. Cromley. All I can say is, thank heavens you're retired." God, please end this damn conversation and let me go inside, Hirsch thought.

"I do freelance work to keep me out of trouble, you know. Mostly human-interest pieces these days. I do get the itch for bare-knuckles journalism. Give it some thought. Remember—

you always want to be out ahead of the story," Cromley said, flashing a thin smile followed by a drag off his cigarette. Two columns of smoke filtered out of his nostrils as he stared at Hirsch and shook his head in disapprobation.

"I'll bear that in mind. Like I said, it's the last thing I want to think about right now."

Cromley nodded. He flicked his burnt-down Winston out into the garden to join the thousands of others decaying amidst the weeds and dead flowers.

"I'm glad you moved back to town, Ben. Life's a helluva lot more interesting with you around."

"Interesting's one way to put it." Hirsch walked toward his house. "I gotta get going. I'll see you around."

"Yes you will, Ben. Mark my words," Cromley said, followed by a disconcerting laugh that reverberated across the empty street. From the aviary behind the house, the shriek of a peacock echoed Cromley's laugh.

Exhausted, Ben retreated into the relative sanctity of his adopted home. For the first time in weeks, he collapsed on the couch, no longer in fear of being shot in the back. The boarded-over window shrouded the room in welcome darkness. The gash on his forehead stung, but he no longer cared. Hirsch crossed his arms over his head and fell into a trance-like sleep.

The buzz of his phone minutes later wrestled Hirsch awake from what promised to be a night of vivid dreams. Without bothering to check the number, Hirsch answered the call.

"Hello," he groaned.

"Not surprised I woke you, Mr. Hirsch. I'd be catching up on rest too after what you went through."

Not this shit. Not right now. Detective Springer was the last person he wanted to deal with.

"What can I do for you, detective? I suppose you've heard this news."

"That I have, Ben. That I have." Springer's habit of repeating certain phrases grated on Hirsch's nerves. "Word travels quick in a small town like this. I'm not going to keep you any longer than I have to, so let me get on with what I have to say."

"All right." Hirsch hoped Springer meant what he said.

"Let me preface this by saying it's my belief you're a liar, you're a schemer, you're an opportunistic ne'er-do-well who came home because you had nowhere else to go. You've conned people with this whole good-guy 'I'm rehabilitated and starting over' routine. Personally, I don't buy it. Most of all, I believe you lied to me the entire time I interviewed you last month. Meth houses don't burst into flames for no reason and siblings of deceased meth dealers don't hunt down witnesses in their trucks. You're lying to protect someone. I don't know who it is yet, but I know you're not alone. By God, if I ever find out, I'll come after them with all I've got.

"Here's the deal though. Despite everything I've said, I'm not going to recommend charging you—for now. Fact is, with your truck riddled with bullets and you damn near killed, I don't think there's much of a case. Not to mention the medivac just airlifted my only living witness to a Green Bay hospital for spinal surgery. Even if he survives—well, I don't need to tell you he won't make the most compelling witness on the stand. You following me here, Hirsch?"

"Yeah, I am."

"Good, I thought so. Don't think you're out of the woods quite yet. If Shaw lives, there'll be a preliminary hearing to charge him. You'll be called to testify. Who knows, you may even get a second bite at the apple if this whole mess goes to trial. Knowing the perp's family, it wouldn't surprise me. My point is, you have two opportunities to perjure yourself. I'm warning you, one wrong word out of your mouth and I won't hesitate to put you in bracelets and nail you with charges. Is that clear?"

"I wouldn't expect anything else, Detective."

"Can I give you a piece of free advice?"

"Sure, why the hell not." Hirsch all but gave up on trying to rest—the universe was clearly conspiring against him. Humoring the detective for a minute might help.

"If I were you, I'd pack your shit up in that shot-to-hell truck of yours, hightail it over the bridge, and go back south where you belong."

"I thought about that," Hirsch said. "Problem is, I like my job here. I guess I feel like I'm useful for once in my life—doing good even."

"If this is what you consider 'doing good,' I'd hate to see you at your worst. Anyway, I could try to explain all this to you, but it probably won't make a difference. I'll be watching you, Hirsch. Stay if you like, but don't screw up."

"I appreciate the sentiments. It's Friday night, you should go home and enjoy yourself. They say it'll be a glorious summer weekend here," Hirsch said.

"Aren't they all these days. The same to you. Good night."

Hirsch ended the call and let the phone clatter to the floor. In a flash of insight, he snatched the phone up and powered it down. He'd had enough of this shit for one day. If it's that important, they'd leave a message.

As he waited for sleep to claw him back into unconsciousness, Hirsch reflected on the past three months. He'd started out as a disgraced, divorced, financially ruined former attorney seeking shelter in the only place he could think to go. A quarter of a year later, he'd destroyed the lives of two men he'd never met before. One was dead and—from Springer's comments—the other may as well be. Still, he couldn't deny he felt more alive than he had in years. He recalled Detective Springer's warning. You're on the last of your nine lives, Ben. Time to steer clear of the flame.

Chapter 18

AN ORANGE AND CRIMSON GLOW rippled across the eastern horizon as Saturday dawned over Manistique. Now in the early days of July, tourists and downstaters flooded into the UP, seeking the panacea of summer and distractions of wilderness. They flung open the shutters of mothballed summer cottages and breathed deep the crisp north air. Boaters and fishermen crowded Lake Michigan, their watercraft zipping to-and-fro across the lake's surface. Families crowded into Kitch-iti-kipi, hungry for a glimpse of the pellucid waters of the ancient spring. The world-weary resident Yoopers began the annual ritual of girding themselves against a spectacle more menacing than winter—the onslaught of visitors who knew nothing of their struggles and resilience the remaining nine months of the year.

Two weeks had passed since Hirsch's showdown with Lionel Shaw. He faced north atop the steel landing of the Manistique lighthouse, sheltered by the fire-engine-red tower from the brisk breeze borne aloft the lake's dark waters. His forearms rested along the powder-coated black railing suspended over the boulders below. The morning light gathered over town across the harbor. An ant-line of visitors silhouetted against the eastern horizon crept along the breakwater toward the lighthouse. For the moment, he had the landing to himself.

It felt like a lifetime ago that Hirsch cowered in the shadow of the lighthouse on a gloomy early-spring day, nursing a hangover and a budding nervous breakdown. That morning now felt like the nadir of his life. Despite falling short on his pledge to abstain from alcohol, he'd emerged from the past few months of ordeal stronger than when he fled Lansing. After his confrontation with Lionel Shaw, he'd taken a much-needed vacation in the Soo visiting his mother and renewing long-fallow relationships with his family. It was his first full day back home.

The vibration of Hirsch's phone jarred him out of his daydreaming. He groaned at seeing who was bothering him this early. Hirsch had never bothered to block Kyle's number.

"What do you want?" he said, answering the call. "I figured we were done with each other after our last meeting."

Kyle chuckled. "Maybe I let my emotions get the better of me." Hirsch offered nothing in response but the ruffle of the wind blowing about him. "Where the hell are you, Ben? It's windy as hell."

"I took a walk this morning along the lakeshore. Not many tourists this early. The wind's nice—keeps the mosquitoes away. What is it you want anyway? I suppose you've heard everything. Word travels quick whenever you're involved."

"I have, but that's not why I called. I've been trying to reach you the past week. I have a couple things to share with you." Hirsch had shut his phone off while in the Soo and never bothered to check his messages.

"Well, go for it, I guess. I'm listening."

"Lionel Shaw's in a spinal-rehab hospital in Green Bay. It doesn't sound good from what I've heard. Word is he's paralyzed from the waist down."

"All right, I already knew that. Do you expect me to be happy? I never wanted a damn thing to do with the man in the first place, let alone cripple him."

"Sure, sure, I get it," Kyle said. "There's another development you might've heard. The sheriff's office raided Shaw's farm on a search warrant after the crash. They found a shit-ton of stolen property tying him to dozens of crimes across the peninsula. Even if he walked on the attempted vehicular-murder charge, we have enough to put him away for years. Not even his sister can weasel him out of this mess. Ten to one he'll take a plea on it all and do time. I wanted to thank you, Ben. In a roundabout way, you did what I asked you to do."

"Wow, Kyle. I'm sure-as-shit glad to hear that. Too bad they nearly killed me, Marcus Shaw is dead, and your *half-brother* is in a goddamn hospital likely never to walk again. But hell, none of that matters since you'll get the conviction you needed. But here's the icing on the cake—Shaw's name is mud. There's no way anyone would believe him if he tried to ruin you or your father's name. Oh, not to mention no more blackmail money. Congratulations, my friend, well played."

Kyle was silent for a moment. "Look, all I'm trying to say is thank you and no hard feelings. I hope we can put all this behind us. Hell, maybe we can still have you over for dinner. I'll do my best to forget you wanted to screw my wife."

"We'll see about that," Hirsch said. Fat chance of him setting foot in the Severson house anytime soon. "Anything else I can do for you? I'd like to get back to enjoying the sunrise."

"Well, there is one more thing I should tell you. Word is Catherine Winslow's looking for you. I don't have a clue what she wants, but I'd be on your guard if I were you."

Hirsch sighed. "Seems to be my life as of late."

"Thought you should know. Do with it what you will. This is a strange place we live in, eh?"

"That I can't argue with." Hirsch ended the call without waiting for any more of Kyle's empty pleasantries.

Hirsch took a moment to review his messages from the past week. He stopped when he came across a two-word text from Lauren.

"Call me," it read.

Intrigued, he did as instructed. Lauren answered after a couple rings.

"Hello, stranger," she said.

"Hey there. I hope I didn't wake you."

"Nah, I'm up early grading test papers. Final grades are due Monday."

"I got your text. I'm a little surprised. I figured I'd never hear from you again."

"Yeah, about that—I read what happened. Maybe I jumped to conclusions last time we talked. I didn't know everything." Hirsch's run-in with Lionel Shaw had made the regional news. The attention accelerated his escape to the Soo.

"It's my fault, Lauren. I screwed up," Hirsch said. "I should've leveled with you about that asshole from the bar. Needless to say, I pissed off his family something bad."

"I guess what I'm trying to say is, maybe we could give it another shot—if you're still interested."

"Well you know, I never took you to Marquette for the

weekend like I promised." A shiver of anticipation ran through him at the thought of an entire weekend in bed with Lauren. He longed to trace his fingers along the contours of her figure as they lay overlooking Lake Superior.

"That does sound nice. It's just with work and all ..." Hesitation clouded her voice.

"Or we could do dinner in Escanaba," Hirsch offered.

"Dinner's perfect. I'm working at Lily's tonight, but I'm free tomorrow."

"Well in that case, how about I pick you up around seven?"

"Sounds delightful." Lauren lowered her voice and said, "Look, I have to get back to grading. I have another dozen midterms to get through, and some are real doozies. But here's one thought—maybe you could stay the night at my place if things go well."

"Now that I'll really look forward to. See you tomorrow evening."

Hirsch ended the call and slumped onto the landing, reclining his back against the cool wall of the lighthouse. The breeze died down, and the Zen-like repetitive crashing of the waves against the shore made him sleepy. At peace for the first time in months—if not years—Hirsch shut his eyes to enjoy a well-deserved respite. As the sensation of sleep trickled through his brain, his phone rang. He jolted into consciousness. *I'm ready to throw this fucking phone in the lake if it rings one more time,* he thought.

"Ben, this is Milo. Where the hell have you been?"

"Over east for a few days visiting family. I'm on vacation, remember? Just made it home last night."

"Oh, yeah, I forgot about that." Hirsch's whereabouts were

the least of Milo's worries. "Look, we had our supervisor in from corporate yesterday. We're running out of work checking lines, but I found enough in the budget to keep you on through September—if you want the work, of course."

Hirsch never banked on becoming a gas company employee, but he couldn't justify turning down work. The chance of recovering his law license in the near future was nil. Besides, it'd give him a couple more months before he'd need to flip burgers to make ends meet.

"That's one generous offer, Milo. Thank you," Hirsch said after taking it all into consideration. "Count me in."

"Good, I'm glad to hear that. Corporate wasn't thrilled at the added expense, but I dug in my heels and told them you were the best crew member we had."

"Well, I appreciate the vote of confidence," Hirsch said. "Milo?" he added after a pause.

"Yeah, what is it?"

"I want to thank you for taking a chance on me. Most folks wouldn't have."

"Don't mention it, Ben. I've been in this business long enough. I know talent when I see it. Keep it up and we'll be fine. Besides, if you want to thank someone, it's our friend Edgar. He told me I'd be a damn fool to offer the job to anyone else. I gotta run but enjoy the rest of your weekend over there."

"Will do, thanks."

Hirsch ended the call. Sitting in the shadow of the lighthouse, the radiant mercy of redemption cast his transgressions in a new light. Were these trials not all but a means of leading him to a state of grace? He gazed out across the harbor, and the profile of the townsite beyond drew his attention. A warm glow burnished the forest-green obloid of the water tower looming over the tree-studded horizon. Cleansed in spirit and emotion, Hirsch saw his hometown for all its worth—the crumbling pavement, the decay of the weather-beaten company-town houses, the silence of the shuttered papermill, the tattered but resilient perseverance of the town's remaining merchants, and the countless souls who, for better or worse, looked past the veneer of corruption to celebrate the ineffable mystery shrouded from the outsider. And it was in that moment Hirsch accepted his destiny lay not in material and carnal distractions, but in the embrace of humanity. *It's time to begin your life, Ben,* he told himself. The sun emerged from behind a passing cloud, painting a golden hue across the mouth of the Manistique River—a point of light shimmering in each of the thousand ripples it brushed.

Hirsch's phone vibrated in his pocket once again. *Jesus, I haven't been this popular since my days in practice,* he realized. *Too bad I can't bill for it.* An unfamiliar 906 number appeared on the caller ID. He answered the call.

"This is Ben."

"You're a difficult man to find, Mr. Hirsch. This is Catherine Winslow. I need your help."

Acknowledgments

The people and landscape of Michigan's Upper Peninsula were instrumental to this work's creation. Multiple visits to Manistique, Escanaba, the Garden Peninsula, and other points across the UP contributed to my background research for *The Blue Flame*. A special thanks to Brett Olin, whose experiences walking the gas lines in Montana inspired my protagonist's occupation following his return to Manistique. I want to express my appreciation to Onur Burc for his sublime jacket-cover design.

Above all, my deepest gratitude to my wife, Jennifer. Without her support, patience, and feedback as one of my earliest readers, this book would not have been possible.

About the Author

Nathan Shore is an attorney and higher education administrator. He lives in southern Arizona with his wife and Siamese cat. *The Blue Flame* is his debut novel.